'R

He turned. Suki was framed in the doorway of her dressing room, clad only in a towel. Her face glowed a light pink from her shower and her damp hair tumbled around her naked shoulders. With no make-up, no sexy lingerie or perfumed skin to entice, Ramon wondered how she could still be the most captivating woman he'd ever encountered.

Because, *Madre de Dios*, she was.

Blood and lust thrumming wildly through his veins, he slowly moved towards her, watched her fingers twist in a death grip on the knot of the towel.

Her gaze flitted from his to the French doors before rushing back to him—as if, like him, she couldn't look away for long enough. 'Did you just break into my bedroom?'

He gave a low laugh. 'I was trying to make sure you hadn't broken out and made a run for it.'

He stopped before her, breathing in the intoxicating scent of woman.

His woman.

Maya Blake's hopes of becoming a writer were born when she picked up her first romance at thirteen. Little did she know her dream would come true! Does she still pinch herself every now and then, to make sure it's not a dream? Yes, she does! Feel free to pinch her, too, via Twitter, Facebook or Goodreads! Happy reading!

Books by Maya Blake

Mills & Boon Modern Romance

Signed Over to Santino
A Diamond Deal with the Greek
Married for the Prince's Convenience
Innocent in His Diamonds

One Night With Consequences

The Boss's Nine-Month Negotiation

Rival Brothers

A Deal with Alejandro
One Night with Gael

The Billionaire's Legacy

The Di Sione Secret Baby

Secret Heirs of Billionaires

Brunetti's Secret Son

Seven Sexy Sins

A Marriage Fit for a Sinner

The Untamable Greeks

What the Greek's Money Can't Buy
What the Greek Can't Resist
What the Greek Wants Most

Visit the Author Profile page
at millsandboon.co.uk for more titles.

PREGNANT AT ACOSTA'S DEMAND

BY
MAYA BLAKE

MILLS & BOON

First Published in Great Britain 2017
By Mills & Boon, an imprint of HarperCollins*Publishers*
1 London Bridge Street, London, SE1 9GF

© 2017 Maya Blake

ISBN: 978-0-263-92534-0

Our policy is to use papers that are natural, renewable and recyclable products and made from wood grown in sustainable forests. The logging and manufacturing processes conform to the legal environmental regulations of the country of origin.

Printed and bound in Spain
by CPI, Barcelona

PREGNANT
AT ACOSTA'S
DEMAND

To Sandy Baron, the perfect next-door neighbour.
Thank you for your invaluable support over the years.

CHAPTER ONE

'DON'T LOOK NOW, but the stuff of your torrid dreams—and my nightmares—just walked in.'

Predictably, at the droll words of caution, Suki Langston's head swivelled towards the entrance of the Ravenswood Arms pub. From their corner booth, she watched the newcomer's incisive gaze sweep the room until it narrowed on reaching them.

Just as predictably, she went from hot to cold. Then blistering hot again as her senses went completely haywire at the sight of Ramon Acosta.

'*Dios mio*, I don't know why I bother.'

She turned back to Luis Acosta, her best friend and the man she held directly responsible for her current state of breathlessness. 'Yes, why do you? You didn't have to tell me he was here!'

He caught her hands in his and gripped them tight, his hazel eyes mercilessly teasing. 'I was trying to spare myself the woeful spectacle of watching you jump and twitch like a cornered mouse when he came up behind you. The last time you two met, I thought you were going to swallow your tongue and spit out your spleen at the same time.'

Heat punched up her face. 'Why do I tolerate you? You're a horrible, horrible human being.'

He laughed and held on tighter when she tried to pull away.

'You tolerate me because by some cosmic stroke of genius we were born on the same day and even though you face-planted in my lap the first time we met at uni, I'm also the best thing that's happened to you since… I don't know…

for ever?' Luis replied, his tone extra dry as he waggled his eyebrows at her.

'Are you going to ever let me forget that? Or the fact that you saved me from Professor Winton's roasting the first day of Business Studies because I hadn't drawn up my pre-class plan yet?'

'Let's not forget the numerous times I've saved that pretty behind since then. Which is why I still think you should thank me by coming to work for my family firm.'

'And have you in my ear all day? No, thanks. I enjoy working for Chapman Interiors because I like designing the interior of *homes*, not five-star hotels.'

He threw out a careless shrug. 'Six-star, but who's counting? Whatever, you'll come round one day.'

'Your crystal ball telling you tales again?'

'I don't need one. Just like I don't need a magic ball to tell me you would get on so much better with Ramon if you dealt head-on with that crush that's flattening you—'

'I don't have a crush on him, Luis!' she hissed, darting a frantic look over her shoulder.

Luis sighed dramatically. 'Sure you don't. I think I'm going to change your nickname from mouse to ostrich.'

'Do that and I'll change yours from friend to ass.'

He shrugged. 'I've been called worse.'

Suki watched his gaze move over her shoulder, then return to hers, a resolute look that always made her hackles rise entering his eyes. 'Whatever crazy ideas you're thinking of, burn them now,' she muttered urgently.

He stared at her, a slow smile spreading on his face as his fingers curled tighter around hers. 'Don't worry, little mouse, Luis knows best.'

Suki tried to think of some smart comeback, some wicked put-down that would for once put her overconfident friend in his place. But she knew she was fighting a losing battle. Apart from the useless talent of coming up with the perfect retort hours or even days after she needed it, she was also cursed with a shyness gene that chose moments like these to bloom into life and tie her up in knots.

The other reason she couldn't quite think straight was the man who'd entered the pub two minutes ago.

She could feel him approaching, cutting through the thick Friday night crowd with minimum exertion. She didn't need to look to know that people would be moving out of his way, creating whatever path he wished with a simple commanding look from brooding sea-green eyes. She could already smell that incredible mix of dark earthy spice and alpha male that exuded from him. In the past she'd only needed a quick inhalation for it to fill her nostrils, her senses, turn her into a mumbling wreck around him.

She was twenty-five years old today, for goodness' sake, long past the wide-eyed-teenager stage. She needed to act accordingly…emulate a little bit of the sophistication Luis oozed and Ramon commanded from his very fingertips with such effortless ease.

She needed to raise her head. Yes, that was right. Take in the six-foot-four tower of masculine sleekness and suppressed power who'd arrived at their booth. Stop herself from ogling the square, rugged jaw, the sculpted perfection of his face. Meet his gaze—

'*Felíz cumpleaños, mi hermano.*'

Dear God, he was too much.

A weird sizzle racing down her back, she lowered her head again, swallowing at the sound of that dark, smoky voice caressing the Cuban Spanish words.

'*Gracias*, although I was beginning to think I'd only get belated birthday congrats from you, seeing as the day is almost over,' Luis replied, a trace of tension twining his sardonic tone.

Ramon's strong, capable hands slid into his pockets. 'It's barely eleven o'clock and I made it, as I said I would,' he said, an even deeper throb of tension in his voice.

Suki's gaze darted up in time to catch his narrow-eyed

gaze on their joint hands before it shifted to his brother. After a second, Luis gave a slight grimace and released her before he shrugged.

'In that case, take a seat. I'll go and fetch the champagne I had the bartender put on ice.'

He slid out of his seat, but despite the slight strain between them, the brothers hugged briefly, Ramon murmuring something to his brother Suki didn't quite catch. Luis nodded, his features relaxing as he murmured back.

Face-to-face, their striking resemblance was unmistakable, the only differences being their eyes, Luis's inch shorter height and hair that was a dark chocolate to his brother's jet black. But where Luis's face and stature evoked keenly interested second glances, Ramon's completely captivated, hypnotising every human being who made the mistake of glancing his way.

It was why, several seconds after Luis had left the booth, and despite urging herself otherwise, Suki couldn't look up. She tightened her hold on the glass holding her wine spritzer, willing her fingers not to shake. But reassuring herself that he was mere flesh and blood seemed utterly useless.

Her breath emerged hard and choppy, when, contrary to her thinking he'd take Luis's seat, he slid into the booth next to her.

Another minute crawled excruciatingly by. A minute when the power of his fixed gaze burned her averted face, when every nerve screamed at being the object of his scrutiny.

'*Felíz cumpleaños*, Suki.'

Unlike the birthday wish he'd delivered to his brother, this one held a little extra…something. Hot and mysterious. Dark and dangerous. Or was it just her stupid, fevered imagination? A shiver went through her. She managed to free one hand from around her glass, long enough to tuck her hair behind her ear before it returned to its death grip around her drink. 'Thank you,' she murmured.

'It's the done thing to look a person in the eyes, at least once, when they're talking to you, is it not?' he drawled. 'Or is your drink infinitely more interesting than I am?'

'It is…I mean…it's the done thing, yes, not my drink—'

'Suki.' Her name was a rigid demand.

One she couldn't have denied even if she'd wanted to. And absurdly, now she was commanded, she didn't have any qualms about turning her head, meeting the gleaming, intense green eyes that focused on her.

She'd met Ramon Acosta a handful of times over the last three years. From the first time when Luis had introduced them at their university graduation ceremony and every occasion since, she'd been struck progressively speechless. Because almost impossibly, her best friend's older brother grew more captivating, the force of his raw magnetism intensifying every time she saw him. Far from Luis's tireless mocking acting as the impetus she needed to kill her senseless crush, her traitorous emotions heightened and sparked even more explosively with each meeting, the stern talking-to she gave herself before each meeting a useless exercise once in Ramon's presence.

It was becoming a problem. But not one she wanted to deal with right now. It was her birthday, after all.

Besides, even if Ramon Acosta were anywhere in her league, he would still be out of bounds on account of his very public, very serious engagement to Svetlana Roskova, the drop-dead gorgeous Russian model.

But, having met his gaze, she couldn't look away. Couldn't think beyond the affirmation of how completely irresistible he was. From the olive-toned vibrancy of his skin to the strong column of the throat exposed by the top two buttons left undone in his dark navy shirt, to the slim fingers resting dangerously close to hers, she was absorbed by him.

'There you are,' he murmured, a trace of dark satisfaction in his voice that triggered alarm within her. 'I'm infinitely pleased that I don't have to spend the rest of the night addressing your profile.'

'You are?' she blurted, then cringed.

Seriously, get a hold of yourself!

One side of his full mouth tilted upward, although Suki didn't spot a single scrap of mirth on his face. 'Contrary to what is widely believed, it turns out that looking into the whites of someone's eyes doesn't guarantee insight into their true nature, but I still prefer that mode of communication.'

This time she caught a definite thread of bitterness, wrapped in thinly veiled fury. 'Is...is something wrong?' she ventured. 'You seem agitated.'

The mocking laugh was unexpected. 'Do I?' he enquired lazily.

His tone grated, morphing, perhaps fortunately, her bemusement to irritation. 'You find my concern amusing?'

Dark green eyes tracked her face, lingered on her mouth. 'Is that what this thing is I'm sensing from you, little mouse? *Concern?*'

'What else could it be? And I wish you two wouldn't call me that,' she replied sharply. 'I'm not a mouse.'

His eyes narrowed again, the trace of distemper thickening. 'Far be it from me to be as predictable as my brother. Rest assured, I will fashion a suitable moniker for you.'

'Or you can use my given name, like everyone else, and just call me Suki?'

For some reason, the request made him tenser. He stilled, his eyes growing even more intense, scrutinising her from forehead to jaw to throat. '*Sí.* I guess I could, Suki,' he rasped.

Her name rolled like an unexploded sensual grenade off his lips, tumbling to a charged stop between them. She stared at him, fighting to breathe, watched his gaze drop and linger for long, unnerving seconds on her mouth. Time ticked away. It might have been a minute. It might have been five. The noise of the pub receded but she could hear his steady breathing, feel the condensation from the glass coating her fingers, the cold a deep contrast to the fire burning inside her.

'Are you and my brother involved?' The question was grim and rapier-sharp.

'Involved?' she parroted, still caught in the grip of the electrical storm brewing between them. 'I don't know what—'

'You wish me to be explicit? Are you screwing my brother?' he demanded.

She exhaled in a horrified little rush. 'Excuse me?'

'Pretended outrage at my language isn't necessary. A simple *yes* or *no* will suffice.'

Another healthy bout of irritation flared, saving her jumbled senses. 'I'm not sure what's up with you, but you obviously woke up on the wrong side of the bed today, so—'

The low curse was uttered in Spanish, but she knew it was potent nevertheless. 'Indulge me and let's refrain from the mention of beds and who woke up where for the moment, *cara.*'

She frowned. 'Well, you're sort of proving my point with that statement. Which begs the question why did you come here to celebrate your brother's birthday if you're in such a terrible mood?'

The skin bracketing his mouth pinched white as his nostrils flared. Suki watched, her spine stiffening with dread as his fist balled on the table. 'Because I'm *loyal.* Because when I give my word I keep it. Because Luis trusts me to be there for him and it's my duty to honour that trust.'

The icy fury with which he delivered the words robbed her of breath, but only for a moment. 'I wasn't questioning your loyalty or—'

'You still haven't answered my question.'

She shook her head, struggling to follow the mercurial swing of the conversation. 'Probably because it's none of your business.'

His fist tightened further. 'You think it's none of my business? When he treats you like you belong to him but you look at me with those gorgeous, *greedy* blue eyes?'

She gasped, her insides clenching tight with mortification. 'I don't!'

His laughter was mocking and cruel. 'You pretended you needed the encouragement to acknowledge me, but your eyes haven't stopped devouring me since I sat down. Fair warning though, even as much as Luis means to me, I don't share my women. *Ever.* So a *ménage à trois* will be out of the question.'

'I… God, you're despicable,' she replied, horror dredging through her, because he'd not only so easily witnessed the stupid feelings she'd been desperate to hide, but had also felt no qualms about calling her out on them.

'Am I? Or are you just disappointed because whatever hot little scenario you concocted in your head has been rumbled?'

'Believe me, I have no earthly idea what you're talking about. And I'm sorry if someone misplaced a few of your billions or kicked your puppy because clearly something's happened today to put you in this filthy mood. But, regardless of that, *I* should warn *you* that I'm two seconds from throwing my drink in your face. So unless you want a cold drenched body to go with that deplorable attitude, I suggest you shut up right now! And also, how dare you speak to me of sharing and…and *ménages*? Aren't you *engaged* to—?'

'*Madre de Dios*, how long was I away for?' Luis slid into the seat and nodded thanks to the waitress who set the ice bucket and champagne flutes down. 'Because I could've sworn it was only five minutes. And yet you two look like you're about to come to blows? I'm surprised at you, little mouse.' Although his tone was jovial, his eyes were shrewd as they slid from her to his brother.

Suki shook her head, unable to believe what was happening. 'Trust me, I'm not—'

'I was setting your girlfriend straight on a few things,' Ramon interjected.

Luis's eyebrows shot up, then he laughed. 'My *girlfriend*? Where did you get that idea?'

Silence reigned at the table. Suki glared at her supposed best friend.

Ramon's tight jaw eased a fraction before he shrugged. 'Are you saying she doesn't belong to you?'

Suki's teeth clenched. *'Excuse—?'*

'Sí, she belongs to me—'

'Can you please stop talking about me as if I'm some ornament?' she interrupted.

Ramon ignored her, his keen gaze fixed on his brother.

Luis's lighter eyes narrowed. 'Like a sister belongs to a brother who cares for her. Like a friend owns the entitlement of kicking *someone's* ass if they so much as whisper a threat of harm her way. Like—'

'Understood,' Ramon said, his voice firm and grave.

'Good, I'm glad that's settled,' Luis replied, then reached for the champagne.

Suki turned her head, met the newly gleaming gaze Ramon turned on her. 'Is it? Is it *settled*?' she hissed.

One corner of his mouth quirked, as if now his brother had explained he found the whole subject amusing. 'I got the wrong end of the stick, it seems, *gatito*.'

'Is that supposed to be an apology?' she snapped.

A fleeting expression darkened his eyes. 'Permit me some time to find the right words.'

Considering Ramon Acosta was lauded worldwide as possessing the Midas touch with every venture he turned his hand to, she found it impossible to believe he was lost for anything.

He'd single-handedly turned his parents' half a dozen Cuban-based hotels into the world-renowned Acosta International Hotels chain while pursuing a private but deeply passionate artistic talent. When Svetlana Roskova had accidentally on purpose let slip during an interview that she was a muse for, and involved with, an artist, the media had clamoured to know who had won the heart of the Russian beauty.

After several sources had speculated that it was indeed Ramon, he'd given a single exclusive interview confirming himself as her lover and the man behind the wildly successful Piedra Galleries. Overnight, his already highly sought after paintings and sculptures had become priceless collectors' items, with commissions from monarchs and world leaders placed on a waiting list that stretched into years, according to Luis.

But the man Suki had placed on a lofty pedestal was far removed from the one now watching her with wild, unsettling eyes. A fact his own brother noted as he peeled the foil off the champagne cork.

'You seem wound up tighter than normal, Ramon. I can virtually see the smoke curling from your ears. It's quite a sight to behold,' Luis observed dryly.

Ramon's mouth tightened. 'Is this how you wish to spend the rest of your birthday, lobbing jokes at me?' he asked without taking his eyes off Suki.

She suppressed a shiver, wondering what was going on behind the hooded green eyes.

'I was just trying to lighten this heavier than normal mood, seeing as it's *my* birthday and I can do what I want, but if you're not going to explain yourself, at least answer that damn phone that's been buzzing in your pocket for the last five minutes?'

Ramon shifted his gaze from her long enough to flick his brother an impatient look before reaching into his jacket. Extracting the sleek phone from his pocket, he barely glanced at it before powering it off.

Luis's jaw dropped. 'You're *actually* turning off the power source to the empire? Are you unwell? Or are you ignoring someone specific?'

'Luis…' His voice held patent warning. One his younger brother didn't heed.

'*Dios*, is there trouble in paradise? Has the great Svetlana tripped over her stilettos and fallen from grace?'

Ramon Acosta's face iced up, his eyes turning a shade of turbulent green. 'I was waiting until later to share the news, but if you must know, as of this morning, I'm no longer engaged.'

He was no longer engaged.

As if his words had caused the planet to stop turning, silence descended on the booth. The three of them remained frozen in place, even as the words ricocheted through her brain.

He was no longer engaged.

Suki jumped at the sound of the cork forcefully ejecting from the bottle. Frothy, expensive liquid spilled. The sounds and smell of the pub roared back into her consciousness. But still the words pounded through her head.

Ramon was no longer committed to another woman.

She frowned at the giddy relief swirling through her, then started as a flute of champagne was thrust into her hands.

'Drink up, little mouse. Now we have two…no, *three* reasons to celebrate,' Luis said, eyeing her with even deeper resolution.

'I'm glad my broken engagement brings you such sublime joy, *hermano*,' Ramon replied, his voice arctic cold.

Luis sobered. 'I chose to respect your relationship, but my views on your engagement never changed. She was the wrong woman for you. Whether the move to end it was hers or yours—'

'It was mine.'

Luis's smile returned. 'Then either celebrate with me or drown your sorrows. Either way, we're finishing this champagne.' He poured two more glasses.

Ramon waited a beat, then raised his glass and recited another clipped birthday toast before tossing back the drink.

Luis, his point made, proceeded to drink most of the bottle, while Suki sipped hers.

All the while tension reigned, heightened even further by the looks Ramon kept casting her way.

She breathed a sigh of relief when Luis rose just after midnight, his predatory gaze on a stunning redhead smiling at him from two seats away.

'Time to make a significant start on my second quarter-century.'

Suki pushed away her half-finished glass. 'I think I'll head home—'

'Stay,' Ramon said. Before she could reply, he turned to his brother. 'My limo is outside. Have the driver deliver you wherever you want to go.'

Luis clapped his hand on his brother's shoulder. 'I appreciate the offer but I'm going to tread delicately with this flower. We don't want her overwhelmed and bolting at the sight of all those Acosta billions before I get the chance to close the deal, now, do we?'

Ramon's jaw tightened before he shrugged. 'Very well. I'll leave you to serenade your paramour on the night bus.'

'*Dios*, everything is such an extreme with you, isn't it? There's such a thing as a black cab, you know? And even with the lowly salary you pay me as junior marketing executive, I can still afford one.'

'If you say so. Either way, I expect you to report to the office sober and whole on Monday morning.'

'As long as *you* promise to deliver Suki home, safe and sound.'

She shook her head, grabbing her handbag as she rose. 'There's no need. I'll be fine getting home by myself.' Although she *would* be relying on the maligned public transport, the reason to keep a close eye on her spending casting a sudden grey shadow on her birthday. Her phone hadn't rung in the four hours since she'd called the hospital to check on her mother so she must be having a relatively restful night. At least she hoped so.

'Sit down, Suki,' Ramon drawled, his tone throbbing with implacable power. 'You and I aren't finished.'

She ignored him. Or at least she tried. She cast a desperate look towards Luis, but her friend merely reached across the table and hugged her close, murmuring in her ear, 'It's your birthday, Suki. Life's too short. Give yourself a break and live a little. It'll make you happy, and it'll make me infinitely ecstatic!'

Before she could respond, he was headed for the redhead's table, smiling that smile that made women trip over themselves.

'I said, sit down,' Ramon pressed.

There was no way to leave the booth while he blocked her exit. With Luis's words ringing in her ears, she slowly sank back into her seat. 'I can't imagine why you'd want me to. I have nothing more to say to you.'

His gaze gradually defrosted from arctic cold to heated green as he scrutinised her face with that unnerving intensity. 'I think we established that I owe you…something.'

'An *apology*. Is that a difficult word for you to say?'

He shrugged and opened his mouth, just as raucous laughter fuelled by hours' long hard drinking erupted from a group nearby.

Distaste crossing his face, he rose and stationed himself at the mouth of the booth. 'Come, we'll continue this conversation elsewhere.'

Despite his imperious tone, Suki stood, telling herself she was obeying just so she could make a quick getaway once they were outside. Ramon Acosta had revealed a part of himself tonight that scraped her giddy dreams raw. She'd seen the ruthless man the financial papers wrote about, the insufferable deity-like brother Luis complained about. She'd also seen a bitter man turned lethally furious by his broken engagement.

Whatever had happened between Ramon and Svetlana still pulsed ill-feeling through his veins. Even now, she felt him loom like a dark lord behind her, quiet fury pouring off him.

The glimpse into his character was a timely reminder that Suki grabbed and held close. Her experiences of men, including her own father, had left her with a deeply ingrained distrust that, unfortunately, received further validation with each interaction with the opposite sex.

Thus far, Luis was the only one who'd breached that distrust. He was the reason why, believing there were other exceptions like him, she'd attempted, despite her mother's bitter warnings about men, to date six months ago.

Stephen turning out to be a two-timing louse had left her hurt, but not surprised. The part of her that still stung now warned her that whatever was going on with Ramon, she wanted no part of it.

Exiting the pub into brisk October air, she breathed in deep. And started to walk away.

A firm hand caught her elbow before she'd taken three steps, dragging her to a halt. 'Where do you think you're going?' Ramon breathed.

With the sounds of the pub now in the background, her every sense was filled with him. She took a step back, fighting the insane sensations that warred inside her. He tracked her move, crowding her with his smell, his overwhelming body, that ferocious look in his eyes.

Much too much. Despite the pathetic weakening in her limbs, she met his gaze. 'It's late.'

'I'm aware of the time of night,' he murmured, moving closer, brushing her legs with his.

The weakness intensified. 'I need to… I should go.'

He took another step forward, bracing both hands either side of her head and trapping her against the pub wall. '*Sí*, perhaps you *should*. But you don't want to.'

She shook her head, frantically calling on her common sense. 'Yes, I do.'

He leaned closer, until she could see the tiny gold flecks in his eyes, feel the warm, faintly champagne-tinged breath on her face. 'You can't. I've yet to give you my apology.'

'So you admit to owing me one?'

His gaze dropped to her mouth, spiky hunger that fused with hers flaring in his eyes. 'Yes, but I'm not giving it to you here.'

She managed the almost impossible feat of laughing. 'You know what birthday I'm celebrating so you *know* I wasn't born yesterday.'

One hand left the wall, his fingers drifting down her cheek. 'I can tell you what you want to hear right here and you can walk away. Or you can let me take you home as I promised Luis I would while giving you that apology. Surely you want to give your friend that peace of mind?'

She shook her head against the magic he was weaving with his low, husky voice and sizzling touch. 'I'm a big girl. Luis will understand. All I want is that apology,' she insisted.

'You want more than that. You want to give in, reach out and take that forbidden thing you've been craving for a while now. Don't you, Suki?'

No.

She opened her mouth, but the word stalled in her throat.

Ramon pushed away from the wall, took a bold step back, then another, robbing her of his closeness, dangling the possibility of loss in her face.

No.

This time the word was in objection of the temptation she knew she shouldn't surrender to. Suki wasn't aware she'd followed him to the edge of the kerb until a sleek black limo rolled to a stop behind him. Reaching for the handle, he pulled the door open, his eyes not leaving her face. 'You will get in the car and I'll take you home, Suki. What happens beyond that will be up to you. Only you.'

CHAPTER TWO

INSTINCTIVELY SHE KNEW her path was set the moment she murmured, 'Okay.'

Life's too short. Give yourself a break and live a little.

Suki knew that there would be no turning back the second she let Ramon help her into the car and he slid along the soft leather bench seat after her. The door slammed behind them, cocooning them in silence and edgy lust.

'Your address?' he rasped.

'167 Winston Street, Vauxhall.'

He relayed the information to the driver, then his mouth firmed. 'There are two dozen pubs between where you live and Luis's residence in Mayfair. Why do you choose one so far outside of the city?' he asked, casting an irritated glance at the establishment that stood on a quiet street in the middle of Watford.

'A uni friend of ours just inherited it from his parents. Luis promised we'd stop by for birthday drinks,' she said, a little relieved at the harmless tone of the conversation.

He'd activated the privacy partition and tinted the back windows, and now, trapped in the dark expanse of the luxurious car, his scent once again sliding intimately over her senses, she needed something to alleviate it.

Unfortunately, the reprieve didn't last long. 'And do you always do what my brother says?' he asked, a different type of edge lining his voice.

Her fingers tightened around the strap of her handbag. 'Are you about to pick another fight with me? Because if I recall, we haven't resolved the last one to my satisfaction yet.'

In the space of one breath and the next, he closed the

gap between them. Her bag was plucked from her fingers and tossed onto the adjacent seat. Firm fingers speared into her hair, the grip firm enough to direct her gaze up to his.

Electricity vibrated from his body, the dark, purposeful gleam in his eyes rendering her mouth dry. He stared down at her for an age, their breaths mingling.

'*Lo siento.* I'm sorry for my less than admirable assumptions. I am not in the best mood tonight, but that was no excuse, so accept my apologies.'

The words were deep and genuine, momentarily silencing the voice screaming a warning at her. 'I... Okay,' she mumbled.

His fingers moved, slowly massaging her scalp in lazy, masterful rotations, triggering a low heat in her belly. 'Are you satisfied?' he asked.

'That...that depends.'

One eyebrow rose but the rest of his face tautened with expectation. 'On what?'

'On whether or not you're about to start another fight with me.'

'No, *querida*,' he breathed. 'I'm about to start something else entirely. And you know it.'

'I don't...'

'Enough, Suki. I told you what happens next is up to you. But I get the feeling I need to move things along before one of us expires from impatience. So the only word I want out of that delectable mouth right now is *yes* or *no*. I want you, *gatito*. Do you want me? Regardless of my sub-exemplary behaviour tonight. Yes or no?'

Her heart leapt into her throat. For three long years she'd harboured a growing crush on this man. But nowhere in that secret longing had there been a possibility that he would be here, in front of her, saying these words to her. She'd always believed she would wake up one day to find herself cured. She'd dated a handful of men like Stephen who, even before they'd proved themselves faithless, had fallen victim to not being *dynamic* enough, *confident* enough, tall enough or dark enough—hell, even *Spanish* enough.

Stephen's betrayal had triggered a numbness of her emotions, had finally pressed home every warning her mother had relayed since she turned sixteen. A desperate part of her wished for that numbness now, yearned for a clap of thunder to deliver her from the ferocious lust threatening to swallow her whole.

Because, staring into Ramon Acosta's eyes, she didn't think she was anywhere near numb. Anywhere near cured of her foolish crush.

And now that he was free...

Oh, God.

She shook her head; the voice whispering that this was the worst idea she'd ever had grew into a scream. Swallowing, she slicked her tongue over her lower lip.

His fingers convulsed in her hair and a strangled sound escaped his throat. About to utter the word that would free her from this madness, she dropped her gaze. His velvet-smooth lips were so close. And good heavens, she was so hungry for a taste.

One. Just one.

Then she would satisfy herself that he was no god, that the lofty status she'd afforded him in her mind was nothing more than dreams spun from loneliness and long-forgotten fairy tales.

'Suki.' Her name was a fierce, demanding whisper. A silken, alluring chain winding her closer.

Her breasts grew heavy, the slick, damp place between her thighs clenching with a manic need she'd never experienced before.

'Yes.' The word poured from her in a swell of surrender.

Ramon didn't need further encouragement. With a rough exhalation, he tugged her closer to meet his descending mouth. A hot, demanding mouth that slanted over hers, fusing power and pleasure into her fired-up senses.

His tongue stroked against her lips, tasting boldly, over and over before he demanded entrance. Entrance she gave with a shaky wonder at the thought that she was kissing Ramon Acosta. That wonder melted away in the next instance when he licked his way into her mouth.

Sensation lashed her from head to toe, the onslaught eliciting helpless whimpers that started from deep within and were crushed between their melded lips. The knowledge that she was whimpering sent another bolt of shock through her. She'd been kissed before. Enough times to know that no one kiss was the same, that some were better than others.

But *nothing* compared to the kiss Ramon was delivering now. Each slide of his tongue against hers, each bold nip of her swelling flesh rained sizzling delight on her, making her strain closer, silently pleading for more.

When the need to breathe forced them apart, he only permitted a second, smoothing his thumb across her lips in a hungry caress. '*Dios mio*, you taste incredible,' he growled before he took her mouth again, unbelievably deepening the kiss.

The words freed her from a hold she wasn't even aware of, the guttural utterance lending her enough feminine confidence to unfold her hands from the death grip on the seat. To raise one hand and settle it on his thigh.

He tensed, hard muscles bunching beneath her hand. He tore his mouth from hers to spear her with a rabid look, the light in his eyes sending a thread of apprehension down her spine. Not the kind that made her fear for her safety. The kind that informed her he was stroking the edge of his sensual limits and was determined to take her down with him.

She started to move her hand. He caught and trapped it against his heated flesh, his eyes flashing as he stared down at her. 'You want to touch me, then touch me.'

'Ramon…'

He inhaled sharply. 'I think this is the first time I've heard you say my name.'

'I…what?' It couldn't be. She'd said it so many times…
in her fantasies.

The hold in her hair propelled her closer. 'Say it again,'
he breathed against her lips.

'Ramon,' she whispered feverishly.

A light tremble vibrated through him. Diving back down,
he sealed his mouth to hers. The hand covering hers released her to slide up her arm, stopping every few inches
to explore her bare skin. Halfway up, he changed course,
his caress gliding over her hip to her waist to the under-
side of her breast. It stayed here, tantalisingly close to the
needy weight that yearned to be touched, the nipples that
screamed for attention.

Her breath hitched as hunger ploughed through her. Beneath her hand, his thigh shifted, demanding her attention.
She caressed him through the material of his expensive tai-
lored trousers. Higher. To the enormous bulge behind his
zipper. And froze at his tight, tormented groan.

'No. Don't stop, *querida.* Touch me,' he commanded
against her mouth.

She smoothed her hand over him, tightened her fist
against his virile girth. Thick, inflamed Spanish words
spilled from his lips, bruising her mouth with their heat.
When one ravenous hand cupped her breast, squeezed and
tortured, she returned the words with needful moans. One
lane of pleasure rolled into the other, delirium swelling high
as he moulded and caressed and kissed.

Suki wasn't sure when he pushed her back against the
leather upholstery or when he tugged her hips to the edge
of the bench seat. Not sure when the side zip of her black
wool dress was lowered or when he pushed up the hem.
But at some point between one potent kiss and the next,
he was on his knees between her thighs, his hands sliding
up her legs, over the silk stockings she'd treated herself to
in a mad moment of weakness last weekend. More fevered
words spilled when he encountered their lace tops.

His fingers traced over them, then trailed over her bare skin. A shudder raked her from head to toe. With one last forceful kiss, he raised his head.

'I need to see you, Suki,' he rasped, his voice barely recognisable. His hip flexed against her hold, the power of his erection thickening in her hand. 'Touch you as you are touching me.'

At the back of her mind a warning blazed. A kiss. This was supposed to be *just a kiss*.

But already her head was moving in a nod, her blood thrilling to the new, unexpected turn the night had taken. There was no way what was happening between them would be sustainable beyond tonight. For one thing, she was too emotionally bruised, her instinct even now shocked at her behaviour. For another, her mother needed her.

Lastly, Ramon divided his time between the many Acosta hotels and his homeland of Cuba. The likelihood of her seeing him again for a very long time, especially once Luis took over the New York flagship hotel, as he was being groomed for, would be low to nil.

And despite the insanity of the sensations Ramon evoked in her now, she knew the shine would wear off sooner rather than later. So maybe she would allow more than just a kiss. Maybe, she would heed Luis's words, and live a little. Just for tonight—

The fingers tracing the outer edge of her satin and lace panties dragged her back to the exhilarating present. To the looming presence of the powerful man crouched over her.

'I must be losing my touch if your mind chooses this moment to go for a wander. What were you thinking about?' he demanded, his thumb sliding dangerously close to her sex.

She shivered. 'I…nothing.'

He doubled the caress with a thumb on the other side. 'Don't lie to me, Suki. I've had enough of those in the last twenty-four hours. Were you thinking of another man?' he sliced at her, his nostrils flaring with quiet fury. 'While you

lay ready and open for me, were you thinking of someone
else? A boyfriend, perhaps?'

Her eyes widened and she tried to scramble away. She
didn't succeed because he refused to let her go. 'You think
I'd be here, like this with you if I had a boyfriend?'

'Answer the question, Suki,' he challenged, his tone
growing even more arctic.

She shook her head. 'No, I don't have a boyfriend. If…
you must know I was thinking of you.'

The tension gripping him eased. His eyes gleamed.
'What exactly were you thinking?' he probed as his thumbs
slid under the thin barrier and caressed her damp flesh.

A moan ripped free, her shaky exhalation rushing
through her lips. 'That I won't see you again after tonight.'

He stilled. His fingers dug into her. Eyes turned almost
black regarded her in abrasive silence. 'And is that what you
want? For us to use each other for one single night and forget
the other one exists come morning?' There was something
darkly condemning in his voice, but also enough sexual
anticipation that said he wasn't completely averse to that
scenario. The opposing forces of that view left her speechless, unable to decide which one would most please him.

He leaned in closer, bringing his power and might to bear
on her. 'Answer me, Suki. Is that what you want?' Blade-
sharp eyes searched hers.

'Isn't it what you want too?' She forced a laugh. 'Please
don't tell me you see anything more beyond…whatever this
is happening tonight?'

He was silent for an interminable age. Then his gaze
dropped to her shoulders and upper breasts exposed by the
gaping dress. Lower to the rapid rise and fall of her torso.
To the restless hands on the seat beside her hips, twitch-
ing with the need to touch him. Finally to her splayed legs
and the black panties whose thin, insubstantial material
framed her core. His thumbs caressed again, drawing another shameless shudder from her.

'*Sí*, you're right. Nothing more can come out of this. Nothing *will*.'

The sharp dart of hurt somewhere deep beneath her breastbone disappeared at the pleasure pain of her panties cutting into her flesh one moment, then ripping free of her body the next.

Suki gasped, the move so audaciously erotic, she felt her folds dampen further.

Ramon's eyes remained on her for a further intense second. Then they dropped to her core.

Heat scoured his cheekbones, his lips parting as he breathed her in. She wasn't sure whether it was the sight of him on his knees before her or the power of sensations ploughing through her. But the urge to touch him grew too big to contain. She cupped his jaw, slid her hand along over the masculine stubble to his strong throat, then around to his nape. A tight smile whispered over his lips, gone in the next breath.

Then he was lowering his head, his intent very clear. Her grip tightened, pulling him away, her eyes widening at the blatant act he was about to perform.

'Ramon, I don't…' she started. Her train of thought dissolved at the firm kiss he delivered to her core, her fingers convulsing in his hair as pleasure jerked through her. 'Oh!'

Raising his head, he blew gently on her. 'You want me to stop?'

The anxious part of her that had rejected what he was about to do frantically begged for more. 'No,' she blurted.

At his husky laugh, heat washed up her face.

But laughter and all trace of embarrassment evaporated beneath the deluge of rapture his next kiss brought. He tasted her and pleasured her with bold, possessive strokes, ramping up her pleasure until her eyes rolled in bliss. Until hoarse, alien words fell from her lips and her fingers sank deep into his hair, urging him on, begging for more.

He gave generously, his tongue and lips drawing untold

delight from her. When he finally concentrated his attention on her tight, swollen nub, Suki's back arched off the seat, a ragged scream ripping from her throat before her whole body was gripped in wave after wave of ecstasy.

She resurfaced to the scent of sex and leather and the sight of a virile, hungry, half-naked man. He'd disposed of his jacket, his shirt hung half open and his trousers were unzipped. Black luxurious hair looked sexily dishevelled as if someone…*she*…had run her hands through it in mind-less caresses.

Her barely decelerated heartbeat kicked up again as she watched him slide on a condom with one hand and roughly push down her dress and free her arms with the other. Next, he unclipped and eased off her bra.

At the sight of her exposed full breasts, he swore low and hard. '*Santa cielo*, you're exquisite.'

As if testing the reality of her skin, he smoothed his hand down from her neck to her stomach, bypassing the needy, screaming peaks of her breasts. On the upward caress, his other hand left his sheathed manhood. Both hands cupped her breasts, his thumbs mercilessly teasing her nipples for a mindless stretch of time before he sucked one into his mouth. Hard on the heels of her expended climax, renewed pleasure surged. High and heady and unthinkably surreal.

Was she really here, about to—?

'*Oh, God,*' she moaned, her mind fracturing as he grazed his teeth over her nipple.

Still torturing her, he wrapped one arm around her waist and dragged her lower until her buttocks hung off the seat. She was a heartbeat from tossing herself over another cliff into another mind-blowing climax when he lifted his head.

Fervid green eyes met and trapped hers as he drew her legs over his shoulders. Then, with a grunt, he gripped her waist and thrust hard and deep inside her.

Her strangled scream was kissed away, urgent hands holding her in place for his second thrust. '*Dios*…so wet…so tight.' His voice was gravel-rough hoarse, the words barely coherent.

Suki gave up trying to decipher them, her mind fracturing into useless pieces as she was fully submerged in the fiery enchantment of Ramon's possession. He commanded her body like a masterful virtuoso, driving her to the peak and pinning her there, over and over, but not letting her fall.

As the limo ate up the miles they writhed beneath streetlights thrown intermittently into the car.

'Ramon… Ramon…'

She wasn't sure how many times she moaned his name to his thick encouragement. But she was fully astride his kneeling form, their bodies slick with sweat and his implacable arms around her when he raised his head one final time, looked deep into her eyes and instructed, 'Now, Suki.'

Glorious pleasure and pressure burst wide open. She could do nothing but hang on as it sucked her deep into a bottomless vortex.

He caught her earlobe in a sharp bite a second before he was hurled into his own release, muttering hot, torrid words that drew out her own pleasure as he jerked inside her.

They were still breathing hard when the car swayed round a corner and drew to a stop. He caressed her for another minute before he set her back on the seat and zipped up her dress.

Unable to meet his eyes or stop the flames of disquiet eating her up, Suki snatched up her panties and bra and stuffed them inside her handbag.

Beside her, having straightened his own clothes, Ramon lounged back in the seat.

'Um…thanks for the lift,' she said after a full minute when it became clear he didn't intend to speak.

He didn't reply, just stared at her with hooded dark eyes. *Okay...* Clutching her handbag, she edged closer to the door. 'Goodnight, Ramon. Have a safe trip back to…wherever.'

She reached for the handle. He beat her to it, catching her hand and tugging her round to face him.

'No, I'm not about to have a safe trip back to...*wherever*. Because we're not done, *guapa*. Far from it,' he said.

Exiting the car with the grace of a sleek, powerful animal, he held out his hand to her.

She had no choice but to get out. She knew that. But suddenly what awaited her outside was more daunting than the mind-bending sex she'd just enjoyed in this car. For one thing, her heart and mind hadn't stopped racing. And the voice screeching in her head that this was over and she needed to walk away was growing weaker under the one howling harder in greedy, grabby need. The one telling her she wanted more. *Needed* to live a little for longer. Experience more of what had just happened. Of everything.

'Come out, Suki,' he ordered.

She told herself that she complied because she couldn't stay in the limo for ever. Not because the unabated hunger in his eyes called to hers.

The moment she stepped out, he slammed the door shut and tapped twice on the roof. As the limo pulled away he yanked her close, delivered a hard, searing kiss to her mouth. That single spark was enough to ignite the erotic conflagration again. Long moments later, he raised his head, glanced up at the small Victorian terrace house she called home, then back at her. 'Invite me in.'

She invited him in.

But even before he'd stepped over the threshold into her sanctuary, Suki knew that this was nowhere near the forgettable experience she had convinced herself it would be.

CHAPTER THREE

Ten months later

SUKI READ THE email one more time, the shaking in her hands nothing compared to the pain lacerating her heart as she took in the stark words that blended with soul-breaking ones. Halfway through the first paragraph, her vision blurred. She blinked and tears spilled down her cheeks. Swiping them away, she closed her eyes for a moment, vainly wishing the words would be different when she opened them again.

They weren't.

Private memorial for Luis Acosta and his parents, Clarita and Pablo Acosta. A strictly family affair. Unless expressly invited, please do not attend.

Lawyers request your presence for the reading of his last will and testament followed by a private meeting with Ramon Acosta. Attendance strictly necessary.

Her throat clogging with fresh tears just waiting to be shed, she looked away from the words she didn't want to read, never mind accept, and clicked on the attachment. A slight bolt of shock went through her when it sent her to an airline website. Swallowing, she clicked on further links until she arrived at the page holding the first-class return e-ticket to Cuba under her name.

The email and attachment had come from a firm of lawyers in Havana, the ones she'd been desperate to contact ever since she received the horrendous news of Luis's and his parents' deaths.

The same lawyers who'd refused to take her calls or answer her letters for two months, but were now reaching out to her. She knew they wouldn't have contacted her without the express permission of Ramon Acosta, their client.

This email giving consent for her to visit Cuba to pay her respects wouldn't have come from anyone else because Ramon was the only one left of the Acosta family.

Despite the turn of events after their night together, she'd reached out to him after Luis died. At first Suki had respected his deafening silence, knowing that he was grieving the family he'd tragically lost in a car crash. Until she'd learned via social media that several of their university friends had been invited to attend Luis's funeral three weeks after his death. The date had come and gone without any of her frantic calls being returned by Ramon's office or his lawyers, forcing her to grieve her best friend's burial alone in her bedroom. Every single email she'd sent after that had also gone unanswered.

Until today.

She wanted to hate Ramon for denying her something so fundamental as a goodbye to the only true friend she'd known. But her emotions, already scraped raw by everything she'd endured these past ten months, were too shredded to accommodate another detrimental emotion such as hate.

Although she'd already been through a gamut of them. For weeks, she'd cried, begged, then railed against fate. And science. And her own weak body.

When she'd finally reached acceptance, she'd cried for days. Those tears had sapped the last of her will to fight, dropped her to what she'd foolishly thought was rock bottom. Until Luis was also ripped from her. Then she'd known true devastation.

Devastation she'd had to deal with on her own, while grappling with her own loss and remaining strong for her mother. The multiple blows fate had dealt her still possessed the power to disrupt her sleep and trigger bouts of tearful sadness.

Like when she'd dissolved into floods of tears during her meeting with the head of HR at her workplace last week. Even before she'd finished the return-to-work interview, she knew things hadn't gone well.

Her boss had insisted she take the full three months of her sick leave, the need to protect themselves from professional liability overshadowing her protests that, with only one month remaining, she was ready to return to work.

She'd petitioned. With her finances fast dwindling and her mother's medical bills piling up, she'd appealed the decision and been granted the interview. Only for her overwhelmed state to get the better of her.

She hadn't been surprised when her HR manager had sympathetically ended the interview and called a taxi to take Suki home. What she hadn't expected was a letter a few days later stating that her sick leave had been extended by another month with half pay because she wasn't deemed fit to deal with clients in her current state.

Suki had been too drained to fight the assessment. And deep down she knew that, as much as she loved her job as an interior designer for one of the most prestigious firms in London, her passion had been depleted.

She didn't need a psychologist to tell her she needed to find closure before things got better. Or barring that, a different avenue for the cocktail of emotions bubbling beneath the surface of her heart.

Closing her laptop, she rose from her small desk and trudged to the kitchen to dispose of her barely touched cup of tea. Mechanically, she washed the mug and set it on the draining board.

Outside, birds chirped and wasps buzzed as Vauxhall basked in the August bank holiday sunshine.

Suki turned her back on it, her hand sliding as it so often, so painfully did to her stomach, to the child that had never managed to thrive there. The urge to walk upstairs to her bedroom, curl up under her duvet and slide into perpetual oblivion was almost catatonically irresistible.

She fought the temptation, her mind returning to the email and the airline ticket. Although she'd been prepared to dig into her meagre savings to pay her last respects to her best friend two months ago, her resources had dwindled even further owing to her mother being readmitted to hospital. With confirmation of her cancer, Suki had had to use almost all her remaining funds to keep her and her mother's heads above water.

Travelling to Cuba had fast become a distant dream.

The arrival of the ticket, although it bruised her pride a little, wasn't one she was about to refuse. For a chance to say goodbye to Luis, she would set aside her ego for the moment. Once she was back at work, she would pay Ramon Acosta back every penny she owed him for the ticket.

The decision eroded a little bit of her apathy, made her half turn back towards the window, allow the sunshine to touch her face. Warm her.

She wasn't aware how long she stood there, making careful plans, her soul mourning the vibrant, charismatic man she'd been lucky enough to call her friend.

The soft beeping on her laptop, reminding her of the appointment at the hospital, finally roused her. On automatic, she dressed, left home and made the short drive to the hospital that held far too many harrowing memories.

Fighting the ravaging pain that attacked her, Suki blocked out the smell of disinfectant and death, forced a smile, and entered her mother's ward.

Moira Langston was dozing lightly, her shrunken form lost in stark white sheets. Sensing Suki's presence, she opened her eyes. For a second, they just stared at each other.

Then her mother gave a soft, shuddering exhalation. 'I told you not to visit. I know how hard it is for you to come here.'

Suki laid her hand over her mother's. 'I'm okay, Mum. It's not that bad,' she lied.

Moira's lips pursed. 'Don't lie. You know I can't bear lies.'

Tension rippled in the air, twisting through pain churning inside them both. Broken trust fired by a thousand lies was what had shattered her mother's heart long before Suki was born. It was the reason Moira Langston had never again let another man close enough to hurt her, the reason she'd drummed into Suki the need to protect her own heart at all costs.

It was the reason her mother had been bitterly angry with her when Suki had told her about her pregnancy. Her mother had come round eventually, even put aside her own health issues to support her after she lost the baby, but the look of mournful regret still lingered.

Suki swallowed, and tightened her grip on her mother's hand. 'I can't *not* visit you, Mum.'

Moira sighed, her face softening. 'I know. But I'm feeling better, so I should be home very soon.'

Suki didn't argue, although her mother's notable weight loss told a different story. They chatted about neutral subjects for a while, before her mother's shrewd eyes settled on her one more time. 'Something's bothering you.'

She started to shake her head, but, not wanting to upset her mother, she took a deep breath. 'I heard from Ra…from Luis's brother's lawyers.'

Moira's eyes narrowed. 'And? What did Ramon have to say for himself?' she demanded sharply.

'I…nothing. The lawyers sent me a ticket to Cuba. To attend Luis's memorial.'

'Are you going to accept it?'

Slowly, she nodded. 'I want to say goodbye properly.'

For a long moment, Moira remained silent. 'Luis was a good man. That's the only reason I won't tell you not to go. But, be careful, Suki. Stay away from his brother. He's caused you enough grief as it is.'

Her mother had been quick to lay the blame for everything at Ramon's feet when she found out Suki was pregnant and alone. Ravaging pain and the need to mourn her lost baby in isolation had made her hold her tongue against telling her mother that Ramon had no knowledge that he'd fathered a baby. That was an assumption she would rectify in the future, when her heart didn't shred every time she thought of her baby.

'Mrs Baron will visit you every day, and I'll be back before you know it.'

As if conjured up, their next-door neighbour walked into the ward. The widow, easily fifteen years older than her mother, was nevertheless spry and full of life. Her cheery demeanour was infectious, and her mother was soon chuckling.

An hour later, Suki left the two women chatting, and returned home, thoughts of the email and of Luis darkening her spirits as she opened her front door.

The sight of mail on her doormat roused her from her blanketing sadness. Welcoming the tiny distraction, she walked through to the kitchen.

Two of the three pieces of post were junk mail. The stamp on the third envelope shot her heart into her throat, and her hand was trembling as she ripped the letter open.

Frantically, her gaze flew over the words. Her shocked, tearful gasp echoed through her small hallway. Forcing herself to calm down, she read them again.

You've been accepted...first appointment 15th September...

Folding the paper, she pressed the heels of her hands into her eyes. Seriously, she needed to stop crying. Tears didn't solve problems. Besides, things were beginning to look up. In the last few hours she'd been given a chance to say a proper goodbye to Luis, and granted a once-in-a-lifetime opportunity.

Losing her baby after months of frantically trying to sustain her pregnancy had wrecked her. When the discharge nurse had given her the packet of leaflets the day she'd left hospital, Suki had almost thrown them away. It'd been days before she'd bothered to sift through the brightly coloured pamphlets prescribing various ways to move on from a loss she knew she would never get over.

At first, she'd dismissed the charity offering women in her situation a new alternative. She hadn't planned to get pregnant, nor had she imagined that her one night with Ramon would result in such a staggering roller coaster of joy and turmoil.

All she'd craved was solitude to mourn her lost child and lick her wounds. But those wounds had grown larger every day, with the hole in her heart widening until she feared it would swallow her whole. When she woke up one morning clutching the leaflet, she chose to believe the same fate that had ripped her child from her was offering her a way to heal. Her child would never draw breath, but she had more of the joy she'd felt for that child to give to another.

She hadn't planned on motherhood the first time round. But this time, she would do things her way, without the fear of a man who wouldn't stick around, as her own mother had experienced from her father, or, even worse, infidelity from someone she opened her heart to.

It had been a long shot because the charity accepted only twenty-five non-paying cases a year, so, although she'd secretly hoped, she'd been prepared for a rejection.

She opened the letter again, her mouth slowly curving in a whisper of a smile as she absorbed the soul-saving words.

She retrieved her laptop from the dark nook and took it into the kitchen. Fully immersed in the brilliant sunshine, she first answered Ramon's lawyers giving the time and date of her arrival in Havana, then sent an email confirming the appointment at the fertility clinic.

Then with the hopeful smile on her face, Suki flew up the stairs to her room, dragged the suitcase from her closet, and began to pack.

Havana in early September was a sweltering vision of vibrant colour. The brief rain shower that had engulfed the plane as they came in to land had already disappeared by the time Suki retrieved her suitcase and made her way through Immigration. Travelling first class had been a singularly unique experience, one she would've appreciated even better had the purpose of this trip not weighed so heavily on her heart. She was thankful that for the most part she'd been left alone to grab what sleep she could, which meant she arrived a lot more refreshed than she had on any other previous plane trip.

Spotting her name on a whiteboard held by a sharply suited chauffeur further hammered home the fact that she was in Luis's homeland. That she was about to come face-to-face with Ramon, the man she'd shared a torrid night with only to wake up alone with no inkling as to the devastating trail of consequences of her actions. The man who still had no clue what had happened to her after he'd walked away in the early hours of the morning.

As she often did when thoughts of Ramon surged, she shoved them back into the box labelled *out of bounds*.

She stood by the decisions she'd made regarding her pregnancy, even the ones involving swearing Luis to secrecy about the fact that she was carrying his brother's child. He hadn't been pleased, but he'd respected her wish to inform Ramon at a time of her own choosing, once she'd come to terms with the new direction her life had taken.

As it turned out, there'd been no need to involve Ramon because fate had had other ideas…

Following the chauffeur who had taken control of her

case, Suki emerged into blinding late afternoon sunshine and a cacophony of Spanish and blaring horns.

Outside José Martí International Airport, the iconic brightly painted nineteen fifties' style taxis lined up in rows next to buses and private cars. Sliding on her sunglasses, she hitched her handbag onto her shoulder and summoned a smile as the driver held open the back door of a stretch limo.

Unlike the luxury car she and Ramon had shared that night a lifetime ago, this car was a silver affair, gleaming in the sunlight and catching the eyes of passers-by. Fighting the strange urge to refuse the ride and find her own, she slid into the car. The tinted windows and the bench seats were identical, the scent of leather engulfing her and catapulting memories she didn't want to remember straight to the forefront of her mind.

Except this time she was alone, reliving every single moment of that night. Just as she'd been alone when she'd learned that her baby would most likely not survive.

Resolutely, Suki turned her thoughts outside, looking out of the window as Havana unveiled itself. It was just as Luis had described often and passionately. Most of the buildings were stuck in their pre-Communism era, with many severely dilapidating as a result of a less than thriving economy. But at every corner there were signs of restoration, pride in a rich heritage exhibited in statues, mosaic-tiled squares, a baroque cathedral and even in the graffiti that littered centuries-old buildings tucked between narrow lanes.

The two-line response from Ramon's lawyers to her email had informed her she would be staying at one of the Acosta hotels in the city. Suki wasn't ashamed to admit to her relief when she'd read the email.

She welcomed the chance to arm herself thoroughly for the next meeting with Ramon.

Traffic was light, and the limo slid beneath the porticoed entrance of the hotel a little over half an hour later.

The Acosta Hotel Havana was a stunning ten-storey building holding pride of place on a palm-tree-lined street that dissected modern Havana City from the world-renowned Old Havana. Straddling the best of both worlds, the six-star hotel had been painstakingly converted from a baroque palace, the designers having retained as many of its original breathtaking features as possible.

Inside, a stunning gold-leaf ceiling depicting an intricate map of the world was highlighted by huge, staggeringly beautiful half-century-old crystal chandeliers, while across the potted-palm foyer, several groupings of stylish leather chairs invited guests to sit and enjoy the formidable architecture.

Suki dragged her avidly exploring gaze away long enough to cross gleaming black and white mosaic tiles to the intricately carved wooden reception desk where a petite, dark-haired receptionist smiled in welcome.

'Miss Langston, welcome to Havana. We hope you will enjoy your stay with us.' She waved over a middle-aged man dressed in burgundy and gold monogrammed uniform and handed him the plastic room card. 'This is Pedro, he'll be your personal butler for the duration of your stay. If you need anything else, please let us know.'

She didn't ask how the receptionist knew her by sight. On the few occasions she'd ventured into Luis's world while he'd been alive, she'd quickly realised that the wealthy and powerful led very different lifestyles. One she got a taster of when, upon arrival in the luxury suite, two additional members of staff unpacked her clothes and a light lunch was set out on a sun-drenched private terrace within minutes.

Suki refused the welcome champagne and mostly picked at her grilled seafood salad. The preoccupation of readying herself for the trip to Cuba had briefly suppressed the jangling nerves that the thought of meeting Ramon again awakened.

They clanged harder now, questions she'd resolutely driven out of her thoughts resurging with brutal force. No matter how many times she tried to tell herself what happened that night had been on equal terms, she still couldn't understand why he'd left her without a word. Was that the done thing? Had she misstepped somehow?

Was that why he'd fast-tracked Luis into moving to New York?

But one question burned most of all, one question she knew deep in her heart had informed some of the decisions she'd made regarding her pregnancy.

Why had he lied about no longer being engaged?

Finding out that Ramon was still engaged to Svetlana after their night together had filled her with numbing disbelief, then horror when Luis had confirmed it. The shock and resulting bitterness at being made an accomplice to infidelity had stayed with her for a long time, and even risked her friendship with Luis. Only her confession about her pregnancy and the associated problems with it had brought a much-needed perspective and support from her best friend.

But now those questions, and more, crowded her brain.

Although her butler spoke perfect English, Suki was reluctant to ask him anything about his employer. The fact that Ramon was choosing to deal with her through his lawyers also indicated that he wished to maintain a distance.

That was fine by her. It should make the decision to tell him about the child they'd lost much easier.

Abandoning her meal, she retreated into the cool suite. A quick check of her emails showed another message from Ramon's lawyers, telling her she would be picked up at nine a.m. for the memorial.

Suki spent the rest of the evening laying out her clothes and taking a bath, after which she slid into bed for an early night.

The soft knock on her door came seconds before her phone's alarm went off at eight the next morning. After trying and failing to swallow more than a bite of the scrambled eggs and toast or stop the ever growing butterflies in her stomach, she took a quick shower and donned her simple black dress and heels. Tying her hair in a knot, she picked up her black clutch just as another knock came on her door.

The butler beat her to it. Which was just as well because the sight of Ramon Acosta filling the doorway wasn't one she could've withstood well up close. Because even across the vast distance of the living room, every single particle in her body clenched tight on seeing him.

He prowled into the room, tall and powerful, his strides measured and predatory. Eyes that had never been soft were now even harsher as they mercilessly raked over her. His mouth, still sensual, still unsmiling, had developed a layer of cruelty and, almost impossibly, his shoulders seemed broader, as if they'd had to expand to accommodate the harrowing circumstances thrown at him.

Even though a part of her heart went out to him for the unthinkable loss he'd suffered, Suki was too busy building the foundation of her own self-preservation as the ground beneath her feet tilted crazily.

Many times before and even after the doctors had informed her of the state of her pregnancy, she'd wondered what their child would look like. She'd eventually discovered she was carrying a girl. Imagining a female version of Ramon had been a little harder than a male version, and perhaps a blessing in disguise in the long run, a way the cosmos chose to help her cope.

Because the man dressed from head to toe in bespoke black standing in front of her was every inch as formidable—goodness, even more so—than her imagination had conjured up.

He stopped before her, eyes of chilled green glass fixed on her. 'Are you not going to greet me, Suki?' he asked icily.

Her gut clenched harder at the sound of his voice. Although it was now arctic, she didn't need much prompting to recall it in a different tone. A huskier, headier timbre. A tone she had no business recollecting right now. She bit her tongue against informing him that he'd entered her domain and therefore etiquette dictated he needed to greet her first. There was no use because men like Ramon played by their own rules. And for her own peace of mind, she wanted the next two days to go as smoothly as possible.

Clearing her throat, she strove for an even tone. 'Good morning, Ramon. I…I wasn't expecting to see you.'

'Were you not?' he countered, unforgiving eyes still hooked into her. 'What were you expecting, *exactly*?'

'Well…not you…here…' She stopped, silently cursed the silly stammering she'd thought was far behind her. 'I mean, I was expecting your driver, not you…to come in person.'

'Then I guess you'll just have to suffer the inconvenience of my presence,' he bit out.

His tone raked across her hackles, making her own chin rise. 'It's not an inconvenience, but surely you have better things to do than personally escort me to the memorial?'

'Indeed, there are many demands on my time. But perhaps everything else paled in comparison to my wish to see you. Perhaps I couldn't wait to clap eyes on you again, reassure myself that you're indeed flesh and blood.'

Something about the way he spoke the words stamped cold, hard dread onto her soul. Frantically she searched his gaze, but his face was an inscrutable mask, the only indication of his demeanour the darkening eyes that continued to regard her with unnerving intensity. 'Flesh and blood? As…as opposed to what?' she asked, her voice not as steady as she craved it to be.

His firm lips flattened. 'As opposed to the many other descriptions whose veracity I will test once the memorial is over. And believe me, Suki, there are many.'

Her hackles rose higher, her breath shortening as ice filled her spine. 'Well, I don't know what that means, but I assure you, I'm made of the same flesh and blood and bone I possessed when you last saw me.'

Cold eyes grew even more remote, his nostrils pinching

white before he took a step back. 'Should I find it curious that you neglected to mention your *heart*?'

Her breath strangled. No, her heart wasn't the same. It'd grown into twice its size when she'd found out she was carrying a child. Then it'd been lacerated beyond repair at the harrowing events and the decisions that had led to the loss of her child. Suki was sure that were she to pluck it out of her chest right this moment, she wouldn't recognise the battered organ.

'Since the contents of my heart are none of your business, no, I don't believe it's a matter for discussion.'

He exhaled slowly, his chest expanding then settling as he regarded her. 'For both our sakes, we will set this aside for now. We will go and remember my brother with our best memories. Then after that, we'll talk.'

She recalled the paragraph in the email that had demanded her attendance at a meeting involving Luis's will, and her heart lurched. 'If this is about Luis's will, please know that if there's any contention I'm willing to relinquish whatever it is that involves me.'

One corner of his mouth twitched with a cruel non-smile as he turned and strolled for the door. 'It's about much, much more than that, Suki. But rest easy, you'll find out soon enough.'

Of course, his assurance achieved the opposite effect. The journey to San Augustino Cathedral in Old Havana took a little over ten minutes, but it felt like several lifetimes with the deadly silence at the back of the limo dragging each second to infinity.

Inside the cathedral, life-size pictures of Luis and his parents were set on easels, their sometimes laughing, sometimes serious, always vibrant faces striking a deep well of sadness and grief inside her. Suki wasn't aware she was silently weeping until a white handkerchief was briskly presented to her. The grateful look she sent to Ramon dissolved when she met his stony profile.

The ceremony was over in a little more than an hour with the two dozen guests lighting candles and saying a final goodbye to lives cut short too soon.

Suki was setting her lit candle back into its cradle when Ramon appeared beside her. Hoping the acrimony she'd sensed in him had receded, she cleared her throat and faced him.

'Thank you for allowing me to be here, and for sending me the ticket. I promise, I'll pay you back as soon as I'm back at work next month.'

His lip curled. 'Such consideration. Tell me, where was that consideration when you decided to get rid of my baby without so much as a text message informing me?'

Her heart lurched to a stop. She felt the blood drain out of her head as she swayed on her feet. Opening her mouth, she strove for words, for anything to explain. But her brain had closed off in utter shock, her whole body drenched in ice-cold dread as he stepped closer, his body throbbing with menace and rage and dark promises of retribution.

'Nothing to say, Suki?' he scythed at her a second before one hand jerked out to imprison her wrist. With a merciless tug, he brought her flush against his body. To anyone watching it would've seemed as if he were comforting her. But he was leaning close, his lips a hair's breadth from her ear as he whispered, 'Don't worry, I have *plenty* to say. And if you think the repaying of an airplane ticket is the only worry you have, then you're seriously deluded.'

CHAPTER FOUR

NOTHING ABOUT HER disturbed him, Ramon assured himself as his driver pulled away from the cathedral and into traffic. Not the prolonged paleness of her frozen face, the ephemeral fragility of the fingers twisting in her lap, the intermittent shudders that racked her body.

She wasn't cold. Or in pain.

No. Not at all.

It was all an act. Suki Langston was nothing but a stone-hearted liar. One he'd had the misfortune of tangling with for one single night. Long before that night, he'd wondered what Luis saw in her, why their so-called friendship had stretched into years.

He'd concluded that his brother had been fooled as concisely as he had. Not only that, Suki had lured Luis into keeping a secret that shouldn't have been his to keep.

In his darker moments, Ramon wasn't sure he would ever be thankful that his brother had finally gone against his vow and told him the truth. Because what use was it to be told that something you hadn't even known you possessed had already been ripped from your life? What good did it do when it left you with a gaping wound further compounded by deeper losses?

At first he'd been stunned at the news, even doubting Luis. He'd used condoms the three times he'd taken her. Granted that last time in her bed had been a very close call but he hadn't taken complete leave of his senses to forget protection. But he was aware that prophylactics weren't one hundred per cent foolproof. And very quickly he'd accepted the consequences of that mishap.

What he hadn't accepted then and couldn't accept now

were the decisions Suki had taken with regard to what belonged to him.

His fist balled, the rage and grief in his chest multiplying a thousandfold.

It was unfortunate that she chose that moment to flick those wide, duplicitous blue eyes at him.

'How…how long have you known?' Her voice was little above a murmur. As if the strength had been bled from her vocal cords. He believed no such thing. Unfortunately, he was well versed in such female tactics, was accustomed to women who often pretended emotional weakness to gain advantage. In his younger days it'd been a mere irritant if it meant the woman in question ended up in his bed. With the passage of time, he'd grown to abhor it. Svetlana had been a master at it. Little had she known that he'd been onto her games very early on in their relationship.

'That's what you're concerned about? How long I was in the dark before I found out the truth?' he demanded. 'Not how I feel about you getting rid of my child?'

She paled even further, but he was in no mood to show mercy. She'd showed him none and dragged his brother into colluding with her lies. 'I—'

'Are you aware of what you robbed me of? Do you know that tying Luis into your web of lies put a strain between us and deprived me of time with my brother in the months before he died?' The words ripped fresh wounds on top of barely healed ones.

A broken sob tore from her. 'Oh, no! Please, please don't say that.'

White-hot rage and shredding grief scorched him from the inside. 'Why not? Because it's too *difficult* to hear?'

She bunched a fist against her mouth, her eyes shining as she stared at him. 'Yes! It is,' she admitted brokenly.

The car drew to a stop at the private heliport. On the tarmac his aircraft waited to transport them to the easternmost point of the island that acosta his true home. The rotor blades were already turning, but he wasn't quite done with her. Wouldn't be for a very long time.

'What right had you to ask that of Luis, hmm? What happened that night was between you and I and no one else. The consequences should have been borne by both of us.'

She squeezed her eyes shut and shook her head. 'I know, and I didn't want to…to tell Luis.'

'Why not? Because it was a dirty little secret you wished to dispose of but couldn't quite accomplish on your own?'

'No! My God, no. Stop twisting my words. Ramon, please listen…' Her mouth trembled as she opened her eyes and sucked in a deep breath.

He inhaled a breath that didn't quite replenish his lungs. Right in that moment he felt as if nothing would ever be right again. He'd lost too much, too soon.

'I have the medical bills from the private clinic, the ones you let my brother pay for. I know *exactly* how much it cost to get rid of my child.'

'Oh, my God,' she whispered.

'No. You're out of luck, *cara*. Not even a higher power is going to save you now.'

She stared at him with wide eyes before her gaze flicked past him, and out of the window at their surroundings. Seeing the readying aircraft, she turned back to him.

'Where are we going?'

'To my villa in Cienfuegos. My lawyers are waiting for us there.'

A wave of apprehension washed over her face. 'I thought we were going back to the hotel. Do…do I need to come with you?'

Another emotion sliced through him. 'You don't wish to know what your so-called best friend bequeathed you?'

She hesitated. 'I do, but…'

'You suddenly fear for your safety?' He couldn't help but mock.

Her chest rose and fell in a steadying breath. 'I fear for

the mood you're in. I prefer for us to continue this conversation when you're more rational.'

'The only thing that would make me *irrational* is you choosing to remain in this car one moment longer. Get out, Suki.' He jerked his chin towards the door his driver was holding open for her and waited, teeth clenched, as she slowly stepped out.

Grabbing his own handle, he threw the door open, the space suddenly too small to contain the power and might of his volatile emotions.

Striding across the tarmac behind her, he wondered how he would bear to be in close proximity to her during the helicopter ride when everything in him wanted to shake answers out of her. No, not everything. A small, intensely illogical part of him wanted to curl his hand over that delicate nape of hers, stop her in her tracks and demand that she stop shaking. That she stopped being so damned pale and fragile. Demand to know why she was no longer as curvy as she'd once been.

Madre de Dios...

Ramon was half thankful when his driver helped her into the helicopter. The same part watched her scramble to the farthest seat and buckle herself in, her body throwing up *keep off* signs.

Climbing in beside her, he saw to his own belt, then nodded to his pilot.

Despite the state-of-the-art noise-cancelling interior and the headphones with microphones they donned, he chose silence over continuing their conversation. He needed time to collect himself.

Losing control now would be counterproductive. He'd set a specific plan in motion when he'd instructed his lawyers to bring her here. And he would carry those plans through.

They completed the twenty-five-minute air ride in silence but he noted that she continued to tremble, her fingers twisting one way then another in her lap.

They landed at the purpose-built heliport at the south end of his villa's garden. Emerging to the small gathering of people at the edge of the tarmac, he caught the questions in her eyes although she refrained from speaking.

Ramon addressed them, shook hands, accepted hugs and fought debilitating emotions that bubbled up when heart-felt condolences were offered up. All through it, Suki stood by in silence, her hands clutching her purse in front of her.

Eventually, when the last of the visitors left, he continued towards the house.

'Who were those people?' she asked as she hurried to keep up with him.

His jaw clenched. 'Our neighbours and Luis's childhood friends.'

The shadow that crossed her face could've been real pain. Or a carefully crafted gesture meant to fool him into thinking she had genuine feelings. *Dios*, he'd had it with calculating women. He clawed his fingers through his hair.

He needed a drink. Badly.

But first there were the lawyers to deal with.

Striding across the terrace, he made a beeline for the hallway that led to his study.

Three of his trusted legal team waited, suits sharp and pens poised to carry out the plan he'd formulated. But first he had to sit through listening to his brother's last words to the woman who had cheated him out of something he hadn't even known he craved until it was gone.

He made quick introductions, ignored the curious stares his lawyers cast her way as he sat at his desk and indicated the chair opposite.

She strode forward, her slimmer hips swaying in the simple but stylish black dress.

Ramon found his gaze lingering over her neatly tied car-amel-blonde hair, then lower, scrutinising other areas where her body had changed. Her jawline was more pronounced, her cheeks hollower. Her lightly glossed mouth was still full and attention-grabbing, but her waist was even trimmer, its slightness easily spanned by his hands…

Realising what he was doing, he ruthlessly reeled himself in, but not before he caught the lingering gaze of the youngest member of his legal team on her. A sharp look redirected the man's focus to the papers he held.

'We will conduct the meeting in English. Miss Langston doesn't speak Spanish…' Ramon paused, one eyebrow raised at her '…unless I'm mistaken?'

She shook her head as she sat down, summoned a whisper of a smile. 'Nothing beyond hello and goodbye.'

Neither of which she would be using on him any time soon. They were light years beyond cordial greetings and he had no intention of letting her out of his sight for a very long time.

His chief legal representative opened the folder before him. 'The reason you're here, Miss Langston, is because of the late codicil attached to the personal will Luis had drafted earlier this year.'

Ramon's nape tightened. 'When was this done?'

'In May, four months ago. On the fifteenth to be exact.'

Suki's breath caught, her throat working furiously.

'What?' he demanded, although he suspected he knew the answer.

'It was the day after…' She stopped, firmed her lips.

He didn't need to hear more. He knew it was the day after she'd first checked into the private clinic. The time and dates Luis had told him were seared into his brain. And if for any reason he needed hard proof, the report from his private investigators was locked away in the top drawer of his desk.

He dragged his focus back to his lawyer. 'Carry on.'

'Miss Langston, I believe at the time the codicil was added you were pregnant?' his lawyer asked.

Still tight-lipped, she nodded.

'Well, Luis didn't alter it so the original document stands. In it, your child was to receive a lump sum of money on his or her eighteenth birthday. But in the event of altered circumstances like what subsequently ensued, half of that sum was to go to you but only at his brother's discretion.'

She shook her head, her eyes finding his. 'You won't need to decide whether I should have the money or not. I don't want it.'

The lawyer's eyebrows rose. 'But you haven't heard how much—'

'I don't care how much it is. I don't want it. Feel free to give it away to Luis's favourite charity.'

Fresh anger boiled in Ramon's gut. 'That's how you're choosing to honour his memory? By tossing away his gift so carelessly?'

The eyes that met his were darker than normal. Bruised. Perhaps she cared about his brother to whatever extent her stone heart was capable. But in the end, her caring hadn't been enough. Luis had assured him he'd tried to talk her out of her decision to no avail.

'That money was never meant for me, Ramon, and you know it. It isn't right,' she murmured, her voice husky.

'Whatever my thoughts are on the matter, this was Luis's wish. You will honour it.'

Her mouth firmed. 'Okay, fine. If I choose to accept it, what then? Will you just hand it over?'

He shrugged. 'That will be one of the subjects of our private discussion.'

A tiny flame lit through her eyes, a spark of anger lightening the dark blue depths that seemed even more vivid against the stark black she wore. 'You just wanted me to say yes so you'd make me jump through hoops, didn't you?'

'I'm not in a habit of handing over a quarter of a million pounds on a fickle whim, Suki, so yes, there will be some hoop-jumping.'

She gasped, her gaze swinging from his to his lawyer's. At the man's nod of confirmation of the sum, she subsided back into her chair. 'That's…a lot of money. Why?'

'You were carrying his niece, and Luis was big on family. As his friend, surely you knew that?' he taunted.

The fire dimmed a little, but her chin elevated. 'Yes, I knew.' Her gaze swung to the lawyers. '*If* Mr Acosta decides to release the money to me, I would still like to donate it. Can I contact you if I need to?'

Temper rising, Ramon watched his lawyer nod, his expression softening.

'*Sí*, of course, Miss Langston.'

Suki started to rise, throwing further fuel on Ramon's mood. 'Sit down, we're not done,' he snapped.

Her gaze reverted to him, then back to his lawyer. The older man cleared his throat. 'Luis also left you two works of art to be handed over on whatever birthday followed his passing. I believe your twenty-sixth birthday is coming up.'

She nodded.

The lawyer continued, 'They're commissioned and paid for, but not yet completed. The artist will let us know when it is ready and you will be informed.'

A tiny frown marred her eyebrows. 'I...who's the artist?'

Ramon hid his sizeable bolt of shock. 'I'm guessing that would be me,' he supplied lazily, both irritated and saddened by Luis's meddling. He looked at his lawyer. 'Correct?'

Her head snapped in his direction, her breath stopping. 'You...why?' she asked for a second time in the space of three minutes.

'Because according to my brother, you *adore* my work. I believe his paraphrased words after a visit to one of my galleries were, "She rhapsodised over your sculptures for a solid hour and needed to be dragged out of the gallery. I think the poor girl deserves a couple of her own." I never thought he'd actually put the thought to deed in his will.'

Her face reddened, her eyes sliding away from his. 'I didn't... Luis liked to exaggerate. I wasn't that taken...'

'Does that mean you're about to refuse this gift, too?'

he enquired, the turbulence inside him curiously emerging in a soft whisper.

Her gaze returned to his. Her lips parted. Ramon found himself holding his breath, unsure whether he wished her to accept or refuse.

'You would still do it? Despite…everything?' Her voice was equally soft, but tinged with bewilderment, not the rage burning beneath his skin.

He allowed himself a twisted smile. 'I loved my brother. I believe in honouring his wishes. The question is, do you?'

Her bewilderment intensified, her tongue sneaking out to lick her lower lip. 'Of course, but, Ramon…'

He actively despised the hot little tug to his groin as he followed the action. 'Is that all of it?' he snapped at his lawyers.

They got the hint, straightened their ties and shuffled papers. 'Yes, that's Miss Langston's part of the meeting concluded. When it's decided what to do with the inheritance, we will be on hand to carry out your wishes.' His chief lawyer switched to Spanish, handing over the papers Ramon had requested with a puzzled expression.

Ramon ignored his concerns. Almost overnight, he'd had everything that meant a damn taken from him. His parents and Luis's loss was unavoidable. The steps Suki had taken were deliberate. He would not be swayed from the path he'd chosen.

The moment the lawyers left he returned his gaze to her.

Watched her gather herself with a deep breath, her eyes fixed on the painting on the far wall of his study. A little colour had returned to her cheeks and she seemed better composed. She was nowhere as vibrant as she'd been the last time they were together, but she didn't look deathly pale any more.

Which he chose to see as an advantage. For what was to come she would need all her strength. Or perhaps she would acquiesce simply to get her hands on the money she purportedly didn't want. He knew different. She was in severe dire straits financially.

Rising, he rounded his desk. Her head immediately swung to him, her expression growing wary as she tracked his slow stride. Hitching his thigh on the corner of his desk, he sat down.

Silently, he watched her. Waited.

Her tongue darted out to worry her lower lip again. 'Ramon, I think I need to explain a few things—'

'Explanation is necessary when there's a misunderstanding, an omission of facts, or outright *lying*. There is no such misunderstanding or omission here. You got pregnant with my child and chose to keep that fact to yourself. Then took specific steps to get rid of it. Have I *misunderstood* or *omitted* anything?'

She flinched then slowly her gaze narrowed, the fire returning to her eyes. 'No, you haven't. But you're also forgetting one thing.'

'And what's that?' he asked.

'That it was my body and ultimately *my* decision. Not yours.'

The truth in that statement was inescapable. And while the civilised part of him accepted it, the part steeped in deep mourning and inextinguishable anger couldn't swallow it in that moment. 'So I didn't matter at all in this scenario?' he breathed.

Her hand flew to her forehead, rubbing restively over her smooth skin. 'I didn't say that. The trouble is that you seem to think I took the decision lightly, when it was the last thing I did.'

'How would I know? I wasn't there.'

Her hand dropped, her delicate jaw clenching. 'I know! And you can berate me about that all you want. But I can't change the past. I'm… I'm trying to put it behind me.'

That terrible vice around his heart squeezed tighter. 'Well, I'm not ready to put it behind me. And no, you can't change the past. But you can change the future. And you will.'

Her breath expelled in a little rush of apprehension. 'What's that supposed to mean?'

'It means it's time to discuss the next item on the agenda.'

He reached for the bound papers his lawyers had drawn up and tossed them into her lap.

For long seconds, she looked down at them. Then, slowly, she picked them up, scrutinised the pages with a frown. 'What is this?'

'It's an agreement between you and me.'

She leafed through a few more pages. 'I can see that. But for what? It just says it's an agreement for my *services*. I'm an interior designer and you're a hotelier and artist. What service could you possibly want from me?'

'I don't need your professional services, *cara*. What I want is for you to provide me with what you took deliberate steps to deprive me of. My whole family was wiped out in a single night. I want a child, Suki. An heir. As soon as possible. Preferably in the next nine months. And you're going to give me one.'

CHAPTER FIVE

DEEP SHOCK AND confusion held her frozen in the chair for countless seconds. Then Suki surged to her feet. She tossed the papers back onto the desk, unable to get her fingers off them quickly enough.

'Are you out of your mind?' She should've posed the question rhetorically because she was one hundred per cent sure that he had gone insane. From grief or from something else, but definitely unsound.

Except he didn't look crazy. Only brutally determined, eerily controlled. 'Far from it,' he confirmed. 'In fact, this is probably one of the sanest decisions I've ever made.'

Her already racing heart tripped over itself to speed up even more. 'Then I'm terrified to imagine what you class as sane!'

A cold smile curved his mouth. 'Let's concentrate on one item at a time.'

'We will not concentrate on any items because what you're…*suggesting* isn't going to happen,' she returned. She didn't realise she was backing away from the chair, from him, until he rose to his imposing height and prowled after her.

'Where do you think you're going?'

'Where do you think? I'm leaving!'

'No. You are not.' His voice was deadly soft.

Goose bumps rose on her skin but she kept moving away. 'Watch me.'

'I am watching you. And I don't think you realise how very little options you have here.'

'I have the option of *not* staying here to continue this in-sane conversation with you.'

His hands slid lazily into his pockets, but there was nothing indolent in the eyes that tracked her backward trajectory with narrow-eyed intensity. 'You can leave this room, but how do you propose to make your escape from this house?'

Her back touched the study door and she froze. 'You… I seriously hope you're not suggesting that you intend to keep me here against my will!'

'That entirely depends on you. You can walk out of here and attempt to make the three-hour journey back to Havana on your own or we can finish this conversation.'

She shook her head, knowing deep inside that things weren't that simple. The alarming suspicion that he'd planned all this with meticulous precision grew with each second he stared at her.

'I'll make the journey on my own, thank you.'

She needed to get out of here. The trip back would be costly, but she'd stick it on her credit card and think about the consequences later.

Reaching behind her, she grasped the handle, turned it. Relief flooded her when it yielded. It occurred to her that once she turned and walked away, this would probably be the very last time she set eyes on Ramon. A tiny second was all she needed to take in the sculpted beauty of his face, the square designer-stubble jaw, the impossibly wide shoulders that Luis had once told her had been honed from his days playing quarterback at college in the States, the lean, hard-packed body that stretched over pure, streamlined muscle.

She took all of it in, stored it in a file somewhere deep in her subconscious, unwilling to admit that some time in the future she would revisit it. Just as she'd revisited their night together more times than she felt comfortable admitting even to herself.

Pulling the door wider, she stepped through it. 'Goodbye, Ramon.'

'Is your hurry to get back to do with your appointment

with the sperm donor agency or your mother?' he enquired in an almost indifferent voice.

Suki turned back so swiftly she almost tripped over her feet. The way he leaned so casually against the doorjamb, legs crossed at the ankles, made her believe she'd misheard him. Because surely he wouldn't look that bored while informing her he'd callously invaded her privacy. *'What did you say?'*

He remained silent, those all-knowing green eyes pinned on her.

'Did you not hear me? I said—'

'I heard you, and you know exactly what I said. I just prefer not to conduct this conversation in the hallway in the hearing of my staff, especially if you insist on using that shrill voice.'

Suki swallowed down the scream that rose; squashed the urge to march up to him, take him by his expensive designer lapels and shake the living daylights out of him. It would be useless because she suspected he would remain just as unmoved as he seemed now.

She shook her head in abject confusion. 'What gives you the right to invade my privacy?'

'You don't seem to have grasped the reality before you, Suki.' He stepped back from the door, his hands leaving his pockets to hang almost menacingly against his masculine thighs. 'So come back in and let's discuss this rationally. Now,' he added after a handful of seconds when she remained frozen.

'All this…the ticket, the hotel, coming here to meet with your lawyers…it was all one giant plan, wasn't it?'

'*Sí*, it was,' he confirmed, not a trace of apology in his face or voice. 'Oh, and I forgot to mention. Your things were moved here from the hotel while we were at the memorial. So bear that in mind if you decide to make another grand exit.'

Her mind sped with the thinly veiled threat in his voice.

Her things…including her passport and airline ticket. 'Oh, God. You…'

'Need your undivided attention *without* the histrionics.'

The reality of what was happening rammed home in that instant. She could try to leave but she wouldn't get very far. So really, she was going nowhere until he deemed it so.

On leaden legs, she returned to the study. The sound of the door shutting felt like the slam of prison gates.

She tightened her fingers around her clutch to stop their trembling. 'I can report you to the authorities. You know that, right?'

He raised a mocking eyebrow. 'For having a simple conversation with a guest after my brother's memorial?'

'There's nothing simple or remotely funny about this, and you know it,' she replied heatedly.

All traces of mockery evaporated from his face, leaving a harsh, bleak mask. 'On that we're agreed,' he bit out. One hand rose to spear agitated fingers through his hair. 'Did you stop to think that, had I been in the picture, things could've turned out differently?'

Suki didn't want to admit that the thought had crossed her mind when the doctors had first given her the diagnosis. But in those initial harrowing weeks, she'd clung vainly to hope. Then the tabloids' timely confirmation of Ramon and Svetlana's still very much *on* engagement had usefully reiterated why any reliance on the man who'd slept with her while still committed to another woman, who'd proven most categorically that he was untrustworthy, was out of the question. Father of her child or not, the knowledge that she couldn't trust Ramon with so momentous a decision had kept her silent. 'How?' she asked, despite knowing they wouldn't have been.

'For a start, had you come to me, you would be in a financially better place now than you currently are.'

She frowned. 'Financially better place? What are you talking about?'

'Luis helped you with your medical bills, did he not? Did you stop to think that going ahead with the pregnancy, that presenting me with my child, would have made you rich beyond your wildest dreams?'

She staggered, actually staggered back at the accusation. 'Are you telling me you think I deliberately got rid of the baby because it wasn't *financially viable*?'

'I had my investigators look into your financial history, Suki. I know you're broke.'

She struggled to take a breath. 'I understand that we were little more than strangers. And we didn't even like each other very much,' she ventured. 'But I would never… never dream of—'

'Drop the excuses, Suki. Nothing you say will excuse your actions. Having my child was an inconvenience you took care of without bothering to tell me,' he cut across her, jaw clenched into stone. Turning, he headed back to his desk and picked up two files and the bundle of papers she'd discarded minutes ago and strode towards her, savage purpose in every step.

He casually opened the file he held. Suki recognised the charity's logo on the letterhead immediately. 'Which begs the question, why would you get rid of my child, then make yourself a charity case for a sperm donation four months later?' There was something dangerously deadly in his voice. A scalpel-sharp control that said he was stroking the very edge of his endurance.

She swallowed, knowing instinctively that the *none of your business* line was the last thing she wanted to throw at him right now. A tremble shivered down her spine. Retreating until she had the grouping of studded leather sofas and a coffee table between them, she attempted to reason with him. 'Ramon, the past is the past. This thing…what you're suggesting…it doesn't make sense.'

His harsh exhalation stopped her stuttering. He glanced up, eyes like the frozen wastelands of Siberia blasting her.

'Why, Suki? Why, for some unconscionable reason, have you decided you want a child now?'

She raised her chin. 'I don't have to explain myself to you.'

A thousand expressions flitted through his eyes, not a single one of them decipherable. Slowly, he shut the file and, without taking his eyes off her, tossed it on the coffee table.

'Okay. Let's talk about something else. Your mother is currently in a private hospital with health complications triggered by stage two cervical cancer, yes?' he pressed.

Her heart lurched painfully. 'Yes,' she murmured.

'With her insurance about to run out this month and her doctors all set to throw in the towel, nothing short of a miracle will bring any hope.' There was no malice in his voice, but neither was there any warmth or sympathy. For reasons she knew were coming, he was laying out the facts of her life in bare chunks.

A spike of anger tunnelled through her bewildered emotions. 'And let me guess, you suddenly have the power to grant miracles?'

'I have more than that. I have the financial power that fuels *particular* miracles. I'm also trying to discover what your goals are. Is this baby you're hoping to have a means of alleviating future loss? Having decided that you didn't want a child before, you're now desperate for one so should your mother not make it you won't be left alone?' he demanded chillingly.

'I don't know what kind of monster you think I am, but what you're suggesting is detestable.'

'Is it?' he enquired, his tone a touch softer, a touch more...vulnerable.

Her eyes widened as what he'd said before made clearer meaning. 'That's why *you* want a child? So you're not alone?'

Pain flickered over his face. 'I want a family, yes,' he confirmed.

'And digging up my mother's records, what does that achieve except to make me think you're leveraging my mother's health against me?'

'It's not leverage. It's an offer of help so, when we reach agreement, you have one less thing to worry about. Those miracles you scoffed about can happen.'

She laughed. She couldn't help herself. 'You actually expect me to believe that you'd do that out of the goodness of your heart, after going to this trouble to bring me here?'

He didn't answer for a long minute. When he did, his voice was bleak. 'For some reason Luis held both you and your mother in high regard, and yet you were prepared to walk away from the inheritance he left you just to make a point when that money could've helped your mother. Luis isn't around any more to make you see sense. But I am.'

She shook her head. 'That money was meant for the child I never had.'

'It was meant for you. But like everything else, you threw it away without a second thought. You think Luis just *overlooked* the fact that you were no longer pregnant when he chose not to amend his will? He knew your mother was ill. Did you not think this might be his way of helping you?'

'I don't know. I had no idea what he was thinking—'

'Perhaps this! What is happening here right now. Maybe he rightly believed that you owe me answers. That *you owe me*, full stop.' His fist was bunched, his nostrils pinched in a tight leash on his control.

She refused to back down. 'Regardless of that, I don't deserve that money.'

'Does your mother deserve your abandonment?'

'I haven't abandoned her! I've done everything I can for her—'

'Have you? Or did you make the barest minimum effort then stop, just like you did with our child?'

Fresh whips lashed her heart. 'You have no right to say that to me—'

'I have every right. And more. For what you did there is no coming back. Only reparations.'

'I'm sorry I didn't tell you the moment I found out! Is that what you want to hear? Do you want me to get down on my knees and beg your forgiveness?'

'You know what I want.'

She flung her clutch on the sofa, every cell in her body too agitated to contain her. 'How can you even propose something like this…how can you contemplate doing something so *life-changing* when you stare at me with such hate? And have you even paused for a second to think about *my* feelings?'

He swivelled towards the window, his features carefully schooled as he raked a hand through his hair. For a long time, she thought he wouldn't answer her questions. When he turned back, his features were set even harder, his eyes completely inscrutable.

'I don't need to like you to take you to bed,' he replied. While she was grappling with that, he added, 'And vice versa. I believe right before our last connection we were less than impressed with each other. Yet, we still proved that we were compatible where it counted.'

Her senses reeled with the enormity of his reasoning. 'You think that tipsy interlude compares in any way to this…*clinical* exercise you're proposing?'

'Yes, I do. And this time we're going into this with clear minds and a finite purpose. And you mistake me by thinking this is something you can argue away.'

'And you do likewise by thinking this is something you can force on me. My answer is no.'

'There won't be any force involved. You'll stay here, take the night to sleep on it. Come morning, you will give me an answer. And I prefer that answer to be yes.'

'Or what?'

'Or nothing. And by nothing I mean we will both walk away empty-handed. You will not be returning to England to get yourself impregnated by some faceless sperm donor. I suggested that your place be given away to another needful applicant as of this morning.'

She gasped. *'What?'*

'You're not deaf. On top of that, I have personally put in place a facility for an additional fifty women to receive similar funding. The charity is beyond thrilled. They won't take your name off the list without your express confirmation, but I dare say you're no longer at the top of their list. Not once I informed them that you'd be giving the traditional way another try with me.'

The ground shook beneath her feet. 'You…you can't do that!'

He nodded to the discarded file. 'You underestimate how much I want this, Suki. You're still on the waiting list with the charity, but if you truly wish to get pregnant any time soon, I'm your only option.'

'That's…that's blackmail.'

'You'll be good enough not to fling disparaging labels around, *cara*. What you did was far worse.'

The urge to scream again rose. She barely managed to keep it together to raise her hands in a placatory gesture when she wanted to find the nearest letter opener and stick it in his black heart. 'Ramon. Please hear me out. What I did…my decision…I didn't think I had a choice…' Her voice broke. Swallowing, she shook her head. 'I didn't have a choice…' she repeated.

Ramon's face paled, his features slackening for a brutal, painful moment, before it clenched back into a tight, furious mask. The eyes that stared back at her were almost black with volcanic rage. 'You had a choice. Me. But you were too selfish to bring me into the equation. You made the decision on your own.'

'My God, you accuse me of so many things, but what about you?'

His brows clamped tight. 'What about me?'

'You told me you were no longer engaged, and yet weeks later I found out it was a lie!'

His jaw flexed for a second. 'And that is the reason you called my brother when you should've called me? That is why you handed him the responsibility when it should've been mine to bear?'

Her breath shuddered out. 'I didn't hand anyone the responsibility. I didn't call Luis. My mother did.'

He stilled, straight eyebrows clenched tighter in a dark frown. 'Your mother?'

She nodded, her head barely able to perform the movement. 'She was home from hospital but weak from her chemo. She knew what was going on and she felt bad that she couldn't help me. I told her I didn't need help but she... she wouldn't listen. She thought she was letting me down. She knew Luis and I were close friends but she assumed our relationship had grown into something more. Anyway, she assumed he was the father and called him. Apparently, she had a long go at him for shirking his responsibilities. Luis didn't say a word to refute the claim. He just...turned up at my house the next day and refused to leave.'

'And let me guess. That was when you swore him to secrecy to keep me from my own child?' His voice bled fire and ice.

'I was going to tell you. I didn't think you would appreciate hearing it from him. And I thought I had time. But then things just...unravelled.'

He breathed in a harsh breath. 'You say that and yet you found time to call on Luis a second time to hold your hand through the procedure.'

It staggered her how much detail he knew. And how things looked from his side of the fence. 'I didn't ask him to come, Ramon. But he wasn't prepared to take no for an answer.'

He gave an arid laugh. 'You found it so easy to give in

to him, the same way you found it easy to make up excuses not to contact me.'

'How dare you—?'

His hand slammed on the desk, making her jump. 'I dare because I am without my child, and you're to blame!'

Pain shook her from scalp to toes. 'You preach at me from your lofty pedestal about doing the right thing. Did you stop to think that after lying to me about Svetlana that I'd want nothing to do with you? Or are you going to tell me that those pictures in the papers of the two of you taken in the weeks after we were together were your doppelgängers?'

His jaw worked for a long moment before he exhaled. 'What happened between you and I was a one-night thing. If memory serves it was what you wanted, what we both wanted.'

The fact that he was justifying his actions shouldn't have come as a surprise. Wasn't that how she had come into this world? Hadn't she heard a version of the same story from her mother about her father's justification for his infidelity? The only difference here was that Ramon had apparently wanted the seed he'd unwittingly planted in her womb. Suki's father hadn't even stuck around for the pregnancy test announcing she was on the way.

The end result of that had been a mother steeped in so much bitterness she'd never trusted another man long enough to move on from the past. From a very early age, Suki had vowed to learn from that lesson, until she'd met Luis and had eventually chosen to hope that all men weren't the same.

Luis had been one in a million, and she'd trusted him with her life. Unfortunately, she'd been foolish enough to transfer some of that faith to his older brother.

She didn't plan on making the same mistake again.

Refocusing on Ramon, she shook her head. 'There's no way this can ever work. Too much has happened. Besides, what about Svetlana? Won't she have a huge say in what you're proposing?'

'She and I have been over for several months.' The words were clipped. Final.

Suki told herself the fluttering in her stomach was a side effect of the strain of the conversation. 'The same kind of *over* you meant the last time?'

His eyes gleamed, his focus unwavering. 'The kind of over that means she has no bearing on this conversation.'

She wanted to press for more. Why, she had no idea. Whether Ramon and Svetlana were over or not had no impact on her life. There were more important things to focus on, like the reason he had a file on her mother.

'Did you know about Luis's financial bequest before today?'

'No, but he was fond of you. It doesn't surprise me he would take such an action.'

Her head still reeled from that. 'I don't know what to say…'

Another bleak expression darted across his face. 'If he were here right now, what do you think he'd say with regard to your mother's condition?'

Suki's heart twisted, her best friend's vibrant face rearing up vividly in her mind's eye. 'He would help me beg, borrow or steal to help her.'

'*Sí*, he would. And what do you think he would say to you helping me to continue his family line?' he countered smoothly.

She gasped at the skilful way he'd cornered her. 'That's not fair.'

'Is it not, or are you being a hypocrite? He's left you a means to help your mother. Should her treatment exceed what he left for you, I'll pick up the slack.' He paused, his eyes still fixed on her. 'Are you going to let pride and stubbornness stand in the way of your mother's health?'

'No, of course not! But I can't help but think this is…a cold transaction.'

'It's a transaction where we both win.'

Her heart shuddered. 'But her doctors say there's nothing else they can do.'

'They were wrong.' Returning to the sofa, he picked up the last file and handed it to her.

Hands shaking, she opened it, started to read. The names that jumped out at her were from some of the best teaching hospitals and medical research facilities in the world. She recognised them because she'd come across several of them in her own research. Letters from acclaimed doctors with countless abbreviations after their names had personally answered all of the pertinent questions Ramon had posed them. Without offering guarantees, at least half a dozen different doctors had given her mother far better odds than her current doctors had.

'Everything in there has been double and triple checked. All that's required for your mother to get the help she vitally needs is to say yes.'

Suki closed her eyes, three unshakeable truths becoming crystal clear. Her mother's case wasn't hopeless. Luis, in his own inimitable way, was caring for her even from the grave. But by doing so, he'd also put her directly in his brother's debt.

And there was only one means by which Ramon Acosta wanted payment.

CHAPTER SIX

SHE WENT THROUGH the paperwork, noting the recommendation for her mother's treatment to be started immediately, preferably at a state-of-the-art facility in Miami. Closing the file, Suki walked to the sofa and sat down.

The pressure that had been building since Ramon walked into her hotel room this morning intensified. Her pulse raced and in a fit of agitation she reached up and tugged the pins from her hair. The simple of act of unknotting her hair brought a tiny bit of relief. But her mind continued to spin at the sheer enormity of what he was asking of her.

Spiking her fingers into her hair, she briefly massaged her scalp, then raised her head to the dominating figure poised like a dark overlord before her. His gaze was on the heavy tresses gliding over her hands and down her shoulders. He seemed momentarily fascinated with what she was doing, but, too soon, dark unwavering green eyes locked on hers once more.

'Are you ready to discuss this properly?'

She took a deep breath. 'You can have any woman you want. You only have to click your fingers to have them lining up outside your gate to have your baby. Why go to these lengths? And why me?'

This time the trace of pain was fleeting, very hurriedly controlled. 'I can't just pluck a surrogate off the Internet. These things take months, sometimes even years to find a right match.'

'What about your little black book? Surely you have conquests that went beyond a one-night stand, who will be happy to bear you a child?'

His full lips compressed. 'I haven't yet come across a

woman who, no matter how much she initially claims otherwise, doesn't start imagining a deeper, more meaningful relationship with me at some point. I'm not interested in that.'

'Right. You were so not interested in that that you were once engaged to be married?'

He ignored her sarcasm. 'I was once engaged because I believed a relationship was a viable option for me. I no longer believe that. Marriage is not for me. And why you?' He shrugged. 'Because you require a sperm donor and I happen to need a surrogate. The timing couldn't be better. Besides, with you I know exactly what I'm getting.'

'And what's that?'

'A black-and-white transaction with no frills, no insincere platitudes and one hundred per cent commitment signed in ink.'

Her chest squeezed tight. 'I'm not just going to hand over my baby to you the moment he or she is born, Ramon. You can forget that right now.'

Two things happened right then. All six feet four inches of him froze in rigid attention. And Suki realised just what she'd said.

'So you agree to bear my child?' he clipped out after a long moment, his voice strangely hoarse.

Her breath shook out. 'I…no. Not yet.'

'This is very much a yes or no situation.'

'And I very much would like five minutes to think about what I'm agreeing to before I say yes to bringing another child into this world!'

He rocked back on his heels, then turned towards his desk. 'While you think about it, I'll get the kitchen to bring you some refreshments.'

Her raw laugh scraped her throat. 'Canapés aren't going to make deciding any easier.'

'Neither will starvation and dehydration. You're much thinner than you were the last time I saw you.'

'Yes, I've been through a trauma or two,' she replied.

'I'm aware of that. But we still need to remedy that,' he countered.

'Fine, let's fatten me up for the slaughter,' she muttered under her breath, because he was already lifting the phone, relating instructions in rapid Spanish.

That done, he returned to his position as silent, merciless master in front of her. After several minutes had gone by, he crossed over and sat down next to her. Elbows on his knees, he angled his body towards hers.

'What is it, Suki? Spit it out.'

She didn't want to say the words out loud, but the fear in her heart wouldn't dissipate. 'I'm…are you not afraid that something will go wrong?' *Again.*

A muscle ticced in his jaw. 'You were about to get yourself artificially inseminated. What guarantees do you have that that pregnancy will proceed smoothly?'

Her heart twisted. 'None.'

He nodded. '*Muy bien.* Then we are in the same boat. But rest assured we will have the benefit of the top obstetricians in the world monitoring you round the clock.'

The assurance eased the constriction around her heart, followed swiftly by the realisation that she was seriously contemplating agreeing to Ramon's wishes.

'What do you think he would say to you helping me to continue his family line?'

Her heart tugged painfully, the belief that Luis would've urged her on so strong, her breath caught. Whether that was the reason the constriction further eased in her chest, or because she now had fresh hope for her mother, she didn't know. And even if she seriously considered refusing, with Ramon determined to throw himself in the way of her having a child any other way but with him, her options for a child of her own were limited, considering she had very little financial resources left.

But another child…with Ramon? Her insides clenched with apprehension at the thought of creating another child, this time deliberately with him. But next to that apprehension, a tiny quiver she refused to label as hope and excitement began to unfurl. She pushed it back down, unwilling to let it spring forth when there was so much more to consider.

'How will we manage this? You work and travel all over the world. I live in England. You know I'm not about to hand over my child to you the moment it's born. So how is this going to work?'

'Our child will be born here in Cuba. Once he or she is old enough, relocating my offices anywhere in the world will not be a problem. We will decide when the time comes how that will be handled.'

She frowned. 'I have a job, Ramon. You expect me to what…just give it up to sit around while waiting to have your baby?'

'I would prefer that you do not work while you're pregnant and of course in the first few years of the baby's life—'

Her stunned laughter stopped him. 'You're joking, aren't you? That's not how the real world works. I have bills to pay, my mother to look after once her treatment is over.'

'How do you intend to do that when your latest request to return to work was denied?'

Her mouth dropped open. 'Is there any part of my life that you haven't dug up yet?'

'I don't know what your favourite colour is or which brand of toothpaste you prefer. But we have time for that.' He picked up the agreement and held it out to her. 'Read the agreement, a little more carefully this time. Pay attention to clause five.'

She eyed him for a few seconds before she accepted the papers. The clause he mentioned was on the third page. Shock bolted through her, blurring her vision after she'd counted six zeros. 'You can't…this is another joke, right?'

'This is to ensure that our child remains your number one priority. To ensure you don't have to think about bills or work or anything beyond our baby's welfare. Your mother too will be well taken care of.'

'I hadn't planned on anything else superseding my child's well-being but…this is an absurd amount of money.'

His sensual mouth pursed. 'You seem to have trouble grasping that nothing about this discussion is humorous, Suki.'

'Probably because I'm still finding it hard to believe that you truly want this.'

He grabbed the papers from her and once again shoved them aside. His hands cupped her shoulders, bringing her close enough so she didn't miss every flicker of emotion that crossed his face.

'I want a child, Suki. You will be the woman who bears me that child. Is there some other way you wish me to say that before you believe that I mean it?' he rasped in a deep, fervid voice.

Perhaps it was the electric burn of his hands on her bare skin. Or the minute tremble in his voice that spoke of soul-deep intent and yearning. Whatever it was, it cut through the fog of her remaining indecision. Even before her head had fully grasped her intent, her heart had accepted that this was what she would do.

For her mother.

For herself.

Perhaps most of all for Luis. The knowledge that she would play a hand in ensuring her friend's bloodline lived on filled her with the same sense of joy she'd been honoured to receive from Luis. Through her child, she would always have a piece of her friend.

'No, you don't need to say anything else,' she whispered.

'So you agree?'

She nodded again. 'Yes.'

He stared down at her for another long spell, his thumbs absently sliding back and forth on her skin before his gaze dropped to her lips. As if he'd touched them, they tingled wildly, the blood plumping them until she slicked her tongue over her lower lip to alleviate the sting.

'What time frame do we have to work with?'

She frowned. 'I...what?'

'Is the window closing on this month's cycle?' he demanded.

That wasn't a question she'd expected. Because those weren't questions near strangers asked each other.

She closed her eyes as heat flared up her face. 'I...I'm... God, I can't believe I'm discussing my menstrual cycle with you.'

'It's a naturally occurring event and nothing to be embarrassed about,' he replied.

'I'm not embarrassed, I'm just...'

'Being very English about it?' he enquired with a dry tone. 'Would you have preferred us to discuss the weather first before we got to the nitty-gritty?'

She shrugged. 'Maybe. There's absolutely nothing wrong with discussing the weather.'

One side of his mouth quirked. 'Maybe I will oblige you next time,' he answered. Then waited.

'Yes, I stop ovulating in three days,' she eventually murmured.

His gaze dropped back to her mouth, his nostrils flaring lightly as he leaned closer, filled her personal space with his larger-than-life aura. 'Then you will come to me tonight.'

Too soon. Much too soon. Suki swallowed. 'No.'

He stilled. *'Perdón?'*

She shook her head. 'I said no. Not tonight. I just... I need a little time to take all of this in.'

A frown gathered at his forehead. 'Nothing will change with more time,' he warned.

'I know that, but I'm still taking the time I need.'

His mouth pursed into a forbidding line. But any response coming her way was halted by the knock on the door. A handful of seconds passed before he released her. At his command, a member of his kitchen staff entered wheeling a serving trolley piled with trays of hot and cold beverages, pastries and neatly cut sandwiches.

The middle-aged woman smiled affectionately at Ramon before setting the tray on the coffee table. 'This is Teresa. She's my housekeeper.' He repeated the other side of introduction in Spanish, to which Teresa smiled and responded, adding a few more words Suki didn't understand.

Ramon shook his head and dismissed her, then reached out to place several pieces of pastry on a plate. Passing it to her, he indicated the drinks. 'Which would you prefer?'

She wanted to laugh at the mundaneness of eating following the tense last hour.

'Coffee, please. Thanks.'

He poured two cups, adding sugar and cream to hers at her request before passing it over.

For a few minutes he drank his coffee without making conversation while she nibbled on a finger sandwich. Unable to stand the tension, she picked up another triangle of pastry, and bit into it. The unexpected flavoursome guava and cream cheese filling made her mouth water, her very empty stomach reminding her how long it'd been since she last ate.

'What are these?' she asked, more to make conversation than anything else.

'They're called *pastelitos*. Teresa makes the best ones.' He nudged the tray towards her. 'Have another one.'

She didn't refuse. A barest trace of amusement whispered over his face as he watched her devour a second one.

'After we finish eating, I will show you to your suite. When you're rested, I'll introduce you to the rest of the staff and give you a tour of the villa.'

Grateful for the first normal conversation she'd had since he'd turned up at her hotel this morning, she took another bite. 'Thanks, that would be good.'

'Tomorrow morning, Suki. I will not wait longer than that.'

The thought of him and her...in broad daylight...threatened to send the *pastelitos* and coffee down the wrong way. 'Tomorrow *night*,' she countered quickly after swallowing.

He didn't frown, but the air of displeasure once again shrouded him as he set his cup back onto the saucer. 'Any reason why you wish to waste a further twenty-four hours?'

She tried a shrug, but it didn't quite come off as smoothly as she would've wished. 'Isn't it enough that we've agreed to do this thing? Is there any reason why we need to...umm do it during the *day*?'

The slight widening of his eyes was the only indication that he was surprised. That surprise turned swiftly into sardonic amusement. 'Are you trying to tell me that you only engage in sex at night, Suki?' he drawled.

She set her cup and saucer on the table. 'We've discussed my monthly cycle. There is no way I'm discussing my sexual history with you.'

'How many lovers have you had?' he asked in the next breath.

'Perhaps you didn't hear me—'

'I heard you. Answer my question.'

She stared back at him, the need to challenge burning inside her. 'You go first,' she said, knowing it would put an end to the absurd line of questioning.

He gave her a number. A number much lower than she'd anticipated. 'Close your mouth, Suki. Not everything you read in the papers is accurate. In fact I'll stake my fortune on the fact that ninety per cent of what's said about me is false. Now, it's your turn.'

She closed her mouth, knowing the number she was about to reveal would scream her woeful inexperience. 'Two,' she muttered.

An expression sparked through his eyes, gone far too quickly for her to decode. 'Two?' he pressed.

'Yes.'

When he continued to regard her with probing eyes, she dropped her gaze. He caught her chin, redirected her gaze to his. '*Including* me?'

She jerked out a nod, then pulled away. She was a touch surprised when he released her. 'Including you.'

'Was the other a long-term boyfriend?' he demanded.

Dear God…

'No, a *very* brief, very much regretted one-time thing that was over almost before it started.' Setting back her empty plate, she stood. 'There, are we done with the questions? Can I go now?'

He rose beside her, immediately towering over her. Even in her heels, she didn't come up to his shoulders. Recalling how overwhelmed she'd been, how much more fragile being in his arms had felt that night when she'd invited him to her bedroom, she took a hasty step back.

He saw the action and his lips thinned.

Scattered around them were the papers and files of her life, reminders of the reason Ramon Acosta had brought her here. Reminders of what she'd agreed to do. The apprehension that hadn't quite died rose again.

'If you're thinking of changing your mind about this, you're wasting your time,' he warned softly, accurately reading her thoughts.

She sucked in a breath. The tiny wisps of amusement that had briefly lightened their simple meal were gone.

'I gave you my word, Ramon. And I meant it. I know what's at stake here.'

Dark satisfaction glinted in his eyes, giving her a glimpse of the ruthless streak that had made him the powerful man he was today. He'd done his homework, searched out her weak points and presented her with an unbreakable deal.

He waited until she'd retrieved her bag before he led her from the study.

The multi-arched hallway leading to the giant entry

turned out to be one of several. Even while her mind grappled with her current situation, the interior designer in her was bowled over by the stunning architecture of Ramon's villa.

Large swathes of baroque had been blended with surprising Moorish designs that should have been out of place here, but oddly complemented the building. Along the upper parts of the walls and windows, over two dozen shades of stained glass let in multi-coloured light. Suki wasn't aware her steps had slowed to a halt until he retraced his back to her.

She'd been too distracted to take in more than a glimpse of the majestic stonemasonry of the villa from the outside, but now she was up close, she couldn't resist, reaching out to trace her hand over salmon-coloured carvings set into the nearest arch. 'How old is this place?'

'The original building is fifteenth century. It's been altered a few times since then, hence the eclectic nature of the architecture,' he replied.

She nodded. Wanted to ask more. But she wasn't here for a guided tour into the past.

No. Her presence here was all about the future. Advancing the progeny of the Acosta family.

Her hand dropped from the wall, her senses lurching in wild alarm again at the enormous responsibility she'd undertaken. With a touch of desperation, she pushed it to the back of her mind.

She wouldn't think about it right now. She had more immediate hurdles to overcome. Like informing her mother of what she'd agreed to on her behalf. Like dealing with her boss.

The latter could wait a few more days. Her mother couldn't.

She turned from the wall to find him watching her. 'What is it?'

'I need to call my mother, let her know what's happening.'

He weighed the request for a moment before he nodded.
'There's a phone in your suite you can use. Come.'

He led her through two more hallways, passing an inner
courtyard complete with iron trellis, balconies and mosaic
fountain before they reached a grand central staircase leading to the upper floors. Ramon turned right at the top of the
stairs, past several doors to the last but one set of double
doors at the end of the corridor.

Throwing it open, he took a few steps in and stopped.
'You should find everything you need in here. Teresa doesn't
speak much English but the younger members of staff do.
Dial zero on the phone if you require anything else. I'll ensure one of them is on hand to answer your call.'

'Are you...will you not be around?' she asked.

'I have a few things to attend to in Havana. I'll be back
tonight.'

The part of her that had conjured him up as her permanent shadow until she was successfully impregnated didn't
know what to do with the fact that he was leaving, albeit
only for a few hours.

'Right...okay.'

They stared at one another for an age, the silence between
them still fully charged. But after the torrent of words they'd
exchanged, there seemed to be nothing more to say. Except
there was something else that needed to be answered.

'Umm, what happens after...after I get pregnant?'

'You mean, will I still want to share your bed?'

She jerked out a nod.

His gaze swept down for a spell before it reconnected
with hers. 'Once you're pregnant, there won't be any need
to have sex.'

A sensation rolled through her she had a hard time de-
fining. But she nodded briskly. 'Good. Great.'

His gaze eventually swung past her, looked around the
room, his thoughts completely turned off to her. But Suki
caught that look of bleakness she'd spotted intermittently

through the day. As he turned towards the door, his profile highlighted that expression even further.

'Wait,' she said before she could stop herself.

He stopped, looked over his shoulder. 'What is it?' There was a hint of weariness. And a lot of wariness.

Her fingers twisted the strap of her handbag. 'You never answered my emails. I guess I know why now. But in case you didn't get round to reading them, I think you need to know what I said in all of them. I'm very sorry for your loss. Luis was a very special person. I'm sure your parents were too.'

He stood stock-still, his face tightening for an infinitesimal second. Then he gave a curt nod. *'Muchas gracias,'* he murmured softly.

A second later he was gone. And she was left in the middle of the most incredible suite she'd ever seen.

The small living room was decorated in tones of cream and burgundy. Heavy drapes were counterbalanced with white muslin curtains that fluttered in the light breeze from the open shuttered windows. Beneath her feet, luxurious cream carpeting muffled her footsteps as she walked to the light-coloured sofas facing each other in front of a small stone fireplace.

The fireplace itself was an exquisitely carved masterpiece, another testament to the skill and dedication that had gone into the villa's design. Setting her bag down on the low wooden coffee table, she walked through another set of doors.

The four-poster queen-sized bed was an eye-catching work of art of wood and iron and expensive linens that made the interior designer in her stop and stare and sigh with pleasure. Kicking off her heels, she padded over and ran her hand over the cream coverlet. At the foot of the bed, a cream-and-burgundy-striped scroll-lipped chaise followed the colour scheme of the room. A theme that was repeated in the adjoining dressing room and bathroom, right down to the burgundy-coloured tubs and bottles holding some of the most exclusive beauty products on the market.

A quick look in the dressing room confirmed the presence of her clothes. Deciding to take a shower before making the phone call, she slid out of her dress and returned to the bathroom. The urge to linger, foolishly hoping that the comforting water would wash away her troubles, was entertained for a single minute before she turned off the shower.

This wasn't the path she would have chosen for herself. For as long as she could remember, she'd relied on herself. Even her mother had warned her never to rely fully on her. The one time she'd pushed aside that warning, and thought to seek out emotional support elsewhere, namely through her absentee father, the situation had backfired spectacularly. What Ramon was demanding of her pushed all of her control-freak buttons. But she truly had no choice. Not with so much on the line.

Towelling herself dry, her hand lingered over her stomach, the constant ache in her heart still very much present, but it held one less layer of the dark despair that had triggered tears a handful of days ago. She didn't want to give in to hope. Mother Nature had dealt her the worst blow she could suffer, so hope was still a scarce commodity to her. But if nothing else, she was glad her ache was less tormenting.

Returning to the dressing room, she retrieved the nightshirt, tucked it over her head and stopped to survey the meagre contents of her wardrobe. Yet another thing she needed to deal with. Besides the light blue sundress and sweater she'd worn to travel, she'd only packed a further two dresses, her nightshirt, a handful of underwear and sandals for her three-day stay. Even she couldn't make that last for nine months.

The hysterical bubble nestling just beneath the surface of her emotions threatened to expand again.

Squashing it back down, she climbed into her sumptuous bed, picked up the bedside phone and punched the familiar number.

It was answered on the third ring. Taking a deep breath, Suki said, 'Mum, I have something to tell you.'

CHAPTER SEVEN

As POTENTIALLY LIFE-CHANGING phone calls went, her mother took the news that there could be hope health-wise for her with quiet but flat acceptance, although Suki suspected the secret fondness her mother held for Luis played a part in her accepting his offer.

Suki had deliberately left her return date vague, not wanting to overly distress her mother.

'Did you speak to your mother?'

Ramon's voice and question dragged her back to the present, to the immense dining room and the highly polished teak banquet table and high-backed chairs that could easily seat an entire state cabinet. Here too, soaring ceilings held magnificent arches and stained glass.

Before her an exquisite setting of multiple plates, glasses and silverware had been laid out for their meal, making her once again feel out of her depth.

Unbidden, Luis's face rose up before her. He would've had a laughing fit at her expense by now. Struggling to contain her sadness, she nodded at Ramon.

He'd changed out of his suit into more casual clothes, his slicked-back hair still damp from a recent shower. Although his attire was still funeral black, the long-sleeved T-shirt, pulled up to exhibit brawny arms, gave him a slightly more approachable air. Although that air was put in serious jeopardy each time she looked into his stormy eyes.

'Yes. I couldn't really tell her too much because I don't know all the details.'

'I spoke with the specialists this afternoon. They will be in touch with her doctors tomorrow and arrange to fly her to Miami in the next three days.'

Surprise spiked through her. 'That soon?'

'I'm sure you'll agree that the sooner things get moving, the better?'

He wasn't just referring to her mother.

'Yes.'

'Good. Then you'll be pleased to know I've made an appointment for us to visit a doctor in Havana tomorrow,' he said calmly as he draped his napkin over his lap. 'After that we'll fly to Miami for the day.'

Suki paused in the act of picking up her spoon to taste the heavenly smelling beef and garbanzo bean soup Teresa had served them. 'Why? My mother wouldn't have arrived by then.'

'Since we won't be busy making a baby first thing in the morning, I scheduled a meeting for the morning, while you take the necessary time to replenish your wardrobe. Unless you intend to recycle the clothes in that weekender you brought for the next year?'

The fact that she'd pondered the same problem didn't stop her lips from pursing. 'I was going to sort something small here in Havana and organise some clothes when I returned to England.'

He put the fork in his hand down carefully, his jaw set. 'You won't be returning to England until you're pregnant and since the child is to be born here, it makes sense for you to remain here. Besides, your mother will be in Miami— you can visit her any time you want.'

Suki wasn't sure whether it was his complete certainty in his own virility or the high-handed way he'd taken over her life that stuck in her craw. 'Do you intend to dictate every single second of my life from now on? Because if that's the case you and I will have a big problem.'

'Accept that I will be taking a huge part in making sure this pregnancy goes smoothly and we won't have one.'

Her fingers tightened around the spoon. 'I'm not even pregnant yet!'

'You could be by now if you weren't so touchy about having sex in broad daylight.'

She cursed her flaming face almost as much as she silently cursed him. 'Oh, my God, you really think you're a stud, don't you?'

His shrug was pure male arrogance. 'I got you pregnant the first time despite using contraceptives. I choose to believe we'll be equally lucky in conception this time round.'

'And if I don't get pregnant immediately?' she challenged.

His teeth bared in a smug smile. 'That's the great thing about sex. As long as we have the necessary functioning equipment, we can keep trying. Again and again. Now eat your soup before it goes cold.'

'I think I've lost my appetite,' she returned.

'Eat it anyway. You need to regain your full health.'

Suki wasn't sure whether to be thankful that he hadn't added *for the baby's sake* to his statement. She wasn't even sure whether it was wise to borrow a little of his dogged assurance. And although her doctors had assured her that her baby's condition wasn't in any way genetic, she couldn't dissipate the fear that continued to live in her heart.

With her mind churning anew, she didn't notice she'd finished her soup until she looked up and saw Teresa's beaming smile of approval.

Her gaze went from her empty bowl to Ramon's cocked eyebrow. 'Let's hope you've *lost your appetite* for the main course too,' he mocked.

Her eyes rolled before she could stop herself. His deep chuckle twanged, then lightened something in her midriff. Unwilling to examine what that *something* was, she sipped her water, nibbled on a piece of thick bread and searched for neutral conversation that didn't involve sex or babies.

'I thought you couldn't fly into the States from Cuba?'

'Until recently, no, you couldn't. But things are beginning to change.

She caught a note in his voice, a blend of pride and anticipation.

'I noticed a bit of regeneration going on in Havana. Is this change why you're choosing to remain in Cuba?'

His expression darkened a touch but he answered her question with a nod. 'Partly, *sí*.'

She didn't need to ask what the other part was. The deep loss he felt was stamped in his expression. His way of somewhat assuaging that loss was why she was here.

Teresa walked in then with the main course of chicken stuffed with roasted peppers and coconut rice. Again they fell into silence and Suki polished off every mouthful on her plate.

They were waiting for dessert to be served when he reached into his pocket and placed an envelope in front of her. 'I'll be taking care of your mother's medical bills, so this is yours to do with as you please.'

She picked it up and slid the folded flap open. At the sight of the cheque, she caught her breath. Then, sending a thankful prayer to her best friend, she nodded. 'Okay.'

If he was curious as to what she intended to do with it, he didn't show it. The charged atmosphere that lurked beneath the surface of their dealings kept conversation to a stiff minimum. Her questions about the doctor in Havana were answered.

The thought that she was of no further interest to Ramon save for her reproductive purpose attempted to cause a level of hurt she wasn't comfortable with, so she ruthlessly pushed it to one side.

'I know we didn't discuss this fully, but I would prefer not to give up working altogether. Sitting around all day will drive me insane.'

She fully expected another disagreement, but to her surprise he pushed back his chair and rose.

'I have a project you could work on, once everything else is taken care of.'

Her eyes widened, a tiny spurt of pleasure welling inside her. 'You do?'

He nodded. 'Come.'

Dropping her napkin on the table, she followed him out of the dining room. Her nap and his late arrival had put a spanner in the tour he'd promised earlier but she'd conducted a mini tour of her own when one of the staff members had led her down for dinner. Each room she'd glanced into had been more spectacular than the last. So she was sure Ramon's project didn't involve the villa.

Until she walked into the room in the west wing. The difference was so jarring, so very *wrong* that her jaw dropped.

'My God, who did this?'

'Someone I had no business trusting,' he replied.

The room, another salon but this one opening onto a terrace facing the sparkling pool and designed to catch the best of the evening sun, had been turned into a futuristic minimalist nightmare completely at odds with the rest of the villa. Everywhere she looked blinding white furniture clashed with chrome and chintz.

'Why did you give them the project, then?' she asked, unsure whether to shut her eyes against the garish design or cry for the indignity the room had suffered.

When he didn't answer immediately, she looked away from the aluminium hanging fireplace to where he leaned against the lintel.

'I went against my better judgement. I also, erroneously, gave them carte blanche. When I realised my mistake I called a halt to it. As you can see, everything came to an untimely standstill.'

She glanced at the far wall, noticing that it was only half done. 'How did they take you firing them mid-project?'

His mouth twitched but it was with something other than humour. 'I got them to see that our differences of opinion were deeply ingrained in fundamental issues and that it was best we parted ways immediately.'

She walked further into the room, mourning the plain walls where beautiful stained glass and intricate carvings should've been. 'I can't believe they did…this! Did you manage to save any of the original features?'

To her surprise, he nodded. 'Teresa's husband, Mario, is the caretaker. He had the wherewithal to ensure everything taken from here was kept intact. Are you interested in a restoration project?'

She gasped. 'Of course! My last big job was a restoration on a country house in Sussex. It wasn't as big as this or anywhere near as intricate but I'd love to sink my teeth into this, if you're okay with that?'

'I'm okay with that. Mario will show you where he stored the stone and other features. But this will happen only—'

'When I've fulfilled my other duties. I know.'

His lids descended over his eyes for a minute before he walked further into the room. Stopping before her, he said, 'The tour I promised will have to wait. I have a few more calls to make and we have an early start tomorrow. I want you rested.'

Despite the heat crawling up her neck, she returned his gaze. 'You don't need to keep doing that, Ramon.'

One eyebrow lifted. 'Keep doing what?'

'Reminding me that we'll be…that I'll be…'

'Taking my seed into your body come tomorrow night?' he finished helpfully, not an ounce of embarrassment in sight.

She reddened fiercer. 'Oh, my God, who talks like that?'

He ignored the question, his fingers rising to trace her hot cheek. 'You blush so readily, *guapa*. One could be fooled into thinking you're one step removed from the very angels.' The observation was flat, but tinged with a definite thread of censure.

And just like that the lighter mood was gone.

'If anyone chooses to make assumptions about me, that's their problem. I never claimed to be angelic. But I'm also not the heartless devil you think I am. I'm sorry that you see me that way.'

His fingers snaked past her jaw and beneath her loose hair to cup her nape. 'Are you?'

Having seen the pain he was in, a part of her understood his emotions. 'Yes, I am.'

'That remains to be seen, I guess.'

Her heart quaked. Resolutely, she stepped away. 'Don't forget those calls you need to go and make.'

He stayed where he was, watching her for a further minute. '*Buenas noches*, Suki.'

She didn't respond. The emotions surging into her throat wouldn't let her. So she stood silently as he walked out of the room. Then, unable to stay in the starkly minimalist apology for a room, she walked out of the French doors onto the pillared terrace.

Down a short flight of stairs the under-lit swimming pool glinted invitingly. The night air cooled her on the outside but, inside, she was still reeling from Ramon's words. By the events of the day.

Ramon had never answered her question about how long he'd known about the baby, but if he'd discussed it with Luis then he'd known for a few months. She shuddered to think how long he'd held on to his anger. How long he intended to hold her in such an unforgiving light. Until she gave him another child?

How could they even make love when there was such acrimony between them?

I don't need to like you to take you to bed. And vice versa.

Recalling the words sent another shiver through her, along with the disarming acceptance that it was true. Although he'd apologised for his uncouth comments, he hadn't exactly been bursting with poetry and roses that night ten months ago.

And she, regardless of his lack of warmth, hadn't minded in the least. Her body had thrilled to his touch, had lapped up every particle of attention he'd generously delivered to her.

Her escalating heartbeat now mocked her with that remembered thrill. Mocked her with the fact that he only had to touch her for her senses to threaten to dive into free fall. The cold, hard truth was that making love with Ramon even for the clinical sake of conceiving a child wouldn't be the most difficult thing she would ever do.

But the risk to her soul, the knowledge that this could all emotionally backfire spectacularly if she wasn't careful, stayed with her long after she'd returned to her suite and slid beneath the sheets.

She was up and showered and in the dining room by eight the next morning, one of the maids having gently woken her a little after seven with the instruction that the *señor* wished to leave by nine. She chose to see it as a blessing that Ramon hadn't hammered on her door himself with that command.

She had almost finished her breakfast when he walked in. Today, his attire was a little less severe, the dark grey suit and lighter grey shirt bringing out the vibrancy of his skin and eyes. Those eyes, however, were no less sombre when they raked over her simple off-white, off-the-shoulder sundress and the neat ponytail she'd tied her hair in.

'*Buenos días, cara.* You look as well rested as I feel,' he observed dryly.

Since she'd spent most of the night tossing and turning, she knew his statement was less than flattering. Her chest tightened. 'I see you're brimming with compliments this morning.'

'Perhaps I'm feeling less than generous because our night could've been put to better use than counting sheep.'

She shrugged, experiencing a tiny burst of pride when it came off smoothly. 'I didn't count sheep. The spectacular wall carvings in my room were a much better visual distraction.'

He paused in the act of pouring steaming black coffee,

a flash of something dark and carnal passing through his eyes. 'I hope you enjoyed them because you won't be inspecting them tonight,' he promised, the raw intent in his eyes making her belly quiver.

Suki refrained from voicing another objection to the blatant reminder. Hadn't she woken up this morning thinking exactly the same thing? And hadn't that knowledge sent darts of secret anticipation straight between her thighs?

Carefully, she set down her half-finished cup of tea and stood. 'I'm done. I'll go and grab my bag and I'll be ready to go.'

Without looking at her, he picked up the folded newspaper next to his plate and snapped it open. 'Changing the subject won't make the event disappear, *cara*.'

'No, but discussing it ad nauseam will definitely make it tedious.'

He perused the inside of the first page. 'Are you calling me boring, Suki?' he murmured.

'I'm calling you out on the fact that, for someone who is lauded for his intelligence, you seem to have developed a one-track mind.'

That got his attention. He looked up from the paper, ferocious green eyes lancing her. 'I get that way when there's something I'm passionate about,' he replied in a low, ardently dangerous voice. 'And on this subject, rest assured that I am *extremely* passionate.'

He returned to his paper, the silently dismissive gesture freeing her to leave the room. She did so swiftly, perhaps even admitting she was fleeing from contemplating what it would feel like to have Ramon be passionate about something other than sex. Be passionate about *her*.

No. Her stupid crush had died long before she'd been beset with the heartbreaking news of her unborn child's illness. It had taken a giant knock when she'd woken up alone the morning after their night together. It'd died the day she'd discovered he'd lied to her about Svetlana.

That welcome reminder threw cold water on her rioting emotions, thankfully, as she freshened up and collected her bag.

He was on the phone when she returned. He got off long enough to attend the lawyers who'd once again been summoned, this time to witness her agreement with Ramon. For a startling second she wondered which other agreements Ramon had got them to draw up that they didn't seem in any way surprised by hers, but then she pushed the useless thought away. Her situation was hers alone to deal with.

Ramon stopped long enough to lock the agreement in the safe in his study. Then, with the next few years of her life committed to the man who looked at her with a fair amount of dislike, she followed him out onto the helipad.

For most of the helicopter flight back to Havana, he made one call after another. For the sake of discretion, Ramon informed her, the trio of doctors were summoned to the Acosta suite at Ramon's hotel. For a solid hour, she answered questions about her health, had her blood drawn and her pressure recorded.

She believed they were done when the doctor powered down his tablet, only to see Ramon taking his place in the chair she'd just vacated. Surprised, she watched him roll his sleeves up in preparation for his own vitals to be taken.

He caught her look and returned it with a steady one of his own. 'My last health check was satisfactory. But it doesn't hurt to be doubly sure, does it?'

Numbly, she shook her head. When he turned away to answer the doctor's questions in low-toned Spanish, she retreated to the far side of the living room. Staring down at the bustling street below, Suki refused to entertain the strange sensation zipping through her stomach.

Not only was Ramon deadly serious about having this child, he was going the extra mile to ensure he was in optimum health. Why that should make her insides sing, she didn't want to examine too closely. Or at all. So she wouldn't.

Unfortunately, her senses weren't in a listening mood. She was veering down the path of wondering what sort of father Ramon would make when she sensed him coming up behind her.

She turned to find him lowering his sleeve over a thick, tanned, hair-sprinkled arm. And for the life of her she couldn't stop staring at it. At him. Like that night in the limo, her senses were swerving into dangerous territory, her nostrils flaring wider to breathe more of his intoxicating scent as he stopped in front of her.

'We're done here. Are you ready to go?'

'Yes,' she said, cringing at the huskiness of her voice.

Get yourself together!

She stepped to one side and smiled her thanks at the doctors before they took their leave. Then she headed for the door herself. Lingering in this suite with Ramon wasn't safe. Not when every move he made drew its own brand of fascination from her. Not when there was a more than adequately functioning king-sized bed so close by.

If he sensed her fresh agitation, he didn't give an indication of it. By the time he joined her at the lift, his impeccable clothes were in place.

'The tests will be expedited. We should have the preliminary ones by this evening although I'm not expecting any surprises.'

Or anything to stand in his way.

She chose not to touch the unvoiced words.

They emerged into sunlight and the awaiting limo. Half an hour later, they were at the airport. This time she didn't need prompting to get out of the car. The tension of yesterday underlined newer, even riskier tension. The kind that made her stomach flutter wildly each time Ramon so much as glanced her way.

Something he seemed to do often, despite the long phone call he was engaged in for most of the journey.

As for that beautifully lilted Spanish that fell so smoothly from his lips?

Dear heaven, she was losing it.

It didn't help that she was robbed of further breath the moment she stepped into his private jet. Every corner of the plane was decked out with unapologetic comfort and luxury in mind. Silky leather suede in soft accents covered all three separate groupings of sofas and armchairs. Light-coloured marble lined the table tops and flat-screen TVs broadcasted the latest financial and world news from two different screens. The two attendants and pilots who greeted them wore the same Acosta Hotels logo on their uniforms that she'd seen previously, and the English they greeted her with was impeccable.

Feeling more than a little out of place in her simple dress and sandals, Suki slowed as she reached the middle of the plane. The touch of a firm, warm hand at her waist made her jump, her senses screeching as Ramon turned her to face him.

'You need to take a seat so we can take off.'

Nodding stiffly, she started to move towards an armchair. The hand at her waist checked her progress and steered her towards a two-seater sofa. Pressing her into it, he buckled her in and sat down next to her, bringing one lean, powerful thigh much too close to her own. Under the pretext of crossing her legs, she shifted away.

A quick glance at him showed he'd caught the movement. And wasn't terribly impressed with it.

'Ramon…' She wasn't exactly sure what she'd hoped to say but one attendant approached them with drinks. She accepted a fruit punch, took a sip of the refreshing drink while Ramon chose a mineral water.

He waited until they were alone again to slice her with a

dark look. 'It would be good if you didn't jump like a startled rabbit when I touch you in public.'

'I wasn't aware that we would be doing public outings together,' she replied.

His mouth twisted. 'Did you think I was going to hide you away for the next nine months?'

She hadn't thought of that. To be honest, the swiftly ticking clock, racing towards what would happen tonight, hadn't given her much thinking room since she woke up this morning. 'But aren't you worried that it'll send out a certain impression?' she asked, a little bubble of bemusement taking root inside.

'What sort of impression?'

She licked nervous lips. 'Well…people are going to think we're together.'

He shrugged, eyeing her with a steady look. 'I don't have a problem with that. Do you?'

No. *Yes.* She shook her head in confusion. 'But we're not. I don't like people assuming something that isn't true.'

'What would you suggest? That we take out an ad in the paper stating that we're having sex simply to have a child together?'

She glared at him. 'No, of course not.'

'You and I know the truth. That's all that matters.' The words held a ring of intractable finality.

Suki was reeling long after their plane had launched itself into the sky. For better or worse, her life was tied to Ramon's for the foreseeable future.

CHAPTER EIGHT

HE WASN'T GOING to demand to know what was going on in her head. Nor was he going to demand conversation. And the need to reach out and free her thick caramel-blonde hair from the ponytail was certainly one he wouldn't be indulging.

He had achieved his purpose where Suki was concerned. Or as near enough to it without having performed the act itself.

She'd subsided into near silence after their conversation on the plane, only acknowledging him when he deposited her in his private suite at Acosta Hotel Miami and left for his meeting. By then he'd concluded that talking was no longer necessary, or even a pleasurable experience with her. Half the time she argued with him. The other half she offered sympathy or touched on subjects that he found difficult. All the time his attention was absorbed by her animation, the little gestures with her hand she probably wasn't aware she was making.

All distracting and frankly irritating.

So for now, he would enjoy the peace of mind afforded to him as he sat in the VIP dressing area of the top Miami stylist his assistant had scheduled Suki to visit.

A visit he'd accompanied her on simply because his mid-afternoon meeting had wrapped up early. Grabbing a copy of the financial paper he hadn't been able to finish at breakfast this morning, he tuned out the three attendants' hushed debate about which signature style to create for Suki.

The woman in question was seated on a chaise longue at the opposite end of the room, her shapely legs neatly crossed at the ankles. She was choosing not to participate in the conversation. Even looked borderline bored, a shrug very much in her expression each time she was asked a question.

Ramon's irritation grew. Every woman he'd dated previously, without exception, had been an utter slave to shopping, the more exclusive, the more fervent the rhapsody. And the more adoring gratitude had come his way.

Suki looked as if she would have more fun watching paint dry.

Her gaze met his. Her lips pursed and her eyes stayed wide and unblinking. The distinct notion that she was fighting the urge to roll her eyes startled, then amused him.

Fighting the sudden twitch of his own lips, he returned his attention to his paper.

Eventually, the whole ensemble headed for an inner sanctum.

For five minutes he read and re-read the same article on the price of soya. The door opened. He tossed the paper aside.

The dress was a bold blood-red, the material a floor-length affair that clung to her body from chest to knees, leaving her shoulders bare and outlining her hourglass figure to perfection. Absently he heard one stylist refer to it as a Bardot-style evening dress.

With her hair caught back, her elegant neck and delicate shoulders gave off a fragile look he knew was false. Suki Langston had a backbone of steel. And as much as the reason for her presence in his life disturbed him, he couldn't deny the fact that her beauty was enthralling. That the hot tug in his groin that had perturbed and then shamelessly dogged him with each subsequent time they'd met wasn't going to go away.

He caught her full reflection in the mirror as one attendant stepped out of the way. She was smoothing her hand down her midriff. When it paused at her stomach, the place where his child had briefly been cradled, something hard and agonising pierced his chest.

The need to see his seed grow there, watch her belly expand with his child, filled every cell in his body.

The hell he'd lived in since finding out about his child, and the further agony of losing the family he'd never thought would be taken from him so suddenly, reared up and knocked him sideways.

He didn't realise he'd made a sound until all four women froze and glanced his way. Suki's gaze met his in the mirror and he caught the faintest tremble in her lips and sympathy in her vivid blue eyes.

He wanted to reject it, wanted to snarl that he didn't need it. But his eyes stayed on hers, silently and secretly absorbing the sentiment.

'She'll take that one,' he rasped into the silence.

The innocuous words altered the mood. A flurry of activity ensued. Having achieved success with the first dress, the stylist decided his opinion was needed for every subsequent ensemble.

He approved another half a dozen evening dresses, growled his dislike of a metallic gold cocktail dress that clung a little too tightly and showed off a little too much skin. At some point it was decided she would take her hair down to better judge the true style of one dress. The sight of her free-flowing hair sent another burst of heat through his bloodstream.

He was nodding at her selection of swimsuits and daywear when his phone rang. The doctors' news sent a bolt of satisfaction through him. Followed closely by ramped-up anticipation.

The next call was to his American pilot to ready his plane.

Suki caught the tail end of the conversation. Enquiring blue eyes met his. He infused purpose in his gaze and watched her swallow.

Rising, he quickly brought the spree to a conclusion and led her out of the boutique with more than a little haste.

'Any reason why we're hotfooting it out of here like we're

fleeing the scene of a crime?' she asked, but the hitch in her
voice and the furtive glance his way suggested she already
guessed the answer.

'Our preliminary tests have returned with a green light,'
he answered as they settled into the car.

'So…?'

'So we're returning home, Suki. I've waited long enough.'
Once he'd dragged himself from the depths of grief and accepted that only the promise of an heir would assuage him,
he'd been planning for this event. He felt zero qualms about
the swiftness with which he was moving now success was
in his sights. The yearning stamped in his blood needed to
be answered. Right now.

He couldn't bring his brother or parents back, but he
could ensure their memories lived on through his child.

The journey back was swift and uneventful. Not so much
the palpable tension that rose between them the moment
they stepped off the plane and onto his helicopter.

Ramon told himself that the anticipation firing through
his veins was born of the primal need to ensure his family and legacy survived the tragic circumstances that had
befallen him.

But as the rotors beat relentlessly towards his villa, he
realised the woman too counted. For whatever reason nature
saw fit, the chemistry between Suki and him transcended
all logical explanation. Svetlana might have committed the
physical act of cheating on him with other men, but in the
handful of times he'd interacted with Suki when Luis had
attended a function with her, the evidence of the unmistakable chemistry between them had caused Ramon more than
a hint of discomfort.

Perhaps that had been the reason he'd acted so deplorably
on the night of her birthday. Entering the pub and seeing
Luis holding her hand had unexpectedly jarred. Recognising the emotion as dark rancid jealousy hadn't improved a
mood that had already been in a black pit after discover-

ing the true extent of Svetlana's infidelity. Perhaps taking Suki to bed that night had been his own way of salving the indignity to his manhood and pride.

For sure, he'd woken up in the early hours more than a little unimpressed with his behaviour. Not enough that he'd regretted the hours he'd spent in Suki's bed. But enough to know that retreat was best for everyone in that moment.

He glanced at her now, completely certain there would be no retreat now.

She was his.

At least until she bore him a child. What came after that would be decided when the time was right.

He took her hand the moment the helicopter landed in Cienfuegos. He noted the slight lag in her steps and suppressed the apprehension that rose within him. She'd barely touched her food on the plane and her eyes had grown steadily darker and her face pinched.

Dios. Anyone would think she was a virgin headed for the slaughter. Wasn't she though, to all intents and purposes? She'd only had one previous lover bar him. One sexual encounter. The primitive part of the alpha male in him had been more than thrilled at that admission, but he hadn't failed to notice her lack of experience on their first night together.

His racing libido throttled down a notch. Entering the main salon, he pulled her to a stop before him. Despite her heeled sandals, she needed to tilt her head to meet his gaze.

So small.

Yet so strong.

His gaze drifted over her, fresh hunger clawing through him, but he couldn't ignore the obvious.

'You're nervous,' he observed.

She laughed self-deprecatingly. 'Give the man a prize.'

'Have you forgotten that we've done this before?'

If anything, her tension increased. 'After which you left my bedroom without so much as an *adios*, if I recall.' Her voice was hushed, but there was a strained note in it that was more than the hurt he sensed.

Ramon got the distinct impression he'd been judged and found wanting, which shouldn't have surprised him considering his own admission of his less than stellar conduct. But still, a thousand tiny pinpricks dragged over his skin. 'A lot of what happened that night was...unfortunate.'

Her face tightened. Her eyelashes dropped to fan her cheeks. 'I see.'

He caught and lifted her chin with his finger. 'But not what happened in the car, or in your bed,' he clarified firmly.

Her face remained closed. 'I don't really see the point in dissecting it any more. What happened...happened.'

Ramon should've been pleased. He wasn't.

Letting go of her, he walked to the drinks cabinet. About to pour them both a drink, he hesitated. Alcohol was a hard *no* for her considering what they were trying to achieve. And he would do well to keep his wits about him.

About to suggest an alternative, he stopped when she glanced at the door. 'I'm going upstairs to...um...take a shower.'

Great idea, he wanted to say, but one look at her face told him she intended it to be a solo mission.

Suppressing the torrid images, for now, he nodded. 'I'll be up shortly.'

She opened her mouth, as if to contradict him, but, face still set in unhappy lines, she walked out of the room.

He shoved a hand through his hair.

Dios. Maybe he would have that drink after all.

The shot of cognac did nothing to bring clarity or calm his raging need.

He'd spent the months after Svetlana's betrayal burying himself in work and avoiding any and all liaisons. Not because he'd been heartbroken, but because he'd realised how jaded the idea of relationships had grown for him.

He and Luis had been lucky enough to grow up in a stable and happy home. Although not wealthy, their parents had ensured they got the best education, his half-American mother smoothing the way for them to attend top universities in the States.

It was this solid foundation he'd foolishly thought to emulate with Svetlana, despite the clear evidence that successful marriages, especially among wealthy men like him, were rare. How many of his silver-spoon college buddies had come from broken homes and were themselves intent on living duplicitous lives even before they'd entered the real world?

After Svetlana, he'd even been a little disconcerted to realise sex had grown boring for him and the idea of pursuing a woman had dropped to an all-time low on his list.

All that apathy was nowhere in sight right now. He paced the salon, nursing a second drink while keeping an eye on the clock.

Ten minutes later, he set the crystal tumbler down and strode from the room. The knock on her door produced no response. That unsettling irritation that was never far off dogged him again. Turning the handle, he tried the door, exhaling when it yielded to his push.

He was getting somewhere if she hadn't locked him out. Except she wasn't in the bedroom and there was no sound from the bathroom.

The absurd idea that she'd made a run for it had him charging for the French doors that led to her private terrace. His hand was on the doorknob when he heard a faint sound behind him.

'Ramon?'

He turned.

She was framed in the doorway of her dressing room, clad in only a towel. Her face glowed a light pink from her shower and her damp hair tumbled around her naked shoulders. With no make-up, no sexy lingerie or perfumed skin to entice, Ramon wondered how she could still be the most captivating woman he'd ever encountered.

Because, *Madre de Dios*, she was.

Blood and lust thrumming wildly through his veins, he slowly moved towards her, watched her fingers twist in a death grip on the knot of the towel.

Her gaze flitted from his to the French doors before rushing back to his, as if, like him, she couldn't look away for long enough. 'Did you just break into my bedroom?'

He gave a low laugh. 'I was checking to make sure you hadn't decided to make a run for it.'

He stopped before her, breathing in the intoxicating scent of woman.

His woman.

'And if I had?'

'I would've chased you down,' he vowed.

A shiver trembled through her. He wanted to trace his fingers over her satin-smooth skin, elicit another delicious shiver. But if he touched her that way, here in this room, he wouldn't be able to stop.

Closing the gap between them, he caught her around the waist. Lifting her high, he banded one arm around her and started to walk.

One hand landed on his shoulder to steady herself as her eyes widened. 'Where…where are we going?'

He passed through the open door and took a right towards the end of the corridor. 'I've had you in my car and in your bed. This time I'm taking you in *my* bed.'

Her breath hitched in a sexy little rush that went straight to his groin. Striding through his private living room into his bedroom, he kicked the door shut with his foot and set her down.

'Let go of the towel,' he rasped in a voice he barely recognised as his own.

She blinked, then looked around wildly before her gaze returned to his. Whatever she saw in his face made her draw her lower lip between her teeth and worry it mercilessly.

Ramon barely managed to stop the torturous groan that rumbled up from his chest.

'Drop the towel, Suki. Or I'll do it for you,' he growled.

Despite the alarming widening of her eyes, she shook her head. 'You take something off first.'

He sighed. 'Are we going to argue about every single thing?'

The hand gripping the towel tightened defiantly. 'Equality is a very big thing for women these days.'

His mouth attempted to lift without his permission but the severity of his need killed his mirth. His jacket came off and hit the floor, followed by his tie and shirt.

When his hand went to his belt, she froze, her gaze following the movement. He slowed the slide of the belt through the loops. Something about having her eyes on him turned him on even harder.

He hadn't forgotten his paramount objective but, *Dios*, he was also going to take a little bit of pleasure in his task.

'*Do it*, Suki. I won't tell you again.'

Slowly, she let go of the towel.

Everything locked inside him, save for the electric zap of lust that powered his every cell. Maybe he was going to take more than a little pleasure in bringing his child into the world.

Discarding the belt, he pulled her into his arms, fisted one hand in her thick hair, angled her face up to his. The wave of anxiety that crossed her face pulled him short for a moment.

'This can be the clinical exercise you accused it of being. Or we can attempt to enjoy it. Which would you prefer?'

Her mouth fell open in shock, then she blushed fiercely. 'I…how can I answer that without…without…?'

He glided his thumb over her lips. 'It's fine, you don't need to incriminate yourself. *I* would prefer the latter. And I will proceed accordingly unless you indicate otherwise.'

'Or we can stop dissecting it and just get on with it?'

she muttered, her colour heightening as her gaze dropped from his.

Ramon wanted to bring it back to his. But he couldn't resist the prompt to *just get on with it*. Not when his hands were gliding over her glorious skin and her breathing was altering in that heady way again. Not when the sight of the tip of her tongue caressing her inner lip was threatening to drive him insane.

The distance to his bed was mercifully short. Laying her down, he quickly disposed of his remaining clothes. When her wide-eyed gaze took in his erection, he swallowed a groan and brought himself under fierce control.

Stretching out next to her, he pressed her body to his, caressed his hand down the delicate line of her spine.

She arched against him, bringing the tips of her sweet breasts against his chest. When the sensitised tips brushed him, she whimpered. The sound, like every single one she made, drove blood straight between his legs.

Unable to resist, he bent his head and took one pink peak into his mouth. Her whimper turned into a cry as her fingers spiked through his hair.

Sí, there was absolutely no reason why they couldn't enjoy making this baby that would ensure the continuation of his family's legacy.

In pathetically few minutes, the insane hunger threatened to annihilate him.

Pressing her onto her back, he braced himself over her.

Suki didn't think she had any more air in her lungs to exhale with as Ramon parted her thighs. But apparently the sight of him, crouched so masterfully over her, could elicit another giddy rush of air.

She couldn't…*shouldn't* be enjoying this. Every particle in her body shouldn't be craving what was coming so much. And yet wild, dizzy anticipation continued to ripple through her as his fingers slid between their bodies, located that needy place between her thighs and delivered wicked caresses.

Her head was rolling restlessly on his pillow as he started kissing his way down her body. Open-mouthed kisses that branded her skin and left a trail of fire she was sure would never be extinguished. She wasn't aware her nails were digging into his shoulders until he hissed encouragement.

Dragging her head off the pillow, she looked down to find his ferocious gaze pinned on her, tracking her every response.

He got to her belly and he paused, his lips hovering over her womb. An enigmatic expression washed over his face. Then his head dropped one last fraction, anointing her belly with a kiss. Something heavy and indefinable moved through her, wrapped around her heart.

Suki shied away from it, her intuition pushing her towards emotional self-preservation. His mouth brushed lower and she stopped thinking altogether.

She resurfaced from her first climax long enough to feel him tug her resolutely beneath him.

'Open your eyes, Suki,' he rasped above her.

She dragged heavy lids open, her chest rising and falling rapidly. His eyes were a dark, primitive green. The turbulence surging through her was reflected perfectly in his gaze.

His hand barely slid beneath her to hold her steady before he thrust inside her. 'Oh!'

His harsh exhalation reverberated in the room. Burying himself to the hilt, he held himself still, fine tremors shaking through his body as his teeth clenched. The sight of him fighting for control thrilled a shamelessly feminine part of her.

Enough for her to raise her hand and slide her fingers over his rigid stubbled jaw, through his hair, drag her nails along his scalp, sink them into his nape.

A guttural groan ripped free from his throat as he began

to move. Powerfully. Relentlessly. His possession was masterful and thorough, commanding every single cell in her body by the time the glorious pressure threatened to stop her breathing.

Frantic for an anchor, her hands found his waist, dug in and stayed as he hurled her relentlessly to the edge.

'Ramon…'

'*Sí, guapa.* Give in,' he encouraged throatily.

She didn't need a second bidding. Shameless cries ripped from her own throat as bliss burst wild and free from deep within her.

Seconds later, Ramon gave an animalistic growl above her before he rammed deep…deeper than he'd ever been inside her. The sensation of his seed filling her, flooding her, shook new, alien feeling inside her long after their breaths had returned to normal. Long after he'd rolled to the side and tucked her against him.

That band around her heart, the one that held apprehension and a whole lot more sensation than she could fathom right now, tightened even further. She tried to will it away. But it loomed larger until she couldn't stem the feeling morphing into naked fear in her chest.

When she pulled free, he let her go.

Her duty was done. At least for tonight. She moved to the edge of the bed, swung her legs down.

Before she could stand, a thick arm snagged her waist, dragged her back against the sheets.

'Where do you think you're going?' he demanded. His sculpted cheekbones were still flushed and his hair was in total disarray. But he remained sinfully, impossibly gorgeous, his face threatening her equilibrium all over again. She fought it with every spare ounce of control she could summon.

'I'm returning to my room.'

'No, you're not. Until we get a positive result you're

sleeping in this bed every night. I will have your things moved here tomorrow.'

She was shaking her head before he'd finished. 'I…I would rather not.'

His face closed, his displeasure evident. 'If you think I'm hunting you down every night, think again.'

'Hunting me down? I'm right next door.'

'Then save us both the trouble of maintaining separate rooms.'

She shook her head again, her instincts screaming that this was a terrible idea.

He exhaled impatiently. 'If you insist on your feminine independence, you can shower and dress in your own suite. But when I'm in this room so will you. Agreed?'

This was his idea of a compromise. She could waste her breath arguing. Or she could take the offer. She took the offer. 'Agreed.'

His expression changed into one of hard satisfaction. Leaning down, he delivered a firm, swift kiss on her lips before he raised his head a fraction. 'One more thing.'

'Yes?' she replied shakily.

'You attempting to leave my bed so soon leads me to think you believe I'll be taking you just once a night.' His lips brushed hers as he spoke, trailing little bursts of fire on her tingling mouth. 'Am I right, *cara*?' he enquired huskily.

Her face flamed. 'I wasn't…I didn't give it that much thought.'

His tight-lipped smile mocked her. 'Well, in case it crossed your mind, revise that impression, *guapa*. And also revise the notion that I will be restricting myself to only nights from now on.'

She was flailing under the torrent of his words when his hand slid down to boldly cup her hip. Before she could so much as take a breath, he had once again taken control of her body.

CHAPTER NINE

RAMON ACOSTA WAS a man on a mission. That became very clear, very quickly. If she slept for more than two or three hours at a stretch during the night, she called that a victory. And he didn't restrict himself to just the bedroom. Discovering her enjoying a mid-morning decaf coffee on his private terrace after lingering in bed for the morning, he'd calmly reefed off his T-shirt and paint-splattered sweat pants, stretched out beside her and pulled her negligee off her body. Afterwards, he'd carried her back to bed and started all over again.

The shower in her own suite had been another scene of his mastery. He'd tracked her there under some now forgotten pretext, invited himself into the steamy cubicle and proceeded to make her shower an unforgettable one.

That had been a week ago. A week when, in between bouts of intense lovemaking, he either spent equally intense hours ruling his kingdom from his study or disappearing into his studio on the boundary of his villa.

He'd given Suki the grand tour of all twenty-eight rooms of his villa the morning after they returned from Miami. Room after room had produced gasps of awe, as priceless antiques vied for attention beneath even more exquisitely carved stone and wood and beautifully cut glass, but, although he'd told her what the glass-roofed structure was, he hadn't invited her inside his studio. What he had revealed was that his parents had also lived in this villa with him. The west wing where they'd had their rooms was slowly being cleared by Teresa and Mario, and Suki had chosen to stay out of their way.

It was also during that tour that she'd discovered there

were two further rooms—a smaller dining room and a drawing room—that needed to be restored. Although her heart mourned the atrocity done to the rooms, she welcomed the opportunity to dwell on something else other than whether she was even now carrying Ramon's child.

But by mutual tacit agreement, neither of them had brought up the subject of pregnancy tests. Suki shied away from the wicked voice that suggested that she didn't want to know just yet so she didn't have to give up her presence in Ramon's bed. They would know soon enough when her cycle rolled around next week.

Until then, she busied herself by compiling a list of Cuban architects and restorers, conducting videoconference interviews to see who would be a good fit. And when her mother arrived in Miami, she made the trip, spending all day with Moira and Mrs Baron. Suki had been shocked to find her retired neighbour at her mother's bedside in Miami, but the older woman had been full of praise for a 'considerate' Ramon, who hadn't thought twice about making arrangements for her to accompany her friend. Suki's expressed gratitude when she'd met Ramon at the hotel afterwards had been shrugged off and quickly dismissed before he'd whisked her into the bedroom.

Her own mother had, predictably, reserved judgement, more concerned with why Suki was still in Cuba. The half-lie that she was working on a commission for Ramon hadn't sat well with her. But the bald truth would've distressed her mother even more.

So instead she'd discussed antique wallpapers and colour swatches and rhapsodised about the beauty of Luis's childhood home.

The call to her boss to request an extended leave of absence had gone more smoothly than she'd hoped. Whether or not it was aided by the tabloid pictures of her and Ramon, first at the memorial and then coming out of the boutique in Miami that had the paparazzi speculating about their relationship, she didn't know.

Charlotte Chapman, the tough but fair boss who'd hired her straight after her internship, had all but offered to keep her job open for as long as Suki needed. Unsure what the future held for her, she'd expressed her gratitude to Charlotte and promised that, yes, she would update her on a regular basis.

She was still bemused by the call when Ramon found her in the living room shortly after. A raised-brow query had prompted a retelling of the phone call. He'd given a very Latin shrug and deftly changed the subject.

That had been the first inkling that there were some subjects Ramon would pursue to the ends of the earth and others he wouldn't waste a single breath on. One such subject was the amount of clothes that had arrived two days after their visit to Miami. Even the clothes he'd initially disapproved of were included in the dozens of boxes that arrived by helicopter.

And tonight, he'd specifically picked the metallic gold dress he'd all but sneered at in the boutique.

They were supposed to be dining by candlelight on his private terrace, yet half an hour after Teresa had set out their meal he hadn't turned up.

Walking to the edge of the terrace, she glanced over to his studio. Lights blazed through the glass. She debated for a second, then went back into the bedroom. Throwing a light shawl over her dress, she left the suite.

Her flats were almost noiseless on the stone path as she approached the studio doors. The hand she raised to knock froze at the steady stream of Spanish curses that ripped through the air, followed by the sound of wood breaking. Then another.

Biting her lip, she remained caught between the urge to find out if Ramon was all right and the urge to flee.

That was how he found her minutes later when he almost ripped the door off his hinges in restless fury.

Green eyes latched on to her. '*Por el amor de*—what are you doing here?' he growled, low and dangerous.

She glanced behind him, caught a glimpse of the carnage on the studio floor. 'I…we were supposed to have dinner forty minutes ago. I came to see if you…are you okay?'

He continued to stare at her as if she were an alien. Stepping out, he pulled the door shut behind him. 'I'm fine. My apologies for keeping you waiting,' he said stiffly, clawing a hand through his hair. 'Give me five minutes and I'll be with you.'

Questions tripped on the tip of her tongue, but the dismissal was clear. She returned to the villa, and, true to his word, he joined her five minutes later.

She turned from the terrace wall, and for a moment she thought he'd been struck dumb when he saw her.

The risqué cut of the dress negated the use of a bra, but, of course, what had looked a little daring but ultimately controllable in front of her mirror soon became a clingy, body-exposing and heat-inducing scrap of torture the moment Ramon laid his sizzling eyes on her.

Calmly he strode forward, pulled out her chair and saw her seated. But despite his attempt at easy conversation, tension poured off him. Whether it was from what she'd witnessed outside his studio or what she was wearing, she didn't dare ask, seeing as she was fighting her ultra-sensitive body's reaction to his every look.

When she attempted to surreptitiously hide the fact that her nipples had peaked to blatant points beneath the sheer silk, he set his wine glass down and decisively drew away the arm she was attempting to use to hide her body's reaction.

'We're alone, Suki. Stop hiding yourself from me.'

Her lips twisted in a tight grimace. 'This dress was a bad idea.'

'Only as a test of fortitude and patience, *belleza*. But we will persevere,' he replied drolly, although she noted the tightness of his jaw and the way he shifted in his seat every few minutes when his gaze dropped to her chest.

He waited until she'd returned to using both hands to tuck into her spicy chicken and sautéed potatoes served with a mango and avocado sauce before he returned his attention to his own food. Pleading with her body to calm down, she attempted to be content with the fact that wherever her appetite had gone it was coming back with gusto.

Ramon, on the other hand, ate less and drank more, his jaw clenching and unclenching until she resolutely set down her cutlery.

'Either my dress is bothering you more than you want to admit or something's wrong. Maybe something that involves you smashing up your studio?' she enquired boldly.

He tensed further. When he didn't reply immediately, she thought he meant to ignore her. But then he shrugged. 'I'm an artist. I'm allowed a temperamental outburst every now and then.'

'I suppose, except you look like you want to have another one right now. So I'm guessing it wasn't cathartic?'

His eyes narrowed on her, but he answered, 'I get that way when my vision and my process don't converge as they should.'

'Artist's block?'

He grimaced, his gaze sweeping her body before he glanced away. 'I prefer…frustrated.'

'How long has it been?' she asked, then mentally kicked herself. With all he'd suffered, was it a surprise?

'I drew my last painting eight months ago. My last sculpture has been even longer.'

Before his devastating loss. *But after his break-up with Svetlana?*

The food in her mouth congealed. Had the break-up affected him to the extent his art had suffered? As she watched him gulp back another mouthful of red wine, his features set, Suki's chest tightened.

Silence reigned while he took another sip.

'Since we're sharing intimate subjects, which of your parents decided to name you Suki?' he asked.

She looked up, a little startled at the unexpected question. Then, glad for the change of subject, she smiled. 'My mother. It was her favourite teacher's name. She decided from a young age that she would name her daughter that.'

'And your father didn't raise any objection?' he asked.

The pleasing memory of how she got her name disappeared. Her gaze veered off him, a sudden interest in her meal meant to disguise the mingled anger and anguish that flashed through her each time she thought of the father who'd chosen to ignore her existence.

'I didn't have the privilege of meeting my father for the first decade and half of my life. He decided to do a runner after being with my mother for one night,' she said. 'When she found out she was pregnant and eventually tracked him down, it turned out he'd lied about his single status. And, surprise, he wasn't interested in the child he'd helped conceive.'

An expression passed over Ramon's face, almost curiously resembling fury. Although why he should be furious on her behalf was puzzling. Or maybe it was directed at her?

'And you've never sought him out all these years?'

'Not in the past ten years, no. I attempted to when I was sixteen. I skipped school one day and went to his office. Perhaps it wasn't the best place to confront him, but what the heck do I know? Anyway, he didn't want to know me. He made it clear he wasn't interested in engaging with me on any level. So I drew a line under that.'

'Perhaps things might be different now.'

'Perhaps. But he knows where I am. He's always known where I was. He's not been inclined to seek me out. That says it all, really.'

His expression turned inward. A little bleak. A lot serious. Again his mouth tightened with a hint of fury. 'Such a waste.'

Something moved in her throat. Her hand found the back of his before she'd fully registered the move. He gave a sharp exhalation, his gaze dropping down to their touching hands before returning to her face.

'Don't take this the wrong way. Your family was a close-knit one so you may think my not knowing my father was a waste, but I don't think I missed a great deal by not having him around,' Suki said.

He tensed, his eyes narrowing on her face.

Suki bit her lip as the powder keg of the subject of denied father threatened to blow up again. 'I don't believe that about everyone, Ramon, only my own. From the little I saw of him, he and my mother would never have been compatible in the long run. I think she fell in love with the idea of falling in love more than anything. And he, of course, would never have left his wife for a one-night stand.'

'Are you saying that knowledge didn't in any way inform your own actions?' he pressed. His tone wasn't as harsh and condemning as it had been on the day of the memorial. As unyielding as the question was, this time it was powered more by the subtle need for assurance and thin layer of vulnerability than anything else.

But still she drew her hand away before she answered. 'Think about it, Ramon. We had a one-night stand too and, as you reminded me, we didn't even like each other much. But would I be here, trying to have another child with you, if I didn't want this? The doctors reassured me that the likelihood of the congenital heart failure reoccurring was low, but it's still scary—'

'*Perdón?* The what?' He cut across her, his voice a deadly blade.

Her breath strangled. 'The baby—'

'*Our* baby.'

She nodded jerkily. 'Our baby was diagnosed with congenital heart disease.' She frowned. 'You said you had me investigated. I thought you knew…'

Her words trailed off as his glass dropped onto the table, spreading red wine on the white cloth. *'Dios mio,'* he muttered through lips gone ashen. He stared at her for an infinite moment, then he jerked to his feet, paced away from the table.

'Ramon…'

He swerved back around. 'Tell me what…how…' He stopped, swallowed.

Pain shook her from scalp to toes. 'We used protection so I didn't suspect I was pregnant…for a while. I was still spotting. Anyway, when I eventually had the scan, it showed the defect, I was told the chances of her living through the very risky surgery were appallingly low. I did *extensive* research. No one could guarantee success.'

'That's why you terminated the pregnancy?'

Brokenly, she nodded.

'So you intended to keep it all along?' he pressed.

'*Yes.* You really didn't know?'

He exhaled loudly. Then his face contorted in a pained grimace. 'No. After Luis told me you'd terminated the pregnancy, I didn't have much room to hear anything else. I admit I didn't treat the messenger very well. We didn't speak for a few weeks, and, when we did, we chose not to discuss it further. My investigation was to verify time and dates and your finances, not *why* you'd terminated…' He shut his eyes and shook his head. *'Madre di Dios.'*

'I'm sorry.'

His eyes opened, spearing her with fierce remorse. 'No, I am the one who is sorry. *Lo siento mucho,*' he repeated solemnly in Spanish.

A stone lodged in her throat, and her eyes prickled. Muttering another curse, he came and crouched before her chair, his thumb brushing her tears. 'This time we will succeed,' he rasped harshly. Whether it was a command to the cosmos or a plea couched in typical Ramon arrogance, she found herself nodding, adding her own silent prayer to the statement.

He caught her hand, drew her up and walked her to the terrace. His tone subdued, he probed her gently for more information, which she freely gave, finding the sharing of the pain she'd carried for ever a little easier to bear.

An eternity later, they returned to the table. Their dinner dishes had been cleared, and the table was now set with dessert.

Ramon offered her a plate of *pastelitos* and *yemitas*. 'Eat, they're your favourite,' he instructed before heaping ice cream onto the side of the dessert bowl.

She stared at the large, mouth-watering dish. 'You're trying to fatten me up.'

'No, I'm trying to get this meal over as quickly as possible so I can drag you to the bedroom and get that damned dress off you,' he returned gruffly, stormy eyes ablaze with lust and a large dose of regret pinning hers.

He stayed true to his word. Except the dress didn't survive the inferno of his lust. Suki suspected he'd intended to rip the dress to shreds all along and didn't mourn the loss for too long. They were too busy mourning, and then reaffirming life.

But as she scooped the ripped material off the floor the next day, her mind tripped back to the night before and the disturbing subject she'd left untouched.

Svetlana. And why Ramon had lied about having broken his engagement with her. Although Luis had informed her without prompting the last time she'd seen him that Ramon and Svetlana were no longer together, the thought that he'd still been with her when he'd slept with Suki had triggered a fresh bout of bitterness.

It still did. Her fingers gripped the tattered material harder as the admission lanced her.

Why?

Because she wanted to be able to trust the father of her child completely? She didn't doubt that Ramon would be fully committed to his child. Family held a premium place in his priorities. Perhaps even the ultimate.

So why did she need other assurances that didn't... *shouldn't* matter to their agreement? Because her child would one day look up to his father and find him wanting, just as she'd found her father wanting.

Even before she fed herself that answer, Suki knew it wasn't the complete truth. She wanted to know *for herself.*

'I'm one hundred per cent sure that dress is out of commission for ever. Glaring at it quite so intensely isn't really necessary.'

She whirled around. He stood in the doorway to their— *his*—suite, the fists he'd thrust into stone-coloured chinos making his well-developed biceps, left visible by his short-sleeved V-necked shirt, bunch in eye-catching glory. A trace of tension stiffened his shoulders, and lingered in his eyes. Clearly, some of last night's subjects bothered him too.

She dragged her gaze from the spectacular sight he made to the torn dress in her hand. 'Yes...I was about to dispose of it.'

'After delivering its last rites?' he teased.

She shook her head, the alarming direction her thoughts seemed intent on taking preventing any humour from filtering through. 'No.'

His face turned serious. Striding forward, he caught her chin in his hand and tilted her face up to his. 'What's wrong?'

She started to shake her head, unsure of where this conversation would go if she started it.

He stopped her. 'Tell me, Suki.' The even tone of his voice didn't diminish the implacable demand.

'Why did you lie to me about your engagement being over the night of my birthday?' she blurted.

His whole body froze, his jaw tightening as his teeth clenched. 'I didn't lie to you,' he bit out after several tense seconds.

Her heart squeezed with disappointment far too acute for her to fool herself into thinking this conversation didn't have rippling repercussions for her emotional state. 'What does that mean? Things weren't over with her though, were they? You didn't deny that you were photographed together after you and I were…'

'Together? No, I don't deny it. And yes, she was still in my life, but we were not engaged.'

Pain she had no right to feel lanced her. But she fought to keep it from showing. 'That's just semantics, Ramon. Whether you were engaged or not, you were with her when you were with me. You weren't just a cheater, you also made me a cheater!'

His head went back at the hot accusation. His hand dropped, leaving her cold, far colder than common sense warranted she should be.

And yet the shiver that went through her was so strong, she rubbed frantic hands up and down her arms as she watched him walk away. When he reached the French doors, he turned around to face her. The look on his face was chillingly forbidding.

'That day, your birthday… I found out that she was cheating on me.'

Her gasp fell into the wide chasm that had sprung up between them. Whether he heard her or not, she wasn't sure as he continued.

'When I confronted her, she swore that it wasn't true. I didn't believe her so I ended it.'

'That's why you were in such a foul mood that night?'

He scowled at the carpet for a moment. 'That's why I jumped to conclusions about you that I shouldn't have.'

The admission salved a little, but there were gaps she needed filled. 'Right. Okay…'

'A few weeks after you, she begged me to give her the benefit of the doubt. I refused. But she had a debut movie coming up and she pleaded with me to maintain appearances until the premiere. Her morals turned out to be questionable but I didn't see the benefit in ruining her so I agreed. Besides, it also got the press off my back for a while.'

'So you maintained a relationship just for appearances' sake?' Suki wasn't sure how she felt about that.

He shrugged. 'We'd been together a year but we both led busy lives and hadn't seen each other more than a handful of times those last two months. Turning up for a three-hour premiere in exchange for a quiet exit to the relationship seemed like a good bargain.'

She frowned in remembrance. 'But that wasn't the end, was it? There were more pictures of the two of you. Even Luis believed you were still together.' She was aware she was coming across like a rabid stalker who had tracked his every move. But she couldn't stop the questions that spilled out. Or the need to understand.

'She tried to get me back after that. She refused to take off the engagement ring and turned up at a few places she knew I would be.'

'But you sent her packing?' she asked, with a lot more hope than she knew was wise.

Ramon's expression didn't alter, but his silence told her he was weighing his words. 'She continued to plead her innocence. When she proved an allegation false, I decided to hear her out.'

Because he'd been in love with her.

'Because you...cared about her?'

A frown twitched between his brows. 'We were engaged to be married. Of course I cared.'

The hollow sensation in her gut shortened her breath. 'Then why aren't you with her now?'

His face twisted in a grimace of deep bitterness and unforgiving reprehension. 'Because only *one* of the allegations was untrue,' he answered in an icy voice.

When the penny dropped, her mouth gaped. 'She cheated on you with different men?'

His jaw worked for several seconds. 'Apparently, she was lonely and I wasn't there for her enough so, yes, she turned to other men while convincing herself that I would be okay with it.' Impatient fingers charged through his hair, ruffling the jet waves. 'Are we done with the questioning, Suki? Are you satisfied that I didn't make a cheater out of you the night we slept together?' he asked.

Although she managed to convince herself that the part of her that had felt battered and wronged was appeased, the sinking sensation in the pit of her stomach presented an even greater problem.

'Yes, I'm satisfied,' she murmured.

He exhaled, his stride steady and assured as he retraced his steps back to her. 'I came up here to tell you lunch is ready. Teresa has made *boliche*.'

For the first time since she'd started sampling his house-keeper's incredible dishes, Suki couldn't summon the appe-tite for the delicious Cuban pot roast. She pushed her food around her plate, forcing down bites for the sake of eating rather than enjoyment.

Also for the first time, Ramon didn't complain, his own thoughts seemingly turned inwards as the meal progressed. When another furtive glance showed his gaze in the middle distance, Suki had to bite her tongue to stop herself from asking what he was thinking of. *Who* he was thinking of.

The idea that she'd opened a vault of memories for him sat like a heavy weight on her chest. One she could no lon-ger bear by the time their plates were cleared away.

'Do you mind if I skip dessert? I want to go for a swim in a little while and I'd rather not fall asleep in the pool.'

'If you wish,' he said, his usual droll response patently absent.

When he failed to deliver the narrow-eyed warning for her to be careful at the pool, Suki walked away from the table, the weight sitting heavier on her chest.

It stayed with her as she traversed the hallways to the room where the decorators were beginning to re-plaster the walls in readiness to replace the centuries-old carved stone that had been removed. After a short discussion with the foreman, she made her way to her suite.

The light tan she'd acquired gave her the confidence to don the canary-yellow bikini she would normally have avoided as being too eye-catching for her pasty skin. But the way she looked was the last thing on her mind as she stepped out onto the terrace and headed for the pool.

Submerging herself beneath the cool water did nothing to erase the image of Ramon's face as he spoke of Svetlana. The bitterness. The pain.

Acrid jealousy rose to choke her as his words joined in her torment.

We were engaged to be married. Of course I cared.

Did he still care? Was he still so in love with her it'd stunted his artistic passion?

She burst from beneath the water, her breath coming in pants as she clung to the edge of the pool. What was wrong with her that she couldn't get off the subject? Who Ramon cared about shouldn't feature anywhere on her emotional landscape. What she should be giving thanks for was that her integrity hadn't been compromised.

She hadn't inadvertently stolen another woman's man, even if it'd been for a single unforgettable night.

And yet, she continued to cling to the tiles, her mind tripping forward to the nights she would soon *not* have. To the time when she would be relegated to sleeping alone, should her job of conceiving succeed sooner rather than later.

Deep in her heart, she knew it would be sooner. But the joy of that knowledge was crushed beneath the boulder sitting on her chest.

Ramon emerged from the salon and for a moment the weight lightened. Her gaze met his as he joined her at the poolside, her senses barely registering the kitchen staff who followed a moment later with a tray holding fruit punch.

Ramon too had changed into a lighter T-shirt that hugged his impressive torso and a pair of swim shorts that framed his powerful thighs.

Tall, proud, virile and impossibly handsome.

His gaze obscured by aviator sunglasses, he stretched out on a lounger. She stared, unable to help herself, unable to fathom why the sight of him did such unimaginably crazy things to her. Why, even when he was with her, a part of her mourned the future loss.

How can you mourn something that never truly belonged to you?

Because she was only borrowing for a while, wasn't she?

Frustration and confusion battling through her, she pushed away from the wall, dived under the water in the vain hope that the exercise would bring her some clarity.

It didn't.

When she eventually gave up and walked up the shallow steps, he met her at the edge of the pool, wrapping a towel around her before leading her back to the loungers.

He waited until she'd patted herself dry, then poured her a drink. Thirstily, she drank the punch, eyeing him as he grabbed sun protection, squeezed a portion into his palm and tugged her foot into his lap. In silence he massaged the protection over her ankles and up her calves.

Her breath hitched when he slid those sure hands over her thighs, but, although his movements were firm and efficient, his touch didn't linger.

Fighting the hunger that was never far off when he touched her like this, she took a deep breath. 'I'm sorry if I brought back memories for you earlier.'

A handful of seconds passed, then he shrugged. '*No es*

nada,' he dismissed. 'Your peace of mind is more important than my past liaisons.'

'Is it? I guess we're making progress, then.'

With the shades obscuring his eyes, she couldn't tell their expression. But she felt tension bouncing off him as his hands froze on her thigh. 'Is there something else on your mind, Suki? I thought we were done, but perhaps you wish to air whatever troubles had you clinging so tightly to the pool tiles ten minutes ago?' His voice was even, but it held the barest hint of a storm that intensified her floundering.

'You were watching me?'

'You decided you wanted to swim directly after lunch,' he replied, as if that explained everything.

'You know that those theories about cramps from swimming after a meal have been proven groundless, right?' she snapped.

'I know that you seem to be spoiling for a fight. Are you?'

The laughter that emerged was dry. 'I don't know. Maybe let's blame the past few hours on crazy hormones.' Words that were meant to be offhand suddenly grew leaden, dropped like anchors between them.

Ramon went completely still. Suki was sure he'd stopped breathing. 'To which type of hormones are you referring?' he asked, that storm powered by a different kind of energy now.

'Which do you think?' Her voice was little more than hushed sound, her instincts clamouring.

He reached up and slid off his glasses, as if he wanted no barrier between them when he asked, 'Are you sure?' His accent was pronounced; a deep husk throbbing with a maelstrom of emotions.

Suki willed her racing heart to calm. 'I…I think so.'

He stood and held out his hand in silent command. 'There's only one way to find out. Come.'

Her head tilted higher to read his face. 'Where are we going?'

'Upstairs. Unless you wish to perform the tests down here?'

Her eyes widened. 'You bought pregnancy tests?'

'*Sí*, of course. A dozen of them when we were in Miami.'

'But you didn't say anything…'

His hand extended again impatiently. 'I was waiting for you. And now you're wasting time, Suki.'

She slid her hand into his, secretly grateful for the support when she rose on shaky legs.

For a moment, they faced each other, saying nothing as hardly a breath passed between them. Then he was leading her away from the pool, through the salon and down the endless hallways to the grand staircase.

His fingers tightened around hers for a second before he made an impatient sound. The next instant, he swept her into his arms. Her already non-existent breath completely evaporated at the sizzling skin-to-skin contact. But while her senses went into free fall, he was taking the stairs with quick, purposeful strides, barely exerting himself as he carried her into his suite.

In his large, luxuriously appointed bathroom, he set her down on the cushioned vanity seat, pulled open a drawer and scooped out the long, rectangular boxes. With uncharacteristically unsteady movements, he started to rip open the boxes.

Suki stopped him when he reached for the fifth one.

'I think we have enough.'

He paused, looked as if he wanted to disagree, then gave a tight nod. 'Do you need anything else?' he rasped, casting a searching look around the bathroom.

'N-no. I'm fine.'

Still he hesitated. Finally, he nodded again, and left the bathroom.

Heart in her throat, Suki reached for the first white and

blue stick. The handful of kits he'd bought were far superior quality to the ones she'd used previously, but the basics were the same.

An excruciating three minutes later, she had her answer.

She emerged to find him pacing the bedroom in tight circles, one hand clamped on his nape. He spun around immediately.

A vein throbbed at his temple. Eyes ablaze with rabid, expectant light fixed on her. His mouth worked, but no sound emerged.

The equally soul-shaking cocktail of emotions rampaging through her weakened her limbs. Leaning against the door frame, she slowly held up the sticks. 'I'm…I'm pregnant.'

His hand dropped from his neck, his eyes turning a dark, dark green she was associating with deep emotional upheaval. When after a full minute he said nothing, she nervously licked her lips. 'Did you hear—?'

'*Sí, querida.* I heard you,' he croaked.

'And?' The blend of joy, hope and naked fear in her voice was very easy to discern.

Coming to life again, he ate up the distance between them and cupped her face in his hands. She'd seen a ruthlessly determined Ramon more times than she cared for. The expression that crossed his face was nothing short of a man on a crusade.

'And this time things will be different. We will succeed this time.' He repeated the words he'd said last night.

And because she needed that assurance more than she would've thought possible, because she wanted to hold on to something…anything that affirmed the belief that things would be different this time, she took a deep breath, and, just like last time, she nodded. 'Yes.'

CHAPTER TEN

RAMON ENTERED THE sunlit space that was his studio one week later and drew to a stop.

The temperature was the same as it had been yesterday, the blue sky visible through his glass roof just as cloudless. The floor bore evidence of his deep frustrations. And yet, the light was almost blinding. And he felt more invigorated than he had in…hell, he couldn't remember.

Sure, there were a million other emotions bubbling beneath the surface of his skin that he didn't want to name, never mind examine, but the energy surging through him was so overwhelming, he experienced its sizzle to the very tips of his fingers.

A father. He was going to become *a father*.

He'd plotted, planned and executed it. But he hadn't allowed himself to fully embrace its possibilities. Same as he had never thought himself particularly invested in evolution or been hell-bent on leaving his mark on the Earth the way some men were obsessed with. Not until Luis had dropped the news of his lost unborn child in his lap. Not until precarious conditions on a rainy night in Mexico had caused a lorry to smash into his parents' car, ending the lives of the three people who meant the world to him.

The dark gloom and relentless anguish that dogged his days hadn't suddenly lifted, but for the first time in a long time Ramon was able to take a breath that wasn't drawn from a place of complete despair.

He knew part of that stemmed from what Suki had told him. She'd wanted their child. Fate had forced her to make a different, harrowing decision. One he couldn't fault her for. Absurdly, mourning for his lost child too now felt a little easier.

He took another deep, soul-restoring breath. He wasn't naive to the risks involved in every pregnancy, had probably over-educated himself on the subject. But the unfamiliar sentiment he first witnessed in Suki's face and was beginning to entertain himself—*hope*—had been bolstered by the requisite doctors' tests and reassurance.

All of which had turned him into the very laughable, very unrecognisable cliché of a *reborn* man.

Fairly certain it was that same alien sentiment that was leading him to re-examine other ideas he'd sealed in the *never again* vault, he'd left a napping Suki in her suite and retreated to the studio.

He looked around him at the half-finished works that had documented his turbulent state of mind.

Pieces he'd promised to his galleries for fast-approaching exhibits lay abandoned, giant hunks of metal, stone and marble enshrouded beneath black cloth.

Ignoring them, he crossed the cavernous space to the back of the studio where untouched slabs of stone and marble were lined up on wheel brackets. Running his hands over the raw material, he settled on the smooth Carrara marble.

Wheeling it to the middle of the room, he yanked off his T-shirt, powered up his tools and started to sculpt.

Three hours later, the frame of his idea had begun to take shape. Unsettlingly, so had the idea that the parameters of the bargain he'd struck with Suki could…*should* be altered.

Like the master strategist the world claimed him to be, he stepped back from fully embracing it, weighing the pros and cons as the days passed.

In many ways it wasn't a road he wanted to go down again. But there was more than himself to think about now. And his child outweighed any con that stood in his way.

So he chipped away, until the one that remained was Suki herself.

* * *

The first six weeks of pregnancy rolled by in a dizzying tumult of blinding joy, hopefulness and inevitable moments of abject fear. The urge to make plans, choose a nursery and start decorating immediately was tempered by the need to exercise brutal caution. With each day that passed, Suki counted her blessings. Hell, she even welcomed the double bout of morning sickness that plagued her this time round.

Through it all, Ramon remained a steady presence at hand to see to her general well-being. Just as he'd made it his mission to get her pregnant, he took on the role of ruthless overseer with aplomb, never straying far when she was awake, reciting bare but reassuring statistics when worry threatened to take over.

He found excuses to be in the room when she tested colour swatches on walls and supervised the staining of the new mantelpiece. He threw a casual arm over her shoulder and held her at a distance when the restorers reinserted the mosaic windows and even helped her re-plaster the priceless tiles.

The belief that he would be committed to his child was indelibly cemented into place. Between that, the doctors' continued reassurance about her healthy pregnancy and the fact that her mother had undergone the first round of treatment and come through with flying colours should've placed her somewhere on cloud nine.

Except for one large hole in the fabric of her contentment.

She and Ramon no longer shared a bed. Despite knowing the day was coming, his immediate and complete withdrawal following confirmation of her pregnancy had lodged a nasty little ball of anguish in her chest she hadn't been able to destroy no matter how much she tried.

And she'd tried.

By reminding herself how her presence here came about. By summoning up Svetlana's drop-dead gorgeous form, comparing it to her own and reiterating that she would always be found wanting.

And if that wasn't enough, she had Ramon's own words to remind her why she needed to find a way to deal with the silly torment of her crush.

We were engaged to be married. Of course I cared...

Except Suki couldn't hide from the fact that this time, it was more than a crush. Her crush had been unwieldy and inconvenient. So much so she'd given in at the first true lesson in temptation in the hope of getting rid of it.

But this…

This ache grew mockingly bigger, churning more anguish with each passing day. And it stemmed from the simple knowledge that she missed him. Missed his sometimes acerbic tongue. Missed him teasing her about her love of Teresa's cooking.

Most of all, she missed falling asleep in his arms. A fact she readily accepted was her most foolish yearning of all.

'What's wrong?'

She jumped at the sharp demand, her heart racing as her hand stilled from the light gloss she'd been applying to the frame of an antique painting that had once hung in the drawing room that was being restored.

Carefully she modulated her voice so her feelings wouldn't bleed through. 'What do you mean? Nothing's wrong.'

'Then why were you standing there with your face contorted and your hand on your stomach?' came the sharper query.

Realising the direction of his thoughts, she dropped the rag, set the painting against the wall, and turned. 'Ramon, there's nothing wrong, I prom—' The rest of the words died in her throat at the sight of him.

He was shirtless. Again. A light sheen of sweat covered his insanely chiselled torso and dampened the trail of hair disappearing beneath the waistband of weathered trousers that were stained with specks of marble dust and the special oil he used on his tools when he was sculpting.

Suki wanted to blame pregnancy hormones for the way her senses went into meltdown at the sight of his half-naked form, but she knew that would be false. Her stupefying re-action to Ramon was nothing new. But it would seriously get out of hand if she wasn't careful.

'You were saying?' he pressed, one hand reaching into his back pocket to pluck a towel to wipe his grimy fingers on.

The sight of those slim, capable fingers, the sweat on his skin, the earthy, sexy smell of him.

Dear God, he was too much.

'I was saying I'm fine,' she replied, her voice waspish. 'And do you have to go around half naked all the time?'

One eyebrow spiked. 'Does the sight of me offend you?' he drawled.

She wanted to laugh. And cry. Maybe throw in a scream or two. Instead, she chose the high road paved with com-posure and dignity. 'On second thought, forget it. It's your house. You can come and go as you please, I suppose.'

'*Gracias*…I think,' he returned dryly.

With nothing more to add, and the even more urgent need to do something other than give in to the temptation to stare at his glorious half-nakedness, she picked up the painting and started walking towards the door. She'd barely taken a few steps when he intercepted her and took it from her.

'I hired an additional team so you didn't have to do your own carrying, Suki,' he grumbled.

Once her morning sickness had abated, a second team of architects had arrived. With the detailed photos from the room, they'd come up with a schedule of when the restora-tion works would start. She'd been forbidden from any lift-ing so Suki set up a temporary office in one of the many bedrooms on the second floor and contented herself with choosing the antique furniture, wallpaper and drapes to finish the room with once the work was done.

'That painting weighs less than my laptop and, besides, I need the exercise.'

His scowl was pure storm clouds. 'Not one that involves you going up and down the stairs a dozen times a day.'

She stopped herself from pointing out that she'd only been down twice today, both times at his bidding, to share a meal with him. 'Was there a particular reason you came looking for me? Or are you gracing me with your grumpy presence just for laughs?'

He paused at the top of the stairs and eyed her. 'Now who's grumpy?'

'You haven't answered my questions.'

He observed her pursed-lips response for a minute before he started walking down the stairs.

Following a step behind him, she couldn't avoid staring at his gladiator-like physique, the beautiful musculature of his back and the light bounce of his slightly unruly hair as he moved in that deeply animalistic way unique to him.

One of the restorers was coming out of a hallway as they reached the ground floor. Ramon handed over the painting with a flurry of Spanish that received several quick and agreeable nods, before he turned to her.

'Let's go.'

'Go where? And what did you say to the contractor?' she asked.

He turned in the direction of the main salon and she, with no choice, followed. 'I suggested that perhaps they would be better off making less trips to the kitchen to take advantage of our housekeeper's culinary skills and more manpower keeping you from having to traipse around with antiques. He was kind enough to agree.'

'Ramon!'

He stopped, turned to face her. And she noticed that, despite his casual tone, he was highly vexed. 'We had a deal, *guapa*. One that I'd hoped wouldn't need us to have this conversation.'

'You're overreacting.'

He stepped closer, bringing more of that irritated, hard-packed body into her personal space. 'Am I?' he enquired softly, his gaze raking her face before it locked on her mouth.

'Yes, you are,' she said. And then because she lived with the same fear every single second, she cleared her throat. 'But I have it on good authority, they will be done before the end of the week, so they will be out of your hair.'

His eyes didn't move from her mouth. '*Bene*. I will not have to tear my hair out after all.'

Her gaze tracked to his full head of vibrant hair. 'You can spare a few, I'm sure. And seeing as I've saved your mane, maybe you will start wearing a shirt?' she asked, hoping her tone was less pleading and more irritated.

Green eyes flicked up to meet hers. Then a low deep laugh rumbled up from his throat. Unfettered. Sexy. Spell-binding. The sound, rarely heard and not at all recently, wrapped around her. It only lasted a handful of seconds but every cell in her body lifted, strained towards the incredible sound.

'You agree to no more carrying heavy stuff around and I'll think about it,' he replied.

'Okay, fine. I agree.'

He muttered something Spanish under his breath before resuming his stride down the hallway. When they reached the salon, he held the door open for her. The sun-drenched beauty of the room never failed to soothe her. She walked around, trailing her fingers over priceless antique furniture steeped in history.

Ramon stayed at the entrance of the salon, leaning against the door frame and studying her for a long moment. When his scrutiny got too much, she dropped her hand from the bronze bust she'd been examining. 'Is there any reason you're staring at me like that?'

'I've started working on the first piece he made me promise to do for you,' he said, his voice containing a solemn tone that made her heart kick.

'He…you mean Luis?'

Ramon nodded. 'Yes.'

'You're sculpting and painting again.'

His face was unreadable. '*Sí*, it seems I am.'

Suki wanted to ask how…when…*why*? Too scared of the answer, she ventured softly instead, 'I…am I allowed to know what it is?'

'It's a sculpture. But I haven't decided what it'll be yet. I sketched out a few ideas. But I need a live representation. I choose you.'

Shock slayed her. 'Me?'

'To be the subject, *sí*.'

A shiver went through her. There was something viscerally exposing about what he was asking. 'I'm not…are you—?'

'Don't think up excuses.'

'I wasn't. I was just going to ask if you were sure.'

He shrugged. 'I have tried several inanimate objects. They're not working. You are the most convenient living test subject.'

'Wow, suddenly I don't feel so special,' she muttered.

A heavy and bleak expression fleeted through his eyes. 'You were special to him. I should've considered you first and saved myself much wasted time.'

Her hurt abated a little even though she knew she would need a scalpel to dig out the precious meaning hidden in his words.

'Will you do it?' he rasped.

It would be a gift from her best friend from beyond the grave. One she could cherish for ever. 'Yes, of course I will.'

He gestured her forward. 'Good. Let's go.'

She looked down at the white cotton, short-sleeved tunic she'd thrown on hastily this morning to meet the restorers. Beneath it, she wore the canary-yellow bikini that had fast become her favourite swimsuit. 'Do I need to change?'

He conducted a long scrutiny from loose hair to sandalled feet. 'No, you're fine as you are.'

They left the villa by way of a little-used hallway at the back of the villa. Like everywhere in the villa and on the grounds, the winding stone path dissecting the back garden and leading to Ramon's brick and glass studio was immaculately kept. He punched in a code and the sturdy double doors sprang ajar.

Her preconceived idea of what Ramon's artist's studio would look like was smashed to smithereens the second she walked in. He'd cleaned up the carnage, obviously, but still, expecting the stereotypical, paint-splattered chaos of a passionate artist's creative space, she froze to a halt at what confronted her.

On either side of the whitewashed walls, rows of tall and short objects were covered with black cloth. And on the long bench that held dozens of pots of paint and brushes, each one was laid out at a precise angle.

The floor beneath her feet had been painted a pristine white too, the light pouring in from the windows giving the space an almost other-worldly dimension.

A dimension where everything was set in its place. Almost chastely so.

Everything except the raised platform at the end of the space and the single black armchair that served as an observation point for the platform. On the floor next to the chair, a half-empty bottle of dark rum stood next to a crystal tumbler containing dregs of amber liquid.

As if that weren't awe-inspiring enough, her gaze rose higher, her eyes widening as she walked further forward to better see the untouched slab of solid black granite suspended from the ceiling.

Against the white walls and floor, the platform and the piece that would form a stunning sculpture one day was wildly hypnotic, commanding and receiving attention. Suki stopped behind the chair, unable to take her eyes off it.

The mental vision of Ramon watching that piece of stone, sketching, viscerally connecting with his subject… his muse…breathing life into the piece was so visually mesmerising, she didn't hear him speak above the growing buzzing in her blood.

'Suki?'

She snatched a quick, restorative breath and faced him. 'Yes?'

'Are you okay?'

She nodded quickly, dragging her gaze from the spectacle before her. 'I'm fine. Umm…why is everything covered?' she asked, hoping to cover her flustered senses.

'I don't like distractions when I work.'

Distractions or *reminders*?

Unbidden, the memory of how Ramon and Svetlana had met rose to her mind. According to Luis, he'd seen her on a catwalk in Milan and had been so struck with her, he'd asked to paint her. Within days they were lovers. Before their first month was over, he'd asked her to marry him.

Emotion she recognised as naked jealousy spiked through her blood. 'Do you have other studios?' she blurted before she could stop herself.

The unexpected question drew a frown. 'No, this is my only one. Why?'

So he'd brought Svetlana here. Painted and sculpted her here. Suki shook her head, swallowing down the sick feeling that surged high. 'I'm just…curious.'

He continued to stare at her for probing seconds. Unable to stand it, she turned around, walked closer to the steps leading up to the platform. This time the noise in her ears was the creaky churning of her heart. And again she didn't hear him when he addressed her.

'I'm sorry, what did you say?'

He prowled to the edge of the platform, stared down at her with narrowed eyes. 'I said, take off your dress.'

Her heart skidded, then jumped into her throat as heat engulfed her. 'I...what?

'The dress, Suki. Take it off. Then lie down on there.' He indicated behind her with his chin.

Turning, she saw that the slab had somehow been lowered to hip level. From where she stood it looked like a narrow bed. A bed from which would be hewn a magnificent piece of art from Ramon's hands. The same hands that had thrilled her so thoroughly when they'd made love.

Sizzling heat flowed over her body, singeing the apex of her thighs and tightening her nipples in remembered torment. Crossing her arms in front of her to hide her body's weakness, she slipped off her thongs and climbed up the three shallow steps of the platform. Behind her, Ramon tracked her movements, towering over her as she slowly reached out to touch the stone.

There was no give in the chains holding it in place.

'Don't be concerned—it will hold your weight.'

She wanted to say that wasn't her concern. She wanted to say she didn't want to lie down because she was afraid of what she would reveal from being this close to something so powerful. Of what he'd see when she was exposed to him.

And she would be. Ramon had been right when he recounted Luis's imitation of her the one time they visited Piedra Galleries in London. Every single one of Ramon's pieces of work had held her in thrall. Touching his pieces had been like touching the man himself.

And that was even before she'd shared his bed, taken him into her body. Been impregnated with his child. Now the sensation was ten times more potent. Because all those feelings were beginning to take a certain shape, make a terrifying kind of sense.

Sensing her prevarication, he stepped closer.

'Now, Suki,' he commanded huskily from behind her.

She wanted to refuse. But, of course, she didn't. Because the slavish compulsion to give him what he wanted also made a terrifying kind of sense.

She caught the hem of her tunic, her hands efficiently tugging the flimsy material over her head.

His harsh exhalation echoed through the space as he caught the dress from her weak fingers and flung it away.

'Now the rest,' he instructed thickly.

Her breath strangled in her lungs but refusal never crossed her mind. Fingers shaking, she tugged the strings of the bikini top and bottom free until they fell away, until she stood naked, her head bowed, her tumbling hair flowing over her shoulders.

Slowly, she sensed him circling her, tracking her every shiver, her every breath.

When he stopped directly in front of her, she raised her head, met his gaze straight on.

Saw for herself that he too was affected.

Hectic colour tinged taut cheekbones, his bare chest rising and falling in ragged breathing. Both hands came up and wrapped around the chains securing the slab, his knuckles showing white as his red-hot gaze flew over her body.

'Lie down, Suki.' Again the instruction was thick, his voice barely discernible.

Two short steps brought her to the raw ingredient that would form his masterpiece. Reaching out, she touched it, familiarised herself with its texture. Lowering herself onto it, she stretched out on her back. The heat of her body meeting the cold drew a shiver and a gasp from her.

Ramon stared down at her, her feet a scant inch from his powerful thighs and the potent reaction to her that currently bulged behind his zipper. Suki wasn't sure whether it was the fire from his gaze or the blaze from her body that soon warmed the stone beneath her.

Ferocious need clamouring through her, she couldn't stop

the sinuous movement of her body or the hand that slid over her midriff to rest on her belly.

Although she'd gained weight in the last several weeks, her stomach had remained flat. And yet she felt different, her not-yet-visible pregnancy powering a change she felt from head to toe.

Now, as Ramon's eyes lingered at the place where their child grew, a tumult of emotions wove over his face.

'*Dios mio,*' he breathed as his gaze raked over her, absorbed the subtle changes in her body.

After a long minute, he lurched away from the slab. Going to the long workbench, he grabbed a large sketchpad and a thin wedge of grey charcoal. Returning, he threw himself into the chair, poured a finger of rum and knocked it back.

Then his hand began to fly over the surface of the pad.

Time sped up. Or slowed to a crawl. She lost the ability to judge as she was caught up in a singularly transcendental experience.

When Ramon instructed her, she turned this way and that, making sure not to jar her body. Finally, he set the pad down and poured himself another drink.

Eyes gone almost black with unfathomable emotions regarded her as he rolled the tumbler between his palms.

Had she not lived through his effortless rejection of her these past few weeks, or known that everything he did was in pursuit of his heir, Suki's heart would've soared high.

But the knowledge was inescapable. And with it came an agony that drew a rough sound from her throat. Probing eyes that saw way too much shifted from where they were stalled on the rise and fall of her stomach to snag her own.

Tossing the drink back, he stood and came up the platform, caught her hand and helped her upright. 'Are you okay?' he rasped.

Attempting to speak past the sensation clogging her

throat was hard, but she barely managed. 'Did you get what you needed?'

For some reason the question made him tense.

One by one, the emotions disappeared from his face and he brought himself under rigid, effortless control. Resolutely, he stepped back and left the platform, once again rejecting her. 'Yes. You can get dressed now.'

As Suki slid off the slab, retied her bikini and pulled on her tunic, her heart finally accepted the truth and tumbled into deep mourning. But even the monumental knowledge of what had happened didn't stop her from caressing the granite one last time.

Because whether or not Ramon used the sketches he'd made of her, she would associate this studio, this platform, this piece of stone with the moment she'd accepted that her stupid crush had turned into something much, much bigger for ever.

CHAPTER ELEVEN

'I THINK WE need a change of scene.'

'A change of scene to where?' Suki asked without turning around from where she was basking in the spectacular sunset. In the two weeks since he'd taken the sketches of her, she'd barely seen Ramon. Each morning after breakfast, he disappeared into his studio.

His presence at lunch and dinner had been replaced by an extra attentive Teresa, who had even attempted to learn a few English phrases in order to engage her in conversation.

As much as Suki appreciated the housekeeper's efforts her appetite had been reduced to forcing food down merely to maintain a healthy pregnancy.

She was in love with Ramon Acosta.

He was only interested in the baby she carried.

No matter how many times she told herself the latter to mitigate any further pain, her heart lurched harder, the pain growing more acute. Her hand tightened around the metal banister that edged the villa's flat roof terrace.

Suki had taken to escaping up here when the worst of the day's heat abated to enjoy the sunset, and the cast-iron bench seats with plump cushions set beneath a simple ivy-covered gazebo were the perfect place to retreat. Either with a book or with the thoughts that were determined not to leave her be.

Hearing the clatter of crockery behind her, she turned to see one of Teresa's minions was heading their way holding a tray. Suki had stopped wondering how the housekeeper knew when to strike with her snacks but then discovered there was actually a twenty-four-hour roster in the kitchen ensuring the endless supply of food.

The unexpected appearance and steady approach of the man who dominated those thoughts sent a skitter of alarm over her skin.

And equally punishing, he was once again shirtless.

She couldn't hide her reaction to the electrifying stimulus or stop the breath that caught dangerously in her midriff, all of which Ramon clocked with perceptive eyes.

'Come and sit down.' He indicated the chairs, murmuring an order to the maid before relieving her of the tray of refreshing drinks and a plate of *yemitas*.

Leaving the balcony, she took a seat on the sofa, numbly accepting a cup of decaf coffee she had no interest in drinking and a small platter of pastries.

Ramon helped himself to an espresso before he snagged one pastry for himself. Sitting back, he chewed and swallowed, his inscrutable eyes on her. 'My art foundation holds a month-long talent-sourcing contest for Cuban artists every September. It's open to twenty-five entrants. The final selection is made in mid-October and we showcase ten of them at my galleries over a two-week period.'

The unexpected subject that had nothing to do with food or vitamins piqued her interest. 'Here in Cuba?'

He nodded. 'Initially, but also in other Piedra Galleries. Teresa tells me you've stopped eating and are a whisper away from going stir crazy. Now your mother is back in London undergoing the second stage of her treatment, I think we should visit the galleries together. We can stop in London to see your mother after Madrid.'

She didn't clock the middle part of his statement immediately because she was too busy being giddy at the thought of time spent on something else other than her tormenting thoughts. Even if that time involved seeing Ramon's work again. 'That would be—wait, you've been having Teresa spy on me?' Her voice rose almost comically.

He gave an unapologetic shrug. 'She's just as invested

in your welfare as I am. And I'm hoping we'll get you out of here before that situation fully blooms.'

'I'm not going stir—' She stopped as the maid returned, holding something in her hand. Rising fluidly to his feet, Ramon took it from her and returned tugging a dark sea-green T-shirt over his chest. Absurdly, even though her senses screamed at the torture of being subjected to the breathtaking masterpiece of his body, she mourned its disappearance once he covered himself up. It was probably why she was still staring at him as he returned, sat down and drained his coffee.

Setting his mug on the tray, he cocked an eyebrow at her. 'Are you happy now, *belleza*?' he drawled.

Tuning off her observation of the amazing things the colour did to his eyes, she finished her own decaf coffee. 'It's a good start,' she declared briskly.

Her senses were too jumpy to ascertain whether she caught a trace of laughter before he inclined his head. 'The first exhibition is this Friday. My assistant will put together an itinerary and put the medical team on standby.'

Her heart performed a sickening lurch. 'Do we need to take them with us?' The twice weekly visits by the team of doctors had been bearable before but were beginning to wear on her nerves.

Grim resolve crawled over his features, his body tensing in preparation for a fight. 'Yes. It's non-negotiable, Suki.'

She rose from the sofa, her agitated steps taking her back to the balcony. Below her lay the beautifully manicured gardens, carefully and attentively tended by Mario. Beyond the boundaries of the villa, the captivating port city of Cienfuegos, which had been awarded World Heritage Site status, went on as normal, unknowing that she was falling in love with its rich culture, thriving art and vintage cars, falling in love with one of its most dedicated citizens.

When she felt Ramon's approach, she turned, met the penetrating eyes that seemed to see into her soul. 'Even if their presence taunts me with the possibility that something could go wrong at any moment?' she blurted.

A tiny flash of shock sparked his eyes at her naked admission. Then he frowned. 'I hadn't quite thought of it that way.'

Of course he hadn't. Her heart twisted painfully. 'You ran a global empire and are used to having teams troubleshoot problems sometimes before they happen. It's a natural reaction for you. It's not for me.'

He reached out and tucked a strand of hair behind her ear. Although the gesture was a gentle one, his body remained tense, his gaze calculating and direct. 'It's the most efficient way to mitigate potential problems.'

Her fists balled, but she struggled to keep her voice even. Her emotions where he was concerned might be slipping out of her control but she could control this. 'I'm not a potential business problem, Ramon.'

His hand dropped, his hands shoving into his pockets. The gaze that had hers captive swept down, shutting her out. When it rose again it was charged with double the purpose. 'No. I've lost too much. I won't risk this baby's safety.'

Pain lanced her. 'And you think I will?'

His jaw clenched tight. 'I think you should remember our agreement. You agreed to the presence of a medical team for the duration of the pregnancy. You won't go back on your promise now,' he finished harshly.

The finality of that statement, the reminder that she was just the vessel incubating his heir, hollowed out any last vestige of the hope that she foolishly clung to in the dark of night. The hope that if they'd been as compatible in bed as she recalled, then perhaps, once the baby was born, they could go forge something out of the bones of that compatibility. It'd been a shameless, desperate wish. But a wish that she'd thought had foundations.

The look in his eyes told a different story.

Chemistry might prompt his body to react a certain way

to hers but the most important part of him, his heart, would never be hers.

Slowly she unfurled her fists. 'Fine. Since that's what your piece of paper states, then, by all means, have them come.'

Skirting his imposing form, she hurried away from the terrace.

Ramon watched her walk away, wondering if the tempestuous upheaval that best described his current state of being was pushing him into taking decisions that weren't entirely sound.

No, he concluded in the next breath. What was more sound than ensuring the optimal well-being of Suki and their baby? He knew the statistics. He also knew that expert care and quick action during a crisis would be the difference between saving the ones he cared about and having his heart ripped out all over again.

He couldn't take that.

But what about her fears?

Discomfort irritated beneath his skin, the voice very much like his brother's sparking a deep vexation.

She'd signed the agreement, yes, but did a piece of paper take into account the true reality? For the first time he'd allowed himself to truly hear her. Had he allowed himself to see the torment that always lurked in her eyes? The same torment she must have felt when faced with the diagnosis of their baby the first time round.

She'd lived through it. He hadn't. Did he not owe her the benefit of a little peace of mind?

But at what cost?

Gripping his nape, he looked to the heavens, seeking clarity. But as with everything else, he knew he would only find it within himself. And yet the instinct he'd trusted all of his life was flashing with an *out of order* signal. Because the options it was throwing out were laughable.

Or perhaps you don't want to trust what it's saying?

'Shut up, *hermano*,' he sneered under his breath.

Dios, he was losing his mind.

Folding his arms, he leaned against the balcony and attempted to calm his racing thoughts. But nothing would be calmed. Nothing had been calm since he first set eyes on Suki, he realised. She managed to consume his thoughts with very little effort.

Day or night.

Except he'd found a minimal outlet in the form of the nearly finished sculpture residing in his studio.

The sculpture you're tipping into obsession over?

He growled under his breath. So what if he was obsessed? He'd made a promise and he planned on keeping it. No matter that he was pouring a part of himself into the project than he'd never done before?

No matter that he fell into bed and dreamed about the subject of the project and woke up with a hollow feeling in his chest?

Suficiente.

Taking his phone from his pocket, he dialled his assistant's number, relayed precise instructions and hung up. Then he turned around, intent on taking a moment's peace of mind to enjoy the last of the blazing sunset.

Thirty seconds later, he was reaching for his phone again, and delivering slightly modified instructions.

The mocking laughter that rang in his ears, Ramon studiously decided to ignore.

Their journey to Havana two days later went without a hitch. As did the first exhibit of the talented artists who'd made the cut of his programme. The eclectic mix of local artists, avid collectors and overseas gallery owners interested in the thriving Cuban art scene meant the event was fully attended.

Already he'd fielded calls from other galleries in the States and Europe interested in featuring three of the artists.

He'd finished delivering the news to the artists in question when she caught his eye from the corner of the room. Hell, who was he kidding? His body's radar had known where she was at every single moment, even after she'd politely excused herself on arrival and made sure to put the width of the room between them from then on.

From across the room of Piedra Galleria Havana, he watched her converse with one of his artists. The short-sleeved lace dress hugged her upper arms and slim torso before flaring in a full calf-length skirt. With her hair caught up and delicate silver jewellery complementing her style, she was easily the most captivating woman in the room.

A fact evidenced by the volume of male attention directed her way.

The powerful hit of pure possessiveness didn't surprise him. Nor did the recognition that part of his irritation stemmed from the fact that her full skirt prevented him from seeing her belly. He didn't care that her pregnancy wasn't outwardly visible yet.

The caveman in him wanted his claim on her in plain sight.

Mine, he wanted to growl. But the word stayed locked in his throat. Because to utter that, he would need another word to give truth to the situation. *Temporarily.*

So the claim stayed down, and he watched as she nodded eagerly in conversation, then replied. The young artist, clearly thrilled to have a captive audience, proceeded to elaborate whatever point he was making with animated hand gestures. Ramon watched a smile break over her face, the first he'd seen for a while. The knot in his stomach annoyed him almost as much as the ever-closing gap between Suki and the artist.

A server approached them. Ramon watched the man snag two glasses of champagne and hand her one. Another smile accompanied her refusal, which should've made him back away. Instead, he leaned ever closer to catch what she was saying.

Ramon was moving across the floor before he'd fully registered the movement of his limbs. He reached them in time to hear his cocky cajoling.

'Come on, a simple drink for the man who put the first smile on your face tonight, *sí*?'

'When a woman states that she doesn't want a drink, you need to be a gentleman and respect her wishes,' Ramon cut in coldly.

Diego Baptiste's attention jerked his way, whatever objection he'd been about to put up dying when he saw Ramon.

He took a hasty step back, almost tripping over his feet. '*Sí, lo siento*. I did not mean any disrespect…enjoy your evening, *señorita*.' Turning on his heel, he struck a straight route into the busy crowd.

Stunning blue eyes, holding distinct accusation, glared at him. 'He was being nice. Did you have to put him down like that?'

A hovering waiter approached. Ramon chose a peach mocktail he knew she would enjoy and handed it to her, then grabbed a glass of cognac for himself, after which he walked her out of Diego's *papier-maché* exhibition into one more pleasing to him. 'He was encroaching where he had no business encroaching. So yes, the put-down was necessary.'

Her eyes snapped. 'Encroaching? We were just talking. And you're the host of this event. If you insist on glaring at everyone who walks past, don't do it in my presence.'

'You're the most beautiful woman in the room. No man wants to *just talk* to you,' he bit out. 'And I can glare at whomever I damn well please.'

She gave a dry laugh, but even that sound attracted more stares. 'What's got into you? If I didn't know better I'd think you were jealous.'

'Then I hate to be the bearer of bad news because you don't know any better,' he replied.

The glass in her hand wobbled. Her eyes widened adorably before heat flared up into her face along with a healthy measure of the confusion firing through his own bloodstream. 'Ramon...'

'You look stunning, *querida*, but I hate that dress you're wearing.'

Her peach-glossed, deliciously kissable lips pursed. 'Blame yourself, you chose it.'

'Well, at the time I didn't know that I would crave seeing your body bloom with my baby.'

She gave a soft gasp, then her forehead creased in puzzlement. 'Are...are you okay?'

He gave a dry laugh of his own then, unable to resist, he stepped forward and slid a hand around her waist. 'No. That skirt you're wearing covers you a little too well.'

'I'm not showing yet. And can we drop the wardrobe preferences for a minute?'

Splaying his fingers on her lower back, he pulled her closer until the top of her head was just below his chin, and he was breathing in the alluring scent of her apple shampoo and heady perfume.

'I wasn't as accommodating to your concerns as I should've been two days ago.'

She tensed, but she didn't move away from him. Ramon chose to see that as a victory.

'I feel like we've been here before but this time on a much grander scale. Is this your way of apologising?' she asked.

He allowed himself a small smile. 'If I say I need time to find the right words will you ride in my limo again?'

'Been there, done that,' she quipped. 'I'm wearing the metaphorical T-shirt right now.'

His hand left her waist to catch her feisty chin in his hand. 'You wear it beautifully and bravely. And your concerns have been noted and acted upon.'

Her gaze searched his. 'Really?'

'*Sí.*'

'How?'

'Leave the logistics to me. Just rest assured that, should we need them, the doctors will be there.'

She nodded after a handful of seconds, relief lightening her eyes. 'Thank you.'

'De nada.'

She started to step away. He scrambled with a reason to hold her close. When no coherent ones punched through the atmosphere of his confusion, he simply splayed his hand over her belly, feeling the slight firmness where his child was beginning to establish its presence.

She froze. A light quivering transmitted through his fingers. Her lowered gaze remained on his chest. Hiding from him.

'Look at me, Suki.' He waited for her gaze to reconnect with his. 'This baby matters. But you matter equally. *Entiendes?*'

Her eyes grew bright. Then she nodded.

The tightness in his chest eased a fraction. Not enough to give him peace, but it was a start. 'Are you ready to leave?'

She glanced around, clocked the people hovering nearby. 'There are about a dozen people waiting to talk to you.'

'They're not important. Besides, every single piece sold out an hour ago and commissions are flooding in for the artists. My work here is done.' His pride in his fellow artists and the work his foundation was doing was undeniable. But right now he wanted to get out of here. Wanted to test the waters with the daunting plan that loomed larger in his brain with every passing minute.

'If you're sure?' She set her untouched drink down.

The faint shadows beneath her eyes sealed his answer. 'I'm sure. Let's go.'

He meshed his fingers through hers, kept the inevitable interaction between the room and the door to a minimum. He felt her slight hesitation as his limo pulled up.

Their interactions in the back of his limos had so far

been…memorable. The hot tug of need to his groin confirmed which of the experiences he would repeat given the choice.

Helping her into the car, he slid in behind her and gave the instructions for the airport.

She glanced at him in surprise. 'We're leaving right now?'

'I thought we'd kill two birds with one stone. You're tired and need to get some sleep. I need to catch up on Acosta Hotel business before we land in Madrid. We can do both on the plane.'

And once she was awake, he would proceed.

She looked out of the window for a second before her gaze met his.

A little apprehensive. A lot alluring, with a swathe of hair falling over one eye. The urge to reach out and slide the wavy silk through his fingers raked through him. He settled for securing her seat belt as the car moved off.

Either she was too tired to protest or his idea wasn't unwelcome, but the yawn that overtook her superseded everything else. Kicking off her shoes, she rested her head against the seat. 'Okay,' she said simply, before her eyes drifted shut.

Her easy acquiescence kicked a pulse of worry down his spine that lingered all the way to the airport. Once he had confirmation that his instructions had been carried out, he allowed himself to relax a touch.

She awakened long enough to get out of the car when they arrived at his plane. Swinging her into his arms, he strode up the stairs. Felt more tension leave him again as she curled into his chest. His plan was the right one.

In his grief and anger, he'd only seen things short term, a quick way to stop the agony of his loss. It was time to think long term.

Take-off was smooth, and they were halfway over the Atlantic by the time she woke up. From his armchair in the large cabin bedroom, he watched her sit up, push her silky hair back from her face. Warm, sleepy, beautiful, she blinked in the soft lamplight for a minute before she spotted him.

Her hand dropped from her hair, the deliberate action obscuring her face from him. Ramon forced himself to stay put. 'Did you sleep well, *belleza*?'

'I slept well.' She looked down at herself, saw the half-slip she wore and tensed. 'You undressed me?' Her voice held the guardedness he'd been subjected to in varying forms for the last two weeks.

'*Sí*, your dress was too restricting. I wanted to make you more comfortable.'

She nodded, still not looking at him. The tension he'd thought he'd talked himself out of ramped up his spine. Leaning forward on his elbows, he took a breath.

'Suki, we need to talk.'

Her slim shoulders stiffened, the square inch of coverlet caught in her fingers twisting over and over. 'So talk,' she invited. But her voice lacked warmth, her throat working as she swallowed.

Dios, this was insane.

He'd faced some of the toughest negotiators in the world and hadn't felt as nervous and out of his depth as he did right now. 'It's time to discuss our baby's future. *Our* future,' he said.

Her head snapped up, her eyes finding his. A deep, bruised wariness lurked in the blue depths and that drowning pain was back in his chest. Expanding.

'We *agreed* we would discuss it after the baby was born. That's months from now.'

He nodded. 'I know, but—'

'I won't give up my baby!' She was leaning forward, her chin jutting out in challenge as she placed one protective hand over her stomach. 'You should know that right now. It's non-negotiable. I will fight you in court for as long as I live, if need be.'

Her fierceness lit a fire in the cold, hard places in him. But that jealousy he'd felt earlier tonight reared its head. The knowledge that this time it was directed at his own child was shameful. But, *sí*, he wasn't perfect. He wanted that fierceness for himself.

'I'm not asking you to give him up. I'm asking that we join forces. That whatever platform we launch from, we do it together.'

She frowned, her fingers twisting even more frantically. He wanted to go to her, take those hands in his. Kiss her. Tell her about every insane emotion that prowled within him. But how could he, when he didn't know it himself?

'I'm sorry, Ramon. You lost me.'

He took a deep breath and rose. Partly because he couldn't sit still any longer. Partly because he needed to be near her when he said the words. 'I want to make this permanent. I want you to marry me.'

CHAPTER TWELVE

SUKI WAS GLAD she was sitting down because she was sure his words—and the sudden bolt of turbulence that hit the plane—would've flattened her.

'What?'

He opened his mouth, but she shook her head quickly, holding up her hands, needing time to absorb what he'd said.

'It's okay, you don't need to repeat it. I heard you. What I meant was *why*?'

A look curled through his eyes and his nostrils flared as if he was gathering himself. The very deep, very real quicksand she'd been sinking in since she admitted the depths of her feelings for Ramon, threatened to suck her down even faster.

Because it was clear he was up to something.

'Our current circumstances are a strong reason to advocate marriage, are they not?'

Her heart lurched harder, and she fought ready tears that prickled her heart. 'When only a few weeks ago you fully denounced it? Your exact words were...*marriage is not for me*, if I recall correctly?' Knowing now what she didn't know then, the statement hurt even more.

He'd been betrayed by the woman he loved and had closed himself off for ever. For him to force himself back down that road...

'Things have changed. *I* have changed. And we're coming from a different place this time.'

She wanted to admire that earth-shaking sentiment. Perhaps, she even did somewhere deep within her. But the seething pain of her wrecked heart didn't give her enough room to feel magnanimous right then.

'Are we?'

He surged to his feet, moving towards her with speed that belied his overpowering presence.

'*Si.* If we're both committed to making this work, we will succeed. I want to try.'

He stopped at the side of the bed, his green eyes blazing down at her with a light she wished with all her heart were hers to own. Hers to love. But she knew it wasn't.

All this was for his child.

Heart mourning, she shook her head. 'I...I don't think I—'

His hand shot out, stopping her answer. 'Perhaps this wasn't the best timing in the world.' He glanced at the lowered shutters then back to her. 'Proposing at thirty-seven thousand feet is unique but it wasn't what I had in mind. Don't give me your answer now. For the sake of what's at stake, take some time to think about it, *si*?'

The light blazed higher in his eyes, his fists lightly bunched at his sides.

Suki nodded because she realised she did need the time. That saying no right then would be diving off a cliff before she'd constructed a safety net.

It was completely selfish, completely delusional, but she wanted to cling to it for just a while longer before it disappeared like mist in the sunlight.

He bent towards her, brushed his lips against her cheek. '*Muy bien.* I'll see you in the living area when you're ready.'

Straightening, he headed for the door, tall, powerful, holding her very life in his hands as he walked out of the room.

Left alone to work through the dizzying highs of imagining his glorious words had been powered by love and the cold lows of knowing the truth, Suki collapsed back against the pillows.

The comforting gesture of sliding her hand over her belly calmed a little of her roiling emotions long enough for the painful but extraneous nuggets to fall away, leaving her with the flags that spelled her reality.

She loved Ramon.

He loved his child.

She would never love anyone else.

Which meant a broken heart was already winging its way to her.

She could run away, wait for the inevitable day to happen and lick her wounds in private. Or she could stay, face it head-on, find a way to move past it while providing her child with the best possible foundation to life?

The thought that she was even considering his proposal sent her back upright, the sheets once again twisting beneath her fingers.

Why not?

She would have to face heartache one day, but was there any reason it had to be right now?

She'd already agreed to co-parent her baby's formative years with Ramon. Just as he'd agreed to restructure his life to suit the baby. And just as they'd gone into conception with their eyes wide open, why couldn't they do the same with marriage?

Because you love him.

Her heart clenched agonisingly. She breathed through it, forcing the pain aside to get to the bare facts. Which were that she would rather spend the next five years with Ramon and their baby than on her own. She would take a single day in his presence rather than do without him.

The inevitable end would hurt like nothing before, but ripping her heart out before she needed to…well, she couldn't…wouldn't do that to herself.

There were no heralding trumpets accompanying her soul-shaking decision, only mild turbulence and the hum of private jet engines.

But she was okay with that.

Rising, she went to the bathroom, splashed water on

her face. It took several heartbeats before she could meet her gaze in the mirror. Several more before her conscience stopped berating her for the path she was choosing.

By the time she slipped her dress back on, her head had accepted the decision her aching heart was still struggling with.

Ramon was on his laptop when she entered the main cabin. Seeing her, he rushed to his feet, dark green eyes brimming with purpose and determination snagging hers as he prowled forward.

'I thought you would rest for a while longer,' he said.

There was a definite question in his eyes. A watchfulness that tensed his shoulders and tightened his jaw. 'You asked me to marry you at thirty-seven thousand feet. Rest after that was out of the question,' she half joked.

He didn't laugh. Heightening tension crawled over him as his probing gaze raked her face. 'I suppose you wish me to apologise for ruining your sleep?' he rasped in a low voice throbbing with notes she couldn't define.

Her mouth would've curved in a smile if debilitating emotions weren't see-sawing through her. 'I know how... cumbersome you find those apologies, so—'

'Lo siento,' he breathed readily. 'The timing of this could've been better. I realise that now.'

'Oh...okay. What about the timing of my answer? Does now suit or should I—?'

He gripped her arms, which was fortunate because the plane chose that second to dip again. She was thrown against him, her hands coming up to brace against his chest. 'Tell me. Now,' he ordered in a half-growl.

With the moment of truth upon her, the words suddenly dried in her throat.

What in goodness' name was she doing?

But then she looked into his face. His strong, too handsome, enthralling, iron-willed face. Beneath her right hand, his heart beat fast and vigorous. Her own heart tripped over

itself. Licking dry lips, she took a deep breath that was nowhere near as steadying as she wished it to be.

'Yes, I'll marry you, Ramon.'

He inhaled, sharp and long, the arms around her tightening for a moment before he nodded. His head lowered.

Suki froze, every cell in her body anticipating his kiss.

But he merely touched his forehead to hers as he said,
'We will succeed in this too. You have my word.'

They wouldn't. Not if he didn't love her. But for the moment, she would fight the demons and bask in that false-
hood.

As was its speciality, Acosta Hotel Madrid was also housed
in a centuries-old building, this one a towering Renaissance
palace taking up a whole block on Plaza de las Cortes.

In honour of its place at the heart of Madrid's cultural
heritage, the walls of the vast marble-floored lobby teemed
with ancient and modern art. Several of Ramon's own sculptures were displayed in prominent places, with Piedra Galleria Madrid's home situated on the first floor.

As she'd found out when Ramon's assistant contacted her
with their itinerary, Ramon chose to stay in private suites at
his hotels rather than own homes across the globe.

If she'd thought the Havana version was spectacular, her
jaw dropped when she walked into their top floor suite.

Taking up almost a quarter of the whole width of the
hotel, the suite was large enough to fit four families with
ease. Four adjoining suites and three double bedrooms took
up the lower mezzanine floor, with a private pool, extensive
living rooms, study and exclusive private spa facilities taking up the floor above it. Signature tones of gold and burgundy themed every elegant room.

As a maid and private butler unpacked their belongings,
she stepped out onto the roof terrace, skirting the pool to
enjoy the early evening breeze and take in the views and
the water display at Fuente de Neptuno.

Ramon found her there ten minutes later, the call he'd needed to make finished. Strong arms planted on either side of her on the terrace wall, bracketing her in. When his mouth brushed the top of her head, her foolish heart soared.

'We have the option of shower and dinner out or swim and dinner in.'

'Hmm, option number two, please. I have the feeling jet lag is just waiting to pounce on me.'

'*Muy bien.* I'll organise it. Before that, you have another decision to make.'

His face remaining cryptic, he caught her hand in his and led her back inside. Two men waited in the living room, one a burly mountain of a man who was clearly a bodyguard. The other was less than half his size, holding a long, thin briefcase connected to his wrist by a chained handcuff.

Ramon exchanged a short conversation in Spanish then indicated the large coffee table in the middle of the room. Still holding her hand, he led her to the sofa and sat her down.

The briefcase was set before her. Opened. It took every ounce of control for her not to gasp.

Some of the biggest diamonds she'd ever seen sparkled from exquisite settings. Rows upon rows of them. Each one bigger than the last.

'You can't stare at them for ever, *guapa*,' Ramon prompted dryly. 'You need to pick one.'

She flashed him a glare. 'Is that *all* I need to do?'

'*Sí*, or you can pick more than one. Make a selection. Decide later which one you prefer.'

'I can't do that!'

He returned her outraged stare with a steady one of his own. 'You can do whatever you want, Suki,' he stated.

She swallowed hard, the implications of his response settling on her.

She was marrying Ramon Acosta. One of the most eligible men in the world. For whatever time she would enjoy at his side, she would be mixing in the big leagues.

Swallowing jangling nerves, she returned her gaze to the gems on the black velvet tray. Bypassing the more ostentatious stones, she settled on a simple oval four carat surrounded by a smaller ring of diamonds.

When Ramon nodded to the merchant, he stepped forward and made a note of her size. Placing her ring choice in a box, he silently left the room with his bodyguard. The near-silent transaction was surreal.

One she would probably have to get used to, she reminded herself as she slipped off her dress and replaced it with a cream and black striped bikini.

Ramon was already at the pool when she arrived. He watched her approach, gleaming eyes raking over her as she crossed to the lounger next to his. Suddenly self-conscious, she hesitated, then sucked in a breath before she shrugged off her filmy black silk kaftan.

The fevered hiss that left his throat made her breath catch. Jerking upright, he captured her hips, turned her fully to face him before he drew her between his splayed thighs.

'You're showing.' His voice was a little shaken. A little awed. A lot powerful. One hand trailed over her hip to gently trace her belly, eliciting a charged shiver through her.

'Barely,' she whispered.

He shook his head. 'No, I can tell. I can *see*,' he muttered. *'Asombroso.'*

Amazing.

Drawing her slowly, inexorably closer, Ramon placed a soft, gentle kiss on her belly.

The power of it weakened her limbs, stung her eyes with emotions she blinked away hard, even as her heart wept with everything she couldn't have.

Another kiss anointed her. Then another.

When her heart threatened to crack wide open there and

then, she stepped back, turned away under the pretext of draping her kaftan on the lounger.

'This baby is going to demand sustenance in T minus half an hour. So I'm hitting the pool now.'

Without waiting for him, she stepped back and headed for the shallow steps, which were, thankfully, on the far side of the terrace, away from his probing eyes. Away from the deceptive bubble that teased her with impossible dreams.

She swam two lengths on her own before he joined her. His powerful strokes easily kept up with her as they lapped the pool, his gaze sliding to her at increasingly frequent intervals.

The moment her arms began to tire, he caught her around the waist and tugged her to the side of the pool. 'You'll not exert yourself,' he murmured into her hair. 'Not even to get away from me.'

Since it was exactly what she'd been doing, Suki thought it wise to remain silent. Or perhaps it was because her vocal cords had stopped working because she was plastered to him from chest to thigh.

Searching for something to take her mind off that thrilling little fact, she asked a question that had been teasing her mind. 'My itinerary shows Dr Domingo and his team are coming in the morning. So they're already here?'

'Yes,' he replied.

'How did you organise that?'

'You didn't want them around, so they'll fly separately.'

Her eyes widened. 'That must be costing you a fortune.'

'A small price to pay for your happiness,' he replied simply, as if they were talking about the price of a latte. But then she realised this was compromise in Ramon's world. She just had to accept it.

Still her breath caught at the ease with which he said that. Then continued catching when his hand slid down her back beneath the water.

'Speaking of which, it's the first ultrasound tomorrow.

It's a little early, but I think we both need the peace of mind?'

A different type of zing went through her heart. As if sensing her distress, he tilted her chin with one firm finger. She met piercing green eyes burning with sure fire.

'Everything will be okay.'

'You don't know that.'

'*Sí*, I do,' he said with breathtaking arrogance, as if he had the ultimate power to make it so.

For some reason that worked. Her worry abated and when the butler came out to announce that their dinner had arrived, she let Ramon lead her out of the water. She even let him dry her, let his hand once again linger on the barely there bump.

And when the diamond merchant, who had apparently been quietly working away in one of the suites, appeared halfway through dinner and presented Ramon with a velvet box set on a sterling silver tray, she let the father of her child crouch down next to her at the dining table, slip the stunning diamond engagement ring on her finger and place a firm, lingering kiss on her knuckle.

But, of course, she knew nothing had changed when he escorted her to the guest suite, and walked away in the direction of the master suite.

The following night was the night of the second exhibit. After sleeping in late, she video conferenced with her mother, who was about to start the next barrage of tests, and listened to the expected prognosis with a lighter heart. Carefully avoiding her mother's probing questions about her own situation, Suki finished the call with the promise to visit the next week on their way back to Cuba.

Her own team of doctors arrived just before lunch. Her vitals were taken and her progress pronounced satisfactory before the ultrasound machine was wheeled in.

Ramon, exhibiting not a single ounce of embarrassment,

climbed into bed with her and took her hand. The tension in his face echoed hers as Dr Domingo spread warm gel on her belly.

The next five minutes passed excruciatingly slowly, the doctor's perfect poker face giving nothing away. Finally, Ramon snapped, firing bullet-sharp questions in Cuban Spanish at him.

Nods and *sí* were batted back and forth, until Suki too snapped.

'Tell me what's going on!'

Green eyes alight with a fiercely pleased fire locked on hers. 'He says the baby is perfectly healthy and thriving.'

A ferocious shudder trembled through her. 'Oh. *Oh, my God.*'

'I said so, did I not?' he muttered gruffly against her ear.

Her burst of relieved laughter turned into tears. When his strong arms enfolded her she held on tight, the cathartic release of weeks of worry triggering even more sobs.

Their baby was okay.

Maybe they would be okay too.

Several hours later, as she dressed for the event, that hope had taken a firm little root in her heart.

Securing her hair on one side with a discreet silver clip, she arranged the heavy fall over one shoulder. The stylist the concierge had sent up had done amazing things with her eye make-up, the smoky shadow bringing out an extra sparkle that highlighted the joy glowing inside her.

Her baby was safe.

She was still smiling when she answered the knock on her suite door a few minutes later.

Ramon's gaze locked on her face, his body growing stock-still before his gaze trailed a blazing path down her body.

'This dress…*this* one is my favourite,' he muttered.

The red evening gown was a little tighter than when she'd first tried it on weeks ago in Miami, especially around the stomach area where her waist had thickened, but even she had to admit it looked amazing on her.

She smiled. 'I know.'

'But it's lacking something, I think.' He stepped inside, reached into his pocket and brought out a glittering necklace.

More diamonds.

Even more spectacular than her engagement ring. Before she could find the right words to express her shock, he was stepping behind her, securing the priceless jewellery around her neck.

Turning her around, he stared down at her. 'Your pregnancy suits you, *guapa*. You're glowing.'

'With all this bling I'm sporting, how could I not?' she joked.

One corner of his mouth began to lift. The buzzing in his pocket made him draw away from her.

Pulling his phone out of his pocket, he glanced at the screen. And tensed.

'What is it?' she asked.

Tucking the phone against his chest, he traced a finger down her cheek. 'Sorry, *belleza*. I have to attend to some business downstairs. Stay here—I'll be back up in ten minutes to escort you down.'

She started to nod, but he was already walking away. Frowning at his abruptness, she picked up her tiny purse and left her suite.

The butler offered her a drink but she refused, on account of the sudden nerves zinging through her stomach. Unable to settle, she slowly paced the living room. As she passed the open terrace doors a breeze blew in. She shivered, hating the disquieting vibes raising goose bumps on her flesh.

When she heard footsteps behind her, she turned gratefully. Only to be confronted with the last person she expected to see.

Svetlana Roskova was a magnificent vision in white.

With her silver-blonde hair perfectly coiled on her crown, her figure-skimming halter-neck dress displaying graceful shoulders and a body that photographers and designers begged for, she was impossible to dismiss.

Bright grey eyes surveyed Suki from head to toe before she glided forward and paused in front of her, her six-foot height on top of her heels making Suki feel like a midget.

'You must be Suzy?' she asked in a smoky voice.

'It's Suki. Can…can I help you?' Suki asked, hating her stumbling voice.

Her smile was shockingly warm. 'Oh, honey, I'm here to help you.'

'I…I didn't realise I needed help.'

'That's okay. I don't mind helping a girl out.' Gliding past Suki, she walked in a small circle, her gaze flitting through the suite. 'I love this hotel. My personal favourite is the Abu Dhabi one, though. Ramon spared absolutely no expense with that one. Which was why it received a seven-star rating, of course. It's also a little less…old-fashioned, shall we say? I don't see the draw in antiques to be honest.' She gave a sultry laugh. 'Which was why I couldn't get the decorators into that mausoleum he calls home in Cienfuegos fast enough.'

Suki gasped, her eyes widening on the supermodel. 'You were the one who changed the rooms?'

For a split second, Svetlana's easy charm dropped. 'He's taken you there, I see.'

'Why are you here?' Suki demanded, the roiling in her stomach predicting unimaginable worst cases.

The Russian beauty moved forward again, her steps faltering when she caught sight of Suki's engagement ring.

'Ah, looks like he's given you one of these.' She held out her right hand, displaying a diamond twice as big as Suki's. 'Did he wine and dine you, then surprise you with a visit from his diamond merchant?'

Suki barely managed to stop herself from gasping again

as a hot spike of pain lanced her heart. 'It's none of your business.'

Svetlana shrugged, continuing forward to circle Suki where she stood. From behind her, Suki felt her lean forward. 'He promised me the world too after I got pregnant,' she whispered in Suki's ear.

She felt the blood drain from her head as she spun on her heels to face Svetlana. 'What?'

The icy blonde gave a sad smile. 'Sadly, it wasn't meant to be. And unfortunately, all the silliness started after that.'

'Silliness?'

'Ramon wanted me to quit modelling. Stay at home and try for another baby. I love him but, boy, he's a typical man when it comes to such things. He got his boxers in a twist when I asked for a little more time.'

'Is that why you cheated on him?'

Svetlana's eyes widened ever so slightly, but she recovered quickly. A little too quickly. 'All of that is behind us now. He's forgiven me and now he's got a mini him on the way, there's no reason why we can't be together.'

'Excuse me?'

'Yes, *excuse* you. He's probably spun you a story about how everything will work out with you and him and the baby. But what he hasn't mentioned is that he still loves me. If you think you're going to walk down the aisle with him any time soon, you're delusional. He's keeping you sweet long enough to get his hands on his kid.'

'Why on earth should I believe you?'

'Because *I'm* the one he can't get out of his head. I'm the one he still paints and sculpts when he's in that studio of his. He's as obsessed with me as I am with him. Has been since the first time we met. If you don't believe me, take a peek under all those black cloths in his studio when you go back. *If* you go back.'

'So you came here to what…warn me off?'

'Ramon is waiting for me downstairs so I'll be quick. I

came to give you a heads up before you started spinning fairy tales that will never come true. You can either break things off with him or content yourself with being the *other* woman in his life. He'll always belong to me.' She smiled and started heading out of the living room. At the last moment, she executed a perfect pirouette. 'Oh, and don't bother asking him. He'll only deny it. Actually, on second thought, ask him. The quicker we get things out in the open, the quicker we can all settle into our places.'

Suki didn't know where she dredged up the strength to ask one last question, when everything inside her was ripped to shreds. 'Are you seriously saying you don't mind sharing him with another woman?'

She smiled a megawatt smile. 'Woman to woman? I don't because I know he'll always come back to me. When I call he comes running, and vice versa. But I hope for *your* sake you choose the path that causes you least embarrassment and pain.'

With a wriggle of her perfectly manicured fingers, she sailed back out in a cloud of expensive perfume.

Not a care in the world about the life she'd just shattered.

CHAPTER THIRTEEN

SHE WASN'T A CHILD. Or a melodramatic actress in a day-time soap opera, choosing sullen silence or dragging things out for effect.

Even before Svetlana had walked out, Suki knew she would ask Ramon. The need to stop the torture ravaging her insides aside, her assumption that he'd lied to her about his relationship with Svetlana was what had delayed her telling him about her first pregnancy. Condemning him again without concrete evidence would not only demean her, it would erode any possibility of trust between them.

Yes, they had to start from a place of trust so, of course, she would ask him if anything Svetlana had said was true—

'Miss Langston?'

She composed herself and turned to find the butler a few feet away. 'Yes?'

'Señor Acosta called. He's been delayed. He says I'm to escort you down to the gallery and he'll find you there as soon as he's free.'

Trust. Trust.

'I see. Okay.'

The butler smiled.

'Umm, you know what, you don't have to come with me. I know where the gallery is. I'll be fine on my own.'

The older man frowned. 'Are you sure?'

Suki forced a smile. 'Yes.'

Without waiting for an answer, she picked up the clutch, which had somehow dropped to the floor, and walked out of the suite.

Half an hour after she arrived downstairs, Ramon was still nowhere to be seen.

Trust. *Trust.*

But the affirmation was growing weaker because, even though the size of the gallery and the number of guests were almost three times bigger than the Havana exhibition, she refused to believe she and Ramon would've continually missed each other. He wasn't here. Neither was Svetlana. Which meant they were together?

Was it true? Was he so madly in love with Svetlana he would take her back even after she'd cheated on him?

Her soul shredding, Suki continued to look for him. Eventually, she arrived at a set of doors marked *Employees Only.*

Biting her lip, she tried to talk herself out it. Then back into it.

She was the fiancée of the gallery owner. Surely that allowed her inner-sanctum access? The pain ravaged, hysteria-stroking demon inside her gave a mocking cackle.

Hand shaking, she pushed the door open. A wide hallway had two offices on either side, all of which were empty. Suki hated herself for the giddy relief that punched through her as she retraced her steps.

About to walk through the doors, she heard the familiar, sultry laugh. Quieter. More illicit? The sound came from the stairwell she hadn't noticed before. She only took one step before she heard Ramon's deep rumbling voice. Another step onto the landing and she saw them, one floor down. Face to extremely close face.

'I've done what you wanted, Ramon. Now it's your turn,' Svetlana murmured.

'You think it's going to be that easy?' There was a throb of anger in his voice, but also something else. Something spine-chilling.

'She's right upstairs. All you have to do is tell her—'

He caught her by the arms, the move so sudden it halted her words. The words snarled in thick Spanish were indecipherable to Suki.

'God, I love it when you're so bossy,' Svetlana groaned. She swayed towards him, closing the small gap between them and sliding her arms up his chest. He didn't push her away. Instead he walked her backward until her back touched the wall. Then he braced his hands on either side of her head.

Suki's stomach threatened to flip.

'Svetlana—'

'I've missed the way you say my name, Ramon. So much.'

Suki stumbled back, the black carpeted floor thankfully dampening her footsteps. She had no recollection of returning to the exhibit floor, had no knowledge of how much time had passed. At some point someone must have offered her a glass of champagne because somehow she held one. When she realised it, she quickly set it down.

She couldn't stay here. She needed to leave. Needed to—

'What's wrong, *belleza*? You look pale.'

She whirled around at the urgent demand. Stared at him, unable to believe he was in front of her. Unable to contain the pain ripping her heart apart. Unable to stand that guilty look in his eyes.

Numbly, she shook her head. *Hold it together.*

She turned, spotted Svetlana on the next wall over.

Please. Please. Hold it together. From the dregs of her whittled emotions, she summoned up a smile. 'Nothing's wrong. Absolutely nothing. Did you take care of your *business*?'

He stiffened, his eyes narrowing. 'Yes.'

'Oh. Good.'

Two guests approached. One grabbed his arm. 'Ramon? There you are. We've been searching everywhere for you. Come and meet—'

'Pardon me a moment,' Ramon rasped, ignoring his guests to frown down at her. 'Suki—'

With her last particle of energy, she waved him off. 'It's

okay. You're the host. Go and do your thing. I'll find you *if* I need you.'

He didn't fail to catch the stress in her words. His jaw clenched, but, short of being rude to his invited guests, he had no choice but to be cordial.

The hot, ragged breath that poured from the depths of her soul strangled when her gaze locked with Svetlana's.

The Russian didn't need to say one word. Her smug smile said it all.

How she managed to get herself up to the suite and into bed would remain a puzzle to her for ever.

At first she thought she was dreaming when she heard him call her name. The firm hand on her shoulder woke her into a fresh recollection of her nightmare. Turning over in bed, she stared at the tall form of Ramon cast in half-shadow from the bathroom vanity light. Beneath the drapes, sunlight filtered through.

She sat up, praying there was no trace of the tears she'd shed. 'Yes?' she croaked.

'You left the exhibition without me last night.'

'You were…occupied.'

He took a step closer, reached for her bedside lamp. 'No!'

He froze. 'It's nine in the morning. Any reason why you prefer to converse in the dark?'

Because seeing you will hurt too much.

'I had…have a slight headache.' And a very large heartache. 'What do you want, Ramon?'

'I've been contacted by your mother's doctors. She wishes to speak to you.'

Her heart lurched as she sat up. 'Is she okay?'

'She's having second thoughts about the next course of treatment. They tried to reach you earlier but didn't get through. Nor did I last night.' The question was clear in his tone.

She'd seen his phone calls but hadn't been able to bring herself to answer them. 'I silenced it so I could sleep.'

Reaching for the phone, she flipped the mute button off, still unable to look him in the eye. 'I'd like to call my mother now, please.'

'Suki, we need to talk—'

'I don't want to keep my mother waiting.'

Grim silence met her request. Then he nodded and left the room.

Suki was one hundred per cent sure the sensation zipping through her wasn't relief. For the moment she pushed her turmoil aside and dialled her mother's hospital.

But it wasn't her mother who answered, but the doctor.

'Miss Langston, we think your mother could use some support to see her through this second stage. Are you able to be with her?'

The lifeline wasn't one she wished for but she grasped it all the same. 'Yes. I can be there this afternoon.'

'Excellent. We look forward to seeing you.'

She emerged from her suite after a quick shower and hastily donned jumpsuit and sandals to find Ramon pacing the living room.

As she'd predicted, seeing him in the sunlight, knowing what he'd been doing with Svetlana in the stairwell last night, was almost too much to bear. Every instinct screamed at her to launch into him, but she needed her energy for her mother. 'The doctors think I should be there for my mother. I want to go.'

Brooding eyes watched her for a second before he nodded. 'We'll head to the airport after breakfast—'

'No, I prefer to go alone. I don't want to overwhelm her with company.'

He frowned. 'Suki—'

'The doctors checked me out yesterday. Everything's fine. You're beginning to smother me and frankly I could do with some room to breathe.'

His jaw gritted and his eyes darkened. '*Bueno*. I have a project to finish in Havana for the next few days. You can have that time.'

'Thank you,' she said stiffly.

Breakfast was a silent affair with Ramon eyeing her darkly in between tossing back steaming cups of espresso. The moment she forced down her toast, she stood from the table.

The porter had already headed down with her single suitcase. Behind her, Ramon prowled hard on her fast-clicking heels.

His hand stayed the door before she could open it. When she refused to look at him, he caught her chin in his hand, raised her gaze to his.

Her breath caught at the dark storms swirling in his eyes. Again she wanted to ask the burning questions that trembled through her. But her mother needed her.

'I'll arrive at the end of the week, Suki. So get as much *breathing* done as possible because come Friday morning, we *will* talk.'

Her hand tightened on her handbag, the alien weight of the ring cutting into her finger. 'I'm sure we will. Goodbye, Ramon.'

He didn't respond, only stared at her for a fistful of seconds before he let her go.

Her body operated on automatic while her mind churned for most of the journey. By the time Ramon's plane landed at London City Airport, she'd worked herself back to her original conclusion. She needed to talk to Ramon, give him a chance to explain. But she was also sure of one thing. Regardless of what he said, there would be no future for them without love.

Svetlana might have thrown a spanner in the works short term but, unless she could find a way to live without Ramon's love, she might be the one to call time on this thing.

* * *

The private hospital where her mother was receiving the next phase of treatment in East London was so state-of-the-art, it was almost futuristic.

Her mother was looking much healthier than Suki had seen her in a long time, but minutes after she arrived Moira Langston dissolved into tears.

'Mum, what's wrong?' she asked after handing her mother a box of tissues.

'It's crazy, isn't it? It's only now, when the possibility of getting better and having my life back is in front of me, that I can't help thinking about the past. Don't get me wrong, this infection I've picked up that could derail the treatment is also responsible for my sorry state, but...' Moira shook her head, silent tears filling her eyes.

Suki reached for her hand. 'Everything will be okay, Mum.'

She eyed Suki. 'Will it? Why have you been crying?'

Suki gave a watery laugh. 'Solidarity?' she tried.

'Has it got something to do with that rock you shoved in your bag before you walked in here? Or the pregnancy glow in your cheeks?'

Suki grimaced. 'I wasn't trying to hide anything. I just—'

'Didn't want to worry me. I know.' She paused a beat. 'So what's wrong?'

'I'm in love with him and I'm not sure he feels the same way.'

Her mother's eyes narrowed. 'And?'

The stern voice of the mother who'd taught her self-worth even before she'd learnt to walk straightened Suki's spine. 'And I owe it to myself to make sure I don't settle for less than I'm worth?'

Moira smiled and rested her head on the pillow. 'If nothing else goes right, at least I know I've done all right with you,' she murmured, then closed her eyes.

They had snippets of conversation over the next three

days as Moira battled her infection. By Thursday night, Suki was struggling not to show her anxiety.

Ramon had stuck to his guns and given her the breathing room she'd demanded. But it was time to take control of her future once more.

The moment her mother was given the all-clear on Friday morning, Suki kissed her goodbye and summoned a taxi. She toyed with the idea of heading to Ramon's hotel before she discarded it. For one thing, she needed a shower and a few hours' sleep before she could function properly. Turning up at Acosta Hotel London dishevelled and with bags under her eyes would probably get her thrown out before she walked through the revolving doors.

Suki didn't know how sound the decision to go home was until she stopped at the corner shop to buy a pint of milk.

The sense of déjà vu that engulfed her felt like a tsunami sucking her under as she plucked the newspaper from the stand and stared at the front-page picture.

He was shirtless, the grimy towel he used when he sculpted hanging from the back pocket of his low-riding chinos. She was wearing the kind of long-sleeved *male* dress shirt that strongly hinted at nothing else underneath. Svetlana's miles-long legs were wrapped tight around his waist, her white-blonde hair tumbled in sexy disarray down her back.

And worst of all, they were standing on the terrace of the villa Suki had had the audacity to hope would be her home one day.

The shopkeeper's ever-increasing demand for payment snapped her out of her shock long enough to hand over the appropriate change before she was stumbling down the pavement and into her house.

Lurching into the kitchen, she discarded everything, raced upstairs, flung herself on the bed and pulled the covers over her head.

The thumping came not five minutes later. Or perhaps

it was five hours. She didn't know or care. Nor did she acknowledge it.

Next, her phone began to ring. She ignored that too.

Then the banging started again. 'Open the door, Suki. I
know you're in there.'

'Go away,' she screamed.

He went away. Then somehow materialised at the bottom of her bed. 'Get up, Suki. Now,' he growled.

She lurched upright in bed. 'Oh, my God! How did you
get in here?'

'I climbed in through the goddamn kitchen window!
We're going to have a serious talk about your security when
we're done talking about us,' he snapped.

Her world lit on fire and turned to ash again in the blink
of an eye. 'There is no us, Ramon. I was delusional in thinking there was a possibility. Trust me, I'm fully awake now
to the type of man you are.'

His face paled a little before his mouth thinned into a flat
line. 'Because you let that bitch feed you poison or because
you've read the tabloids and tried and found me guilty? Yes,
I found out she was in the suite. Why didn't you tell me?'

Hot, angry tears prickled her eyes. Snapping back the
duvet, she surged to her feet. 'Because she was there on
your behalf. And it wasn't poison if it was true! And don't
forget your back-stairwell tryst as well! Did it give you a
little thrill to grope her like that while she moaned in your
ear? *God, I love it when you're so bossy. I've missed the
way you say my name, Ramon. So much.*'

His mouth actually dropped open in shock before he
raked his fingers through his hair. '*Santa Cielo*, you heard
that?'

She wrapped her hands around her arms. 'I didn't stay
for the full performance, if that's what you're asking.'

'Pity. If you'd stayed you would've got the whole picture, instead of the half-baked conclusions you're letting

hurt you now. And let's get one thing clear: she wasn't there on my behalf!'

'Don't you dare turn this back on me. You lied to me upstairs when you said you had business to take care of. You lied again when you came back into the gallery, looking *as guilty as hell*.'

'She *was* business, because she turned up uninvited making a nuisance of herself. I didn't want you stressed so I went down there to deal with her. Somehow she slipped past Security and made her way up to the suite. And I felt guilty afterward for neglecting you for so long.'

'Wow, and you rail me about *my* security?' she snapped.

He paced in a tight back and forth at the end of her bed. 'She's…cunning.'

'You mean she's good at getting men to do what she wants, you included?'

'No. I told you, we're over. We've been over for a very long time.'

'There's a newspaper photo and article that says something very different. And don't tell me the picture is false because I recognised the decorator's scaffolding still on the south wall.'

He let out an exasperated breath. 'It wasn't false. She was at the villa two days ago.'

She'd thought the picture that had torn the bottom out of her world had done all the damage she could sustain. She was wrong.

His words sapped the last strength from her legs. Ramon caught her as she swayed. She fought him as he carried her over to the bed.

'*Madre de Dios*, stop this!'

'No. What about you *neglecting* to tell me she was the one who did the appalling redecoration? Or that she was pregnant with your baby, too? You know what? I don't want to do this. Just…just get out of my house!'

'She's lying, Suki. There was never a baby. And I'm not going anywhere. Not until you hear me out.'

Sitting down, he imprisoned her in his lap. Suki sat stiffly, her every cell fighting not to be consumed once again.

'Think about it rationally. You lived in Cienfuegos for almost two months. In that time, did you ever spot a paparazzo there?'

Her mouth tightened but it was clear he wasn't going to carry on until he had an answer. 'No, but—'

'So, why would they suddenly show up, if they hadn't been fed that information?'

'Ramon. It doesn't matter—'

His hand tightened on her hip. 'It matters because she orchestrated it all from start to finish.'

'Because she wants you back that badly?'

He gave a very masculine, very arrogant shrug.

'But that picture. It was…'

'Nothing. Less than nothing,' he insisted.

'Was…was that your shirt she was wearing?'

'I didn't stop to check. It's probably one she took from when we were together. Mario alerted me that there was someone on the premises insisting on seeing me. She launched herself at me out of nowhere.'

Suki shook her head, unable to stop the tears that brimmed her eyes. With another pithy curse, he took her face in his hands, tilted it up to his.

'Don't do this to yourself, *mi amor*. Can't you see she's not worth it?' he demanded raggedly.

A wet sob bubbled up from her chest. 'I can't get that picture out of my mind.'

'Try. She cheated on me, Suki. But even if she hadn't I doubt that we would've made it to the altar.'

She wasn't going to hope.

She wasn't going to hope.

She…

Oh, hell. Hope bloomed bright and strong. 'You wouldn't?'

He shook his head. 'The initial spark fizzled out very quickly. We both knew it. But she didn't want to admit failure and I initially left it because I felt a little…guilty.'

Her eyes widened. 'Guilty? Why?'

'She overheard me asking Luis about you the day he brought you to the office summer party. Long before we broke up she had a bee in her bonnet about you. She suspected I had a thing for you and she was right. Someone took a picture of us at the Havana event and it made social media. That's what triggered her nonsense.'

Her breath caught. 'You had a *thing* for me?'

'Each time we met I had a harder time getting you out of my head. I think it was partly why—'

'You were so mean to me?'

His low chuckle reverberated through her. 'I couldn't exactly pull your hair.'

'You never know. I might have liked it.'

The humorous moment lingered for a split second before it disappeared under the weight of heavier emotions. 'Ramon—'

His hand tightened in her hair. 'I would *never* cheat on you, Suki. I swear. I love you, only you.'

Her heart stopped, then raced wildly in her chest. Blinking tear-filled eyes, she pulled back, searched his face. 'You love me?'

He squeezed his eyes shut for a second. 'That night after we made love and I left, I couldn't stop thinking about you. I must have picked up the phone at least two dozen times every day to call you. Hell, I may have hated you a little for wrecking my workday for weeks on end. When Luis told me about the pregnancy, my first thought was that I finally had a reason to be in your life. A *permanent* reason.'

'And then it went away?' she whispered.

He leaned his forehead against hers. 'That was one of the worst days of my life,' he whispered back, his gruff voice thick with sorrow.

'I'm so sorry. For both of us.'

'No, I'm sorry. For the way I went about righting what I thought was wrong. You have every right to hate me for the things I said to you. Every right.'

'I tried very hard to save her, Ramon.'

He held her tighter. '*Dios*, I know that now. But losing Luis and my parents on top of losing the baby…it drove me a little insane. I'm not asking you to forgive me now. Just that you'll forgive me some day?' he pleaded hoarsely.

'No, promising to forgive you some day means hanging on to bad feeling now. I won't do that. I forgave you the moment I agreed to have this baby with you.'

Sea-green eyes swimming with heavy, wild, unstoppable emotion met hers. '*Belleza*, I don't deserve you.'

She slid her hands over his five o'clock shadow to cup his face. 'No, you don't, but I'm yours anyway.'

A deep shudder rippled through him. In the next instant, she was on her back, both her hands trapped above her head in one of his as he levered himself carefully over her.

'Tell me again,' he demanded, his mouth hovering a whisper above hers.

'I'm yours,' she whispered fervently.

His free hand trailed down her arm, over her waist to splay possessively over her belly. 'Again,' he growled.

She couldn't stop the tears from filling her eyes again. 'I love you. I'm yours. *We're* yours.'

His own eyes misted as he sucked in a long, unsteady breath. His fingers were equally unsteady as he divested her of her clothes.

He paused when his fingers tangled in her panties. 'The doctors said it was okay, didn't they?'

'They said it was okay *weeks* ago. But you decided to torture us both.'

He grimaced. 'I will make up for that now, *si*?'

She nodded eagerly. '*Sí, mi amor*. Now and for ever.'

EPILOGUE

Eight Months Later

'*CARIÑO*, WE'RE GOING to be late.'

Ramon thought it wise not to raise his voice above a gentle murmur, seeing as, when it came to this particular subject, his wife was prone to falling apart at the slightest provocation.

That plan backfired spectacularly.

'And whose fault is that?' she snapped. 'Just one picture, you said. No one will notice, you said.'

He winced. 'I'm sorry your pictures turned out to be an international sensation, *guapa*.'

'No, you're not. You crow to everyone who comes within shouting distance that you're my husband. That you're the reason I look the way I look in those pictures.'

'Well…to be fair—'

'Don't you dare. I don't want to hear it. And I didn't want to be the star of your silly gallery exhibit.'

'Okay, then we'll stay home.'

The door to the bathroom flew open. And Ramon was eternally glad he was leaning against the bed frame. Because like always, he struggled to catch his breath whenever he looked at her. The love of his life grew more beautiful each day. She'd become his everything. His wife. His muse. The mother of his child.

His most intense lover.

The sculpture he'd made from the sketches of her on the granite slab had turned out to be too intimate to share with the world, so he'd sculpted another, a mother-son one, which now resided in a special garden at their home in Cienfuegos.

Framed to perfection in the doorway, she flipped golden caramel hair over one shoulder. 'No, you won't cancel. I've already been called a diva for showing up five minutes late to the last exhibit.'

Ramon wisely stopped from pointing out that preventing tardiness was why they needed to leave now. Personally, he wouldn't care if they turned up an hour late, or not at all. But Suki was unused to media scrutiny and still sensitive to being the centre of attention.

Sadly, she'd been thrown in the deep end when the semi-intimate black-and-white photos he'd taken of her with their son had taken the world by storm. Pictures where she'd been breastfeeding, bathing or just taking a nap with Lorenzo. The purity of her beauty had publishing houses clamouring to sign her up to coffee-table portrait book deals.

So far she'd resisted all offers, choosing to only exhibit at Piedra's Havana gallery. Even then, she tore strips off him each time she had to appear in public. But as always, Ramon knew he only needed to get her there. Because the moment she saw the super-sized pictures of their son, her heart melted.

He witnessed that transformation forty-five minutes later as she stood in front of the second to largest picture of all. It was another black-and-white print where she was watching Lorenzo sleep. The awe and love on her face was a shining beacon that was impossible to look away from.

He approached her from behind, admiring her post-pregnancy body draped in a white sleeveless floor-length gown. Sliding his arm around her waist, he breathed in her perfume as she leaned back against him.

'He really is a gorgeous baby, isn't he?' she sighed happily.

'Of course. He's my son.'

She rolled her eyes but turned to bestow a kiss on him. One that lingered and lingered some more until a throat cleared loudly nearby.

Ramon smiled indulgently as his mother-in-law joined them with his nine-week-old son cradled in her arms.

The second star of the show was asleep and gently snoring. But his grandmother couldn't keep her eyes off him. 'He really is a gorgeous baby, isn't he?' she sighed.

They all laughed, Suki's eyes shining extra brightly as they lit on her mother. Moira had come through the cutting-edge treatment with flying colours and been given the all-clear six months ago. With a new lease on life, she'd ditched her job in favour of solo world travel four months ago, only taking a hiatus when her grandson had been born. She was headed to Australia in two weeks and was getting as much time with her grandchild as possible.

Ramon didn't mind. He welcomed the extra time he got with his wife. Moira drifted away to show Lorenzo off to guests, and, almost by telepathy, he and Suki drifted to the largest picture of the exhibit.

Luis was smiling at someone off camera, his young vibrant face turned up to the sun. The teasing twinkle in his eyes was captured for all eternity, something Ramon would be grateful for for ever.

'I miss him,' he admitted gruffly, the pain now dulled with happier memories but never forgotten.

Suki turned from her best friend's image and looked into her husband's eyes. 'Me too,' she murmured. 'I'm so grateful to have known him, albeit too briefly. For the beautiful soul that he was and also because he brought you to me.'

He leaned down, rested his forehead against hers as he was wont to do when emotion got too much for him. When the moment subsided, they walked on, hand in hand, stopping to talk about paintings or conversing with guests.

The sudden clink of glasses stopped her in her tracks. A prominent curator and art columnist whose name she couldn't quite remember was smiling at the gathering guests.

'We've been keeping it under wraps, but, since it'll be in

the papers tomorrow, we wanted to formally take the opportunity to announce the formation of the new charity for children's art. It's in honour of Ramon's brother and will be named the Luis Acosta Foundation for Children's Art. Suki Acosta will be its leading patron and has already donated a staggering quarter of a million pounds.'

Rousing applause went through the large crowd. Then she clinked her glass again. 'We also have a special surprise this evening, again, to be announced tomorrow, but I do love letting the cat out of the bag.' She paused for laughter before continuing, 'Anyway, it's my pleasure to announce that the prestigious White Palm Photography Award this year goes to our dear Ramon for the simply named but utterly divine photo known as *Suki & Lorenzo*.'

An image of the very first picture Ramon had taken of her son and her was projected onto the large screen. She'd woken up from a wonderful dream just as Lorenzo too had opened his eyes. They'd been captured staring at each other with eyes full of transcendental wonder and magical hope.

Singularly her most favourite picture in the world; happy tears filled Suki's eyes as she applauded and kissed her husband.

'I'm so proud of you.'

He gave his usual one-sided smile, then caught her hand in his to pull her towards the stage.

'What are you doing? They came here to see you,' she whispered.

'No. You are my true muse because you own my heart. I can't breathe without you, or live without you. I wouldn't want to. So you need to take your bow, *mi amor*, because it's really you they've come to see.'

She stepped up onto the stage beside him, blinking back further tears as more applause broke out. 'Oh, God, you choose the worst moments to say the most wonderful things.'

He gave a very short, very poignant speech, then stepped

off the stage and pulled her close. 'I say them because they're true. I say them because I love you. *Dios mio*, I love you so much, Suki.'

'I love you more.'

* * * * *

If you enjoyed
PREGNANT AT ACOSTA'S DEMAND
why not explore these other Maya Blake reads?

SIGNED OVER TO SANTINO
THE DI SIONE SECRET BABY
A DEAL WITH ALEJANDRO
ONE NIGHT WITH GAEL
THE BOSS'S NINE-MONTH NEGOTIATION

Available now!

'Your father forbade you from seeing me and, like a good little Lady Heiress, you jumped when he clicked his fingers.'

'Don't call me that!' Marnie said distractedly, hating the tabloid press's moniker for her.

It wasn't that it was cruelly meant, only that it mistook her natural reserve for something far more grandiose: snobbery. Pretension. Airs and graces. The kind of aristocratic aspirations that Marnie had never fallen in line with despite the value her parents put on them. The values that had been at the root of their disapproval of Nikos.

'So this is revenge?' she murmured, her eyes clashing fiercely with his. Pain lanced through her.

'Yes.'

'A dish best served cold?' She shook her head sadly, dislodging his hand. 'You've waited six years for this.'

'Yes.' Nikos brought his body closer, crushing her with his strong thighs, his broad chest. 'But there will be nothing cold about our marriage.'

Clare Connelly was raised in small-town Australia amongst a family of avid readers. She spent much of her childhood up a tree, Mills & Boon book in hand. Clare is married to her own real-life hero, and they live in a bungalow near the sea with their two children. She is frequently to be found staring into space—a sure-fire sign that she is in the world of her characters. She has a penchant for French food and ice-cold champagne, and Mills & Boon continue to be her favourite ever books. Writing for Modern Romance is a long-held dream. Clare can be contacted via clareconnelly.com or through her Facebook page.

This is Clare's stunning debut
for Mills & Boon Modern Romance—
we hope you enjoy it!

BOUGHT FOR THE BILLIONAIRE'S REVENGE

BY
CLARE CONNELLY

MILLS &
BOON

First Published in Great Britain 2017
By Mills & Boon, an imprint of HarperCollins*Publishers*
1 London Bridge Street, London, SE1 9GF

© 2017 Clare Connelly

ISBN: 978-0-263-92534-0

Printed and bound in Spain
by CPI, Barcelona

BOUGHT FOR THE
BILLIONAIRE'S
REVENGE

For Dan, my beloved.

PROLOGUE

HIS CAR CHEWED up the miles easily, almost as though the Ferrari sensed his impatience.

He exited the M25, the call he'd received that morning heavy on his mind.

'He's broke, Nik. Not just personally, but his business, too. No more assets to mortgage. Banks are too cautious, anyway. The whole family fortune is going to go down the drain. He's about to lose it all.'

Nikos should have felt overjoyed. There was something about chickens coming home to roost that ought to have brought him amusement. But it hadn't.

Seeing Arthur Kenington suffer had never been his goal.

Using the man's plight to avenge the past, though... *That* idea held infinite appeal.

For six years he'd carried the other man's actions in his chest. Oh, Arthur Kenington wasn't the first elitist snob Nikos had come up against. Being the poorest kid at a prestigious school—'the scholarship boy'—had led to an ever-present sense of being an outsider.

But it had been so much worse with Arthur. After all, the man had paid him to get out of Marnie's life, declaring that Nikos would never be good enough for his precious daughter. Worse, Marnie had listened to her father. She'd dropped him like a hot potato.

Marnie.

Or 'Lady Heiress', as she was known: the beautiful, enigmatic, softly spoken society princess who had, a long time ago, held his heart in her elegant hands. Held it, pummelled it, stabbed it and finally, at her father's behest, rejected it. Thrown it away as though it were an inconsequential item of extremely limited value.

It had hurt like hell at the time, but Nikos had long ago credited it as the fuel that had driven his meteoric rise to the top of the finance world.

A dark smile curved his lips as he navigated the car effortlessly through London's southern boroughs.

The tables had turned; the power was his and he would wield it over Marnie until she realised what a fool she'd been.

He had the power to help her father, to prove his own worth, and finally to hold her heart in his hands and see if he felt like being gentle…or repaying her in kind.

CHAPTER ONE

She shouldn't have come.

The whole way into the city she'd told herself to turn around, go back. It wasn't too late.

But of course it was.

The second Marnie had heard from him the die had been cast. It had fallen into the water of her life, changing stillness to storm within seconds.

Nikos.

Nikos was back.

And he wanted to see her.

The elevator ascended inside the glass building, but it might as well have been plunging her into the depths of hell. A fine bead of perspiration had broken out on her top lip. Marnie didn't wipe it. She hardly even noticed it.

Every cell of her body was focussed on the next half-hour of her life and how she'd get through it.

'I need to see you. It's important.'

His voice hadn't changed at all; his tone still resonated with assuredness. Even at twenty-one, with nothing behind him, Nikos Kyriazis had possessed the same confidence bordering on arrogance that was now his stock in trade. Sure, he had the billions to back it up these days, but even without the dollars in his bank he'd still borne that trademark ability to command.

For the briefest of moments she'd thought of refusing him. So long had passed; what good could come from re-hashing ancient history? Especially when she knew, in the deepest corner of her heart, that she was still so vulnerable to him. So exposed to his appeal.

'It's about your father.'

And the tiny part of Marnie that had wanted to run a mile at the very thought of coming face-to-face with this man again had been silenced instantly.

Her father?

She frowned now, thinking of Arthur Kenington. He'd been different lately. Distracted. He'd lost a little weight, too, and not through any admirable leap into a healthy life-style. She'd become worried, and Nikos's call, completely out of the blue, had underscored those concerns.

The elevator paused, the doors sliding open to allow two men to enter, both dressed in suits. One of them stared at her for a moment too long, in that way people did when they weren't sure exactly where they knew her from. Marnie cleared her throat and looked straight ahead, her wide-set eyes carefully blanked of any emotion. She tried to conceal the embarrassment that always curdled her blood when she realised she'd been recognised.

When the elevator doors swished open to the top floor of the glass and steel monolith at the heart of Canary Wharf, she saw an enormous sign on the wall opposite that pronounced: KYRIAZIS.

Her heart thumped angrily in her chest.

Kyriazis.

Nikos.

'Oh, God,' she whispered under her breath, pausing for a moment to settle her nerves.

The painstakingly developed skill she possessed of hiding her innermost thoughts and feelings from the outside world failed her spectacularly in that moment. Her skin, usually like honey all year round, was pale. Her fingers trembled in a way that wouldn't be stopped.

'Madam? May I help you?'

She blinked, her golden-brown eyes showing turmoil before she suppressed the unwanted emotion. With a smile that sat heavily on her lips, Marnie clicked across the tiled foyer.

More recognition.

'Lady Kenington,' the receptionist said with a small tilt of her head, observing the visitor with undisguised interest from the brown hair with its natural blonde highlights to the symmetrical features set in a dainty face down to the petite frame of this reclusive heiress.

Cold-hearted, the tabloids liked to claim, and to the receptionist there seemed indeed an air of aloofness in the beautiful woman's eyes.

'Yes, hello. I have an appointment with…' There was the smallest hesitation as she steeled herself to say his name aloud to another soul. 'Nikos Kyriazis.'

'Of course.' The receptionist flicked her long red hair over one shoulder and nodded to a banquette of chairs across the room. 'He won't be long. Please, take a seat.'

The anticlimax of the moment might have made Marnie laugh under different circumstances. All morning she'd counted down to this very moment, seeing it as a sort of emotional D-day, and now he was going to keep her waiting?

She moved to the seating area, her lips pursed with disapproval for his lack of punctuality. Behind her there was a spectacular view, framed by a wall of pure glass.

She'd followed his meteoric rise to the top, reading about each success and triumph in the papers alongside the rest of the world. It would have been impossible not to track his astounding emergence onto the world's financial stage. Nikos had built himself into a billionaire with the kind of ease with which most people put on shoes in the morning. Everything he'd touched had turned to gold.

Marnie had contented herself with congratulating him in her dreams. Or reading about him on the internet—except when her heart found it could no longer handle the never-ending assault of images that showed Nikos and *her*. The generic 'Other Woman' he habitually dated. She was always tall, with big breasts, blonde hair and the kind of extroverted confidence that the Marnies of this world could only marvel at.

In a thousand years she'd never be like one of them. Those women with their easy sexuality and relaxed happiness.

As if to emphasise her point, her fingers drifted to the elegant chignon she'd styled her shoulder-length hair into that morning. A few clumps had come loose. She tucked them back into place with care, then replaced her manicured hands in her lap.

Almost twenty minutes later the receptionist crossed the room purposefully. 'Lady Kenington?'

Marnie started, her face lifting expectantly.

'Mr Kyriazis is ready to see you.'

Oh, *was* he? Well, it was about time, she thought crossly as she stood and fell into step behind the other woman.

A pair of frosted glass doors showed a dark, blurred figure that could only be him. The details of his features were not yet visible.

'Lady Kenington, sir,' the receptionist announced.

On the threshold of not just the door but of a moment she'd fantasised about for years, Marnie sucked in a fortifying breath and then, on legs that were trembling lightly, stepped into his palatial office.

Would he be the same?

Would the spark between them still exist?

Or had six years eroded it completely?

'Nikos.'

To her own ears her voice was cool and detached, despite the way her heart was stammering painfully against her ribs. Standing by the windows, he turned to face her at the receptionist's pronouncement, the midafternoon sun casting a pale glow over him that focussed her attention on him as a spotlight might have.

The six years since she'd last seen him had been generous to Nikos. The face she'd loved was much the same, perhaps enhanced by wisdom and the hallmarks of success. Dark eyes, wide-set and rimmed by thick black lashes, a nose that had a bump halfway down from a childhood accident, and a wide mouth set above a chin with a thumbprint-sized cleft. His cheekbones were as pronounced as always, as though the features of his face had been carved from stone at the beginning of time. It was a face that conveyed strength and power—a face that had commanded her love.

He wore his dark hair a little shorter now, but it still brushed his collar at the back and had the luxuriant thickness that had always begged her to run her fingers through it. His dark eyes, so captivating, flashed with an emotion that seemed to Marnie almost mocking.

With pure indolent arrogance he flicked his gaze over her face, then lower, letting it travel slowly across her unimpressive cleavage down to her slim waist. She felt a spike of warmth travel through her abdomen as feelings long ago suppressed slammed against her.

Where his eyes travelled, her skin reacted. She was warm as though he'd touched her, as though he'd glided his fingertips over her body, promising pleasure and satisfaction.

'Marnie.'

Her gut churned. She'd always loved the way he said her name, with the emphasis on the second syllable, like a note from a love song.

The door clicked shut behind her and Marnie had to fight against the instinct to jump like a kitten. Only with the greatest of effort was she able to maintain an impassive expression on her subtly made-up face.

Under normal circumstances Marnie would have done what was expected of her. Even in the most awkward of encounters she could generally muster the basics in small talk. But Nikos was different. *This* was different.

'Well, Nikos?' she said, a tight smile her only concession to social convention. 'You summoned me here. I presume it's not just to stare at me?'

He arched a thick dark brow and her stomach flopped. She'd forgotten just how lethal his looks were in person. And it wasn't just that he was handsome. He was completely vibrant. When he frowned it was as if his whole body echoed the feeling. The same could be said when he smiled or laughed. He was a passionate man who hid nothing. She felt his impatience now, and it burned the little part of her heart that had survived the explosive demise of their relationship.

'Would you like a drink?' His accent was flavoured with cinnamon and pepper: sweet and spicy. Her pulse skittered.

'A drink?' Her lips twisted in an imitation of disapproval. 'At this hour? No. Thank you,' she added as an afterthought.

He shrugged, the bespoke suit straining across his muscled chest. She looked away, heat flashing to the extremities of her limbs. When he began walking towards her, she was powerless to move.

He stopped just a foot or so across the floor, his expression impossible to interpret. His fragrance was an assault on her senses, and the intense masculinity of him was setting her body on fire. Her knees felt as if they might buckle. But although her fingers were fidgeting it was the only betraying gesture of her unease. Her face remained impassive, and her eyes were wide with unspoken challenge.

'You said you needed to speak to me. That it was important.'

'Yes,' he murmured, his gaze once again roaming her face, as though the days, months and years they'd spent separated were a story he could read in it if he looked long enough.

Marnie tried to catalogue the changes that had taken place in her physically in the six years since he'd walked out of Kenington Hall for the last time. Her hair, once long and fair, was shoulder-length and much darker now, with a sort of burnt sugar colour that fell with a fashionable wave to her shoulders. She hadn't worn make-up back then, but now she didn't leave the house without at least a little cosmetic help. That was the wariness she had learned to demonstrate when a scrum of paparazzi was potentially sitting in wait, desperate to capture that next unflattering shot.

'Well?' she asked, her voice a throaty husk.

'What is your rush, *agape mou*?'

She started at the endearment, her fingertips itching as though of their own free will they might slap him. It felt as though a knife had been plunged into her chest.

She flattened the desire to correct him. She needed to stay on point to get through this encounter unscathed. 'You've kept me waiting twenty minutes. I have somewhere else to be after this,' she lied. 'I can't spare much more time. So, whatever you've called me here to say, I suggest you get it over with.'

Again, his brow arched imperiously. His disapproval pleased her in that moment. It eclipsed, all too briefly, other far more seductive thoughts.

'Wherever you've got to be after this, I *suggest* you

cancel it.' He repeated her directive back to her with an insouciant shrug.

'Just as dictatorial as ever,' she said.

His laugh whipped around the room, hitting her hard. 'You used to like that about me, I seem to recall.'

Her heart was racing. She lifted her arms, crossing them over her chest, hoping they might hide the way her body was betraying her. 'I'm definitely not here to walk down memory lane,' she said stiffly.

'You have no idea why you're here.'

She met his gaze, felt flame leaping from one to the other. 'No. You're right. I don't.'

Wishing she'd obeyed her instincts and refused to see him, she began to walk towards the door. Being in the same room as him, feeling the force of his enmity, she knew only that nothing could be important enough to go through this wringer.

Some paths were best unfollowed—their relationship was definitely one of them.

'I don't know why I listened.' She shook her head and her hair loosened a little, dropping a tendril from her temple across her cheek. 'I shouldn't have come.'

He laughed again, following her to the door and pressing the flat of his palm against it. 'Stop.'

She started, and it dawned on him that Marnie was nervous. Her facade was exceptional. Cold, unfeeling, composed. But Marnie was uncertain, too. Her enormous almond-shaped eyes, warm like coffee, flew to his face before she seemed to regain her footing and inject her expression with an air of impatience.

But she *wasn't* impatient. How could she be? The past was claiming her. He was him, and she was her, but they were kids again. Teenagers madly in love, sure of nothing and everything, unable to keep their hands off each other in the passionate way of illicit love affairs.

Sensing her prevarication, he spoke firmly. 'Your father is on the brink of total ruin, and if you don't listen to me he'll be bankrupt within a month.'

She froze, all colour draining from her face. She shook her head slowly from side to side, mumbling something about not being able to believe it, but her mind was shredding through that silly denial. After all, she'd seen for herself the change in him recently. The stress. The anger. The drinking too much. The weight loss. Disturbed sleep. Why hadn't she pushed him harder? Why hadn't she demanded that he or her mother tell her honestly what was going on?

'I have no interest in lying to you,' he said simply. 'Sit down.'

She nodded, her throat thick, as she crossed the room and took a chair at the meeting table. He followed, his eyes not leaving her face as he poured two glasses of water and slid one across the table, before hunkering his large frame into the chair opposite.

His feet brushed hers accidentally beneath the table. The shock of her father's situation had robbed her of her usual control and she jumped at the touch, her whole body resonating before she caught herself in the childish reaction.

And he'd noticed it; the smile of sardonic amusement on his face might have embarrassed her if she hadn't been so completely overcome by concern.

'Dad's...I don't...' She shook her head, resting her hands on the table, trying to make sense of the revelation.

'Your father, like many investors who didn't take adequate precautions, is suffering at the hands of a turbulent market. More fool him.'

He spoke with disrespect and obvious dislike, but Marnie didn't leap to defend Arthur Kenington. At one time she'd been her father's biggest champion, but that, too, had changed over time. Shell shock in the immediate aftermath of Libby's death had translated to the kind of loyalty that didn't allow room for doubt. Her need to keep her family close had made it impossible for her to risk upsetting the only people on earth who understood her grief. She would have done anything to save them further pain, even if that had meant walking away from the man she loved because they'd expressed their bitter disapproval.

Her eyes were cloudy as they settled on his frame. Memories were sharp. She pushed at them angrily, relegating them to the locked box of her mind.

Those memories were of the past. The distant past. She and Nikos were different people now.

'He will lose everything without immediate help. Without money.'

Marnie turned the ring she always wore around her finger—a nervous gesture she'd resorted to without realising. Her face—so beautiful, so ethereally elegant—was crushed, and Nikos felt a hint of pity for her. There was a time when he would have said that causing her pain was anathema to him. A time when he would have leapt in front of a speeding bus to save her life—a time when he had promised to love her for ever, to adore her, to cherish her.

And she'd answered that pledge by telling him he'd never be good enough for her, or words to that effect.

He straightened in the chair, honing in on his resolve.

But Marnie spoke first, her voice quietly insistent. 'Dad has lots of associates. People with money.'

'He needs rather a large sum.'

'He'll find it,' she said with false bravado, unknowingly tilting her gaze down her small ski slope nose.

His smile was almost feral in its confidence. 'A hundred million pounds by the end of the month?'

'A...hundred...' Her feathery lashes closed, muting any visible shock. She was hiding herself from him, wanting to keep her turmoil private and secret.

He didn't challenge her; there was no need.

'And that is just to start,' he confirmed with a small nod. 'But if you want to leave…' He waved a hand towards the door, as though he didn't give a damn what she chose to do.

Marnie toyed with the ring again, her eyes studying its gentle golden crenulations before shifting their focus back to his face. 'So? What's *your* interest in my father's business?'

'His business?' Nikos's laugh was short and sharp. 'I have no interest in that.'

Marnie's eyes knitted together, confusion obvious on her features. Even her hair looked uptight, knotted into that style. Her hands, her nails, her perfectly made-up face: she was the picture of stylish grace, just as her parents had always intended her to be.

'I presume you called me here because you have a plan.' She pinned him with her golden-brown eyes until the sensation overpowered her. 'I wish you'd stop prevaricating and just tell me.'

His smile was not one of happiness. 'You are hardly in a position to issue commands to me.'

Marnie's face lifted to his in surprise. 'That's not what I was doing.' She shook her head timidly from side to side. 'I didn't mean to, anyway. It's just…please. Tell me everything.'

He shrugged. 'Bad decisions. Bad investments. Bad business.' He pressed back further in his chair, the intensity of his fierce gaze sending sharp arrows of awareness and emotion through her blood. 'The why of it doesn't matter.'

'It matters to me.'

He spoke on as though she hadn't. His eyes bored into hers. 'I believe there are not ten people in the world who would find themselves in a financial position to help your father. Even fewer who would have any motivation to do so.'

Marnie bit down on her lower lip, trying desperately to

think of anyone who might have enough liquidity to inject some cash into her father's crumbling empire.

Only one man came to mind, and he was staring at her in a way that was turning her mind to mush.

Unable to sit still for a moment longer, Marnie scraped her chair back and stalked to the window. London vibrated beneath them: a collection of cars and souls all going about their own lives, threading together into one enormous carpet of activity. She felt as if she'd been plucked out of the fibres and placed here instead, in a madhouse.

'Dad's never been your favourite person,' she said softly. 'How do I know you're not making this up for some cruel reason of your own?'

'Your father's demise is not a well-kept secret, *matakia mou*. Anderson told me.'

'Anderson?' The name was like a knife in her gut. She thought of Libby's fiancé with the shock of grief that always accompanied anything to do with her sister. With *Before*.

'We're still in touch,' he said with a shrug, as if that wasn't important.

'He knows about this?' She thought of Anderson Holt's family, the fortune they possessed. Maybe *they* could help? She dismissed the thought instantly. A hundred million pounds—cash—was beyond most people's capabilities. Besides, Arthur Kenington would never let himself be bailed out.

'It is no secret,' Nikos said, misunderstanding her question. 'I imagine the whole city knows the truth of your father's position.'

Her spine stiffened and sorrow for the man who had raised her pushed all thoughts of her late sister's fiancé from her mind. She blinked quickly, denying the sting of tears that was threatening. She was not willing to show such weakness in front of anyone, let alone Nikos.

'He *has* seemed stressed lately,' she conceded awkwardly, keeping her vision focussed on the buzz of activity at street level.

'I can well imagine. The idea of losing his life's work and the legacy of his forebears will be weighing heavily on his conscience. Not to mention his monumental ego.'

She let the barb go by. Her mind was completely absorbed with trying to make sense of this information. 'I don't understand why he wouldn't have said anything.'

'Don't you?' His eyes flashed with anger and resentment as his last conversation with Lord Arthur Kenington came to mind. 'The man prides himself on shielding you from the world. He would do anything to spare you the pain of actually inhabiting reality with the rest of us.'

'You call *this* reality?' she quipped, flicking a disapproving glance around the cavernous glass office decorated with modern art masterpieces and furniture that would have looked at home in a gallery.

A muscle jerked in his cheek and Marnie wished she could pull those words back. Who was *she* to sit in judgement of his success? She didn't know the details, but she knew enough of his childhood to realise that if anyone on earth understood poverty it was Nikos.

'I'm sorry,' she said stiffly, lifting a finger to her temple and rubbing at it. 'None of this is your fault.'

A pang of something a lot like sympathy squeezed in Nikos's gut. Recognising that she could still evoke those emotions in him, he consciously pushed aside any softening towards her.

'No.' He rubbed a hand across his stubbled jaw. 'He stands to lose it all, Marnie. His investments. His reputation. Kenington Hall. He will be a cautionary tale at best, a laughing stock more likely.'

'Don't…' She shivered, thinking of what her parents had already suffered and lost in life. The thought of them enduring yet another tragedy weighed so heavily on her chest she could hardly breathe.

'I would be lying if I said I'm not a little tempted to leave him to his fate. A fate that, as it turns out, is not at all dissimilar to what he predicted for *me*.'

A shiver ran down her spine. 'You're still angry about that?'

His eyes flashed. 'Angry? No. Disgusted? Yes.' He dragged a hand through his hair, as though mentally shaking himself. 'He would spend a lifetime repaying his creditors.'

Nikos was conscious that he was driving a proverbial knife into her. He didn't stop.

'Some of his decisions might even be seen as criminally negligent.'

'Oh, my God, Nikos, *don't*.' She spun to face him; it was like being hit with a sledgehammer.

He ground his teeth, refusing to feel sympathy for her even when her world was shattering. 'It is the truth. Would you prefer I'd said nothing?'

When she spoke her voice was hoarse, momentarily weakened by the strength of her feelings. 'Does this bring you pleasure? Did you bring me here to gloat?'

'To gloat?' His smile was like a wolf's. 'No.'

'Well? Then what *do* you want? Why are you telling me any of this?'

A muscle jerked in his cheek. 'I could alleviate all of your father's problems, you know.'

Hope, a fragile bird, fluttered in her gut. 'Yes?'

'It would not be difficult for me to fix this,' he said with a shrug.

Marnie's head spun at the ease of his declaration. 'Even a hundred million pounds?'

'I am a wealthy man. Do you not read the papers?'

'God, Nikos.' Relief was so palpable that she didn't

even acknowledge the insult. Hope loomed. 'I don't know how to thank you.'

'Delay your gratitude until you have considered the terms.'

'The terms?' Her brows drew together in confusion.

'I have the means to help your father, but not yet the inducement.'

Aware she was parroting, she murmured, 'What inducement?'

The breath burned in her lungs. Her heart was hammering so hard in her chest that she thought it might break free and make a bid for freedom. Tension was a rope, twisting around them. She waited on tenterhooks that seemed to have sharp gnashing teeth.

'You, Marnie.' His dark voice was at its arrogant best. 'As my wife. Marry me and I will help him.'

CHAPTER TWO

SHE'D NEVER UNDERSTOOD how silence could vibrate until that moment. The very air they breathed seemed as if it was alive, crackling and humming around them. His words were little daggers, floating through the atmosphere, jabbing at her heart, her soul, her brain, her mind.

'Marry me and I will help him.'

Only the sound of her heavy breathing perforated the air. For support, she pressed back against the glass window. It was warmed by the sun.

'I don't understand,' she said finally, squeezing her eyes shut. Every fibre of her being instantly rejected the idea.

Or did it?

Briefly, childish fantasies bubbled inside her, spreading the kind of pleasure she'd once revelled in freely.

When she blinked a moment later, Nikos was holding a glass of water just in front of her. She took it and drank gratefully, her throat parched.

'It is not a difficult equation. Marriage to me in exchange for a sum of money that will answer your father's debts.'

'That makes no sense,' she contradicted flatly.

'No?'

'No!'

It seemed like the right reaction. It was an absurd proposal, after all. Wasn't it? She should have felt panicked by the very idea. And perhaps a part of her did. This was the man who had disappeared from her life but never fully from her heart.

But panic and wariness were only tiny components of her emotional tangle. Hope and an intense flare of passionate resonance also filled her.

'Marriage…' Her heart squeezed. Her words were a whisper. 'Marriage…is for people in love. That's not us. How can you be so cavalier about it?'

He took a step closer, curling his fingers around the glass. Instead of taking it from her he kept his hand over hers. Electricity sparked along the length of her arm, shooting blue fire through her body.

'Call it…righting a wrong,' he said darkly, his eyes scanning her face with hard emotion. 'Or repaying a debt.'

Her stomach rolled.

'Your father paid me a considerable sum to get out of your life six years ago.'

Her mouth formed a perfect 'o' and she gasped in surprise. He gathered she hadn't known *that* little piece of information. It didn't make him proud, but he enjoyed seeing her sense of betrayal and outrage before she schooled her features once more. Her mask was excellent, though the more tightly she held on to it the more he wanted to force her to drop it. To shock her, surprise her, make her feel so strongly that she could no longer remain impassive.

He put his thumb-pad over her lower lip, remembering how soft they were to kiss.

'I didn't know.' Her eyes were earnest and it didn't enter his mind to doubt her.

'No.' He shrugged. 'It wasn't necessary, in any event. He obviously didn't realise that you had already conclusively ended things.'

Marnie's heart squeezed. 'I had no choice.'

'Of *course* you had a damned choice.' He controlled his temper with effort. 'You could have told him that you'd fallen in love with me. That no amount of comment about the fact that I didn't live up to his exalted expectations would change how you felt about me. You could have told him to shove his snobbery and his stupidity. You could have fought for what we were—as I would have.'

She sucked in a deep breath. The pain was as fresh in that instant as if it was six years ago. She ached all over. 'You know what we'd been through.' She squeezed her eyes shut. 'What my family had lost. I couldn't hurt him. I had to choose between him and…what I felt for you.'

'And you chose him.' His stare was filled with a startling wave of resentment. 'You switched something in here—' he lifted a finger to her chest, pointing at her heart '—and that was it. It was over.'

She swallowed convulsively. It had been nothing like that. He made it sound easy. As if she'd simply decided to forget Nikos and move on. But she hadn't. She'd agonised over the decision.

She'd tried to explain to her parents that she didn't care that Nikos didn't have money or come from one of the established families they approved of. But arguments had led to the unsupportable—her mother in tears, her father furious and not speaking to Marnie, and the certainty that they just wanted Libby back—perfect Libby—to make good choices and be the daughter they were proud of.

'In any event, the financial…*compensation* for leaving you helped to soften the blow. At first I swore I wouldn't take it. But then…'

He spoke with gravelled inflection, sucking Marnie back to the present.

'I was so angry with you, with him. I took it and I told myself I'd double it—just to prove him wrong. To prove a point.'

Marnie's cheeks were flushed. His hand moved to cup her face. She could have pulled away, but she didn't. 'I think you did more than that.'

His smile was grim. 'Yes.'

So Arthur had given her boyfriend money to get out of her life? A chill ran the length of her spine. It seemed like a step too far. Pressuring her to end it was one thing, but actually forcing Nikos out?

'I'm sorry he got involved like that. It wasn't his place to…to pay you off.'

'Not when you'd already done his bidding,' Nikos responded with a lift of his shoulders. 'Your father forbade you from seeing me and, like a good little Lady Heiress, you jumped when he clicked his fingers.'

'Don't call me that,' she said distractedly, hating the tabloid press's moniker for her.

It wasn't that it was cruelly meant, only that they mistook her natural reserve for something far more grandiose: snobbery. Pretension. Airs and graces. The kind of aristocratic aspirations that Marnie had never fallen in line with despite the value her parents put on them. The values that had been at the root of their disapproval of Nikos.

'So this is revenge?' she murmured, her eyes clashing fiercely with his. Pain lanced through her.

'Yes.'

'A dish best served cold?' She shook her head sadly, dislodging his hand. 'You've waited six years for this.'

'Yes.' He brought his body closer, crushing her with his strong thighs, his broad chest. 'But there will be nothing cold about our marriage.'

Desire lurched through her. The world began to spin wildly off its axis. 'There won't be a marriage,' she said, with a confidence that was completely forged. Already the options were closing in around her. 'And there certainly won't be…what you're…suggesting.'

'What's the matter, *agape mou*? Do you worry that we won't still feel as we did then?'

He ground his hips against her and she groaned as sensations that had long since been relegated to the past flared in her belly. Of their own volition her fingers curled into the fabric of his shirt, the warmth from his chest a balm to her fraught nerves.

'Do you remember how I respected your innocence?' He brought his mouth close to hers, so that his words were a breath on her lips. 'How I told you we should wait until we were married, or at least engaged?'

Shame, desire, misery and despair slid through her like a headless snake, twisting and writhing in her heart. She pulled her lower lip between her teeth and nodded once.

'How, even though I had kissed your body all over, and you had begged me to take you, I insisted that I wanted to wait? Because I thought I loved you and that it mattered.'

He dropped his hands to her hips, holding her still as he pushed against her once more. She tilted her head back as far as she could, the window's glass providing a hard barrier.

'Do you remember how you laughed in my face and told me you'd never marry someone like me?'

Those words! How she'd hated saying them! She'd rehearsed them for days, and when the moment had come only the belief that she was doing the right thing for her family had spurred her on to say them. It was the most difficult thing she'd ever done. Even now, six years later, she wondered at the way she'd been led away from him despite the intensity of her feelings.

'*Do* you?' he demanded, scraping his lips against her neck, sending her pulse rioting out of control.

'Yes!' She groaned as desire and memory weakened her body.

'I have met many people like you in my life—like your father. Snobs who value centuries-old fortune above all else.'

'That isn't me,' she said with quiet determination.

'Of course it is.' He almost laughed. 'You broke up with me because you knew your destiny was to marry someone like you. Somebody that your parents approved of.'

'That's what *they* wanted. I just wanted *you*.'

'Not enough.' He sobered, his mouth a grim slash.

Frustrated, she tried to appeal to the man he'd once been: the man who had known her better than anyone on earth. 'God, Nikos. You *know* what my life was like then. We'd just buried Libby. We were all in mourning. I couldn't upset them like you wanted me to. I *couldn't*. Don't you dare think for a moment it was because I thought you weren't good enough.'

'You thought as your parents wished you to,' he said with coldness, shrugging as though it no longer mattered. 'But they will shortly come to realise there is one thing that carries more sway than birth and breeding. And when you are as broke as your father that is *money*.'

His words fell like bricks against her chest.

'Now you will marry me, and he will have to spend the rest of his life knowing it was *me*—the man he wouldn't have in his house—who was his salvation.'

The sheer fury of his words whipped her like a rope. 'Nikos,' she said, surprised at how calm she could sound in the midst of his stormy declaration. 'He should never have made you feel like that.'

'Your father could have called me every name under the sun for all I cared, *agape*. It was *you* I expected more of.'

She swallowed. Expectations were not new to Marnie. Her parents'. Her sister's. Her own.

'And now you *will* marry me.'

Anticipation formed a cliff's edge and she was tumbling over it, free-falling from a great height. She shook her head, but they both knew it was denial for the sake of it.

'No more waiting,' he intoned darkly, crushing his mouth to hers in a kiss that stole her breath and coloured her soul.

His tongue clashed with hers. It was a kiss of slavish possession, a kiss designed to challenge and disarm. He blew away every defence she had, reminding her that his body had always been able to manipulate hers. A single look had always been enough to make her break out in a cold sweat of need.

'No more waiting.'

'You can't still want me,' she said into his mouth, wrapping her hands around his back. 'You've hardly lived the life of a monk. I would have thought I'd lost all appeal by now.'

'Call it unfinished business,' he responded, breaking the kiss to scrape his lips down her neck, nipping at her shoulder.

She pushed her hips forward, instinctively wanting more. Wanting everything.

Her brain was wrapped in cotton wool, foggy and filled with questions softened by confusion. 'It was six years ago.'

'Yes. And still you're the only woman I have ever believed myself in love with. The only woman I have ever wanted a future with. Once upon a time for love.'

'And now?'

'For...less noble reasons.'

He stepped away, breaking their kiss so easily it made her head spin.

'Your father isn't the only one I intend to prove wrong.'

She narrowed her eyes, her heart racing. 'What does *that* mean?'

His laugh was without humour. 'You said I didn't mean

anything to you. That I had been merely a distraction when you needed to escape grief.'

He brought his face closer to hers once more—so close that she could see the thousands of tiny prisms of light that danced in his eyes.

'You told me you didn't want me.'

'I…' She squeezed her eyes shut. 'I don't remember saying that,' she lied.

'You said it. And I will delight in showing you how wrong you were.'

He stepped away, leaving her cresting a wave of emotion. Striving to sound cool, she said, 'So you've been… what? Pining for me for six years? Give me a break, Nikos. You moved on pretty damned fast, so it's a little disingenuous to be playing the heartbroken ex-lover now.'

'We were never lovers, *agape*.'

Her stomach churned; her cheeks were pink. 'That's not the point I'm making.'

'Whatever point it is you are attempting to make it is irrelevant to me.'

She sucked in an indignant breath but he continued. 'I have not been pining for you. But I *am* an opportunist.' His smile was almost cruel—at least it looked it to Marnie. 'Your father's situation presented me with an opportunity I felt I couldn't resist.'

'Oh, yeah?' she snapped, trying desperately to think of a way out. A way to make him realise how foolhardy this was!

'You will spend every day of our marriage faced with the reality of just how wrong you were.'

Speechless, she fidgeted with her ring, her mind unable to grasp exactly what was going on.

Seemingly he took her silence as a form of agreement. 'A licence can be arranged within fifteen days. I have engaged a wedding planner to oversee the details. Her card is on my desk; take it when you leave.'

She shook her head as the words he was saying tumbled over her. She needed to process what was going on. 'Wait a second. It's too sudden. Too soon.'

He arched a single thick brow. 'Any delay will make it impossible for me to help your father in time.'

'You're saying we have to actually *be* married before you'll help him?'

His lip twisted in a smile of cynical derision. 'It would hardly make sense to prop him up *before* the pleasure of having you… As my wife.'

To Marnie, his slight pause implied that he meant something else altogether. That he wanted to sleep with her before money changed hands. It made her feel instantly dirty, and she shifted away from the window, crossing her arms in an attempt to stem the pain that was perforating her heart.

'Do you think I'd renege on our deal?' she asked, realising only after posing the question that it showed her acquiescence when she hadn't actually intended to agree…*yet*.

'I think you will do whatever pleases you—as you always have done.' His eyes narrowed. 'Forgive me—what is the expression? Having been bitten, I am…?'

'Once bitten, twice shy.' She sucked in an unsteady breath, waiting for relief to calm her lungs. But still they burned painfully. She tried to salvage her pride. 'If I agree to do this, I *will* go through with it.'

'I'm not sure I can put much stock in your assurances,' he said with a shrug. 'I credit you and your father for my scepticism. Were it not for you, perhaps I would have continued to take promises at face value. Now I live and die by contracts.'

'That's fine in business. I'm sure it's wise, in fact. But marriage is different, surely.'

'A *real* marriage,' he conceded, with a tight nod.

'You're saying you don't want ours to be a real marriage?'

His laugh sent a shiver down her spine. 'Oh, in the most important ways it will be.'

'Meaning…?' she challenged—though how could she not understand his intention?

'Meaning, Marnie, that I have no interest in paying a hundred million pounds and tying myself to a woman *purely* for revenge.'

His smile curled her toes.

'There will be other benefits to our marriage.'

Her heart slammed hard in her chest. 'I…' She clamped her mouth shut.

What had she been about to say? That she was still a virgin? That after being so madly in love with him and letting him go she'd found she couldn't feel that same desire for another man? Especially not the men her parents approved of her dating.

'I'm not going to sleep with you just because you appear out of the blue…'

'That is not why you'll sleep with me,' he said.

He spoke with a confidence that infuriated her. But he was right! Despite the passage of time, and the insufferable situation she found herself in, she couldn't deny that the same need was rioting through her now, just as it had in their past.

'This is a deal-breaker,' he said with a shrug. 'These are my terms. Accept them or don't.'

'Wait.' She shook her head and lifted a hand to make him pause for a moment. But she was drowning. Possibilities, questions, wants, needs, doubts were churning around inside her—it was background noise but it was going to suck her under. 'There's so much more to discuss.'

'Such as?' he prompted, crossing his arms over his broad chest.

She tried not to notice the way the fabric strained to reveal his impressive pectoral definition.

'Well, such as…' She darted her tongue out and licked her lower lip. 'Say I went along with this absolutely crazy idea—and I'm not saying I will, because clearly it's madness—where would you see us living?'

'That is also non-negotiable. Greece.'

'*Greece?*' She was in free fall again. 'Greece, as in… You mean Greece?'

He stared at her for a long moment, his eyes mocking her. 'Athens. My home.'

'But I've always lived *here*. I can't move.'

Their eyes locked; it was a battle of wills and yet when he spoke it was with an easy nonchalance she admired.

'I will be spending a considerable fortune to save your father's reputation. You do not think it's fair that *you* should make some concessions?'

'Marrying you is *not* a c-concession,' she stammered in disbelief. 'It's so much more than that. And the same can be said of moving to a different country.'

'You are *so* sheltered,' he murmured. 'What would you suggest? That we live in London? Within arm's reach of your father? A man I will always despise? No.'

'How can I marry you knowing you feel that way about him?'

His expression was rock-hard. 'You will find a way.' He shrugged. 'While it might be difficult for you, it is the only way to spare him—and your mother—from a considerable fall from grace.'

'So this is how it would be? You'd dictate terms and I'd be expected to fall in with them?'

The air was thick between them. He studied her for a

long moment and she wondered if he wasn't going to answer. Finally, though, he sighed.

'I have no intention of being unreasonable. When you make a fair request I will hear you out. But this is not one of those instances. I live in Greece. My business is primarily controlled from Athens. You still live with your parents, who hate me as much as I do them. You have no business to speak of. It is obvious that we should move.'

'Just like that?' she murmured, shaking her head at his high-handed dictatorial manner even when a small part of her brain could see that he was raising a decent rationale for the suggestion.

'These are my terms,' he said again.

'You're unbelievable,' she replied softly, worrying at her fingers.

She spun her ring some more, trying to think of a way to appease him that didn't involve anything so drastic as this ridiculous marriage. But there was nothing. He had the money. And there was no way he'd help unless she made it worth his while.

'Yes.' He shrugged. 'So?'

'I wouldn't want a big wedding.' She was thinking aloud, really, though to her ears it sounded as though she was going along with his proposal. 'If I had my way it would just be us. No fanfare. No fuss.'

'Hmm…' he murmured with a shake of his head. 'And no one need ever know? No. I want the world to see that you are my wife. You—a woman who once felt I was far beneath her. A woman who declared she'd never marry someone like me. I want your father to have to stand beside us, smiling as though I am all his dreams come true, when we three will know that I am the last man on earth he wants his daughter to marry.'

The way he'd been treated by her and her parents was a nauseating truth. She wished—not for the first time—

that she'd been able to stand up to them. That she'd been wise enough to fight for the relationship that had mattered so much to her.

'Nikos…' She furrowed her brows, searching for words. 'You have to understand why I…why I couldn't be with you. You know how my parents were after Libby…after…'

He studied her face, torn between listening and shutting down this hollow explanation.

'I know I never explained it properly at the time. The way I was always in her shadow. The certainty that I was a poor comparison to her. The absolute blinding fact that they wished again and again that I could be more like her.' She swallowed, an image of her sister clouding her eyes and making her heart ring with nostalgic affection. 'They wanted me to marry someone like Anderson—her fiancé. And I wanted their approval so badly I would have done anything they asked.'

He compressed his lips. 'Yes. I presumed as much at the time.'

He brought his face closer to hers, so she could feel the waves of his resentment.

'You walked away from me and what we were to each other as though I was nothing to you. You can blame your sister, or you can blame your parents, but the only one who made the decision was *you*.'

'I'm trying to explain why…'

'And I'm telling you that it does not matter to me.' His eyes flared. 'You were wrong.'

She had been. In the six years since she'd watched Nikos leave for the last time, his shoulders set, his head held high, she'd never met anyone who excited in her even a tenth of the emotions he had. He alone had been her true love. And she'd burned him in a way that he'd apparently never forgive.

He brought the conversation back to the wedding. 'The guest list will be extensive and the press coverage—'

'Nikos!' Marnie interrupted, her voice strained.

Something in the pale set of her features communicated her distress and he was quiet, watchful.

'Please.' Her throat worked overtime as she tried to relieve her aching mouth. 'I can't do that.'

'You do agree to marry me?'

She nodded. 'But not like that. I… You know how I feel about the media. And, more to the point, how they feel about me.' She flashed a look at him from beneath thick dark lashes. 'I'll marry you. I will. But without all the fuss. Please.'

It was tempting to push her out of her comfort zone. To say that it was a big wedding or none at all. She was staring at him with a look of icy aloofness that had no doubt helped earn her the nickname of Lady Heiress. That look of untouchable elegance bordering on disdain that he understood was her tightly held shield in moments of wrenching panic. That same look he was desperate to dislodge as soon as possible, shaking her into showing her real feelings.

'You don't like the press any more than I do,' she said with measured persistence. 'If you insist on a big wedding we'll both know it's simply to be spiteful to me. And you're not that petty—are you, Nikos?'

He felt his resolve slipping and a grudging admiration for her reasoned argument spread through him. Still, he drawled, 'I'm blackmailing you into my bed and you don't think I'm petty?'

Heat flooded her system, warring with the ice that had coated her heart. 'No, I don't. I think you want me to marry you. What does it matter how we do it?'

She had an excellent point. Besides Marnie there was only one other person he really cared about having at the wedding.

'Fine,' he said, with a nonchalant lift of his shoulders. His eyes glittered with determination. 'So long as your father is there the rest does not greatly matter.'

'It's enormous,' she intoned flatly, rubbing her fingertip over the flattened edges of paper.

Nikos's stare was loaded with emotion. 'It needs to be.' His accent seemed thicker, spicier than it had been the night before. Her gaze flicked to his face, then skidded away again immediately. His face was all angles and planes, unforgiving and unrelenting.

Harsh.

She had never comprehended the full extent of that hardness before. Not in the past, anyway. When she'd loved him as much as the ocean loved the shore. She had felt, then, just like that. As if she would spend the rest of her life rolling inexorably towards him, needing to touch him, to wash over him, to feel him beneath her and around her. She had believed them to be as organically dependent as those two bodies—sea and sand. That without him she would have nowhere to go.

Foolishly, she had thought he felt the same.

But Nikos had moved on quickly, despite his protestations of love, and his bed had been such a hot spot it might as well have had its own listing on TripAdvisor.

'Mind if I have my lawyer check this out?'

He shrugged his shoulders. '*Sígoura.* Certainly. But that may cause a delay to proceedings.'

Her eyes narrowed. 'You mean you might not be able to help Dad in time?'

He sat back in his chair, his body taut, his face unreadable. 'I will not apply for the marriage licence until you have signed the pre-nup.'

A frown formed a little line between her eyes. 'Why not?'

His laugh was a sharp sound in the busy café. A woman

at the table beside them angled her head curiously before going back to her book.

Marnie lowered her voice, not wanting to risk being overheard. She was obliged to lean a little closer. 'Does it matter if I don't sign it in the next week or two? So long as you have it before the wedding...?'

'The minute I apply for our certificate there's a high probability the press will pick up on it. Do you *want* the world to know we were hastily engaged and that the wedding was then cancelled?'

Her cheeks flamed. 'As if the journalists of the world have nothing better to do than search the registry for your name, waiting with bated breath until such time as you see fit to hang up your well-worn bachelor belt,' she muttered.

He arched a single brow, his expression making her feel instantly ridiculous. 'If you believe our wedding won't excite media interest then you're more naive than I recall.'

Yes, she definitely felt childish now. She dragged her lower lip between her teeth, then caught the betraying gesture and mentally shook herself. She was Lady Marnie Kenington, and it was not for Nikos to berate and humiliate her.

'Each of us on our own would create a stir of interest. Marrying one another guarantees press interest.'

'I know.' She nodded. There was no point, after all, in arguing the toss. He was absolutely right. 'But we agreed on a quiet wedding.'

'And I will do my best to arrange this,' he promised.

'Okay.' She nodded again quickly.

His first instinct was to feel impressed by her ability to be reasonable in the face of an argument. But he quickly realised that she wasn't reasonable so much as changeable. That she was deferring to him at the first sign of pressure. Was that how it had been with her parents?

His mouth was a grim line in his face. 'There are four pages you need to sign.'

She expelled a heavy breath and tapped the pen against the side of the table.

Memories, visceral and sharp, twisted his gut. How familiar that tiny gesture was! Flashes of her studying for exams, writing lists, pausing midsentence to capture the next, flashed into his mind. When she'd had a particularly large problem to solve she'd chewed on the end of the pen, waiting for clarity to flood to her from its inky heart.

'Nikos...' She lifted her gaze to him. 'Doesn't this all seem a bit crazy?'

He didn't react.

She huffed out a sigh. 'I don't know you any more. And you definitely don't know me.'

He narrowed his eyes almost imperceptibly. 'I know you perhaps as well as ever.'

She bit on the pen again and shook her head. 'I just don't see why we have to rush this.'

'It is your father's financial situation that puts a time limit on matters.'

'But—'

'No.'

He leaned across the table, pressing his hand on hers. Sparks shimmered in her heart. Angered by her body's ongoing betrayal to his proximity, she worked overtime to conceal the explosive desire. Her glare was dripping with ice.

'This is the only way I will help your father. It's not a negotiation.'

Backed against a wall, she wondered why she didn't feel more angry.

She looked down at the thick pile of papers. 'If you expect me to sign this today then you're going to have to explain it to me.'

'Fine.' He flicked a glance at his gold wristwatch.

'Sorry if I'm taking up too much of your time,' she snapped sarcastically, and for the briefest moment he felt the full force of her emotions—emotions she was so good at guarding. Fear, worry, stress, uncertainty.

But he had no intention of softening towards his fiancée. He nodded curtly, his expression rock-hard. 'The first section deals with our assets. Any assets you bring to the marriage will be quarantined against becoming communal.'

'So I get to keep what's mine?' she interpreted.

'Yes. I have no interest in your money.'

The way he said it, with such vile distaste, made Marnie shiver.

'Fine. Just as I have no interest in yours.'

He arched a brow, his face filled with sardonic amusement. 'You mean, I presume, beyond the hundred million pounds I will be giving your father?'

Her cheeks flamed. 'Yes.' She couldn't meet his eyes because she felt the sting of tears in her own.

'Irrespective of that, you will be entitled to a sum for each year we remain married.'

'I don't want it,' she said through clenched teeth.

'Fine. Give it away. It's not my concern.' He reached forward impatiently and turned several pages until he arrived at the end of that section. 'Sign here.'

Pressing her lips together, she scrawled her name, blinking her eyes furiously.

They were still suspiciously moist when she lifted her face to his. 'Next?'

He appeared not to notice how close her emotions were to the surface. 'The next section deals with the moral obligations of our union. Any infidelity will lead to an immediate termination of the marriage. It will also invalidate the financial agreement, and will necessitate your father returning half of the money I have given him to that date.'

She blinked in confusion. 'You think I'm going to cheat on you?'

His lips compressed with a dark emotion, one she couldn't fathom. 'I could not say with certainty.' His smile was wolfish. 'Though I imagine this makes it considerably less likely.'

She ground her teeth together. 'And what if *you* cheat?'

'Me?' He laughed again, this time with real humour.

'Yeah. You're the one who seems to be constantly auditioning lovers. What happens if you get bored in our marriage and end up in another woman's bed?'

'You will just have to make sure I don't get bored.'

Her breath snagged in her throat. The threat weakened her. Her pulse throbbed painfully in her body. 'When did you get so cynical?'

He narrowed his eyes, stunning her with the heat she felt emanating from him. 'When do you think, *agape mou*?'

She shook her head, hating the implication that she'd somehow caused his character transformation. 'Nikos…'

What did she want to say? She'd already tried to explain about Libby, and the burden she'd felt to please her parents—a burden that had increased monumentally after Libby's death. He didn't care. He'd said as much. She clamped her mouth shut and shook her head. It was futile.

'I have a meeting after this.'

She swallowed, shaking her head to clear the tangle of thoughts. 'Fine.'

'The third section deals with children.'

Her eyes startled to his face. 'Children?' Her heart was jackhammering inside her chest.

He turned several pages but Marnie was too shocked to bother trying to read them. He fixed her with a direct stare. 'It stipulates that we won't have a child for at least five years.'

Fire and ice were flashing within her, making speech

difficult. She blinked her enormous caramel eyes, then shook her head, but still it didn't make sense. 'You want children?'

He shrugged. 'Perhaps. One day. It's hard to imagine right now—and with you.'

'Oh, gee, thanks.' She rolled her eyes in an attempt to hide the way his words had wounded her. 'As if I'm just lining up to be your baby-baker.'

'My...*baby-baker*?' Despite himself, he felt a smile tickle the corner of his lips.

'I can't believe you're actually contracting hypothetical children.'

He arched a brow. 'It makes sense.'

'A baby isn't...' She dropped her gaze. 'A baby isn't *Section Three, Subsection Eleven A*. A baby is a little person. A new life! You have no right to...to...make such arbitrary decisions about something that should be magical and wonderful.'

'A baby between us would *never* be magical and wonderful,' he responded, with such ease that she genuinely believed he hadn't intended to be unkind. 'It is the very last thing I would want. As for it being arbitrary...' He shrugged his broad shoulders with an air of unconcern. 'You seemed perfectly fine making such decisions in the past.'

'Not about a child!'

'You just said you don't want to be my...baby-baker. Have you changed your mind suddenly?' he asked cynically, his eyes drifting over her features with genuine interest.

'No.' She bit down on her lip. The lie—and she recognised it as such—hurt. Images of what their children might look like were hard to shake. Instantly she could see a tiny chubby version of Nikos, with his imperious expression and dark eyes, and her heart seemed to soar at the prospect.

'Our marriage is not one of love. I can think of nothing worse than bringing a child into that situation.'

'But in five years?' she heard herself ask, as if from a long way away.

He shrugged insolently. 'In five years we will either have found a way to live together with a degree of harmony, or we will hate one another and have long since divorced. It gives us time to see what's what. No?'

She nodded jerkily. He was right. She knew he was. But as she signed her name on the bottom of the page she felt as if she was strangling a large part of herself.

'Next?' She forced a tight smile to her lips; her tone was cool.

'A simple confidentiality agreement. Our business is our own. The press has a fascination with you, and I have often thought, despite what you say, that you court their interest.'

'You've got to be kidding me!' she interrupted sharply. 'I go out of my way to stay off their radar.'

'Which in and of itself only heightens their attention and speculation.'

'So I flirt with the press by hiding from them?' She crossed her legs beneath the table. 'That's absurd.'

'You are "Lady Heiress". They call you that because of your behaviour—'

'They call me that,' she interrupted testily, 'because I refuse to engage with them. After Libby died they were everywhere. I was only seventeen, and they followed me around for sport.'

She didn't add how horrible their comparisons to the beautiful Libby had made her feel. How Marnie's far less stunning looks had drawn the press's derision. She had refused to court them in order to create the impression that she didn't care, but each article had eroded a piece of her confidence until only the 'Lady Heiress' construct had remained. Being cold and untouchable, a renowned ice queen, was better than being the less beautiful, less popular, less charismatic sister of Lady Elizabeth Kenington.

He shrugged. 'You will not be of such interest in Greece. Here you are a society princess. There you will be only my wife.'

Why did that prospect make everything inside her sing? Not just the prospect of marrying him, but of escaping it all! The intrusions and invasions. Freedom was a gulf before her.

'Your parents are included in this agreement. They are to believe our wedding is a real one.'

'Oh? I would have thought you'd like to throw the terms of our deal in Dad's face, just to see him suffer,' she couldn't help snapping.

'Perhaps one day.' His smile tilted her world off-balance. 'But that is *my* decision. Not yours.'

She furrowed her brow. 'This agreement doesn't apply to you?'

'No. It is a contract for you. So you understand what is expected of you.'

'That definitely isn't fair.'

He laughed. 'Perhaps not. Do you want to walk away, Marnie?'

The sting of tears was back. She lowered her eyes in an attempt to hide them and shook her head. But when she put her signature to the bottom of the page she added something unexpected.

A single teardrop rolled down her cheek and splashed onto the white paper, unconsciously dotting the 'i'. It was the perfect addition to the deal—almost like a blood promise.

She closed the contract and pushed it across the table.

It was done, then, and there was nothing left to do but marry the man. Except, of course, to break the news to her parents.

CHAPTER THREE

'YOU CAN'T BE SERIOUS.' Arthur Kenington's face was a study in apoplexy, from the ruddy cheeks to bloodshot eyes and the spittle forming at the corner of his mouth.

Marnie studied him with a mix of detachment and sadness. Perhaps it was normal to emerge into adulthood with a confusing bundle of feelings towards one's parents. Marnie loved them, of course, but as she sat across from Arthur and Anne in the picture-perfect sunroom of Kenington Hall she couldn't help but feel frustration, too.

She lifted her hand, showing the enormous diamond solitaire that branded her as engaged. Anne's eyes dropped to it; her lips fell at the corners. Just a little. Anne Kenington was far too disciplined with her emotions to react as she wished.

'Since when?' The words were flat. Compressed.

'Be vague on the details.' That had been Nikos's directive when they'd spoken that morning. Had he been checking on her? Worrying she was going to balk at this final hurdle? Did he think the idea of breaking the news to her parents might be too difficult?

'We met up again recently. It all happened very fast.'

'You can certainly say that.' Anne's eyes, so like Libby's had been, except without the warmth and laughter, dropped to Marnie's stomach. 'Is it…?'

'Of course not!' Marnie read between the lines. 'I'm not pregnant. That's not why we're getting married.'

Arthur expelled a loud breath and stood. Despite the fact it was just midday, he moved towards the dumb waiter and loudly removed the top from a decanter of sherry. He poured a stiff measure and cradled it in his long, slim fingers.

'Then why the rush?' Anne pushed, looking from her husband to her daughter and trying desperately to make sense of the announcement that was still hanging in the air.

'Be vague on the details.'

'Why not?' she murmured. 'Neither of us wants a big wedding.' She shrugged her slender shoulders, striving to appear nonchalant even when her heart was pounding at the very idea of marriage to Nikos Kyriazis.

'Darling, it's not how things are *done*,' Anne said with a shake of her head.

Marnie stiffened her spine imperceptibly, squaring her shoulders. 'I appreciate that your preference might be for a big, fancy wedding, but the last thing I want is a couture gown and a photographer from *OK! Magazine* breathing down my back.'

Anne arched one perfectly shaped brow, clasped her hands neatly in her lap. At one time, not that long ago, Marnie might have taken Anne's displeasure as reason enough to abandon her plans. But too much was at stake now. If only her parents knew that the wedding they were so quick to disapprove of was their only hope of avoiding financial ruination!

'You don't like the press. That's fine. But our friends. Your family. Your godmother…!'

'No.' Marnie didn't flinch; her eyes were tethered to her mother's. 'That's not going to happen. Just you and Dad.'

'And Nikos? Which of *his* family will be there?' Anne couldn't quite keep the sneer from her voice.

'As you know, he has no family,' Marnie responded with a quiet dignity. 'Besides me.'

How strange it was to say that, knowing it was the literal truth if not a particularly honest representation of the situation.

'I don't like it,' Arthur interjected, his sherry glass empty now, and his focus on Marnie once more.

Marnie had expected this, and yet still she heard the words with an element of disappointment. 'Why not?' she queried quietly.

'I have never thought he was right for you. I still don't.'

There was nothing inherently offensive in the statement, but it was the reasoning behind it that Marnie took exception to. Six years ago she'd let the implication hang in the air, but now she was older and wiser and significantly less worried about upsetting her parents. 'For what reason, Dad?'

He reached for the sherry once more and Anne Kenington, across from Marnie, stiffened visibly.

'He's just not *right*.'

'That's not a reason.' Marnie's smile was forced.

'Fine. He's different. From you. From us.'

'Because he's Greek?' she asked with an assumption of mock innocence.

'Don't be obtuse,' he snapped.

Anne stood, moving her slender figure across the room towards the large glass doors that opened out onto the rolling green grass of the East Lawn. A large oak broke up the expanse of colour a little way in the distance, casting dark shadows beneath its voluminous branches.

'Is there any point in having this discussion?' she asked wearily.

'Meaning…?' Marnie asked softly.

'Your plans appear to be set in stone,' Anne continued, her pale eyes skimming over the gardens, her face a mask of calm despite the storm Marnie knew to be raging beneath.

Was that the only thing they had in common? Their steadfast commitment to burying any display of emotion? Keeping as much of themselves as possible hidden from prying eyes?

Marnie shifted her gaze back to her father. He looked as if he was about to pop a blood vessel. He was glaring at the sherry decanter, his fingers white around the fine crystal glass.

'One hundred per cent.' Marnie nodded. 'I hope you can put the past behind you and be happy for us.'

Arthur's harsh intake of breath was smothered by Anne's rushed statement. 'You're a grown woman. Who you marry is your choice.' She practically coughed on the statement.

Marnie stood, not sure what else she could add to the conversation. 'Thank you.'

A ridiculous way to end the conversation but, then again, what about the circumstances of this wedding *wasn't* ridiculous?

She slipped from the room, the muted voices of Arthur and Anne chasing her down the long corridors of Kenington Hall. She emerged onto the front steps and breathed in deep. Her cheeks were flushed, her skin warm. She moved deliberately away from the East Lawn, wanting to be far from her parents.

She walked with innate elegance until she reached the edge of the rose gardens. Then she slipped her pumps from her feet and cast one last glance towards the house. She began to move as she'd wanted to since she'd first seen Nikos again. As though the earth had turned to magma and was burning through the soles of her feet. She couldn't stand still; she could no longer be composed and calm.

And so she ran.

She ran as though the ghosts of the past had taken animal form: they were lions and tigers and they were chasing her, making her tremble with fear and terror.

'No daughter of mine is going to throw her life away on a no-hoper like that! You will end it, Marnie, or you will be out of this house faster than you can say inheritance.'

Arthur's hateful declaration was a cheetah, fierce and gnashing its teeth.

'I don't care about money! I love him!'

She sobbed as she remembered her impassioned cry, her belief that if she could only get her parents to understand what a good man Nikos was they would shelve their dislike.

But their dislike hadn't had a lot to do with the man he was so much as the man he *wasn't*.

'He's got no class. He will never make you happy, darling.'

At least Anne had tried to couch her objections gently. But her meaning had been clear. No class. No money. No social prestige.

Even then she'd stood fast. She'd fought for him.

'We've been through enough this year, for God's sake!' Arthur had finally shouted. *'We've already lost one daughter. Are you going to make us lose you, too?'*

Marnie ran until her lungs burned and her eyes stung with the tears the wind held in check. She ran past the lake that she'd fallen into as a child, before she'd learned to love the water and to navigate its murky pull; she ran around the remnants of the tree house where she and Libby had spent several long, sticky summers, pretending they were anywhere but Kenington Hall. She ran to the very edges of the estate, where an apple orchard shielded the property from the curious view of a passer-by.

Finally she came to an abrupt stop beneath a particularly established tree, bracing her palm against the trunk and staring back at the sprawling stone mansion.

Her whole life had been lived within its walls. She'd learned to walk, she'd played hide-and-seek, she'd read book after book, she'd been a princess in a castle. It was her place in the world.

But why hadn't she left when her parents had taken a stand against Nikos? Why hadn't she moved to London like most of her friends?

Because of Libby.

A sob clogged her throat. She swallowed it.

They'd lost Libby. And it had changed them for ever. Maybe they would have been difficult and elitist, anyway. But their grief had made it worse. And it had made Marnie more forgiving.

How could she run away from them and leave them alone after burying one of their daughters?

She groaned now, shaking her head.

So she'd put her life on hold. She'd remained at home, under their roof, managing the gardens, working in her little home office, pretending she didn't resent them for their heavy-handed involvement in a relationship that had been so important to her.

Was this marriage to Nikos a second chance? Might they even fall in love again?

Her heart turned over in her chest as she remembered the exquisite emotions he had evoked in her as a teenager. She had loved him fiercely then—but not enough. Because she'd walked away from him instead of staying and fighting and there was no turning back from that.

Goose bumps danced along her soft skin. 'This is beautiful.'

And it was. The house was nothing like she'd imagined. Set high on a hill on the outskirts of Athens, it was crisp

white against a perfect blue sky. Geraniums tumbled out
of window boxes, creating the impression that the flowers
had sprung to life there and decided to blow happily in the
light, balmy breeze. Clumps of lavender stood proud from
large ceramic pots and the fragrance of orange blossom
and jasmine hung heavy in the air.

'I'll give you a tour tomorrow—introduce you to the
household staff.'

'Staff?' That was interesting. 'How many staff?'

He put his hand in the small of her back, propelling her
gently towards the front door. 'My housekeeper, Eléni, and
her husband, Andréas. Two gardeners...'

'That's good,' she said with a nod.

His laugh was a short, sharp bark. 'Did you think it
would be just you and me?'

Of course she had.

He leaned closer, so that she could see the hundred and
one colours that danced in his irises.

'Don't worry, *agape mou*.'

The heat of his words fanned her cheek.

'They will give us plenty of space in the beginning. We
are on our honeymoon, after all.'

Her stomach lurched. Desire was swarming over her
body, making her pulse hammer. Moist heat slicked
through her. It felt as if she'd been waiting an eternity
to be possessed by this man. The time was almost upon
them, and anticipation was flicking delicious little sparks
over her nerves.

He pushed the front door inwards. A wide tiled corridor led all the way to glass doors that showed the moonlit
Aegean Sea in the distance.

'Are you hungry?'

Despite the fact that it was their wedding day, she hadn't
eaten more than a piece of wedding cake after the ceremony. A sip of champagne to wash it down and Nikos had

whisked her away from the disapprovingly tight smiles of her parents.

Her stomach made a little growl of complaint. 'Apparently,' she said, with an embarrassed smile.

His smile was the closest thing to genuine she'd seen on his face. It instantly offered her a hint of reprieve.

'There is food in the fridge. Come.'

She fell into step behind him, taking in the blur of their surroundings as she walked at his pace. Beautiful modern artwork gave much-needed colour to a palette of all glass and white. The home was obviously new, and it was a testament to minimalist architecture. While beautiful, it was severely lacking in comfortable, homely touches.

The kitchen housed a large stainless steel fridge. He reached in and pulled out a platter overflowing with olives, cheese, bread, tomato and *dolmades*. Another selection of bread was complemented with sliced meats and smoked fish.

'Wine, Mrs Kyriazis?'

The name splintered through her heart. 'I thought I'd keep Kenington,' she said, though in truth she'd barely contemplated the matter.

He poured two glasses of a pale, buttery-coloured wine, his face carefully blank of emotion. 'Did you?'

She shrugged. 'Lots of women do, you know.'

He nodded thoughtfully. 'But you are not "lots of women". You are my wife.'

He said it with such a sense of dark ownership that she was startled. Marnie couldn't have said if it was surprise at being spoken of almost as an object that inspired her sense of caution, or the fact that his passionate statement of intent was flooding her with desire and overarching need. A need that made rational thought completely impossible.

She sipped her wine in an attempt to cool the fire that was ravaging her central nervous system. It didn't work.

She nodded jerkily, at a loss for words.

'I want the world to know it.'

The statement hung between them like a challenge.

Her stare was direct. 'I'm not planning on hiding my identity.'

He reached for a cube of feta and lifted it towards her lips. Surprised, she parted them and he slid the cheese into her mouth, watching with satisfaction as she chewed it.

'No.' His eyes bored into hers, holding her gaze for several long, fraught seconds. 'My wife will bear my name.'

There it was again! That flash of pleasure in her abdomen. A sense of *rightness* at the way he wanted to claim her. To possess her. The desire to subjugate herself completely to his will terrified her. She bucked against it even as she wanted to move to him and offer her submission.

'Will she, now?' she murmured.

'Of course it is not too late to back out of this agreement.' He shrugged. 'Our marriage could be easily dissolved at this point, and I have not yet spoken to your father about his business concerns.'

Something lurched inside her. She stared across at him, needing her wine to banish the kaleidoscope of butterflies that were panicking, beating their wings against the walls of her stomach.

'Are you going to threaten me whenever I don't let you have your way?'

His laugh was without humour. 'That was not a threat, Mrs Kyriazis. It was a summation of our current circumstances.'

'So if I don't take your name you'll divorce me?'

His lips twisted in a wry smile. 'At this point I believe we could simply seek an annulment.'

'You should have put it in that damned pre-nup,' she said with a flick of her lips.

Anger flared inside her and beneath the table she turned the ring on her finger, looking for comfort and relief.

'I would have if I had known you were going to be so irrational about such trivialities.'

'It's not a triviality!' she demurred angrily, tipping more wine into her mouth.

How could she possibly explain her feelings? Explain how essential it was to hold on to at least a part of her identity? How terrified she was that she was married to a man who despised her, who was using her to avenge an ancient rebuff, who was determined not to care for her—a man she had always loved?

'You are my wife.'

'And taking your name is the *only* way to be your wife?' She had to force herself not to yell.

'Not the only way, no.'

His teeth were bared in a smile that sent shivers down her spine. Need spiked in her gut. She wouldn't acknowledge it. She couldn't.

'Fine.' She angled her head away. 'Whatever. I don't care enough to fight about it.'

That bothered him far more than the suggestion she might not take his name. The way she'd rolled over, acquiesced to his wishes at the first sign of conflict. Just like the last time he'd challenged her and she'd almost immediately backed down.

Arthur and Anne had insisted she couldn't be involved with him. Had she argued calmly for a moment and then given up? Given *him* up, and with him their future? Had they invoked her dead sister, knowing that Marnie had never felt she measured up to St Libby? Had they compared him—a poor Greek boy—to Libby's blue-blood fiancé, with his title and his properties? Had she looked from Nikos to Anderson and agreed that, yes, she needed someone like the latter?

'These olives are delicious,' she said quietly, anxious to break the awkward silence that was heavy in the room.

But when she lifted her gaze slowly to his face she saw he was lost in thought, staring out of the kitchen windows at the moonlit garden. It allowed her a moment to study his face and see him properly. He looked tired. No, not *tired*, exactly, she corrected, so much as…what? What *was* the emotion flitting across his face? What did she see in the tightening of his lips and the darkening along his cheekbones? In the knitting of his brow and the small pulsing of that muscle in his jaw?

'Fine.' He blinked and turned to face her. 'I'll show you the house now.'

She nodded out of habit.

It was enormous, and modern throughout. Wide corridors, white walls, beautiful art, elegant lighting…

'It's like a boutique,' she murmured to herself as they finished their tour of the downstairs rooms and took the stairs to the next level.

'This will be our room.' He paused on the threshold, inviting her silently to precede him.

Our room. Did he expect her to argue over their sleeping arrangements? She had no intention of giving him the pleasure.

'It's very nice.' Her almond-shaped eyes skimmed the room, taking in the luxurious appointments almost as an afterthought. King-size bed, bay window with a small seat carved into the nook, plush cream carpet and a door that she imagined led to a wardrobe.

She spun round, surprised to find him standing right behind her. They were so close her arms were brushing his sides.

She stepped back jerkily. 'I'm going to need an office space.'

'An office space?' His laugh was laced with disbelief and it irked her to the extreme.

'Yes. Why do you find that funny?'

'Well, *agape*, offices are generally for *work*.'

'Oh, I see.' She nodded with mocking apology. 'Work like *you* do, I suppose you mean?'

He crossed his arms over his chest, drawing Marnie's attention to the impressive span of musculature.

'Yes, generally.'

Her temper snapped, but she didn't show it. She'd had a lot of practice in keeping her deepest feelings hidden— she could only be grateful for that now.

'I need an office.' She said the words slowly and with crisp enunciation. 'For *my* work.'

'What work?'

Curiosity flared in his gut. Six years had passed and he'd presumed she was still simply Lady Marnie Kenington, daughter of Lord and Lady Kenington, employed only in the swanning about of her estate, the beautifying of herself and the upholding of the family name. It had never occurred to him that she might have done what most people did and found gainful employment. Frankly, he was surprised her parents had approved such a pedestrian pursuit.

'Does it matter? Do you care? Or are you just surprised that I haven't been rocking in a corner over the demise of our relationship since you left?'

Though frustrated by her reticence to speak honestly, he liked seeing the spark that brought colour to her cheeks and impishness to her eyes.

It intrigued him. He far preferred it to the obedient contrition she'd modelled in the kitchen. Instantly he thought of other ways in which he might inspire a similar reaction.

He nodded, concealing his innermost thoughts. 'Fine, have it your way. I do not need to know about your employment if you do not wish to speak of it.' He shrugged, as though the conversation was now boring him. 'I'll have a room made available. Just let my assistant know what you need in terms of infrastructure and he'll see you're set up.'

'*He?* You have a male assistant?'

It was Nikos's turn to act surprised. 'Yes. Bart. He's been with me five years.'

She laughed quietly and shook her head. 'I guess that makes sense. I can imagine you'd run through female secretaries pretty damned fast, given your track record for taking any woman with a pulse to bed.'

'Jealous, *agape?*'

She'd been jealous, all right. For years she'd followed his exploits in the gossip columns. Like watching a train crash, she'd been powerless not to stare at the pictures. They'd come to life in her over-fertile imagination so that she hadn't simply looked at an attractive couple coming out of some hot spot so much as imagined them in bed, or perhaps on the dining table, or the kitchen floor, while *she* lay in her own bed. Alone, untouched, able only to dream of Nikos rather than feel his hands on her body…

'Oh, yes,' she simpered, with an attempt at false sincerity. 'I've spent the last six years *desperately* waiting for you to reappear in my life. I've been missing you and dreaming about you and praying you'd turn up and blackmail me into a loveless marriage. This is pretty much the high point of my life, actually.'

'And we haven't even slept together yet,' he said, in a voice that was honey and dynamite.

Her breath caught in her throat. She spun away from him, her cheeks flushed.

'What is it, *agape*? Suddenly you are shy? It is our wedding night.'

She lifted a hand to her throat and lightly rubbed her skin. 'I… Of course not.' She squared her shoulders.

Hadn't she been dreaming about this for as long as she'd known him?'

'Relax.' His hands on her shoulders were firm. He spun her in the circle of his arms so that they were facing one another, his warmth offering some comfort to her. 'You are shaking like a leaf.'

Tell him the truth!

She fluttered her eyes closed, her lashes dark circles against her pale cheeks.

'You are my wife.' He pressed a finger under her chin, lifting her face to his. His eyes were troubled, tormented. 'Are you...*afraid* of me?'

It was so uncharacteristic of him to show doubt that she raced to reassure him. 'Of course I'm not.' She shook her head, inhaling a deep breath that flooded her system with his spicy scent. 'I'm afraid of *myself,* and of what I want right now.'

He nodded, silently imploring her to continue.

'You hate my father. I think you might even hate me.' She lifted a finger to his lips to stop him from speaking. 'But I don't hate you.' Her eyes were enormous, loaded with fear and desire. 'I don't hate you...'

Her finger, initially placed against his mouth to silence him, dragged slowly across his lower lip. Her eyes followed its progress as if mesmerised.

She knew he was going to kiss her. The intent was in every line of his body. If she'd wanted to she could have stepped away. She could have asked for more time. Instead she lifted herself up on tiptoe, crushing her mouth to his.

In that bittersweet moment all Marnie needed was to right one of the biggest wrongs of her past: she wanted Nikos and, damn it, she was finally going to have him.

To hell with the consequences. They'd be waiting for her afterwards.

CHAPTER FOUR

HER BODY FLASHED like flame when his mouth crushed down on hers with the kind of intensity that spoke of long-held desire. She was powerless to swim against the tide of need: powerless and unwilling.

Her feminine heart was hot and wet, slick with moisture and need. Unfamiliar but instinct-driven urges were controlling her body. Her hands pushed under his shirt, seeking skin and warmth. She traced her fingertips up his hair-roughened chest, splaying her fingers wide. She felt the beating of his heart beneath her touch; it was as frantic as her own.

His body weight pushed her downwards—not to the bed but to the floor, to her knees. He knelt with her, kissing her, his tongue clashing fiercely with hers as his hands pulled through her hair then pushed at her head, holding her against his mouth. She groaned into him, marking their kiss with the desperation that was scrawling a painful tattoo across her being—inking her as his in a way that would never be erased.

He pulled at her as his body pushed at hers until she fell back onto the carpet. His weight on top of her was divine. She curved her hands to his back, digging her nails into his warm skin as she felt the power of his arousal for herself. Hard and firm through their layers of clothing, A bodily ache was spreading through her. She lifted her hips, silently begging him for more. To mark her once and for all.

'Nikos!' She cried his name into the room and he groaned in response. 'Please!' She dug her hands inside his jeans, cupping the naked curve of his arse, pressing him against her and grinding herself intimately against his masculinity.

He laughed throatily. 'You want this, huh?'

He kissed her again—hard, fiercely, possessively—and then roamed his lips lower, encircling one of her erect nipples through the fabric of her dress and her bra. Even with such obstacles in the way the warmth and pressure of his mouth sent sharp arrows of need spiralling within her.

'Yes!' she hissed, arching her back, desperately needing more. 'Please, please...'

'In time.'

He smiled, running his mouth lower, over the fabric of her dress, until he reached the apex of her thighs. He skimmed lower, to the hem of the dress, and finally pushed it upwards, so that only a flimsy scrap of lace stood between him and her most intimate flesh.

Her cheeks were pink, her eyes fevered. Even when he wanted to go quickly he took his time, removing her underpants, sliding them down her soft, smooth legs and discarding them to one side. He let his hands dance patterns along her thighs, revelling in the way she quivered beneath his touch as her body responded instantly to him.

His fingers worshipped at her crease, teasing her, exploring her, aching for her. He was more gentle than he'd known he could be, perhaps afraid that she might regret her decision at any moment. That after years of waiting this was, after all, *not* to be.

Greek words, whispered hoarsely, filled the air. Words that swirled around her, wrapping her in magic and myth.

She didn't have a clue what he was saying, but she loved the sound of his native language.

When he slid a finger into her core she bucked hard, writhing at the intimate touch. Even back then, when they'd been fevered and passionate, he hadn't passed *this* threshold. His invasion was completely, utterly unprecedented.

Sharp, hot barbs of pleasure drove through her body, into her mind, weakening every earthly thought before it could be imagined. He moved slowly, curiously, watching her face as he stroked her sensitive flesh, learning what made her almost incandescent with desire before pulling out of her.

She gasped, the withdrawal of his touch an unbearable pain she could not withstand. But he didn't leave her for long before dropping his lips to her opening. His tongue was warm, but she was more so. Her body was on fire... his mouth seemed to kiss flame into her.

It had been a long time since Marnie had felt anything like this. She was completely unprepared for the insanity that his ministrations would bring. She was digging her nails into the carpet at her sides now, her knees lifted towards the ceiling as her toes curled into the ground and her whole body shook and quivered.

The orgasm was intense. She screamed as it saturated her being in long, luxuriant waves.

Sweat beaded her brow; heat painted her cheeks pink. Her throat, her arms—she was burning up. Her breath was loud in the room as she panted, satiated passion making her lungs work overtime.

Before she could drift down from the clouds that had absorbed her into their heavenly orbit Nikos was straddling her, his arousal pressed against her tingling core.

Marnie stared up at him, and everything in her world was perfect.

He studied her as his hands worked the buttons of his

shirt, and she was powerless to look away. Her tongue darted out, licking her lower lip, moistening it hungrily.

His smile was sexy as sin. She groaned, impatient for more. As he pushed at his shirt her trembling fingers unfastened his belt and pulled it from his jeans. She cast it across the room, wincing apologetically when it hit the wall loudly. He didn't react.

His shirt was unbuttoned, his chest exposed to her greedy eyes, and she stared and she touched and she felt, tracing his muscles, circling his nipples and filling with pride when he sucked in a raspy breath. He rotated his hips, taking back the upper hand, making her weak with the promise of what was to come.

She pushed at his shirt, chasing it down his arms, catching the fingers of one hand as she passed, lifting it to her lips and kissing him. It was a tender moment in the midst of passion. Their eyes locked and the past was all around them, threatening to suck them into the vortex of what had been.

'It might have cost me a small fortune, but finally you are going to be mine.'

His eyes glittered with dark anger, and the moment was swallowed up by cruelty as though it had never been.

Marnie bit down on her lip, trying not to react, trying not to let the pain sour what they were sharing.

She didn't have long to absorb his words, to turn them over in her mind. He shifted his body weight so that he could kick his jeans and boxers off. He was naked. Gloriously, wonderfully naked. She stared at him, her mind disappearing completely at the sight of Nikos Kyriazis. Her husband: the definition of tall, dark and sexy.

She groaned, dropping her hand to her womanhood, her fingers lightly grazing her flesh. His chest heaved as he sucked in a breath, his eyes sparking with hers. He stood over her, incapable of looking anywhere but at her hand and incapable of moving.

Until something snapped—and a desperate need to finally possess her cracked through him.

'You're on the pill.'

It was a statement, not a question. As though it hadn't occurred to him in earnest that she might not be.

Her cheeks flushed pink as she nodded. It had been the first thing she'd done after signing the pre-nuptial agreement. It had been all she could do to prepare for this moment, for him.

'I am safe.'

He straddled her, almost trapping her hand, but she snaked it higher. Tentatively, nervously, as though she had no right, she touched his length. He jerked instantly in her palm. She smiled a feminine, feline smile of innate power.

'You?'

'Me…?' He was long and smooth and so, so hard.

He laughed throatily. 'You've been tested?'

'Oh.' She hadn't been but, having never shared her body with another, she supposed it was the same thing. 'I'm safe, yes.'

He kissed her mouth, squashing her hand, his flesh against her stomach. 'Good. Because I want to feel you, *agape*. *Really* feel you.'

He jerked out of her grip, bringing his tip to her opening, teasing her with his nearness before pulling away. His hands pushed her dress higher, so that he could lift her breasts out of her bra, rub his palms over her flesh. He pushed the dress roughly over her body, the fabric grazing against her over-sensitised skin, pushed it over her face. She shifted upwards so that he could lift it and toss it. Her bra was next.

She opened her mouth, knowing she didn't want to surprise him with her virginity. She had no sexual experience, but even *she* thought it was somehow not good etiquette to spring that on someone.

But his mouth took hers, making speech impossible, driving rational thought from her brain once more. She tried to cling on to her conviction, to the knowledge that she should speak the truth to Nikos, but it was like chasing a piece of shell in eggwhite.

It slipped out of her mind. Only the physical remained.

His hands were insistent on her breasts, his thumb and forefinger teasing her nipples, rolling them, before his mouth dragged down her throat to take a peach areola into his mouth. His tongue lashed it and she groaned, felt pleasure building to another inevitable crescendo.

Her heart hammered against her ribs, so hard and fast she could hear the pounding of it in her ears.

She lifted her legs, wrapping them around his waist, pulling him closer. He groaned, his stubble-roughened chin like sandpaper on her soft flesh as he moved his mouth to her other breast, delighting it with the same treatment. His tongue lashed her, chasing invisible circles around the erect peak until she could bear it no longer.

'Nikos!' she cried out, tightening her grip around his waist. 'Please, please now...'

He laughed, but it was a sound without humour. 'I thought we'd at least get to bed,' he said ruefully, bringing his tip closer.

There was no fear for Marnie. Despite her innocence, and his impressive size, she knew that this coming together was somehow destined. She had waited a long time for him, and she wasn't about to let something as silly as fear or concern take the shine off the moment.

Still... That explanation she owed him...the warning...

'Nikos, I need to tell you—'

'No.' He pinned her with his gaze as he lifted himself

up on his arms so that he could stare into her eyes. 'No more explanations. No more words. Not now.'

'But—'

'This is not the time for conversation.'

She might have argued with him. After all, she had a strong sense that it was an important thing to share. But before she could say another word he parted her legs, pressing them back onto the carpet, splaying them wide, and thrust into her.

Not gently, nor slowly—why would he?

They were at a fever pitch of desire and he had no reason to suspect that everything they were doing was new and therefore held the potential for pain.

Her eyes squeezed shut as he slammed past the invisible barrier of her innocence, discarding it as swiftly and easily as he had her bra. He swore, the harsh sound jarring her nerves, then swapped to Greek and released a litany of words in his own tongue.

The pain, which had been sharp and searing, was quick to vanish. Like a receding shoreline it disappeared, leaving only the surrender to pleasure in its wake. She moaned as her muscles stretched to welcome him, squeezing his length, gripping him at her core.

He swore again and then shifted, moving gently now, slowly, his eyes on her face, watching for any sign of discomfort. There was none. She began to moan as he stoked her fires. His lips claimed hers, his tongue duelling with hers in time with each delicious thrust until she was about to explode. She curled her toes into the carpet and cried out, the sound muffled by his mouth.

She was incapable of controlling the sensation of release. It burst from her through every pore, every nerve ending. It flew from her body like a bubble being released underwater. It burst, spilling her pleasure across the room in an effervescence of cries and hard breathing.

She arched her back in an ancient step in the dance of sensuality. He gripped her hips, holding her there, his fingers digging into her flesh. He pressed his forehead to hers, their sweat mingling.

He didn't let her catch her breath before he was torturing her anew. Nerve endings already vibrating at an almost unbearable frequency began to quake and quiver. She groaned as another orgasm, bigger and scarier, chased the other away. This time, though, when she cried out into the room, he chased after her, his own voice combining with hers as pleasure saturated their surroundings.

It was a perfect moment.

Marnie caught the pearl of memory—the way he felt, smelled, tasted—and wrapped it deep into the recesses of her mind, knowing she would want to visit this feeling again and again and again.

He lifted up from her, and the absence of his weight was a pain she hadn't been prepared for. He pulled away, removing himself from her heart and standing in one swift movement. He paced away, gloriously naked, and for the briefest moment Marnie thought he was actually going to stalk out of the room without a word!

Incensed, she got to her feet, wincing as muscles that had never been tested began to groan in complaint. The sound of running water heaped fuel onto the fire of her anger. He was actually going to shower straight away? Hell, she had no point of reference, but Marnie would have put money on that being an absolutely hurtful thing to do.

The door she had initially thought was a wardrobe must conceal an *en-suite* bathroom.

The shower was running when she stepped into the tiled room, but Nikos was not behind the glass. He stood, naked, his hands braced on the vanity unit, his head bent. She couldn't see his expression in the mirror, but tension seemed to emanate from his strong frame.

It arrested her in her tracks.

Fear that she'd somehow got something wrong swirled through her.

She cleared her throat, uncertain what she wanted him to say but knowing she needed to hear *something*. Some form of reassurance or kindness.

He lifted his head, his eyes spearing hers in the mirror's reflection. His face was strained, his expression otherwise unreadable. He scanned her face, seeming to shake himself out of his own reverie, then turned to look at her.

'Did I hurt you?'

It was so far from what she'd expected him to say that relief whooshed through her. She shook her head wordlessly.

He held a hand out, inviting her to join him. She placed her smaller hand in his palm, feeling as if it was symbolic of so much more, and took a step closer. A small line had formed between his brows; he was scowling. Thinking. Deep in analysis.

'I did not expect...' he said, shaking his head again.

He tugged her lightly, pulling her to his body. His hands ran the length of her back gently, carefully.

'Here.' He swallowed, his Adam's apple bobbing visibly as he tried to gain a perspective on this turn of events. He guided her into the shower without breaking his contact with her.

He had one of those enormous ceiling shower heads; warm water doused her the minute she stepped in and she made a little yelp of surprise. Her dark hair was plastered to her face. But once she became accustomed to it the feeling of warmth on her skin was beautiful.

She watched as Nikos took a soft sponge from the shelf and poured shower gel on it. His eyes clung to hers.

'I do not understand,' he said finally, bringing the sponge to her shoulders and soaping her slowly.

The shower gel frothed against her skin. It smelled of lime and vanilla.

'I'm sorry,' Marnie said, then wished she could take the words of contrition back. She bit down on her lower lip. 'Not that I think I did anything wrong,' she hastened to correct. 'Only that I probably should have warned you.'

'Warned me?' A smile flicked at the corners of his lips. 'You think this is something for which I needed *warning*?'

'Well…' She huffed, crossing her arms over her chest. 'I don't know.'

Her eyes dropped to the tiled floor, where the soapy water was fleeing the scene, racing towards the drain.

'Not warning,' he said firmly. 'Just…explanation. How is this possible?'

Her cheeks were glowing; she could feel them. 'Well, it's not that difficult. I've just abstained from having sex. Hardly rocket science.'

His laugh was thick and throaty. Desire flickered in her abdomen, surprising her into blinking her eyes up at him. The air around them seemed to be supercharged with awareness.

He sponged across her décolletage, then lower, slowly, torturously circling one already over-sensitive breast.

'Was it a decision you made? To remain a virgin?'

She was on a precipice. The question wasn't a simple one to answer. If she responded with the truth it would reveal so much more of her heart than she wished to show him! What if she were to tell him that she'd never met a man who'd made her feel remotely tempted in the way he had?

Instinctively she shied away from handing him such a degree of power. 'Yes. I made a little pre-nup with myself,' she breathed with a hint of sarcasm.

He transferred the sponge to her other breast, his attention focussed on the small orbs and the erect nipples that were straining for his touch.

'You wanted to sleep with me back then.'

She shrugged. Her heart was pounding, though. Why hadn't she realised that he would hone in on that? 'Any chance we can *not* talk about this?'

He opened his mouth to say something, but then he nodded, a muscle jerking in his cheek. 'I was surprised,' he said simply. 'You've had boyfriends?'

'Of course I have,' she said, thinking of the handful of men she'd gone on dates with. The men her father had approved of. Suitable men who had left her stone-cold.

'Then how...?'

'I thought we weren't talking about this?' she reminded him quietly.

He nodded once more, his frustration obvious despite his acquiescence. 'It's just so unusual. You are twenty-three years old.'

She nodded, but speech was becoming difficult as he moved the sponge lower, dragging soapy suds over her stomach and lower still, to the space between her legs.

The warm water was heaven against her body. She moaned as he dropped the sponge to the ground with a splash and let his palm rub against her womanhood instead. After wondering briefly if she should be ashamed of the certainty that she wanted him again, she discarded the thought, pressing herself lower, begging him with her body not to remove his hand.

He watched as a fever of desire stole through her body. 'You must have been tempted. From what I recall you had a healthy sexual appetite when we were together.'

She gasped as he teased a finger at her entrance, incapable of responding.

'I had imagined you to have slept with several men by now.'

How those thoughts had tortured him!

'Yes, well...' She groaned, lowering her hips, begging

him for more. 'We're not all as libidinous as you.' She pushed the words out from between clamped teeth.

'*You* are,' he said simply, marvelling at how her body was clamping around him.

He dragged his lips along her jaw, nipping the flesh just beneath her ear before taking an earlobe into his mouth and flicking it between his teeth.

She writhed against the tiles and he jerked in immediate response.

'I would take you again already if I weren't worried about hurting you.'

'You won't hurt me,' she promised throatily. Her eyes were enormous as they lifted to his. 'I want you. *Now.*'

He arched a brow, moving his mouth to her breasts. The soap had long since been washed away and they were warm and moist between his lips. The feeling of his lips on her flesh made her jerk.

'Nik!' she cried out, digging her nails into his shoulder.

The name jarred. *No.* Out of nowhere, it infuriated him. A white-hot rage slammed against him—completely inappropriate but impossible to ignore.

Just her simple use of that name—as though she was slipping back into the past and forgetting that they were no longer a couple. Yes, they were married, but resentment had led to that. Anger, and even hatred. Referring to him as she had done when they were together wasn't something he welcomed.

Nik she'd called him back then. Never Nikos. And her lips had always curved into a sweet smile, as though his name was an invocation of secrets and hopes.

But that had all been a lie. She hadn't really cared for him then; she'd just made him believe she had. She'd played the part perfectly. And he'd fallen for it hook, line and sinker. Well, not again.

She had married him, but only for the sake of her father.

Just as she'd broken up with him because of her father. This was a business deal, plain and simple, and just as in business he needed to keep his focus. Her virginity, while interesting, did not change a thing about their arrangement.

He lifted her against the tiles and wrapped her legs around his waist, driving into her as though his life depended on taking her, on being one with her. It was just sex, but Nikos didn't want anything else from Marnie, anyway. And, no matter how great the sex was, he couldn't forget that.

It was up to him to remember just who he'd married.

She was cold to the core—except in his bed.

CHAPTER FIVE

MARNIE PADDED DOWN the stairs, her eyes straining a little against the brightness of Greece and the whiteness of his home. It was warm, too, though a breeze shifted through the wide corridor, lifting her Donna Karan dress as she reached the ground floor.

The house was quiet, except for a buzzing noise coming from the direction of the kitchen. Curious, she followed the sound, her tummy making a little groan of anticipation.

She'd slept late.

Then again, she'd been up late, too.

Her cheeks flushed as she remembered making love to Nikos in the shower, and then afterwards, when she'd almost drifted off to sleep, she'd felt his mouth teasing her body, drifting over her breasts, down her abdomen, to torment her one last time.

It had been a fantasy. She could almost believe she'd dreamed the whole thing. Except that she felt a little sore and tender in the light of day.

The sight of her husband in the kitchen made her heart skid to a stop. She swallowed, drinking him in hungrily. Awareness flooded her body. He was dressed in a business shirt, the sleeves rolled up to his elbows, exposing those dark, muscled forearms of his. The shirt sat tucked in at the waist, revealing that honed stomach and firm hips. A burst of adrenalin and desire flared through her.

She bit down on her lower lip in an attempt to stall the smile that was threatening to split her mouth apart.

'Morning,' she murmured, her eyes sparkling with remembered intimacies.

He flicked a gaze to her, then returned his attention to the broadsheet paper that was spread across the bench. 'Coffee?'

Her smile was quick to snap into a small frown. 'Oh… um…yes.'

She wasn't sure he'd heard; he remained perfectly still, his head bent as he read an article. After several long seconds he sipped his own coffee, then placed the mug down and moved to the corner of the kitchen. She'd expected to see a machine, but she saw Nikos had one of those stainless steel coffee pots. He poured a measure for Marnie and she wrinkled her nose, remembering instantly his predilection for coffee so thick it was almost like tar.

'Perhaps I'll have tea instead.'

He shrugged. 'I would be surprised if you find teabags. I don't drink the stuff.' He left the coffee cup on the bench beside her, then topped up his own mug. 'Speak to Eléni about your requirements. She will see the house has whatever you need.'

'Eléni?' Marnie murmured, her voice soft in response to his emotional distance.

'My housekeeper,' he reminded her.

'Right.' She nodded, sipping her coffee and pulling a face at the liquid, claggy against her tongue.

Her eyes lifted to the window, and beyond it to the view. The beach was shimmering in the distance, invitingly cool given the warmth of the day.

'I'm happy to go shopping.' A frown pulled at her brows. She wasn't sure she wanted to leave a housekeeper to run the house completely. 'I suppose we should talk about that, actually.'

He gave no indication that he'd heard her. Whatever he was reading was apparently engrossing. Or he was avoiding her like the plague. But that didn't make sense. Not after what they'd shared the night before.

'Nik?' she murmured, moving to stand right beside him.

There it was again. The word that he hated hearing from her mouth. *Nik.* The name that had given him such pleasure in the past was now like an accusing dagger in his gut. A reminder of what they'd been contrasted with what they were now, of the pain of their history and the resentment that had fuelled this union—all contained in that small, soft sound. *Nik.*

Harsh emotions straightened his spine. He pressed his finger into the page, marking his spot, then lifted his eyes to her face. He skimmed her features thoughtfully, careful not to betray the emotions that the simple shortening of his name evoked.

'I think we should stick with Nikos, don't you?'

The rebuff stung. No, it *killed*. A part of herself withered like a cut flower deprived of water.

She narrowed her eyes, ignoring the tears she could feel heavy in her throat. 'Are you sure you wouldn't prefer Mr Kyriazis?'

A muscle jerked in his jaw but he returned his gaze to the paper and read on for a few moments before closing the pages and turning around, propping his butt against the edge of the kitchen bench. His eyes locked with hers.

'What did you want to speak to me about, Mrs Kyriazis?'

She swallowed, all desire to act the part of his wife for real evaporating in the face of his coldness. Confusion was swirling through her, biting at her confidence bit by bit.

'The housekeeper,' she said finally, knowing the only thing worse than looking overeager was looking like an idiot who couldn't finish a thought. 'I can do some of her stuff.'

He arched a brow, silently imploring her to continue.

'Well,' she said, bitterly regretting embarking on this path. 'I did my own shopping at home. Most of my cooking, too. I also took over the gardens.'

'You? Who can't tell wisteria from jasmine?' he prompted sceptically.

She squared her shoulders. 'That was a long time ago. I love flowers now. Roses especially.'

She was babbling. What was that pervasive feeling of grief? And how could she stem its tide?

'Do you grow roses here? I suppose not. They're more of an English thing, aren't they? But, anyway, you said you have gardeners. In England I…' She tapered off at his complete lack of responsiveness.

'Eléni has been my housekeeper for a long time,' he said finally, his tone as far from encouraging as it was possible to get. 'I am not willing to offend her. She will not want to share her responsibilities.'

Marnie stared at him with rich disbelief. 'Even with your *wife*?'

His smile was not softened by anything like happiness or pleasure. 'My wife has other responsibilities.'

Marnie reached for her coffee. Thick and gloopy or not, it still had the ability to put some fire in her blood. 'What's got into you?' she asked when she'd drunk almost the whole cup. 'You're treating me like…like…'

He waited for her to continue, but when she didn't speak, letting her sentence trail off into nothingness, he prompted, 'Like what?'

He was impatient now. She felt like a recalcitrant child.

'Like you hate me.'

His nostrils flared as he expelled an angry breath. 'Your

words, *agape*, not mine.' He pushed up off the bench. 'I'll be home for dinner.'

'Where are you going?' She stared at him incredulously.

He laughed. 'Well, Marnie, I have to go to *work*. You see, our so-called marriage is really a business deal. You've upheld your end of the bargain spectacularly well so far— even bringing your virginity to the table. Now it is my turn. My assistant's number is on the fridge, should you need me.'

He walked out of the kitchen without so much as a kiss on the cheek.

She stared at his retreating back, gaping like a fish dragged mercilessly from the water. Hurt flashed inside her, but anger was there, too. How could he be so unkind? They were married, and only hours earlier had been as close as two people could be. That had moved things around for her; it had changed the tone of her heart. She wasn't the same woman she'd been the day before, or the week before, or when they'd made this hateful deal.

But for Nikos apparently nothing had changed. *Nothing.*

And he hadn't even told her to call *him* if she needed anything! She was so far down the pecking order that she was supposed to go through his assistant if she needed her own husband for anything.

Well! She'd show him!

She ground her teeth together and wandered over to the newspaper, simply for something to do. The article he'd been reading was an incredibly dry piece on an Italian bank that was restructuring its sub-prime loans.

She flicked out of the finance section and went to international news. Though she generally liked to keep abreast of world events, she looked at the words that morning without comprehension. The black-and-white letters swam like little bugs in her eyes until she gave up in frustration and slammed the paper shut.

She sipped the coffee again, before remembering how disgusting she found it, and then glided across the kitchen floor, pulling the fridge open. The platters from the night before were there; they'd been put back on their shelves. The flavours were reminiscent of childhood family holidays, when the four of them had travelled by yacht around the Med, stopping off at whichever island had taken their fancy, enjoying the local delicacies.

Libby had loved squid. She'd eaten charcoaled tentacles by the dozen. Whereas Marnie had been one for olives, cheese, bread and *dolmades*. Libby had joked about Marnie's metabolism in a way she'd been too young to understand, though now she knew that she'd been unfairly blessed with the ability to eat what she wanted and not see it in her figure.

It was the one small genetic blessing Marnie had in her favour. The rest had gone to Libby. The shimmering blonde hair that had waved down her back, the enormous bright blue eyes, a curving smile that had seemed to dance like the wind on her face, flicking and freshening with each emotion she felt. And Libby had almost always been happy.

Marnie padded across the tiled floor, drawn to the glass doors that framed the view of the ocean. It sparkled in the distance, and she saw with a little sound of pleasure that there was an infinity pool in the foreground. She toyed with the door handle until it clicked open and then slid the glass aside, stepping out onto the paved terrace as though the breeze had dragged her.

She breathed deeply. Salt and pollution were a heady mix for a girl who'd spent much of her time in the English countryside. She grinned, trying to put her situation with Nikos temporarily out of her mind. An almost childlike curiosity was settling around her, and she slipped across the terrace and stood on the edge of pool. The water was turquoise.

Her toe, almost of its own volition, skimmed the surface before diving beneath, taking her foot with it.

Perfection.

Uncaring that her expensive linen dress might get crumpled or wet, and for once not thinking about photographers or what people might think, safe in the knowledge that she was completely alone, Marnie lifted the dress over her head and left it in a roughly folded heap on the tiles.

In only her bra and underpants she slid into the water, making a little moan of delight as it lapped up to her neck. As a child she'd gone swimming often.

She ducked her head underwater, beyond caring that her artfully applied make-up would smudge, and stroked confidently to the far end of the pool. She propped her chin on the edge, studying the bright blue sky, turquoise ocean and faraway buildings for a moment before duck-diving underwater once more and returning to the house side.

It felt good to swim, and she lost count of how many laps she completed. Eventually, though, as she drew to the edge of the pool, her arms a little wobbly, she paused to gain breath.

'You are fast.'

A woman's accented voice reached her and Marnie started a little, her heart racing at the intrusion.

Not knowing exactly what to expect, she spun in the water until her eyes pinned the source of the voice.

A woman was on the terrace, a mop in one hand, a smile on her lined face. She had long hair, going by the voluminous messy bun that was piled on top of her hair, and it was a grey like lead. She wore a dark blue dress that fell to the knees and sensible sandals.

The housekeeper. What had Nikos said her name was? She wished now she'd paid better attention, rather than focussing her mental skills on just what the hell had happened in the hours since they'd made love.

'You swim like a dolphin, no?' the housekeeper said, and when her smile widened, Marnie saw that she was missing a tooth.

'Thank you,' she said, inwardly wincing at how uptight she sounded. She tried to loosen the effect with a smile of her own. 'I'm Marnie.'

'You Mrs Kyriazis.' The housekeeper nodded. 'I know, I know.'

She was tall and wiry and she moved fast, propping the mop against the side of the house before lifting the lid of a cane basket. 'I always keep towels in here. Mr Kyriazis likes his swim after work.'

Dangerous images of Nikos—bare-chested, water trickling over his muscled chest and honed arms—made her insides squeeze with remembered desire. 'Does he?'

'So the towels always are fresh. I can get you one.'

True to her word, she lifted one from the box and placed it on the edge of the pool, beside Marnie's dress. Her hand ran to the item of clothing, lifting it as if on autopilot and draping it over a chair instead.

Marnie was a little shamefaced at the uncharacteristic way she'd discarded it.

'I'm sorry,' she said, her tone stiff. 'Nikos didn't mention your name,' she fibbed.

'I'm Mrs Adona.' She grinned. 'You can call me Eléni, though, like Mr Kyriazis does.'

'Eléni.' Marnie nodded crisply. *That was it.* Curious, she tilted her head to one side, watching as the older woman returned to fetch the mop. 'It's nice to meet you.'

Eléni cackled quietly in response.

'That's funny?' Marnie prompted with a small smile on her face.

Later, she would be mortified to realise that she had big black circles of smudged mascara beneath each eye.

'Oh, it is nice for me to meet you, I was thinking. Nice for him to settle down. In my day men didn't work as hard as him. They had one woman and a simple job. You'll be good for him,' Eléni said, with an optimism that Marnie was loath to dispel.

So she nodded. 'Perhaps.'

Something occurred to her and, spontaneously, she called the woman nearer to the pool.

'Eléni? Nikos is worried that I'll step on your toes if I do the odd bit of grocery shopping or cooking.'

She watched the other woman carefully for any sign of mortification or offence, and instead saw a broad grin.

Spurred on, she continued, 'The thing is, I quite like to cook. And I don't have a lot to do here yet, and shopping kills time. So…well…I hope you won't be upset if you see that happening?'

'Upset?'

Her laugh was contagious and alarming in equal measure. Loud—so loud it seemed almost amplified—it pealed across the courtyard and out towards the sea. Marnie found herself chuckling in response.

Eléni said something in her own language, then rubbed her angled chin as if searching for the words in English. 'I don't know he can like a woman who cooks.'

The sentence was a little disjointed, and the accent was thick, but the meaning came to Marnie loud and clear.

Nikos didn't bring women who cooked to his home.

They had other talents.

And wasn't that just an unpalatable thought?

Well, Marnie would show him.

By the time he returned that night Marnie and Eléni had moved a table onto the tiled terrace and Eléni had set it beautifully. A crisp white cloth fell to the floor, and in its centre she'd placed orange blossoms and red geraniums to create an artful and fragrant arrangement of blooms.

Marnie was just pulling the scallops Mornay from the grill when he arrived. It was difficult to say who was more surprised. Nikos, by the sight of his wife in a black-and-white apron, kitchen glove on one hand, feet bare but for the red toenail polish that was strangely seductive, or Marnie, who took one look at her husband and felt such a surge of emotions that she had to prop her hip on the bench behind her for support.

He placed a black leather bag on the kitchen floor, then crossed his arms. 'I thought we discussed this,' he said finally.

So much for new beginnings.

'*You* discussed it, as I remember.' Her smile was overly saccharine. 'I listened while you told me that I shouldn't get comfortable in your home.'

Her acerbic remark had caught him unawares—that much was obvious.

Choosing not to tackle the bigger issue of her statement, he said thickly, 'I told you—I don't want you upsetting Eléni .'

'Yes, yes…' She moved to the fridge and pulled a bottle of ice-cold champagne from the door. She placed it in his hand and paused right in front of him. 'You also told me that I should save my energy for other wifely duties.'

He had. And he'd enjoyed, in some small part, seeing the way he'd shocked her. But having her say the words back to him switched everything around. A hint of shame whispered across his features.

'Eléni's very happy that you've married someone who enjoys cooking,' she said, with an exaggerated batting of her long, silky lashes. 'I think she finds me surprisingly traditional compared to your usual…*companions*.'

'You've spoken to her?' he said unnecessarily.

'Yes. So you don't need to worry that I've sent her off to cry into her pillows.'

He curled his fingers around the neck of the bottle and unfurled the foiled top, his eyes lingering on his wife's face. Her honey-brown hair was plaited and little tendrils had escaped, curling around her eyes. Her make-up was impeccable, and beneath the apron he could see that she was wearing a simple dress that he was growing impatient to remove.

'You have a smudge on your cheek,' he lied, lifting his thumb to his mouth to wet it before wiping it across her skin. He was rewarded with the sight of her eyes fluttering closed and her full lips parting as she exhaled softly. The same knot of desire that had sat in his gut all day was inside her, too, then.

'I've been busy,' she said softly, her eyes bouncing open and clashing with his. As if consciously slicing through the web that was thick around them, she stepped backwards. 'You open that—thank you.'

A grudging smile lifted half his mouth. 'Yes, Mrs Kyriazis.'

She turned away before he could see the way the name brought an answering smile to her own features.

He popped the top off the bottle, placed the cork on the bench. He reached for two glasses at the same time she did. Their hands connected and she stepped aside quickly. 'You do it. I'll get our starter.'

'Starter?' he murmured, watching as a pink like the sunset dusted her cheekbones.

'Uh-huh. I told you—I like to cook.'

That was new. 'Since when?'

She began to place the scallops in their fan-like shells on a plate, forming a spiral of sorts. 'Some time after we broke up—' she skidded over the words a little awkwardly

'—I discovered it as a hobby. It turns out I love cooking. I've always loved food.'

She reached for a spoon and ran it around the edge of a shell, coating it in the Mornay sauce. She lifted it to his lips and he widened his mouth to taste the sauce. It was as delicious as it smelled.

'Apparently you excel at it.'

'Thank you.' The compliment was a gift. A beautiful gift to cherish in the midst of the turbulent ocean they were stranded in. She lifted the plate and smiled. 'Shall we?'

He turned, two champagne flute stems trapped between the fingers of one hand, the bottle in his other. He began to retreat from the kitchen, but Marnie stalled him.

'Not the dining room,' she said over her shoulder, weaving through the kitchen towards the patio. It was then that Nikos saw that against the backdrop of the setting sun, and the evening sky that sparkled with tiny little diamonds of stardust, a table glowed with candlelight.

Emotions, warm and fierce, surged in his chest. '*You* did this?'

'Eléni helped,' she said honestly, nudging the door with her shoulder.

The night was blissfully warm. She placed the scallops on the table and then stretched behind her back for the ties of the apron.

'Allow me,' he said throatily, settling the drinks onto the table and reaching for her. His fingers worked deftly at the strings but, once they were untied, he kept his hands on her hips. He spun her in the circle of his arms so that he could stare down at her face. In the softness of dusk she was breathtakingly beautiful. But the fragility he sensed in her terrified him.

He wasn't prepared for Marnie's vulnerability. He had no protection against it.

He dropped his hands to his sides and moved to a chair instead. He pulled it from the table, waiting for her to settle herself in the seat. She pushed the apron over her head, not minding that it roughened her hair. She draped it over the timber back of the chair, keeping her eyes on the spectacular view as she sat down.

He glided the chair inwards a little way, his hands resting on her bare shoulders for a moment before he moved to the other side of the table.

At another time, or for another pair, the moment would have been singing with romance. But Marnie knew they didn't qualify for that. And yet the setting was so magical that for a moment she let herself forget the tension and the blackmail, the resentments and regrets.

'Do you remember when we had that picnic in Brighton?'

His eyes skimmed her face, tracing the features he'd stared at that night. It had been only a few weeks before he'd told her he wanted to marry her one day—before she'd told him that would never happen.

'Yes.' He pressed back in his chair. The past was a sharp course he didn't particularly like to contemplate. 'I remember.'

'The sun was a little like this,' she said, obviously not sensing his tone, or perhaps willfully ignoring it.

She watched the glow of the golden orb as its own weight seemed to catch up with it, making it impossible for day to remain any longer. As the sun dipped gratefully towards the sea the sky seemed to serenade it, whispering peach and purple against its outline.

'This is my favourite thing to watch,' she said softly, a self-conscious smile ghosting across her face as she returned her attention to the table.

'Why?'

She lifted a scallop and placed it on her plate, indicating that he should do likewise. But he was fully focussed on his bride.

'I guess I find it somehow reassuring,' she said with a small shrug of her slender shoulders. 'That no matter what happens in a day there'll always be this.'

He arched a brow, finding the sentiment both beautiful and depressing. 'I am more for mornings,' he said after a moment.

'I remember.' She grinned, trying hard to inject their evening with the normality she'd longed for that morning. 'You wake before the sun.'

'I do not need a lot of sleep.'

'Apparently.'

Her cheeks flushed pink as she remembered the previous night—the way he had commanded her body's full attention even when she had been exhausted. And she'd responded to his invitations willingly, rousing herself to join with him, needing him even from behind the veil of exhaustion.

He ate a scallop, though he wasn't particularly hungry. It was divine. A perfect combination of sweetness and salt. He didn't say anything, though, so Marnie continued to wonder if he'd enjoyed it or was simply being polite when he reached for another.

'How was your day?' she asked, after a moment of prickly silence had passed.

He regarded her for a long moment. 'I spoke with your father, if that is your concern.'

Her face slashed with hurt before she concealed it expertly. 'It wasn't,' she responded, shrugging as though he *hadn't* scratched her with the sharp blade of recrimination. 'I was simply making conversation.'

His eyes glowed with the strength of his feelings. Marnie pressed back in her chair, her own appetite waning. She thought of the fish she was baking in a salt crust. What a waste it would be if they couldn't even make it through a few scallops without breaking into war.

'Let us not pretend, Marnie, when there is no one here to benefit from the performance.'

CHAPTER SIX

SHE PLACED HER fork down carefully beside the plate, using the distraction to rally her rioting emotions. His mood and manner were on a knife's edge. She felt the shift in him and wanted to protest. She wanted to address it. But the implacable set of his features thwarted any thought of that.

'I'm not pretending,' she said instead, with a direct stare that cost her a great deal of effort.

'Of course you are.' He was bored now, or at least he seemed it.

'Really? Why? Because I asked about your day?'

His eyes narrowed. 'Because you act as though your primary concern in this marriage is not your father.'

Denying that assertion wasn't an option—at least it wasn't if she wanted to protect herself from seeming motivated by other more personal feelings. What would he say if she told him more than money had motivated her into marrying him? Would he run a mile? Or use her confused feelings to keep her exactly where he had her?

'Well, Nikos,' she said, impressed that she sounded almost condescending, 'given that you used my father's debts to blackmail me into this, are you really so surprised?'

'I made no claim of surprise,' he corrected. 'I intended to point out the futility of your charade.'

'Wow.' She blinked and lifted her champagne, drinking

several large gulps despite the pain of the bubbles erupting against her insides. 'That's spectacularly rude,' she said when she'd settled the glass back on the table.

'Perhaps.' He shrugged insouciantly. 'In any event, your father was both grateful and, I believe, resentful of my offer to help.'

She was startled, her enormous eyes flying to his face. 'You're not saying he turned you down?'

'He has agreed to take the bare minimum from me to stave off foreclosure. That will buy him another month at the most.' A frown crossed his features. 'He is a stubborn man.'

'Remind you of anyone?' she snapped tartly, biting into another scallop.

'I would not be so foolish as to turn away a lifeline if I were in his situation.'

'He's very proud,' she said silkily, and though she'd meant it to be a subtle insult to Nikos it was ridiculous. She'd realised as soon as she'd uttered the words. For there was no man on earth with more pride than Nikos. She'd damaged it six years earlier and he'd moved heaven and earth to make her pay now.

'To a fault.'

'Thank you for speaking to him,' she said quietly.

She meant it. Were it not for Nikos, her father would have no hope. At least he knew now that there was an option. An alternative to bleak bankruptcy and failure.

'It was our deal, remember?'

The deal. The damned deal! She wanted to tear her hair out! But why? One day after their wedding, did she *really* think anything would have shifted? Just because they'd slept together, and her body had begun to vibrate at a frequency that only he could answer, it didn't mean that it was the same for him.

'Nonetheless, you didn't have to do this. Any of it. You

could have left him to suffer and watched from the side-lines.'

He braced his elbows on the table, his eyes pinning her to the chair as though his fingers were curled around her shoulders. 'Where would the fun be in that?'

The air crackled and hummed with the intensity of his statement.

'You find this *fun*?'

His smile was pure sensual seduction. Like warmed chocolate being dripped over her flesh.

'Last night was certainly pleasurable.'

Memories seared her soul. She shifted a little in the chair as her insides slicked with pleasurable anticipation. 'I'm glad you think so,' she murmured, her heart racing like a butterfly trapped against a window.

His smile was pure arrogance. It said that he knew she thought so, too. 'You disagree?'

Damn it. The wedge between a rock and hard place was a little constricting. She dropped her gaze, unable and un-willing to duel with him in a battle she'd never win.

But Nikos wasn't going to let it go. 'You seemed to enjoy yourself…' he pushed, one hand flicking lazily across the tablecloth, trapping her fingers beneath his. He turned her palm skywards and began to trace an in-visible circle across the soft pad of her hand.

'Now who's acting?' Her question was breathy, infused with the hot air in her lungs.

'When it comes to my desire for you there is no neces-sity to lie.'

'Thank heavens for small mercies.' The statement was lacking sass; it fell flat. She cleared her throat and pulled her hand away. 'How much money?'

The change in conversation, and the removal of her hand, confused him momentarily. But not for long. Nikos hadn't built an empire from scratch by being slow on the uptake.

'Why does it matter? Do you want to make sure you haven't overpaid your end of our bargain?'

She made a sound of surprise and shook her head.

'You did offer your virginity. Perhaps you feel anything less than a hundred mill isn't quite fair on you.'

'How *dare* you?' Her voice quivered with the force of her hurt. 'How dare you equate what we did with an amount of money?'

He had gone too far. He realised that, but it was out of Nikos's character to apologise. Instead he came back to the original question, speaking as though he *hadn't* just virtually equated their marriage with prostitution.

'I have helped him enough for now,' he said, his words soft to placate the rage he'd breathed into her. 'He will not go broke, Marnie. I will not allow that to happen.'

She pulled her lower lip between her teeth, her feelings jumping awkwardly from one extreme to the other. Hurt was making her body sag, and her throat was thick with tears that she damned well would *not* let fall. But there was relief and gratitude, too. Because she *did* trust Nikos. Despite all this, all that he'd done, she believed that he would keep her father from destitution.

He lifted another scallop and ate it, then another, and Marnie watched, a frown unconsciously etched across her face.

'Are you going to have any more?' he prompted, reaching for the second-last.

She shook her head. 'I'm fine, thanks.'

He placed his fork down and stared at her. 'Your father has asked us to return to England for his birthday.'

Marnie nodded thoughtfully. 'He doesn't like to do much, but Mum generally twists his arm into a small party.'

His expression was guarded. 'Would you like to travel home again so soon?'

Home.

The word was one syllable that throbbed with an enormous weight of meaning. She reached for the last scallop, despite having just given up her claim to it. She needed to distract herself and to hide her face as she unpacked the impact that single word was having.

Home.

Other than here.

Home.

Not here. Not in *his* home.

She blinked and shook her head a tiny bit, pushing the thoughts away. 'I'd like to see them,' she said cautiously. 'But it *is* soon. I didn't really imagine that we'd go to England again yet.'

Her family complicated matters. What hope did Nikos and she have of forming any kind of relationship with her parents and his antipathy towards them in the foreground?

'You want to refuse?'

She toyed with her ring, turning it round her finger. 'I didn't say that.'

'No. You didn't say anything,' he drawled, the words lightly teasing.

But Marnie was not in the mood to be teased.

'God, Nikos, you're impossible.'

He laughed throatily, the sound doing something strange to her fractured nerves.

'I am honestly asking what you would like. It occurred to me that I would have more success persuading your father to be reasonable if we were to meet in person.'

The tears he'd brought to the surface were closer now, and she had to dig her nails into her palms to stop from weakening and letting her eyes become moist.

Out of habit, she hardened her expression, creating an

air of nonchalance when she tilted her face to his. 'You'd do that?'

His eyes glittered in his handsome face. 'You'd be content if I didn't?'

Damn it. She was being careless. Slowly she shook her head from side to side, her eyes not quite meeting his. 'You told me you'd sort it out. It's the only reason I married you, remember?'

'Good. Honesty is so much better than role-play.'

She cleared her throat and focussed her gaze on the view. What she'd just said hadn't been honesty, but she let it slide. 'Fine. We'll go back for a weekend. In a month.'

And in the back of her mind she really did hope that their difficulties might have been resolved by then. There had been a time when they were so comfortable together. Was it so unlikely to believe they might return to that footing?

She looked at the man opposite, her heart turning over in her chest.

So familiar.

So foreign.

She knew him intimately, and yet she didn't.

He was a stranger, and yet her husband.

The dichotomies kept flowing through her mind, thick and fast.

'You are staring, Mrs Kyriazis, in a way that makes me want to peel that dress from your body and claim you here and now.'

She started, her pulse shearing her skin. 'I was just thinking…' Her voice was thick with the desire he could so easily evoke. 'So much has happened in six years. You're my husband, and at one time I would have said I knew you better than anyone. But I don't know you at all now.'

'You know me,' he responded, standing up swiftly and reaching for her plate.

She watched as he cleared the table, her mind overflowing with questions.

'When we were together, you only had aspirations in finance. How did you do all this so fast?'

He sent her a look of impatience. 'When someone tells you that you will never amount to anything, that you are not worth a damn, it *is* rather motivating.'

Her father's words mortified her. 'He shouldn't have said that.'

'No.' His eyes glittered. 'But that is what you people are like. Do you *really* believe that the blood in your veins is of more value than mine simply because you can trace your lineage back thousands of years and I am not able to do so?'

'Don't do that.' She followed him into the kitchen. 'Don't tar me with the same brush.' A frown drew her brows together. 'I don't really understand why my dad spoke like that to you. He's not—'

'Of course he is,' Nikos interrupted. He tamped down on his temper with effort, stacking the plates neatly into the dishwasher.

He worked with a finesse that made her wonder if he did this simple domestic act often. Though incongruous, it made sense. Nikos hadn't been born with a silver spoon in his mouth. He'd grown up poor. He'd presumably shouldered his fair share of domestic duties for most of his life.

'Whatever you're about to say, make no mistake. He *is*.'

'Anyway…' She made an effort to salvage the situation. 'I understand why you might have felt you had to prove something. But *how* did you do this?'

His eyes skimmed her face. 'In the same way I won a scholarship to Eton and then Cambridge. I worked a thousand times harder than anyone else. I always have. I don't sleep much, *agape*, because I work.'

Admiration soared through her. 'I think you've done something very impressive,' she said quietly.

He propped himself against a bench. 'Your turn. Why did *you* do all this?' He gestured around the kitchen.

Because I missed you. Because I couldn't stop thinking about you.

'It's our honeymoon, isn't it?'

His lips lifted in a half-smile. 'If you say so.'

The rejection hurt, but she didn't show it. 'Why don't you sit down? I'll get the main course.'

He crossed the kitchen so that he stood right in front of her, without touching. Goose bumps littered her exposed flesh.

'I have a better idea.'

She lifted her eyes to his face slowly. Breathing was suddenly difficult. He overwhelmed every single sense in her body. 'Oh?'

'Let's have a break between courses.' His smile was tight. 'I do not usually eat so early.'

'Oh…'

He'd upset her. He squashed the urge to apologise. 'It is a…ritual I have. I swim as soon as I return from the office. I find it rids me of the day.' He reached down and linked his fingers. 'Join me.'

A command or a question?

An order or an invitation?

Whatever the case, she found herself nodding. 'Okay. I'll just go and get changed.'

His laugh was throaty. 'Why?'

Her eyes were wide. She watched as he began slowly to unbutton his shirt until the sides were separated. He pushed it off his arms, then stepped out of his trousers. In just his boxers, he reached over and lifted her hand to his lips.

His kiss breathed butterflies into her veins. She stifled a moan and then pulled at her hand. It was a necessary tool. She felt around for her zip, and when she couldn't immediately catch it he reached behind her and loosened it, sliding it slowly, seductively, teasingly down her spine.

She shivered as his fingers lingered, taunting the flesh at the small of her back. She lifted her gaze to his face again, searching for something there. Kindness? Affection? She saw only lust. Pure and simple.

It was better than nothing.

With a small exhalation she stepped backwards. 'I'll just need a minute.' She took another step backwards to underscore her resolve. 'I'll meet you in there.'

He shrugged indolently and strode across the tiles with that almost feral power that seemed to emanate from his frame. She watched him go, greedily waiting to see him dive into the water. His muscles rippled as he speared through the air then beneath its surface. She held her breath unconsciously until he stood at the other end. His dark hair was slicked to his head like an animal's pelt.

She moved quickly up the stairs and into their bedroom. The sight of her face that had confronted her after swimming earlier that day was hauntingly close to the surface. She didn't want to turn into a panda again. She lathered her hands with soap and washed at her face until every hint of make-up was removed, then changed into a swimsuit with a low-cut vee at the front and delicate beading in the fabric. It was elegant and inviting.

He was swimming laps when she emerged, his strong body pulling powerfully through the water, each bronzed arm worthy of its own sculpture. He was naked. His boxers had been discarded and she could see his whole body as he cut through the water.

She swallowed huskily, her eyes tracing his progress from where she stood at the edge of the pool. A warm breeze drifted past, lifting her hair. She tucked it behind her ears and approached the edge. He turned underwater, his stroke not breaking the surface.

With a smile, she dived in, pulling up beside him. Underwater, their faces were illuminated by the green lights embedded in the side of the pool. He turned to her. Their eyes locked and Marnie almost lost her rhythm, so fierce was the tumble of awareness that accosted her body.

But she quickly regained her focus, racing him to the end and touching the rounded edge of the pool just as he did. She laughed when they both lifted onto their feet, the thrill of adrenalin and the rush of endorphins pumping through her body.

He stared at her with a sense of confusion.

Her laugh.

That beautiful laugh.

It was as if she'd burst through the cracks in his memory, slowly infiltrating him with what she'd once meant to him.

It wasn't only the musical sound, it was her face. Wiped of make-up, radiating happiness, with a little bit of honey in her complexion from the day she'd spent outdoors.

He swallowed and turned to the view, his face unyielding in profile.

'I haven't swum like this in years,' she confided easily, blissfully unaware of the hurricane of feelings that was besieging him.

His smile lacked warmth. He pinned her with eyes that she couldn't read. A sense of loss wiped the smile from her own features and she spun away, kicking to the opposite side of the pool and propping herself against it. The coping was still warm from the day's heat, despite the lateness of the hour and the coldness of his look.

The sense that her husband—the man she'd married and had once loved—despised her, made her heart hurt in her chest. She turned slowly to see him walking through the water towards her, his gaze pinned to hers.

He was going to kiss her. The fine pulse at the base of her throat was hammering wildly in expectation, and yet every sensible thread of her mind was telling her to step backwards and talk to him.

What did it mean that she had such a small understanding of everything that made him tick except his desire for her?

'Nikos,' she said softly, her eyes silently imploring him to help her make sense of it all.

He caught her hips underwater, pulling her the final distance to meet him. Their bodies melded as one. She drew her lip between her teeth, ignoring the warning voice in her mind as she wrapped her arms around his neck. Her fingers teased the wet hair at his nape.

'I know.'

Her breath hitched in her throat. She wasn't alone. This maelstrom of need after six long years was as unsettling for him as it was her.

Good.

For now that would have to be enough.

His kiss was a claim. It was a seal of their union. She kissed him back fiercely, her tongue clashing with his, her body wrapping around his beneath the water. The feeling of his arousal between her legs, straining at the fabric of her swimsuit, with the warmth of the pool water surrounding them was almost too much to bear.

Impatience crested inside her, bubbling out of control.

She made a sound into his mouth as she pushed back a little, her fingers toying with the straps of her swimsuit. They were saturated, and stuck to her body like a second skin; it didn't help that her hands were unsteady.

He had no such difficulty.

With total confidence he slid the straps down her arms,

revealing her breasts. The dusk light bathed her, spreading gold and peach over her flesh. He continued to push the fabric away, and Marnie lifted her legs to make it easier.

Naked in the water with him, she had a blinding sense that she might actually die if they didn't make love. If something were to happen to change his mind she wasn't sure she could recover. Her desperation for him would have terrified her if she'd had any mental space left with which to process it.

He pulled her back towards him, settling her legs around his waist. His eyes showed strain as he paused, his hard cock nestled between her legs without yet invading her womanhood.

'You have not been sore today?'

She shook her head.

'You must tell me…'

Groaning, she repositioned herself, startling him by thrusting down on his length and taking him deep inside her core. Relief spread through her body, weakening and strengthening her in yet another contradictory sensation. He held her hips, his fingers digging into her soft flesh, his lips seeking hers. His tongue was harsh in her mouth, echoing the movements of his body as he made her completely his.

Her orgasm burst over her swiftly; there was no time to prepare.

The entire day had been a kind of torturous foreplay for Marnie. Memories of their night together had tormented her, driving her body to fever pitch, so that the tiniest things—such as the feeling of the apron as she'd wrapped it around her over-sensitised nipples—had almost driven her over the edge.

Nikos watched as she crested the wave, her face a thousand little nerve endings vibrating with pleasure. The answering swelling in his heart was not something he wished to acknowledge.

Telling himself it was simply relief that they'd found themselves to be sexually compatible, he pushed deeper into her, drifting his fingers lower to cup the neat softness of her buttocks. He dragged his lips down her throat, flicking his tongue against the pulse-point that was frantically trying to move blood through her body, then lower still to her breasts. They were lapped by the water, and he had to lift her a little to take one into his mouth. The second he did she cried out, tilting her wet head back into the water so that her hair, no longer braided, fell like a dark curtain.

He moved one hand to tangle in its lengths, holding her head there while he plundered her core in an insatiable rhythm.

His own control was slipping. Her muscles, so moist and tight, were squeezing him as her pleasure spiralled, and when he felt her tremble and knew she was about to crest the wave again he went with her, holding her close, mirroring her movements until they were both panting, drenched in sweat and pool water, satisfaction emanating from every pore.

Their coming together had been as intense as it had essential. But it was just a prelude to the slow exploration he had been distracted by thinking of all day. To the myriad ways he wanted to torment and delight her.

Satiated, Marnie slowly relaxed, her body reassuring her that nothing bad could eventuate when such uncontainable desire abounded.

It was only then that she remembered the fish in the oven. It would be burned to a crisp.

Well, if that was the only casualty of this desire then she could live with it.

In the small hours of the morning, their naked limbs tangled with crisp white sheets, bodies sheened in post-coital perspiration and satisfaction, sleep fogging around the edges of their tableau, Marnie shifted a little, tilting her head to observe her husband.

His eyes were shut, his breathing heavy.

'How can you call this a pretence?' she whispered—to herself more than anything.

Without opening his eyes, he said thickly, 'This is just great sex, Marnie. Do not confuse it with anything more substantive or you will be hurt.'

He rolled over, his broad, muscled back turned to her, his heart apparently closed.

CHAPTER SEVEN

A FORTNIGHT HAD passed and his words were still sharp in her brain, like shards of glass that made her weep blood whenever she ran the fingertip of her mind over them.

'This is just great sex... Do not confuse it with anything more substantive...'

Her coffee-coloured eyes were flecked with gold as they drifted over the view from the window. For her office she'd chosen a room far away from the pool, their bedroom and the kitchen—that was to say far from any of the rooms that distracted her with what Nikos and she had shared there.

It was a small room, but she didn't need a lot of space, and it afforded an outlook of the city, rather than the ocean. In the distance she could see the Acropolis, bathed in early-evening light, and the buildings of the city sprawled almost like a child's model.

Though she took solace and inspiration from the outlook, this was not why she'd chosen this particular spot from which to work. From her seat she could see the curve of Nikos's driveway. The second his car thrummed through the gates she knew. And then she had the maximum time to prepare herself for his arrival, to gather the facade she had perfected around her slender shoulders. A facade that was essential when faced with her husband.

They shared meals and polite conversation. They were

unstintingly civil. But there was a torrent of emotions swirling hatefully beneath all their appropriate conversations. Only when they came together at night did she find an outlet for her rampant emotions. Sex. Passionate, all-consuming sex that explained everything. She was addicted to him. To his body and to the way he made her feel.

Marnie clicked out of her spreadsheet, her mind half-absorbed with the call-list she had for the following day. How grateful she was to have her work! Were it not for the distraction of the behind-the-scenes fundraising she did for the Future Trust she might have exploded already in a scene reminiscent of Vesuvius.

She flicked a glance to the clock above the door. He was late, and nerves that had been stretched tight for two days—since he'd told her about this event—were at breaking point.

For the first time since marrying they were going *out*.

Strange how she hadn't even realised that she'd become a virtual recluse, spending her time almost exclusively within the confines of his home except for brief trips to the markets with Eléni.

Now it was time to meet the world. She was Mrs Kyriazis—billionaire's wife.

What a joke.

Their marriage was little more than revenge and sex, and yet tonight she would play the part of doting newlywed to perfection. If only to show him how little she cared.

She heard his car and rose quickly from her desk. It wasn't that she had intended to be secretive about her work, but Nikos never came into her office. As if that conversation on her first afternoon in Greece had flagged something in his mind and he had subsequently delineated her office as her own space. For all he knew she might be running some kind of international drug ring, she thought with a small smile as she pulled the door shut behind her.

Marnie rarely wore heels, but for the kind of evening Nikos had foreshadowed she knew they'd be a requirement. They did bolster her height nicely, and she felt the picture of elegance when she walked gracefully down the stairs.

She'd spent a long time styling her hair, and her make-up was a masterpiece. Anne Kenington might not have played Cubby House with her children, nor had she read them the books that a nanny had had more time for, but she had insisted both her daughters were drilled in the skills necessary to present themselves as Ladies.

When Marnie emerged into the foyer at the same moment that Nikos entered the house she waited with a small smile on her red lips for him to see her. Pleasant anticipation swirled through her as she waited for the light of attraction to bounce between them.

The second his eyes lifted to her she felt a bolt of something. Not desire. Not happiness. Something else. Something far darker.

His eyes undertook a slow and thorough inspection, but his expression showed only shock. Marnie held her breath as he stared at her, waiting, aching, needing. Wanting him to say something to explain the reaction.

'You look…' He wiped a hand across his eyes and shook his head.

'Yes?' She braved a smile, though her heart was plummeting to the floor.

'Nothing. It doesn't matter.'

He dropped his keys onto the side table and turned away. Only the ragged movement of his chest showed that he was still struggling with a dark tangle of emotions.

'I will be ready as soon as I can. Why do you not have a drink while you wait?'

A frown marred her features for the briefest of moments before she remembered. She didn't *do* that! She didn't betray how easily he could upset her.

'Fine,' she agreed, her smile ice-cold, her pulse hammering. 'Don't be long. You said it starts at eight.'

He didn't acknowledge her rejoinder. Marnie watched with consternation as he took the stairs two at a time, then she turned away and wove her way to the kitchen.

It was another stunning evening. The sun was almost completely out of sight, leaving inky streaks in the sky and a sprinkling of sparkling lights that heralded night's arrival. She flicked the kettle on to brew tea and then thought better of it. She had a feeling something stronger was called for.

She poured a glass of champagne and held it in both hands as she moved to the terrace. The pool was beautiful. The surface, undisturbed by their usual evening activity, had a stillness to it, and it reflected not only the evening sky and the glow of his house but Marnie's figure, too.

She stared down at the watery image of herself, allowing her earlier frown to tug her lips downwards now that she was alone. Why did he disapprove? Though she hated this sort of mix-and-mingle affair, she'd been to enough of them to know the drill. Her dress was the latest word in couture, her shoes were perfect—everything about her was just what people would expect the wife of Nikos Kyriazis to be.

She crouched down, careful to keep the hem of her dress out of the water, and ran her manicured fingertips through its surface, slashing her image so that only swirls of colour remained. Satisfied, she stood and turned towards the house, startled when she saw Nikos just inside the door.

He'd showered and changed into a formal tuxedo, and his dark hair was slicked back from his brow, showing the hauteur of his handsome features, the strength of his bone structure and the determination of his jaw.

A kaleidoscope of butterflies was swirling through her insides, filling her veins with flutters of anticipation. As she stepped closer a hint of his fragrance—that unmistakably masculine scent of spice and citrus—carried to her on the balmy breeze.

The tuxedo was jet-black and might as well have been stitched to his body; it fitted like a second skin, emphasising the breadth of his shoulders and neatness of his waist.

She waited half a beat, giving him an opportunity to redeem the situation. It shouldn't be hard. He simply needed to offer a smile, or compliment her appearance, or ask about her day. She wasn't fussy. Any of the small ways a husband might greet his wife would have sufficed.

But instead Nikos looked at his wristwatch. 'Ready?'

She compressed her lips, the spark of mutiny colouring her complexion for a minute. 'Do I *look* ready?' she asked tartly, swishing past him and clipping across the room.

In the kitchen, she took two big sips of her champagne and then placed the glass down on the marble counter a little more firmly than she'd intended, so that a loud noise cracked through the room.

'Yes,' he said finally, closing the distance between them.

He stared down at her, his eyes flicking across the inches of her face. She didn't back away from him; she didn't let him see that her heart was being shredded by his lack of kindness. With her shoulders squared she walked ahead of him, out of the house and into the warm night air.

He opened the passenger door of the Ferrari for her and Marnie took her seat, careful not to touch him as she slid into the luxurious interior. The moment he sat beside her she was aware of his every single breath and movement. Unconsciously, she felt herself swaying closer to the window on her side, her eyes trained steadfastly on the view beyond the vehicle as they cruised away from his home.

At the bottom of the drive he turned left. Though Marnie was still getting her bearings, she'd ventured to the markets with Eléni enough times to know that he'd turned the car away from the city.

He drove without speaking, and she was glad of that. She needed the time to regain her composure, though she didn't have long. It was only a short distance to their destination: the ocean—and an enormous boat that was sparkling with the power of the thousands of tiny golden fairy lights that zigzagged across its deck. It was moored just off the coast.

'The party's on a boat?' she murmured, shifting to face him.

His eyes stayed trained on the cruise ship. 'As you see.'

She swallowed and bit back on a tart rejoinder. She'd vowed not to argue with him. Even that would show how she'd come to care too greatly. 'Great,' she snapped with acidity. 'I love boats.'

He was out of the car and rounding the side. Marnie pushed the door open and stepped out before he could reach her. After all, she'd opened her own doors all her life; why did that have to change now?

The ramp that led from the shore to the boat looked to have been specially constructed for the event. Though sturdy, it was obviously temporary. They were the only ones on it—though that was hardly surprising given that they were arriving well after the party had started.

'What is this *for*?' she asked as they stepped onto the polished deck.

'My bank throws it every year.'

'*Your* bank?' she clarified, pausing and turning to face him.

'The bank I work with,' he said distractedly. 'I do not own it.'

'I see.'

But from the second they arrived it became blatantly obvious that Nikos enjoyed an almost god-like status with the high and mighty of the institution.

Drinks were brought, food offered and advice sought.

Much of the conversation was in Greek or Italian, which Marnie understood only passably. She stood beside him listening, catching what she could, but her frustration was growing.

What was going on with him? He was acting as though she'd just knifed the tyres of his car or sold the secrets of their marriage to a tabloid. He was furious with her—and for what possible reason? She had done everything right! The clothes she wore, the hair, the make-up—she had put so much effort into being exactly what he needed of her that night. She was the picture-perfect tycoon's wife. And yet that seemed to have angered him.

When the group of men Nikos was deep in conversation with paused for a moment Marnie squeezed his arm. The smile on her face was broad; only Nikos would be able to detect the dark emotions that powered it.

'Excuse me a moment,' she murmured, pulling her hand away from him.

He bent down and whispered in her ear. 'Do you need something?'

'Yes.' She flashed her eyes at him in frustration, then encompassed his companions in her smile, knowing he wouldn't argue in front of them. 'Excuse me.'

She felt his eyes on her as she walked away, and just knowing that he was watching made her walk as though she hadn't a care in the world. Her feet seemed to glide over the deck, despite the crowds that were thick on the ground.

It was a perfect night. Sultry even though it was late in the summer season, and clear. The breeze was warm and soft, providing comfort rather than chill. She wove her way to the edge of the ship, seeking space and solitude. The polite smile on her face and a faraway look in her eyes discouraged conversation, and when she put her back to the crowds and stared out at the view she was all but absenting herself from the festivities.

She stood like that for a long time, enjoying the privacy of her thoughts, until a hand on her shoulder caught her attention.

Expecting to see Nikos, she masked her features with an expression of bland uninterest and turned slowly.

But the man opposite her caused such a flurry of feeling inside of her that tears welled instantly in her eyes.

'Anderson!' She hugged Libby's fiancé, her mind grappling with the question of why he was there even as she acknowledged how thrilled she was to see him. 'Oh! What a surprise.'

'I was hoping you'd be here.' He grinned. 'Nik wasn't sure you'd want to come.'

A frown briefly flashed in her face as she remembered that these two men were still close friends. Anderson was the one who had told Nikos about her father's dire situation, after all.

'Congratulations on the wedding.' He kissed her cheek, then grabbed two glasses of champagne from a passing waiter. 'To happily-ever-after, huh?' He clinked his glass to hers, earning a smile from Marnie.

'Indeed.' She drank the champagne, watching the man who would have become her brother-in-law over the rim of her glass.

'I wish I had been able to come to the wedding,' he said, nudging his hip against the railing and effectively screening them from the other guests.

Marnie studied him thoughtfully. Did he know what a farce their marriage was? 'I would have liked that,' she said finally, earning a laugh from Anderson.

'You sure? You sound ambivalent.'

She laughed, too. 'Sorry. I'm just surprised to see you. I somehow forgot that you and Nikos were close.'

His smile was warm. 'He's my oldest friend.'

Her heart turned over in her chest. She changed the

subject. 'I haven't seen you in a long time. You've been staying away from our house?'

He grimaced. 'I've been meaning to visit. But…'

'But?' she prompted, a smile belying any accusation.

'You know…I feel bad sometimes. Your parents look at me and see only Libby.' His smile was thin. 'I expect you know exactly what *that's* like.'

She sipped her champagne again, and her voice was carefully wiped of feeling when she spoke. 'It's not the same. They look at me and see only my failings as compared to Libby.'

Anderson rubbed a hand over his chin. 'They're wrong to compare the two of you. There's too many differences for it to make sense.'

Colour flashed in Marnie's cheeks. 'Thanks,' she said, with a hint of sarcasm.

'I wasn't being offensive,' he clarified quickly. 'Libby used to laugh and say that you and she were chalk and cheese. But that you were her favourite of all the cheeses in the world.'

Marnie's smile was nostalgic. 'I used to tell her that *she* was cheese and I was chalk. Doesn't that make more sense? She was sweet and more-ish and fair, and I'm a little…thin and brittle.' Her laugh covered a lifetime of insecurity.

'Don't *do* that,' Anderson said with frustration. 'She wouldn't want you to do that. She wasn't vain and she wasn't self-interested and she adored you. I know Arthur and Anne have always made you feel wanting, but that's not a true reflection. You owe it to Libby not to perpetuate that silliness.'

Marnie bit back the comments that were filling her mind. It was all too easy to justify her sense of inferiority, but with Anderson she didn't want to argue. 'I'm glad to see you,' she said finally.

'And I'm thrilled you and Nikos worked everything out. I know he never got over you.'

Marnie's eyes flew to Anderson's, confusion obvious in her features. Was it possible that even Anderson didn't know the true reason for their hasty wedding?

'Don't look so surprised,' Anderson said, sipping his drink. 'He might have played the part of bachelor to perfection but it was always you, Marnie. You're why he did all this.'

She shook her head in silent rejection of the idea, but Anderson continued unchecked. 'One night, not long after you guys broke up, he had far too much of my father's Scotch and told me that he'd earn his fortune and then win you back.'

'I can't imagine Nikos saying that.' But her heart was soaking in the words, buoying itself up with the hope that perhaps he *did* love her; that he *had* missed her.

'Oh, he talked about you all night. How you would only ever be serious about a guy like me. A guy with land and a title. He was determined to prove himself to you before he came back and won you over.' He laughed. 'If you ask me, he went a little far. I mean…a million would have done, right?'

Her smile was lacking warmth. She focussed her gaze on the gentle undulations of the water beneath the boat, her mind absorbing this information. 'It was never about money,' she said gently.

'Oh, I know that. I told him that a thousand times. But he didn't get it.' Anderson drained his champagne. 'Until you see first-hand the uniquely messed-up way Arthur and Anne made you girls feel you can't really understand a thing about you. Right?'

Startled, she spun to face him. Her breath was burning in her lungs and she wasn't sure what to say.

'You think you're the only one who had them in your

head? Libby almost didn't agree to marry me because she knew how *happy* it would make them. She was so sick of living up to their expectations that she said she wanted desperately to do the *wrong* thing—just once.'

'I can't believe it,' Marnie whispered, squeezing her eyes shut as she thought of Libby. 'She was the golden girl, and I never thought that bothered her.'

'It was a big mantle to wear,' he said simply.

Marnie expelled a soft breath and looked away. The breeze drifted some of her hair loose and she absentmindedly reached for it, tucking it back in place. 'I miss her so much,' she said finally.

Anderson was quiet for so long that Marnie wasn't sure he'd even heard her, or that she'd said the words aloud. Then, finally, he nodded and his voice cracked. 'Me, too.'

She wrapped her arms around him spontaneously, knowing that he understood her grief. That even years after losing Libby he stood before her a man as bereft now as he had been then.

From a distance they looked like a couple, he thought. The perfect blue-blooded pair. She with her couture gown and her swan-like neck angled towards Anderson's cheek. Her manicured hand resting on his hip, her flawless arm around his back.

His wife was beautiful, but in this environment, surrounded by Europe's financial elite, she was showcased to perfection—because she was at home. She was completely comfortable, whereas he felt the prestige like a knife in his side.

'If I did not trust you with my life I would be jealous of this little scene.'

Nikos's accented voice sent shivers of sensual awareness down Marnie's spine. She lifted away from Anderson, her eyes suspiciously moist. It caught Nikos's attention instantly. He looked from his wife to his friend, a frown on his face and a chasm in his chest.

'You are upset?'

She rolled her eyes. 'No. This is my happy face.'

He sent her a warning look that was somewhat softened when he reached into his pocket and removed a cloth handkerchief. She took it with genuine surprise at the sweetness of the gesture, dabbing at the corners of her eyes so as not to ruin her eye make-up.

'We were just reminiscing,' Anderson said simply.

Though he was subdued, he appeared to have largely regained control of his emotions.

'Your father was asking for you,' Nikos said to his friend.

'Bertram is here?' Marnie asked, a smile shifting her lips as she thought of the elder statesman. It transformed her face in an expression of such delicate beauty that Nikos had to stifle a sharp intake of breath.

'Yeah.' Anderson extended a hand and shook Nikos's. 'But I suspect your groom just doesn't want me monopolising you any longer.'

He winked at Marnie, obviously intending to make a swift departure.

She put a hand on his forearm to forestall him. 'Are you in Greece much longer? Will you come for dinner?'

'I'd love that,' Anderson said honestly. 'But we fly out tomorrow.'

Marnie's smile was wistful. 'Another time?'

'Sure.' He leaned forward and kissed her cheek, then winked at Nikos.

Alone with her husband, and the hundreds of other partygoers, Marnie felt her air of relaxation disappear. She reached for the railing, gripping it until her knuckles turned white. 'Are you having a good time?' she asked stiffly, her eyes seeking a fixed point on which to focus.

'It is good business for me to be here,' he said, lifting his broad shoulders carelessly.

'I wouldn't have thought your business required this sort of schmoozing.'

'That is true,' he said simply. 'But I do not intend to grow complacent in light of my success.'

She nodded, adding that little soundbite to the dossier of information she'd been building on him: *Nikos: V 2.0.*

This Nikos was determined to prove himself to the world—or was Anderson right? Was it that he wanted to prove himself to *her*? To prove that he deserved her?

No, that couldn't be it.

Had it not been for Arthur's financial ruin, Nikos would never have reappeared in her life.

'He might have played the part of a bachelor to perfection...' Anderson had said, and it had been an enormous understatement. Nikos had dedicated himself to the single life with aplomb. She'd lost count of the number of women he'd been reputed to be dating. And even 'dating' was over-egging it somewhat.

The women never lasted long, but that didn't matter. Each of those women had shared a part of Nikos that Marnie had been denied—a part that she'd denied herself.

Her eyes narrowed as she turned to study her husband. He'd followed her gaze and his eyes were trained on the mainland, giving her a moment to drink in his autocratic profile, the swarthy complexion and beautiful cheekbones that might well have been slashed from stone.

'Do you see that light over there?'

She followed the direction he was pointing in, squinting into the distance. There was a small glow visible in the cliffs near the sea. 'The hut?' she asked.

'Yes. It *is* a hut.' His sneer was not aimed at her; it showed agreement. He pinned her with his gaze; it was hard like gravel. 'That is where I spent the first eight years of my life.'

'Oh!' She resettled her attention on him, curiosity swelling in her chest, for Nikos had never opened up about his childhood even when they'd been madly in love. 'Is it?' She strained to pick out any details, but it was too far away. 'What's it like? Is it part of a town?'

'A town? No. There were four huts when I was growing up.' He gripped the railing tight. 'Two rooms only.'

She didn't want to say anything that might cause him to stop speaking. 'Did you like it?'

'*Like* it?' He lifted his lips in a humourless smile. 'It was a very free childhood.'

'Oh?'

'My father had a trawler. He came out here every day.'

'Squid?'

He nodded. 'Scampi, too.'

'You said you lived there until you were eight. What happened?'

He tilted his head to face her, his expression derisive. 'There was a storm. He died.'

'Nikos!' Sympathy softened her expression, but she saw immediately how unwelcome it was.

He shifted a little, indicating his desire to end the conversation.

'I should have told you he'd be here,' Nikos said only a moment later, surprising her with the lightning-fast change in conversation.

For a moment she didn't comprehend who he was talking about.

'It did not occur to me that Anderson would upset you.'

She drew her brows together in confusion. 'He didn't.'

'The tears in your eyes would suggest otherwise.'

She opened her mouth in an expression of her bemusement. 'This from the man who seems to live to insult me?' The words escaped before she could catch them.

Nikos nodded slowly, as if accepting her charge even

as his words sought to contradict it. 'Hurting you... That is not intentional. It is not what I want.'

She blinked and spun away, turning her body to face the railing. 'I can believe that.' And that hurt so much more! Knowing he could inflict pain without even trying, without even being conscious of her feelings, simply demonstrated how little he thought of her feelings at all.

'Do we have to stay long?' she asked, doing her best to sound unconcerned when emotions were zipping through her.

'No. Let's go. *Now*.'

He trapped her hand in his much bigger palm and led her from the party. Several times people moved to grab his attention, but Nikos apparently had a one-track mind, and it involved getting them off the boat.

At his Ferrari, with the moon cresting high in the sky and the strains of the party muffled by distance, Nikos put his hands on her shoulders and spun her to face him. His eyes seemed to tunnel into the heart of her soul.

'What is it I have done that's insulted you?'

She knew she couldn't deny it; after all, she'd just laid the charge at his feet. She shook her head, yet the words wouldn't climb to her tongue.

'Tell me, *agape*...'

'Nothing. It's fine.' Her eyes didn't meet his.

'Liar!' He groaned, crushing his mouth to hers.

His hands lifted, pulling at the pins that kept her hair in its chignon until they had all dropped to the ground in near-silent protest. He dragged his fingers through her hair, pulling at it and levering her face away.

His eyes bored into hers. 'I was angry with you tonight. I was rude.'

A sob was filling her chest. She wouldn't give in to it. '*Why?* What in the world could you have had to be angry about?'

Was that really her voice? With the exception of a slight tremor, she sounded so cool and in command! How was that possible when her knees were shaking and her heart was pounding?

'This. *You.*' He stepped backwards, as if to shake himself out of the hurricane of feelings. He pulled the door open and stared at her.

Marnie stared back. She wasn't going to let this go just because he appeared to have decided the conversation was at an end.

'*What?*' she demanded, lifting a hand and splaying her fingers against his broad chest. 'What *about* me? What did I do?'

'Do?' His head snapped back as if in silent revulsion. 'You did nothing. You cannot help that this is who you are.'

Her heart was pounding so hard now that it was paining her. 'I don't understand,' she said, with a soft determination that almost completely hid her wounds.

'No? Allow me to clarify. You are Lady Marnie Kenington and you always will be. You are this dress. This party. This perfect face. You are cold and you are exquisitely untouchable. The girl I thought I loved all those years ago never existed, did she?'

CHAPTER EIGHT

FOR THE FIRST time since her arrival in Greece the early morning was drenched by storm. The sky was leaden with weighty clouds, the ocean a turbulent, raging gradient of steel. White caps frothed all the way to the horizon, and the trees that marked the shore arched in the distance, folded almost completely in half.

Marnie, her knees bent under her chin, her eyes focussed on the ravaged horizon, took a measure of consolation from the destruction. Her mind, numb from the exhausting activity of trying to join the dots of what had happened the night before, looked for some kind of comparison in the wasted outlook.

The storm was trashing everything, and yet in time—perhaps even later that day—the clouds would disperse, the sun would shine, and all would look as it once had. Better, perhaps, for the rain had a spectacular way of cleaning things up, didn't it?

Could the same be said for her and Nikos?

Were they in the midst of a storm that would one day clear? Argument by argument, would they wash away their hurts?

She shook her head sadly from side to side, the question that had plagued her at length tormenting her anew.

Why had he married her?

'You are Lady Marnie Kenington and you always will be. The girl I fell in love with all those years ago never existed, did she?'

Had she?

He was right. Marnie had changed so much since then. He seemed to attribute it to her upbringing, to her parents' snobbery. Wasn't it more likely that she'd simply grown up?

She glanced down at her manicured fingernails and the enormous diamond that sparkled on her ring finger.

They were husband and wife, but outside of that, they were strangers. A lump formed in her throat; futility hollowed out her core.

He hadn't come to bed last night. She'd showered and waited for him—hoping, knowing, that their being together would make sense of everything. That when they made love the truth of their hearts was most obvious.

But she had no experience in the matter. Was it as he said? Just great sex? Or was it love? Or memories of love, like fragments of a dream, too hard to catch now in the bright light of reality and daytime?

She scraped her chair back impatiently. The pool was dark today, too, reflecting the sorrow of the skies. Had it been a stormy day like this when Nikos had lost his father? When the ocean had swallowed him up, perhaps as retribution for the fish he'd stolen out of its belly?

He had been silent and brooding on the car trip home, and Marnie had been too absorbed by his statement to try to break through that mood, to get to the heart of what he had meant.

Perhaps this morning they could talk.

She moved towards the kitchen, the thought of a cup of tea offering unparalleled temptation. And froze when she saw him.

It was like a flashback to the morning after they'd first

arrived. Impeccably dressed in a high-end business suit, he had his head bent over the newspaper and a cup to his left, which she knew would be filled with that thick coffee he loved.

'Good morning,' she murmured, her voice croaky from disuse.

He flicked a gaze to her face, studying her for one heart-stopping moment before smiling tightly and returning his attention to the paper.

So that was how it was going to be.

Marnie squared her shoulders and tipped up her chin defiantly. 'Did you sleep well?' She walked to the bench, standing directly opposite him.

Without looking up, he responded, 'Fine. And you?'

It was a lie. He hadn't got more than ten minutes altogether.

'Not really,' she said honestly.

He turned the page of the newspaper. Did she imagine that it was with force and irritation? The admission had cost her. It was an offer of peace—an acceptance of their relationship, faults and all.

'Where did you sleep?' she pushed, determined to crack through the facade he'd erected.

'In a guest room.' Still he read the damned newspaper.

Marnie, trying her hardest to forge past the storm, reached down and put her hand over the article. 'Nikos, we need to talk.'

He expelled a sigh and glanced at his watch. 'Do we?'

'You know we do.' She lifted her hand and moved it to his, lacing his fingers with her own. 'This isn't right.'

He moved his hand so that he could lift his coffee cup and drink from it. 'Talk quickly. I have a meeting.'

Hurt lashed her as a whip. 'That's not fair,' she said, with soft steel to her voice. 'You can't keep doing that.'

'Doing what?'

'Making yourself unavailable as soon as things get tough.'

'I relish obstacles. I relish difficult opportunities. But I cannot see the point in discussing anything with you right now.'

'So what you said last night isn't important enough to talk about?'

'What *did* I say?' he asked softly, his eyes roaming her face.

'Don't be fatuous,' she snapped. 'You made it sound like we didn't love each other. Like we didn't know each other.'

His look was one of confusion. 'But we *don't*.'

Denial! The sharpness of it plunged into her heart.

'I meant back then…' She limped the conversation along even when she felt as if she was dying a little.

'I said that the girl I thought I loved never existed,' he said with a shrug. 'That girl would have stood up for what we were. Would have fought to be with me. But you were never that. Seeing you last night, in that dress, you looked so perfect.' Derision lined his face. 'You've become exactly what your parents wanted.'

'You keep *doing* that! You keep making me out to be some kind of construct of theirs.'

'*Aren't* you?'

'Aren't we all?' she challenged. '*You* are a product of your life just as I am of mine. But if you hate me so much why the hell did you insist I marry you? It *has* to be more than revenge against my father'

He closed the paper and drained his coffee cup before placing it neatly on the edge of the sink. The seconds ticked by loudly in the background.

'Why do you think?'

A thousand possibilities clouded her mind, some of them dangling hope and others promising despair. 'I don't know,' she said finally, warily, shaking her head.

'To prove that I could have you.'

She had to brace her hands on the edge of the bench for support.

Her face flashed with such a depth of hurt that Nikos instantly wanted to call the words back. To defuse the situation and make her smile again. To make her laugh in that beautiful, inimitable way she had.

Laughter was a long way from Marnie's mind, though. 'You're serious?' She pressed her lips together, her mind reeling. 'This was just ego? As a seventeen-year-old I rejected you, and you couldn't handle that, could you? And now you've bullied me into this marriage so—what? So you can make me feel like this? So you can berate me and humiliate me...'

He held up a hand to silence her. 'I told you last night—I do not mean to hurt you. I never did.'

'Yeah, *right*.' She swallowed, her throat moving convulsively as she attempted to breathe normally. 'It didn't occur to you that this whole idea would hurt me?'

A muscle jerked in his cheek. 'Are you having regrets?'

'How can I *not* be? You put me in an impossible situation.' She spun away from him, looking out at the storm. She was at a crossroads. She could tell him the truth—that it was impossible to be married to him knowing he would never love her. Or she could remember that she *had* married him. A thousand and one reasons had driven her to it, and they were all still there.

Worse, Marnie stared down the barrel of her future and imagined it without Nikos and she was instantly bereft. Even this shell of a relationship, knowing he would share only a small part of himself with her, was better than nothing.

She'd faced life without him and it had been a sort of half-life. She'd poured all her energy into her work, and she'd dated men that she'd known her parents would approve of, but she hadn't felt truly alive until she'd seen Nikos once more.

Was it better to feel alive and permanently in pain or to be alone and feel nothing?

She turned to face him slowly, her face unknowingly stoic. 'I didn't hope for much from you, Nikos, but I expected at least that you would respect me. And do you know why? Because of who *you* are. Last night you said that the girl you fell in love with never existed. Maybe you feel that—maybe you don't. I don't know. But I have no doubt that I knew *you*. Who you were then. I think I know who you are now, too. And the contempt you are meeting me with is completely unwarranted.'

Her eyes sparked as she spoke the declaration.

'You say you married me to prove that you could have me. Well, I only married *you* to save my father. Did you honestly expect me to do anything less?'

'Not at all.' His voice was gravelly. 'You are excellent at taking direction.'

She sucked in a breath at the cruel remark. 'My parents were right to tell me to break it off with you. Not because you had no money or family prestige, but because you're a jerk.'

It wasn't funny but he laughed—a short, sharp sound of disbelief.

'I'm serious,' she said stiffly. 'I *am* Lady Marnie Kenington. I am the same woman I've always been. You forced me into this marriage and now you're angry with me just for being who I am. *You're* the one who's trying to make me something I'm not.'

Her words were little shards of glass, all the more potent for she was right. He couldn't fault her behaviour as his wife. She'd done and been everything he'd required of her. She hadn't shifted the goalposts—he had.

The realisation only worsened his mood. How could he

explain to her that he never enjoyed being at events like the party they'd attended the night before? That he hated most of the people in attendance, despised their grandiose displays of wealth and their desire to outdo one another. That he hated that entire scene and she was the very epitome of it? That seeing her amongst her own people—people who'd been born to wealth and prestige—made him realise that they'd never see the world the same way?

'You make an excellent point. I knew what I was getting when I suggested this marriage.' He looked at his wife long and hard. She was a woman who projected an image of being cool and untouchable—except with him. A gnawing sense of frustration engulfed him. 'Now, I really *am* late.'

He stalked towards the door, then turned back to face her. She was staring straight ahead with such an attempt at strength and resolve that something inside him twisted painfully.

'Marnie…' *What?* What could he offer her? 'We can make this work. The way we are in bed—'

'Is just great sex,' she reminded him, hating the words even as she spoke them.

But it was more than that. In bed, in his arms, Marnie was as he wanted her to be. Genuine, overflowing with desire and feeling: a real flesh-and-blood woman. Not the fancy ice queen she showed the world.

'Yes. And many marriages are built on less.'

'Great.' She appeared calm and in control, but her strength was crumbling. 'Don't you have a meeting to go to?'

He walked out of the door with a heavy pain in his gut that stayed with him all day.

His mind was shot. He lost concentration, he sent emails to the wrong people, he inverted figures on his spreadsheets.

He gave up on work in the early afternoon.

When he arrived home the place was deserted. He wandered from room to room, pretending he wasn't looking for Marnie, until he heard her voice drifting from the small space she'd claimed as her office.

By silent but mutual agreement he didn't intrude on her there. She generally only utilised it when he was at work, anyway. But curiosity drove him towards the door now, and he lingered for a moment on the threshold.

'We're in stage three of some very promising trials. Yes…'

She paused, and he could imagine the way she'd have that little line between her brows that showed deep concentration.

'That's true. Human trials are still a way off. But every day brings us closer.' Another pause. 'You're a gem, Mrs Finley-Johns. That's really very generous. Thank you.'

Silence filled the room for long enough that Nikos presumed she'd hung up the phone. He pushed the door inwards silently.

Marnie—his wife—was sitting at her desk, her honeyed hair piled into a messy bun, her head bent over a page as she handwrote something. He watched her for a moment and then stepped into the room.

That feeling in his gut didn't dissipate. He'd thought seeing her might do it. That just the sight of her might make everything slide back into place. It didn't.

When she realised she was no longer alone and lifted her gaze to his face he waited impatiently for a smile to burst sunshine through the room and relax his chest. It didn't. If anything, she was impatient, lifting her eyes to the clock above the door.

'Nikos? Is everything okay?' She reached for her phone, rotating it in her hands.

'Why do you ask?'

'It's so early,' she said with a look of confusion. 'You're usually not home for hours.'

He felt as if the ground was slipping beneath him. 'My afternoon was freed up,' he said with a shrug. 'You wanted to speak this morning and I rushed you. I thought we could go out for dinner and talk properly.'

The suggestion had come out of nowhere but as soon as he'd issued the invitation he'd known it was right.

'We did speak this morning.'

Their conversation had chased its way through her mind all day. Like a maze, it had twists and turns, but no matter which path she chased down they all finished in a dead end of despair.

'Not properly.' The words were gruff. He dragged a hand through his hair. 'Let's have dinner and try to be civilised.'

She arched a brow, genuine surprise obvious. 'I'm working.' She bit down on her lip. 'And I don't think anything's served by going out, do you?'

She sounded prim, and inwardly she winced. *'You'll always be Lady Marnie Kenington...'*

He crossed his arms over his chest, staring down at her. Marnie felt the imbalance in their arrangement and fought an urge to stand, to right it. That would just be symbolic; the true imbalance would remain.

'What is it you are doing? For work?' His smile was an attempt to relax her. To elicit a similar reaction in her. It failed. 'Or is it still a secret?'

'It's not a secret.' She shook her head. 'It never has been. I do behind-the-scenes fundraising for a cancer charity. Specifically leukaemia research.'

It wasn't what he'd expected and that was obvious. He rubbed a hand over his stubbled chin, propping his hip against the doorframe. He was settling in. Marnie swallowed. Her insides were clenching with desire, her mind was sore from trying to figure out what the hell they were doing, and all she could think as she looked at him was how much she wanted him. To hell with everything else.

'Why behind the scenes?'

She blinked, passing her phone from one hand to the other. 'It's more my thing.'

'I would have thought your profile would garner donations…'

'My name does that, too.' She shrugged, placing the phone down on the desk and clasping her hands together in her lap. 'And my contacts.'

He took a step into the office, looking at the computer screen. It had a list of names with donations beside them, tracking various contributions for the last few years.

'You are apparently very effective at this,' he murmured, leaning forward and scrolling down the page.

His body framed hers, trapping her within the circle of his arms. She thought of telling him to stop looking, saying that her work was confidential. But why? Nikos Kyriazis was hardly likely to be indiscreet with the information, and most of her donors released details of their charitable contributions as a way of attracting good publicity.

'Thanks,' she said, allowing herself to extract a small kernel of pleasure from his praise. 'I suppose it's because I feel passionately about it.'

'Yes…' He straightened, but stayed where he was, so that his legs straddled hers. 'How come you have not asked *me* to donate?'

Her smile was a twist of her pink lips. 'You don't think you've donated enough to my cause already?'

That feeling in his gut intensified in a burst of pain. 'This is different.'

She shook her head. 'Not really.' She ran a fingernail over the hem of her skirt, drawing his attention to her smooth, tanned legs.

'Why don't we go for dinner and you can tell me about this? Your charity. Pretend I am a donor you want to win over.'

'But you're not,' she said with a shake of her head. 'And I don't want to ask you to put money into this.'

'It matters so much to you, though,' he pointed out logically. 'Surely you wouldn't turn me down?'

She shrugged, perfecting an air of impatient unconcern. 'If you want to donate, you can. That's your business.'

'Tell me more about it first.'

Marnie bit down on her lip, her eyes drifting to his face. The time she'd spent in an attempt to make sense of their situation had all been a waste, for here was yet another facet of Nikos Kyriazis that wholly renewed the riddle. His ability to set aside their contretemps and the harsh words he'd issued made her head spin.

She nodded finally, expelling a soft sigh. 'Fine. We'll talk at dinner.'

Nikos had dismissed enough people enough times in his life to know that he was being dismissed from her office. Feeling that somewhere in their conversation he'd scored a minor victory, he didn't push it.

CHAPTER NINE

In England, Marnie was used to being recognised. She hated the sensation but she'd come to expect it, so she had long ago given up the idea of eating in glamorous high-profile restaurants without expecting to be photographed and approached by all and sundry.

In Athens it was Nikos who drew the long, speculative glances. Nikos whose name opened doors and inspired attention and curiosity.

Marnie was actually enjoying being an outsider to the sense of celebrity. She'd never craved it, and watching him being fawned over by waitresses and even the manager at the exclusive Athens hot spot from the moment they arrived brought a small smile to her lips now.

He saw it immediately. Of their own volition his eyes dropped to the curve of her pink mouth and fire warmed her belly.

'Yes, Marnie?' he prompted, leaning forward so that a hint of his masculine fragrance teased her nostrils, making her gut clench with unmistakable desire. She tried to ignore it.

She crossed her legs beneath the table and shrugged. 'I was just thinking how nice it is that I'm unknown here.'

'Not unknown,' he said, with a small shake of his head.

'Well, *lesser* known,' she corrected. 'Less relevant. And you're…'

'Yes?' He broke off the query when a waitress appeared with a bottle of ice-cold champagne.

'Compliments of the owner.' She smiled at Nikos, her cleavage exposed as she leaned forward to pour some of the liquid into a long, tapered flute.

'Thank you,' he murmured dismissively. 'You were saying…?'

Marnie waited for the waitress to finish pouring. 'You're who everyone wants to see.' She grinned. 'I'm anonymous and you're hot property.'

His laugh surprised her. It was rich and warm, and reminded her of how long it had been since she'd heard the sound.

'Hot property?' He shook his head. 'I'm glad to hear you think so.'

'You know what I mean.' Colour bloomed in her cheeks. She focussed on the menu. 'What's good here? What do you recommend?'

'It is all excellent.' He shrugged.

She scanned the menu but she was far from hungry. Butterflies had taken up residence in her stomach and their beating wings made it impossible for her to imagine accommodating food into their kaleidoscope.

'What do you suggest?'

His eyes narrowed. 'I can order for you, if you'd like?'

'That won't be necessary.' She shut down his perfectly normal offer, knowing how dire it would be to keep conceding to him.

'As you wish.' He pushed the menu away, his mind apparently made up.

She continued to skim her eyes over the words on the page but they were puddles and blurs.

'How long have you done this work?'

She started, despite the fact his suggestion of dinner had been hung on a desire to learn more about the trust.

'About four years,' she said, reaching for the stem of her champagne flute simply for something to do.

'You didn't go to university?'

She shook her head. 'The timing wasn't right.'

A frown smudged his handsome face. 'In what way?'

Marnie pulled her lower lip between her teeth and Nikos surprised her by reaching over and abruptly swiping his thumb across her mouth, disturbing the gesture.

'Don't think.' He spoke commandingly, his words gravelled. 'You do this too often.'

Her expression was blank. 'I wasn't aware thinking was a crime.'

'It is when you are selecting which words to use to your husband. Just answer my questions directly.'

Marnie gaped, her mouth parted on an exhalation of surprise. 'That hardly seems fair.'

'Why was the timing not right?' He returned to his original question, impatient for an answer.

He was right. She *had* been prevaricating, unconsciously trying to select words that wouldn't apportion blame or imply resentment.

'I wasn't ready to leave home,' she said quietly.

But he understood what she hadn't been willing to say. 'You mean your parents didn't want you to go?' His disapproval was marked, despite the way he spoke quietly.

The waitress reappeared, her smile bright. Was it also inviting? Or was Marnie being paranoid?

She flicked her gaze back to the menu, intent on seeming not to notice the way the waitress lingered a little too close to Nikos as she spoke.

Nikos didn't appreciate the interruption, and his annoyance brought a childish kernel of pleasure to Marnie. She hesitated over ordering for far longer than was necessary, finally selecting scampi followed by chicken, having changed her mind several times.

Nikos glared at her and spoke in Greek, quickly dispensing with the waitress.

'They forbade you from attending university?'

She started, shaking her head softly so that her hair flew around her cheeks. 'Not at all.'

'You wanted to study law. You were passionate about it.'

'Not really.'

He ignored the rejoinder. After all, they'd spent a long time talking about their hopes and dreams. He had not misunderstood her desire to go into law. Nor did he doubt she would have achieved the requisite grades.

'But instead you stayed at home, living with your parents, working for a charity that revolves around your sister's illness,' he murmured, with a directness she hadn't expected.

'Do you think there's something wrong with that?'

'Yes.' He leaned forward and put his hand on hers. 'You are a person, too, Marnie. You are not simply Libby's sister. Nor your parents' daughter. You have your own life to live.'

She compressed her lips and pulled her hand down to her lap. 'You say that even after blackmailing me into this marriage?'

She sipped her champagne but it was too sweet. She didn't want it. She was definitely not in the mood to celebrate. She ran her finger around the rim, staring at the hypnotic, frantic movement of the bubbles as her mind spun over the situation they found themselves in.

'It's not as if I can't move on,' she said quietly, her eyes refusing to meet his. 'But without funds research into leukaemia is slow. It occurred to me that the people most likely to succeed at raising money are probably those who have every reason to passionately pursue it. In ten years—who knows? Maybe girls like Libby won't get sick.'

Finally, she forced herself to lance him with her eyes; they were softened by sorrow.

'It's idealistic, but…'

He surprised her by murmuring, 'Not at all. You are right. Progress does not always happen as you expect it to. Sometimes it is hard-fought, and other times it is overnight, as though a cascade of discoveries slides into place. But without funds neither is likely.'

She nodded, distracted enough by the subject matter to speak naturally. 'I thought I'd do it for a year. As a way of giving back to the trust that was so supportive to us. But it turns out I sort of have a knack for it.'

'I can imagine,' he said. 'Do you regret not studying law?'

It was on the tip of her tongue to deny it, but the truth came to her first. 'Yeah. Sometimes. But that would have been about helping people, too. I'm just helping different people now.'

He let the words sink in and shied away from the intrinsic guilt they evoked. After all, her propensity to help others was what had made it impossible for her to walk away from his marriage proposal.

'And staying at home instead of finding your own place…?'

Her smile was enigmatic. 'You know… Kenington Hall is enormous. I have my own wing. It's much like living on my own.'

'And your parents are your neighbours?' he murmured, his voice ringing with disbelief.

'Yes.' She nodded. 'But apparently I'm a pretty inattentive neighbour,' she said with regret. 'I had no idea about Dad's troubles.'

His desire to comfort her displeased him. 'I imagine he was adept at concealing the truth.'

'Not really.' She shook her head wistfully.

The waitress appeared with their starters, placing them on the table and then disappearing without a word. Marnie wondered if Nikos had commanded her to stop making conversation when he'd switched to speaking Greek earlier.

Nikos watched as Marnie lifted her fork and speared a single scampi. She put it down again almost instantly, and when she looked at him he felt a wave of guilt emanating from her.

'I should have seen the signs.'

'What signs?' he prompted.

'He's been stressed. Angry. He's just not himself.'

Nikos found it hard to find any genuine sympathy for the man, but he realised he didn't like seeing Marnie suffer. *At all.* 'Tell me something…'

She nodded, toying with her fork.

'After your father paid me off, were you angry with him?'

Marnie's eyes flashed with emotion. 'I didn't know about that, remember?'

He waved a hand dismissively through the air. 'Fine. After I left, were you angry with him? With your mother?'

'I…' She shuttered her eyes closed, her dark lashes fanning over her translucent cheek.

'Do not *think*!' He repeated his earlier directive and she grimaced.

'I was furious,' she said, so quietly he had to lean forward to catch the words. 'But they're my parents, and they'd been through so much.' She swallowed. 'My father threatened…' She closed her mouth on the threat she'd been about to repeat. 'My father was devastated by losing Libby.'

'And he threatened you?' Nikos prompted, with a smoothness that spoke of determination.

She thought about lying. But wasn't there so much water under the bridge now?

'They made me choose.'

The anticlimax brought about in him an intense sense

of disappointment. Right when he'd thought he might finally be going to understand just what had led to Marnie pushing him far, far away, she'd gone back to the old lines.

'I mean they *literally* told me they'd disown me if I didn't break it off with you,' she added with a look of grief on her beautiful features.

She was back in the past, her mind far from him in that moment.

'I didn't care when they said they'd disinherit me.' She looked at him—and through him. 'Money meant nothing to me. But they were my link to Libby, and they said they wouldn't have me in their lives so long as I was with you. That I would never be allowed to return to Kenington Hall.' Marnie's voice cracked. 'The house was—is—all I have left of her...'

Marnie woke with a start as the plane pitched a little in one direction. She'd dozed off, despite the fact their flight had been a morning one. She stifled a yawn with the back of her hand, her groggy eyes drifting to her husband's bent head.

He was working.

A smile flicked to her lips with ease, though her stomach churned with a mix of anxiety and an emotion that was so much more confusing.

She didn't have time to attempt to understand it before the plane shuddered and Marnie's panic overtook everything. She dug her fingernails into the armrests, her expression showing distress.

Nikos, attuned to her every move, looked up instantly. 'There is thick cloud-cover over London, that's all.'

She nodded, but her childhood fear of flying was ricocheting through her. Marnie stared out of the window, trying to distract herself with thoughts of her father's birthday weekend—anything to curtail the clear picture she had in her mind of the aeroplane spearing nose-first towards the earth.

Their trip had come round quickly—for Marnie, almost too quickly.

After that one night in Athens when they'd shared dinner she felt as if a new understanding had settled between her and her husband and she wanted to hold on to that, to strengthen the understanding that was building between them. Would a trip back to her parents' unsettle the bridge they'd been building?

They were not a normal couple.

There was no shared love between them—at least not on Nikos's part. Perhaps not on Marnie's part either.

She had spent a great deal of her energy trying to decipher and separate her feelings of lust from love; her feelings of past love from present infatuation. Some days she convinced herself that she'd fallen in love with only the *idea* of Nikos—an idea that bore only a passing resemblance to the ruthless, determined businessman he'd become.

But then he would do something sweet—like bringing her tea in bed when she'd slept late, or calling in the middle of the day to remind her of something small they'd discussed the night before—and her heart would flutter and her soul would know she loved him. Not in a sensible, rational way, but in the way that love sometimes bloomed even when it was not watered or fed.

They barely argued. By tacit agreement each tried to respect the other's limitations. Marnie accepted the dark streak that ran through Nikos—the side of him that was so hell-bent on making her father see how wrong he was to have passed Nikos off as a failure that he'd blackmailed her into marriage. If she thought about it too much it made her queasy, so she pushed it to the recesses of her mind and clung to a sort of blind hope. Maybe one day he wouldn't feel that aching resentment so forcefully?

Their truce was underpinned by a sex life that made her toes curl. He had been right about that. Even if it was all they had to go on it would make their marriage worth staying in. Wouldn't it?

But uncertainty lurked just beyond her acceptance. For they had travelled stormy waters, and weren't there always eyes in storms? The calm that gave a moment's respite before the intensity of the cyclone returned with twice its strength?

Was she in the eye of a storm?

Or was this a lasting peace?

Only time would tell, and Marnie had a lifetime to wait and see.

CHAPTER TEN

THE APPLE WAS as sweetly sun-warmed as those she remembered from childhood. Despite the fact the day was cool, the morning had offered just enough heat to darken the flesh of this one more than the others.

Though it wasn't yet midday, she was tired. They'd been travelling since dawn and the return to Kenington with Nikos by her side had brought with it a sledge-load of emotions.

Juice dribbled down one side of her mouth and she lifted a finger to catch it.

Nikos watched, transfixed.

'I used to love coming down here to the apple orchard...'

'I remember.'

Memories. They were his problem. They were thick in the air around them. Memories of how it had felt then. When he'd been young and in love. He would have plucked a matching apple from another branch and enjoyed its fruity flesh alongside Marnie.

She stopped walking and turned around, her back to the heavily adorned fruit trees. 'I always think this is the best aspect of the house.' She lifted her free hand and framed the building between her forefinger and thumb. Her smile was born of whimsy. 'Until I go to the rose garden or Libby's garden. Then I think *that* view is preferable.'

She crunched into the apple once more.

'Perhaps it is the same from all viewpoints,' he suggested, with a hint of cynicism that was out of place and sounded, even to his own ears, forced.

'Maybe.' She shrugged and began to walk back towards the house.

He resisted the urge to ask her to stay with him where they were a little longer.

'Thank you for coming with me this weekend.'

His laugh was short. 'I presumed my attendance wasn't optional.'

She lifted her face to his. 'I would think almost *everything* is optional for you.'

His smile was without humour—a relic of his twisted laugh. 'Not this.'

She didn't pretend to misunderstand. 'When are you seeing him?'

'We're meeting after lunch.'

Marnie stopped walking, reaching for Nikos's hand. Her fingers curled around his as though they belonged. Familiarity and comfort knotted through her, momentarily putting aside the nausea and anxiety that had besieged her since they'd arrived in London.

'What is it, *agape*?'

A husky question. A promise, too, laced with so many emotions she couldn't translate.

'You know how stubborn he is?'

Nikos's lips curled. 'Yes.'

'I just don't know if he'll let you help. And I'm… I'm scared.'

His eyes held hers, probing her, trying to read her soul. 'Tell me something, Marnie. Why do you care?'

She started, scanning his face. But Nikos wasn't backing off. In fact, he moved closer, welding his body to hers, linking his arms behind her back. His nearness was seductive and distracting.

'Besides the fact he's my father?'

'Blood isn't everything. Your parents don't seem too concerned with your happiness. You're not close to them.'

'Of course I am,' she said with a shake of her head.

He laughed, dismissing her assertion easily. 'You don't speak to them. You don't speak *of* them—except with a sense of obligation and guilt because you survived and Libby died.'

She was startled at his perceptiveness.

'You married a man who saw you only as a means of revenge in order to stave off the financial fate that they deserve.'

'They're my *parents*,' she mumbled, her eyes flicking closed. The pain of his words was washing through her. 'And I'm very grateful to you.'

'Grateful?' He stepped backwards, shaking his head. '*Thee mou.* You offer me *gratitude*? I tell you I see you as a means of revenge and you say thank you?'

She frowned. 'You know what I mean.'

'No, I don't. You have been pushed around by your parents, and by me, and yet you seem to treat us all with civility and thankfulness. I cannot comprehend this.'

She swallowed. 'Do you need to?'

He shook his head. 'No.' He lifted a hand to her cheek and stroked it. 'And I suppose the same could be said for you.'

She pressed a hand to his chest, perhaps intending to put some distance between them, but the warmth of him, the beating of his heart, was mesmerising.

'Do you really believe our marriage comes down to revenge and sex?'

'Our marriage—' He began to speak, the words thick with meaning. He stared into her eyes; he was drowning in them. They were the depths to her soul; the truth to her questions. They mirrored his past, his heart and all his hopes.

They were beautiful eyes. How could people mistake her for being cold-hearted? In her eyes there was always a twisting of emotion and thought, of kindness and concern. Yet he had missed it. He had believed her unfeeling and incapable of true emotion at one point. He'd clung to that; he'd enjoyed believing it of her.

'Yes?'

It was a husk. An invitation for him to say something that would smooth away the pain of their predicament. A contradiction of the fact that he had bought her out of a need to avenge past wrongs.

But they were wrongs he'd carried with him for a long time. Was he willing to let them go? And, if so, what did that mean?

'Marnie?'

The voice was shrill and imperious, cutting across the lawn and breaking through the growing understanding that had been forming between them. He was unwilling to close their conversation, but a cloud instantly seemed to spread across Marnie and she stepped back.

The woman who had pulled a sweet apple from a frothy tree and crunched into it hungrily was gone. Lady Heiress was his companion now—only her eyes showed that Marnie was still in there.

'It doesn't matter,' she said quietly, shifting her gaze to the manor house in the background. 'I'm glad you're going to help him. Only be gentle, Nikos. And…' She turned to face him, hurrying now as Anne Kenington approached them. 'I know you said *you* would decide if you wanted to tell him the truth about our arrangement but…'

It seemed like an age ago that they'd had that conversation, but it had only been a month! Something strange lodged in her mind—a recollection she couldn't quite grab so she pushed it aside.

'But could you not? Not this weekend? I know you hate him, and that it's tempting to throw it in his face. But not now. Please?'

He stared at her without speaking and Marnie continued anxiously.

'I don't think I could forgive that. It would be… It really would be the end of what we used to mean to one another.'

Nikos was perplexed—and something else. Something he couldn't analyse or comprehend. So he spoke honestly. 'I have no intention of telling your father you married me to clear his debts.'

'Don't say that!'

She was visibly stricken, but Anne was almost upon them. Like a consummate professional Marnie blinked and slid her mask into place.

It annoyed him, and he wanted to prise it off again—just for a moment. He was sick and tired of masks and pretence.

'It's the truth,' he replied softly, clinging to that fact for her sake as much as his own.

Did he want her to contradict him? Did he want her to redefine their marriage? How could he expect that of her? A challenge? A gauntlet? One he knew she'd never answer.

'Isn't it?'

Their conversation had left Nikos in a foul mood. The lack of resolution, the constant chasing one another in circles, had given him the feeling that as soon as he began to comprehend a facet of his wife she morphed into something else and slipped out of his grip and downstream from him completely.

Worse was the sense that he was losing his own convictions in the face of hers. To lose one's sister would be hard enough, but to have your parents threaten to cut you completely from their life and support... Even Marnie, who had always seemed to have certainty and strength to her, must have been terrified of what that would mean.

How *dared* they? How had they dared to speak to their own child with such cold disregard?

It was not the ideal mind-set to bring to his meeting with Arthur Kenington. Nor was it the ideal backdrop. This study of Arthur's was familiar, yet different. Since they'd stood here six years earlier many changes had taken place—not least between the two men.

The walls were filled with a collection of books, impressive volumes that had never been thumbed—perhaps carefully selected by an interior designer who had chosen the titles because they would add *gravitas* to a man who was otherwise lacking in it—there was an elegant liquor tray that looked to be well-used, and a family photograph that was framed above Arthur's desk.

Arthur and Anne had barely aged, though Libby and Marnie looked much younger, so the picture must have been taken at least a decade earlier.

Arthur caught Nikos's gaze and grimaced. 'Our last family photo. We used to get them done every year until... we lost her.' He coughed, his slight paunch wobbling a little with the involuntary spasm. 'It didn't make much sense after that.'

Nikos didn't respond. Marnie and Libby stood at the foreground of the photo, Libby's arm wrapped around her sister's shoulders. There was an air of genuine affection between the girls: a sign of true camaraderie. Perhaps it had developed as a result of this environment?

'She was such an angel,' Arthur continued, perhaps misunderstanding Nikos's interest. 'Not a girl in the world like her.'

Nikos felt a possessive protective instinct flash in his gut. Yes, Libby had been lovely. And beautiful in a way that was ordinary and common. Unlike Marnie, with her steely, watchful gaze and determined little chin. Her reserve that made it difficult for her to speak to people unless she really, truly admired them.

'We need to discuss your business,' Nikos said sharply, not wishing to wander down Arthur's Libby-paved Memory Lane a moment longer. 'My information on your situation has me...concerned.'

'And what information is that?'

Nikos leaned forward, bracing his elbows on his thighs. 'It is no secret. You are out of immediate danger, but that is only temporary.'

'I don't believe that.'

'Then you are a fool.' Nikos spoke sharply.

Six years had passed since their last private conversation, and in that time Nikos had become used to having the world obey him. Deference generally met his commands—not dithering indecision.

'Do you want to lose it all, Arthur?'

'Of course I don't. But it won't come to that. Mark my words, there'll be—'

'Nothing.' Nikos eased back in his chair. 'You are overcommitted. There are no more assets left to shore your interests up and the market continues to fluctuate wildly. I am your only chance.'

The silence sparked between them. It was electrified by resentment.

'You're enjoying this, aren't you?'

Nikos didn't pretend to misunderstand; his smile was thin and unknowingly filled with disparagement. 'How I feel isn't relevant,' he said finally.

Strangely, he wasn't enjoying it. He had spent a long time imagining a situation like this. How good it would feel to throw his own success in Arthur Kenington's face. A man who had told him he would never amount to anything! He'd fantasised about it, and he'd done everything he could—even sacrificing his conscience—to achieve this moment.

And he felt nothing. Except, perhaps, a pervasive pity for this man who had let vanity and arrogance get in the way of financial security. His voice was softer when he spoke again, conciliatory.

'You cannot lose your business. Nor this house. It would devastate Marnie.'

'Marnie?' A scoff of surprise. 'She'd recover. This place never meant to her what it did to Libby.'

Nikos's fingers flexed into a fist on his lap, but he kept his face impassive. How was it possible that her own father understood her so little? Did he not see what she didn't say? Didn't he understand that her reticence to express emotions didn't mean that she lacked them?

'It is for Marnie's sake that I offer my assistance, so do not disdain her feelings.'

The statement held a barely contained warning. Nikos, though, knew he had no option *but* to help. It was a promise he had made to Marnie and he would never break it.

Arthur dragged a hand through his hair, his eyes skidding about the room. 'There has to be a way…'

'Yes. There is. *I'm* it. You know I have the money. A single phone call would remove this worry from your life.'

'You have the money?' Arthur spat, his eyes glistening with dark rage. '*You.* A boy I all but dismissed as—' He had the wisdom to cut the sentence off.

'Yes?' Nikos demanded through bared teeth.

'Worthless.' Arthur spat the word with satisfaction.

Nikos stood, his powerful stride taking him to the window. He looked down on Libby's garden and imagined Marnie there. His will strengthened. The papers he'd had couriered to him that morning were heavy in his pocket, begging for attention.

'You were wrong.' He turned, his eyes pinning Arthur where he sat. 'Do you want my help or not?'

A long silence clouded them. Nikos studied his opponent—there was no mistaking the adversarial nature of their relationship in that moment. With no one else to witness their interaction both men had dropped their masks of civility.

'I offer it to you with only one condition.'

Arthur snorted. 'I knew it was too good to be true.'

'Perhaps.' Nikos nodded, knowing for certain now the only way he could make sure Marnie was well-looked-after for the rest of her life. 'But it is your only chance to salvage something of your pride, so I suggest you listen.'

'The gloves are off, eh?' Arthur snapped, but there was weariness in his defiance.

'If the gloves were off you would know about it,' Nikos contradicted. 'The terms of my helping you are to stay between us. Marnie need never know what we have discussed here. Understood?'

Was it any wonder that, hours later, surrounded by formally dressed party guests, Arthur Kenington stayed as far from Nikos as possible? His concessions that afternoon had been hard-fought and potentially confidence-destroying. Evidently he found the idea of celebrating his birthday with his son-in-law impossible to contemplate.

Nikos didn't mind. In fact he barely noticed. Making Arthur eat crow had offered him no satisfaction, and yet he'd thought about the moment for years. How odd that once he'd had the chance to make the man beg for help he'd skated over it and provided assistance on a silver platter instead.

He considered the matter with Arthur closed. He didn't intend to think of it again save for one salient point that would require delicate handling. Would Marnie be angry when she discovered the exact nature of his help? Would she resent what he'd done?

His entire focus shifted to her. He watched her speaking to her parents' friends with the effortless grace that had first captivated his attention. Holding a glass of Scotch cradled in the palm of his hand, he felt the full force of that long-ago afternoon swarm through him.

He had come to Kenington Hall reluctantly. Spending time with Anderson and Libby had tended to leave him feeling like a third wheel, and yet Anderson had been so welcoming to him. He had been the one guy at school who *hadn't* seen Nikos as an outsider, and Nikos had repaid his friendship with unswerving loyalty. So when Anderson had asked Nikos to tag along he'd put aside his own reticence and travelled to the estate of one of England's noble families.

And he'd met Marnie.

She'd been seventeen and utterly breathtaking.

'Don't go near the horses. They're in a foul mood today!'

She had laughed as she'd torn past him, her long hair flowing behind her, the horse moving too quickly to catch more than a passing glimpse. Yet she'd reminded him of a sort of young Boadicea. Beautiful and strong, striking and confident, full of life and vitality.

Had he loved her from that moment? He'd certainly been fascinated.

'Hi.'

Her voice came to him now as if from a long way away. He lifted his head, capturing her in his gaze. But that moment was still around him and before he could question the wisdom of it he smiled at her as though they were back in that time, just Nikos and Marnie, without all the subsequent heartbreak.

She felt the purity of his look and it rang through her,

but she'd been worrying all afternoon and the habit was hard to break. 'Did you speak to him?'

He nodded, his stubborn smile still on his features.

Her hair had caught the sunshine as she'd gone past him that day. It had been like gold. He reached for it now and flicked the ends, bringing his body close to hers. She smelled good. Like apples and desire.

'And...?' Her eyes skimmed his, but her breath was coming fast and hard, making her breasts lift and fall.

'And what?' he prompted, wrapping his arms around her waist.

The band was playing a slow jazz song, the singer crooning gently into the elegant space. The formal dining room was large, and it had been converted into a ballroom for the purpose of tonight. Enormous flower arrangements punctuated the walls at regular intervals.

'Did you...?' She looked around, conscious of their surroundings.

'Yes?' he drawled, though he knew where she was going.

'Did you fix it?'

'Well, I couldn't transfer a hundred million pounds to your father in one afternoon,' he murmured sardonically, 'but, yes, *agape*. He has agreed to accept my help.'

She let out a whoosh of relief and he studied her features thoughtfully.

'You thought he might refuse? Even now?'

She shrugged, her shoulders slim and pale. 'I don't know. Like I said, he's stubborn.'

'You don't need to worry about it any more,' he said gently.

'I know.' She smiled up at him. 'Am I allowed to thank you now?'

'No.' He drew her closer, so that she could feel the strength of his body.

'Why not?'

'My helping him was entirely self-serving. You don't owe me thanks.'

She rested her cheek against his chest, listening to the beating of his strong heart. 'Was he grateful?' she asked instead, changing tack slightly.

His laugh was quiet but she felt it rumble through him.

'He was incensed.'

She grimaced. 'It wouldn't have been easy for him to face you, knowing what a mess his interests are in.'

'No,' Nikos conceded, without feeling the need to point out that Arthur only had himself to blame.

'I don't care.' She looked up at him. 'I'm going to thank you, anyway. How can I not?'

He stared down at her familiar face and the past blurred with the present. 'Fine. Then I can tell you how I wish you to express your gratitude.'

'Yes?' she murmured, her stomach swirling.

'For this night let's not speak about your family. Nor our past. We have spent a month retracing it and I wonder if we'll ever understand one another. Tonight I just want to dance with my wife. To kiss her. To feel her body. To be here with her and not think about the reasons we married. Deal?'

Hope blew open inside her. Surely that spoke of wanting a fresh start—of believing they were worthy of one. She looked at him for a long moment and knew exactly what it was that danced with hope.

Love.

Love for *him*.

Despite everything he'd done to get her into his life, she felt fierce love burst through her. It was not born of gratitude. Nor circumstances. It was the same love she'd always felt for him, only stronger—because it had been scorched by life, loss and disappointment and still it was there.

She stood up on tiptoe and pressed her lips lightly to his. 'Deal.'

The next song was another indistinct jazz tune. The singer's voice was low and husky and they danced slowly, in the middle of the crowd but aware only of each other. Marnie breathed in time with him, her eyes whispering shut, every fibre of her being in sync with her husband. So that when he stopped dancing and dropped his arms to his sides, capturing one of her hands in the process, and began to move towards the large glass doors, Marnie went with him without question.

'Do you know what I was thinking about today?' he asked as they emerged to see the moon casting a silver string from the inky sky above.

'Other than the significant hit your finances are about to take?' she offered with a teasing smile.

'Other than that.' He guided her along the terrace towards a small courtyard he'd seen earlier that day.

'What?'

'I was remembering the first time I met you.'

Marnie's heart was thunder; Nikos was lightning.

'Yes...?' Her voice was a husk.

He moved towards a balustrade, reclining against it with an expression that Marnie couldn't fathom.

'Being back here with you makes it feel like yesterday.'

And yet it wasn't. It was far in the past, with no way of recapturing that time. They could only exist in the moment. What they were now had to sustain them. The past would never be enough.

'I thought we weren't going to talk about our history,' she said with an uncertain smile.

'You're right.'

Marnie closed the distance between them as though a magnetic field was drawing her to him. She stood in front of him, the moon dancing across her face, a small smile on her lips.

'So let's talk about now.' She dared herself to be brave. To look at him with all her hope and want. 'Do you still think that we're just about sex?'

'And revenge,' he murmured, but an answering smile was playing about his lips and it surged her sense of hope higher.

'Of course.' She copied his expression, her look droll. 'Well, if it's meaningless sex you're after, that's fine by me.'

His laugh was warm butter on her frazzled nerves. 'I'm glad to hear it, Mrs Kyriazis.'

His fingers traced the bare skin of her arms and she shivered involuntarily. Anticipation trembled inside her. He caught her hand in his and together they walked. Was he leading her? Or the other way around? Marnie couldn't have said.

They went to the room that had been hers as a child. In the distance, the sounds of merriment could be heard. Wine glasses chinking, music, conversation. But it was all far away from where they were. Their world was their own, their breathing and needs the only noise.

She slipped into the room ahead of him, turning around in time to see him click the door shut and press the ancient lock down. His hands were lifting to his tie, loosening it in one movement so that it hung around his neck, a stunning black contrast to the sharp whiteness of his shirt.

Marnie reached for the zip on her dress, tucked under her arm, but a simple shake of Nikos's head stilled her.

'Let me,' he murmured, stalking towards her with a look she couldn't quite understand.

His face was set in a mask of *something*, and that something made her heart hammer in her chest.

'Let me,' he repeated, though she'd offered no opposition. Was he asking for something else? The air felt heavy with unuttered words, but perhaps they were all inside her.

She swallowed, the fragile column of her neck shifting with the movement. His fingers at her side were gentle, pulling at the zip so that she felt the slow whisper of cool air against her flesh. Goose bumps rioted across her and she drew in a sharp breath as he lowered the dress with a reverence she hadn't imagined possible. Standing before him in just a flimsy pair of knickers and heels, she was trembling—almost as though they were about to make love for the first time.

It was ridiculous. She forced a laugh to break the mood; it didn't work.

'Something amusing?' he queried, sliding his hands beneath the elastic of her underpants and cupping her rear.

It jolted her into a state of hyperawareness. She shook her head but his lips were on hers, stalling any further movement.

It was a slow kiss—a kiss that deepened as his hands roamed her body, a kiss he didn't break even as he removed his hands to strip his own clothes away. He stepped out of his shoes, guiding Marnie towards the bed, all small movements, urgent movements, designed to bring them together as quickly as possible.

They'd kissed in her room before, but they had been different people then. He full of hope and certainty and she so willing to surrender herself to the feelings they shared.

He pushed the past away. It had haunted him long enough.

He was making love to his *wife*—not a figment of his memories. She was a red-blooded woman and she wanted him *now*.

His hands glided over her body, feeling every square inch, paving a way for his mouth to follow. His fingers pulled at her nipples while his lips teased the delicate flesh beneath her breasts, breathing warm air and making her back arch with desperate need. He dragged his mouth higher, running his teeth over her décolletage and then meeting her mouth once more.

There was so much he didn't understand about them—about himself. So much he would say if he knew how to find the words. Instead he kissed her with all the confusion he had become, the contradictions that now filled him.

'Nikos…' She groaned.

Did she understand?

Was this her way of telling him that she, too, was ready to let the past go? To lay those ghosts to rest once and for all?

'Please…'

A soft whisper. A sound of need that he would meet again and again for the rest of his life if he had the opportunity.

He entered her gently but she lifted herself higher, taking him deep and groaning as their bodies were unified once more.

Transfixed, he watched as she rode her first wave, her body quickly adjusting to his possession and welcoming him with giddy delight. He watched her fly high into the peaks of pleasure, so beautiful against this bed from her childhood.

And then he was joining her, his body meeting her questions, taking them, answering them, and cresting with her. Her fingers sought his and laced through them. He lifted their arms above her head, kissing away the pleasure-soaked moans that were becoming louder and more insistent. He absorbed them, but he was an echo chamber for them, for those same cries were deep inside him, too.

He felt her slowly quieten, and her body gradually stopped its fevered trembling so that only the sound of her husky breathing was left. He rolled onto the bed, bringing her with him, cradling her head against his chest. And he stayed like that, holding her, not wanting to speak—finding that he had nothing to say in any event—until her continued silence caused him to realise that she had fallen asleep.

He shifted a little so that he could look at her.

And guilt shot a hole in his heart.

It was Marnie—the Marnie he'd once loved and the Marnie he'd married. How could he think the past didn't matter? The past was a part of them. Her rejection had turned him into who he was. It had happened, but it was over with.

She was *his* Marnie.

His wife, his lover. Just Marnie.

Understanding was chased by bitter recrimination, as though he was waking from the depths of a nightmare.

His eyes slammed shut as acid filled his mouth. Because he'd *forced* her to marry him. He'd taken away any choice in the matter, skilfully applying just the right pressure to ensure she had no way of saying no.

And she'd risen to the challenge. She'd done what he'd asked of her. For her father? Or had there been a part of her that had wanted to see whatever it was they had been through to the bitter end?

The end.

He hadn't thought that far ahead. He lifted his finger and traced a line down her arm. In her sleep she smiled. It was a beautiful smile but it might as well have been a spoken accusation.

What the hell had he done? And why?

He lay there for hours, his mind spinning over the past, his body refusing to move from the closeness of hers. But eventually, somewhere after midnight, he gave up on sleep and shifted from the bed, taking care not to wake her. He dressed in a pair of boxers and a loose shirt before stepping quietly from the bedroom.

The house was in darkness, save for a few lamps placed through the hallway.

In the kitchen, midway through making coffee, he heard a noise and looked towards the door.

Whether Nikos or Anne Kenington was more surprised would have been difficult to say with certainty. Nikos flicked a glance at his wristwatch. Despite the lateness of the hour Anne was still wearing the same dress she'd been in at the party.

'Late night?' he murmured, inserting a pod into the machine.

Anne's smile was tight. 'And for you?'

He shrugged. 'I couldn't sleep.'

Anne expelled a sigh that could only be described as disapproving and moved farther into the kitchen. Closer, Nikos caught the smell of alcohol on her breath and realised her eyes were a little unfocussed.

'You're leaving tomorrow?' she asked.

He nodded. A shorter visit had seemed like a good idea, and nothing he'd seen since arriving had changed his mind. Except Marnie's smile. Out of nowhere he saw her as she'd been in the apple orchard, the sun glinting on her hair, a trickle of sugary fruit juice dribbling down her face, and his gut kicked. If anything, it served as vindication for how he'd handled Arthur's affairs. Her happiness here was no reason to remain longer.

'Such a short trip,' Anne murmured as she walked to the fridge and pulled out a bottle of wine.

Nikos watched as she reached into the cupboard and frowned, running her hands over an empty shelf before reaching lower and pulling out a Royal Doulton teacup. She sloshed Chardonnay into it, then placed the bottle on the bench.

'I'd thought you might be here a few days at least.'

His gaze was narrowed. 'Would you have liked us to stay longer?'

Her eyes met his and for a very brief moment he felt a surge of recognition. He'd adored Libby. She had been different from Marnie, but a beautiful person, and she'd faced her illness with such strength and humour. He saw that same resilience in Anne's eyes—and it surprised him to realise that they must have other similarities, too.

'I suppose not.' She laughed—a brittle sound that made him sad for her.

'Why?' he prompted, pulling his coffee cup from the machine and holding it in one hand.

'You're bad for my husband's blood pressure.'

Nikos laughed with true mirth. 'Am I?'

'He was in quite a mood this afternoon. Some birth-day present…'

Curious, Nikos nodded. 'Did he tell you what we dis-cussed?'

Anne's face was pinched. 'He gave me an indication,' she responded with cold civility. 'I suppose you think I should thank you?'

Another moment he'd thought he would relish. He shook his head, though, brushing her words away. 'It was no hardship for me to intervene.'

'I'm surprised you bothered,' she said quietly, imbib-ing more of her wine.

He shrugged. 'For Marnie…'

He let the rest of the sentence hang in the air, knowing he couldn't speak the bald-faced lie now. After all, it had all been for his own selfish gratification. None of this was really for his wife, was it?

'She loves you,' Anne said, her body so still she might have been carved from stone. 'She always has.'

He heard the words without allowing them to find any

credibility within him. 'She loved me six years ago, when you forced her to end it.'

Anne didn't visibly react. It was as though the past was a ribbon, pulling her backwards. 'She was miserable afterwards. I doubt she ever forgave us.'

It was a strange sense; he was both hot and cold. He didn't want to think of how Marnie had felt. He'd been so furious with her, so concerned with his own hurts, he'd never really given her situation any thought. She'd told him she'd been angry, though. Furious, she'd said. Had her fury matched his? It couldn't have or she would have held their course.

'She moved on,' he said quietly. 'Until recently.'

'But she didn't.'

Anne's eyes were darkened by guilt. She pushed up from the bench and strode a little way across the kitchen, then froze once more—a statue in the room.

'She continued to live and breathe, but that's not the same as moving on. She thought I didn't notice her reading about you in the papers. That I didn't catch her looking at photos of you.' She flicked her head over her shoulder, pinning him with a glance that spoke of true concern. 'She was so careful, but I saw the way she missed you. The way she seemed to wither for a long time. It was almost like losing two daughters.'

Disgust, anger and guilt at the way they had all failed Marnie gnawed through him.

Anne sipped her wine and moved back to her original spot, opposite Nikos. 'We introduced her to some lovely young men—'

'*Suitable* men?' he interjected, with a cynical strength to his words. But Anne's statement was slicing through him. The idea of Marnie having pined for him was one he couldn't contemplate.

'Yes, suitable men. Nice men.' She closed her eyes.

'She never mentioned your name, but I always knew you to be the reason it didn't work out. She never got over you.'

Nikos sipped his coffee but his mind was spinning back over their conversation in his office, when he'd first suggested they marry. She'd been so arctic. So cold!

But wasn't that Marnie's defence mechanism? Wasn't that how she behaved when her emotions were rioting all over the place? And her being a virgin? Was that simply because she'd never found someone who made her body tremble as it did for him? Had she chosen not to get serious with another guy because she still wanted *him*?

'I believed we were doing the right thing.' Anne's smile was tight. 'After Libby, we just wanted Marnie to be safe.'

'You thought I was somehow *unsafe*?' he barked, anger and frustration and impotence to change the past ravaging his temper.

'You *aren't* safe,' she responded sharply. 'The way she feels about you is a recipe for disaster.'

Marnie didn't still love him, did she? How could she after what he'd put her through? She might have loved him a year ago...even two months ago. But the way he'd burst back into her life had been the one thing that must have ruined any love between them.

He closed his eyes briefly.

Anne continued speaking, but she wasn't particularly focussed on her son-in-law. 'You must hate us. I know Marnie did for a long time. But I *love* her, Nikos. Everything I've done has been because I love her.'

'Yet you sought to control her life? You told her you would disinherit her if she didn't leave me?'

Anne winced as though he'd slapped her. 'Yes. Well, Arthur did...' A whisper. A hollow, tormented, grief-soaked admission. 'At the time I told myself that she must have known we were right. She broke up with you. And Marnie knew her own head and heart. If she'd *really* loved you, I told myself, she would have fought harder.'

Nikos felt a familiar sentiment echo within him.

'But she couldn't. We were holding on by a thread and Marnie knew that.'

'And what about Marnie?' he asked with dark anger, though he couldn't have said if it was directed at Anne, Arthur or himself.

'She was *Marnie*,' Anne said finally, drinking more wine with a small shrug. 'Determined to act as though everything was fine even if it was almost killing her.'

Nikos angled his head away, his dark eyes resting on their reflections in the window. Anne appeared smaller there, shrunken. Surprised, he looked at her and realised that the changes had taken place in real time—he just hadn't noticed them. She was smaller, wizened, stressed.

'How could you let her go through this?' he muttered, but his blame and recriminations were focussed on himself.

Anne pinned him with eyes that reminded him once more of Libby. 'Libby was such an easy child—so like me. I just understood her. But with Marnie… She's a puzzle I can't fathom.'

Nikos rubbed a hand across his jaw. 'Marnie is all that is good in the world,' he said finally. 'Often to her own detriment. She wants the best for those she loves, even when it means sacrificing her own happiness.'

Guilt over their marriage was a knife, deep in his gut.

'Yes!' Anne expelled an angry sigh. 'I love that girl, Nikos, but I don't always know *how* to love her. I suppose that sounds tremendously strange to you—she's my child, after all.'

His smile was thin. For Anne's words had lodged deep in his mind and begun to unravel with condemnation and

acceptance. He had loved Marnie once, too, but never in
the way she'd needed to be loved. His faults were on a par
with Anne and Arthur Kenington's.

CHAPTER ELEVEN

MARNIE STOOD UNSTEADILY as the plane pitched yet again, rolled mercilessly by the thick cotton wool clouds that had clogged the entire journey from London to Athens.

Nikos, in the middle of a newspaper article, lifted his gaze curiously. He had been distracted for the entire flight, and he seemed almost to be rousing himself from a long way away now.

'Travel sickness,' she explained, moving quickly away from him towards the back of the plane.

She burst into the toilet, relieved to have made it just a second before losing the entire contents of her stomach. Her brow broke out in sweat and still she heaved, her whole body quivering with the exertion.

She moaned as the taste of metal filled her mouth and finally, spent, straightened. The mirror showed how unwell she'd been: the face that stared back at her was bright red, sweaty, and her eyes were slightly bloodshot in the corners.

She flushed the toilet and ran the cold water, washing her hands and splashing water over her face, enjoying the relief of the ice-cold liquid.

As a child she'd been prone to travel sickness. Even a short journey had brought on a spell of nausea. But it had been a long time since she'd felt it. Years. In fact the last time she'd been sick she'd been ten or eleven.

But what else could it be?

Marnie froze midway through patting her cheeks with a plush hand towel. Mentally she counted back the days to their wedding, her mind moving with an alacrity she wouldn't have thought it capable of a moment ago, while doubled over an aeroplane toilet.

They'd been married just over a month and they'd made love on their wedding night. And since that time a certain something had been glaringly absent.

She'd started the pill in plenty of time for it to have been effective. So what did that mean? Had going on birth control simply changed her normal cycle? Was that it? Or was she pregnant with Nikos's baby? Because what she was feeling felt altogether different, and a little terrifying.

The idea was a tiny seed she couldn't shake. It put roots down through her mind, so that by the time she returned to her seat, looking much more like her normal self, she was almost certain that she was indeed pregnant.

She'd need to do a test to be sure, but there was no room in her mind for doubt.

She barely spoke for the rest of the flight, and she was too caught up in her own imaginings to notice that Nikos was similarly silent. Brooding, even.

Athens was cool but humid when they landed; the clouds that had made their flight so bumpy were thick in the air, making the ground steam.

'I have some business to take care of,' Nikos murmured once they'd disembarked. His Ferrari was waiting on the Tarmac. 'I will need to go straight to my office once we're home.'

Marnie, secretly glad for this reprieve, time to ascertain whether or not she was in fact pregnant, nodded. 'Okay.'

It was all Marnie could do not to tell him of her suspicions as he drove the now familiar roads to his mansion.

But she wouldn't do that. Not until she knew for sure that there was a baby.

It would be a surprise—a shock, really.

But it didn't necessarily follow that it would be a nightmare, did it?

'A baby between us would never be magical and wonderful. It is the very last thing I would want.'

The words circled her mind.

She waited until he'd left, and then for Eléni to arrive, and somehow was casually able to ask for a ride to the markets to pick up some groceries.

The whole way there, making halting chitchat with Eléni, Marnie wondered what it would mean if she was actually, truly pregnant.

She paid for the groceries, stuffing the pregnancy test into her handbag rather than stowing it with the other shopping, and listened to Eléni the whole way home.

Finally she removed herself to her room to find out, once and for all, if her suspicions were right.

The test showed exactly what she had known it would.

Two bright blue lines.

She was pregnant.

With Nikos's baby.

Elation danced deep in her being. She felt its unmistakable warmth zing through her and she treasured it—because she knew that it would not last long. Complications would surely arise soon enough and take away the pleasure she felt.

For it was an incontrovertible truth that no matter what she chose to do she would be a part of Nikos's life for ever. And he of hers.

Where was her despair at that prospect? Her concern?

She looked into her heart and saw nothing—just joy.

Tears ran down her cheeks and for the first time in her

life they were happy tears. Tears that warmed her and blessed her and made her feel as if she wanted to shout her euphoria from the rooftops. It was not a simple joy—there would be complications—but they paled in comparison to the happiness that shone before her.

She needed to tell him—but not on the phone. She would wait until he returned and leave him in no doubt as to how pleased she was with this turn of events. Even though she knew they had broken his cardinal rule…

The minutes of the day seemed to gang up on her, deciding that they'd like to drag their way mutinously towards the hour of Nikos's arrival gleefully slowly rather than with the alacrity she craved.

Just wondering when you'll be home?

She sent the message, her impatience burning through her, fear threatening to take hold of her.

Not for a while. N.

Well, he'd be home eventually, and then she'd just have to put her hope in his hands and pray he didn't crush it.

The first sign that there was a problem was that Nikos didn't drive himself home. A luxurious limousine pulled up out at the front and Marnie, hovering in her office with its view of the driveway, wondered briefly if they had unexpected company.

When Nikos emerged from the back his large frame seemed different. Slightly unsteady. He stood for a moment, a hand braced on the roof of the car, his eyes scanning the front of his house. Why did he look so grim? Had something happened?

Concerned, she moved quickly through the house, reaching the front door at the same time he did. She heard his keys drop to the ground outside and pulled the door inwards, her expression perplexed.

Until she smelled the Scotch and realised that her husband—the father of her tiny, tiny baby—had obviously been drinking. Heavily.

'Nik...?' she said with disbelief, holding the door wide and letting him in.

Marnie had never seen him anything other than in complete control. She was struggling to make sense of what might have happened in the hours since they'd returned from London to lead him to be in this state.

'My wife,' he said, as though it brought him little pleasure.

Confusion thick in her mind, she waited for him to move deeper into the house so she could close the door. 'Have you been out?'

'No,' he muttered. 'I have been in my office.'

Unconsciously, she moved a hand to her stomach. 'Drinking?'

He expelled an angry breath. 'Apparently.'

Marnie nodded, but he still wasn't making sense. The uncharacteristic act jarred with everything she knew about this man. He was a disciplined control freak.

Out of nowhere old jealousies and suspicions erupted. 'Alone?'

His eyes narrowed, but he nodded.

'Why?' she asked finally, putting a hand on his elbow in order to guide him towards the kitchen.

But he pulled away, walking determinedly ahead of her, his physical ability apparently not as affected as she'd first thought.

She walked behind him, and once in the kitchen moved to the fridge. As if on autopilot, she pulled out the ingredients for a toasted cheese sandwich, her eyes flicking to him every few moments. And he stared at her. He stared at her with an intensity that filled her body with fire and flame even as she was laced with confusion and anxiety.

So telling him about the baby wasn't going to happen, she admitted to herself. At least not until the following day, when he might be in a headspace to comprehend what she was saying.

'*Why*, Marnie?' He repeated her question in a tone that was so like the way he'd spoken in the past it made her chest heavy; his words seemed to ring with disdain and dislike.

She tried not to let it fill her heart but it was there. Doubt. Hurt. Aching sadness.

'What's wrong?' she said finally. 'Has something happened?'

He reached into his pocket and pulled out an envelope. 'Your mother believes you've spent the last six years pining for me. That you have loved me this whole time.'

Marnie started, her eyes flying to his involuntarily. Her mouth was dry. 'I…I don't understand why that matters. What my mother says…how I felt. What difference does it make right now to this marriage?'

He spoke slowly, his tone emphatic. 'Did you stay single and celibate because you love me?'

Marnie's heart dropped.

She spun away from him but Nikos raised his voice.

'Damn it, Marnie. You broke up with me. You walked away from us.'

'I know,' she whispered, tears springing to her eyes. The happiness of the last twenty-four hours was being swallowed by old hurts. 'I thought we agreed we wouldn't talk about the past any more?'

He slammed his palm against the benchtop. 'Why didn't you come back? Why didn't you call me when you realised you were still in love with me?'

'You'd moved on,' she said simply. 'And nothing had changed for me.'

'You were so emphatic when you ended it. You convinced me you didn't care for me, that you had never been serious. You completely echoed your father's feelings about me and men of my *upbringing*.' He spat the word like a curse.

She recoiled as though he'd slapped her. 'I *had* to do that! You wouldn't have accepted it unless I made sure you truly believed it was over.' She shook her head and no longer bothered to check the tears that stung her eyes. 'I hated saying those things to you when it was the opposite of how I felt.'

He was not his usual self, but even on a bad day and after a fair measure of Scotch Nikos was better than anyone at debating and reasoning.

He honed his thoughts quickly back to the point at hand. 'You admit you've loved me this whole time?'

Marnie froze, her only movement the rapid rise and fall of her chest as she tried to draw breath into her lungs. She felt that she'd been caught—not in a lie so much as in the truth.

'I would never have done this if I'd known,' he said after a beat of silence had passed—one he took for her acquiescence.

'Done what?' She didn't look at him. Her voice was a whisper into the room.

'This marriage...'

Her heart fell as if from a great height. It was pulverised at her feet, a tangling mass of heaving hopes.

'It was the worst kind of wrong to use you like this.'

She couldn't stifle her sob. 'Is that what you were doing?' She forced herself to look at him—and then wished she hadn't when the intensity of his expression left her short of breath.

He spoke with a cold detachment that was so much worse than the heat of an argument. 'I forced you to marry me. Just as your parents forced you to leave me. I am no better than them. Hell, I consider my crimes to be considerably greater.'

He pushed the back of the envelope open and lifted a piece of paper out. One page. When he handed it to her it was still warm from having been nestled close to his chest all afternoon.

'But at least I can atone for my sins.'

'What's this?' she asked, even as her eyes dropped to the page.

'*Petition for Divorce*' was typed neatly across the top, and as she skimmed lower she saw her name written beside Nikos's. He'd already signed his name. A masculine scrawl of hard intent.

Marnie was still. So still. Briefly she wondered if she might pass out. She felt hot and cold, as she'd done on the flight. She dropped the page and moved backwards until her bottom connected with the bench. She stayed there, glad for the support. Her head was spinning.

'Divorce?'

'I was wrong.' The words were saturated with bleak despair. He was begging her to understand. 'I regret everything I said to you that day in my office. I heard your father was going bankrupt and this idea came to me. I acted on it before I could realise what a stupid mistake it was. I need to undo it.'

She stared at him in shock. 'You can't simply *undo* a marriage. You can't undo what we are!'

'This piece of paper would suggest otherwise,' he said, with a factual determination that left her cold.

'Nikos!' His name was a plea. She looked at the paper. 'Do you want me to leave?'

'I don't want you to stay,' he said thickly. 'Not like this.'

Marnie dropped her head forward. Tears splashed out of her eyes.

'I've had the pre-nuptial agreement voided,' he murmured. 'And you need never worry that your father's finances will be in trouble—'

He thought of the other provisions he'd had enabled, but dismissed the need to discuss them at that point. Actually, he doubted he had the mental wherewithal in that moment to do justice to any of the financial arrangements he'd put in place.

'Listen to me,' she interrupted, her voice unsteady, her tone showing urgency. 'My father has nothing to do with this.'

'He *is* why we married.'

But it was almost a question, a demand for information.

His eyes locked to hers in a way that stole Marnie's breath. It was time to tell him the truth. She didn't believe she'd married for love necessarily, and yet hadn't it always been there? Even when she was furious, wasn't it because she loved him so much and felt so hurt by his actions?

But at that moment her courage was thin on the ground. She tried a different approach, desperately needing to understand what was going on.

'Why don't you tell me what's happened? Last night was fine. Last night was amazing. We danced and spoke as though…as though…we were making progress,' she finished lamely. 'We made love,' she said—an anguished reminder of the beautiful way he'd taken her. It *had* been making love—not just sex, but perfect, intimate love.

'You need to leave me,' he said quietly, taking a step backwards. 'Let me be as clear tonight as you were six years ago, when you ended things the first time. For both our sakes, please leave. Our marriage was a mistake. I should have known better than to even contemplate it.

Now you must go. It is over between us and you should be grateful for that.'

She watched as he strode out of the kitchen in what she considered to be the middle of their argument, and was torn between chasing after him and doing just as he'd said. How easy it would be to numbly pack a suitcase and go—to leave this minefield for the peace of solitude.

Only what followed wouldn't be easy. Leaving him once had hurt like hell and she'd never recovered. And the way she'd felt then was a fraction of what she felt now. She'd lived with him, and beyond that she'd committed her full self to this man and their marriage.

But could she keep trying to make their marriage work if he didn't even *want* the marriage any more? She stared at the piece of paper, anger building brick by brick inside her.

When had her mother and her husband had this *tête-à-tête*? And if Anne knew how badly Marnie had longed for Nikos why hadn't she talked to Marnie about it? Why hadn't she taken back the edict that had led to Marnie ruining her relationship with the only man she'd ever loved?

She caught a scream in her mouth; just a muted sound of frustration erupted into the silent kitchen. She had been pulled in a thousand directions by those she most cared about and now fury was building within her.

She stormed across the room, her feet planted heavily on the tiles, until she reached the sliding glass doors. She pushed them open and went outside. At the pool, she ripped her dress over her head, then leapt in. The water was a balm to her fraught senses and it absorbed the stinging, angry tears that were running freely down her cheeks.

Divorce?

After a month?

When she was pregnant with his baby?

And completely in love with him?

And he loved *her*, didn't he? She was almost sure of it. So why tell her to leave, then? None of it made sense.

But she wasn't going to let history repeat itself. She loved him more than ever before, and that meant staying to fight—not running away.

When Nikos awoke the next morning it was still dark and he was alone in his bed. He sat up, intent on going for his usual run, but a blinding headache shattered his temples.

And then it all came flooding back to him.

His conversation with Anne Kenington… *'I love her. I just don't know* how *to love her.'*

The divorce papers that had seemed like such an inspired idea at his lowest ebb.

Marnie's face as she'd stared at him, tears on her lashes, her slender body shaking as she comprehended his words.

'I want you to go. It is over between us.'

He squeezed his eyes shut, but that only enabled him to remember more clearly. The pain had slammed into her like a wall. Her harsh reaction to his simple solution. His belief that by divorcing her he could erase the barbarism of his behaviour.

He swore loudly and stood, ignoring the blinding pain that spiked in his brain. *Marnie.* Where was she? Had she left?

A cursory inspection of their room showed that her clothes were all in their usual spot. Relief was brief. She hadn't gone anywhere. *Had she?* He moved into their *en-suite* bathroom intent on making himself look slightly more civilised before facing the music.

It smelled of her. Lavender, violets…feminine and sweet. His gut clenched and he swore again.

He showered quickly and wrapped a towel around his waist while brushing his teeth. The toothpaste tube was empty and he tossed it carelessly in the rubbish bin. It missed. When he crouched down to retrieve it, his head complaining the whole time, something unusual caught his eye. A box.

He lifted it out and stared at it in confusion.

A pregnancy test?

That didn't make any sense.

Marnie was on the pill. But it sure as hell wasn't Eléni's. Which meant that somehow, for some reason, Marnie had had reason to believe she might be pregnant. He opened the box but it was empty. Nor was there a test in the trash.

With renewed urgency he pulled on a pair of shorts and shirt and practically ran out of the room and through the house. There were several guest rooms but they were all empty. Fear was building.

What if she *was* pregnant? Would he still be strong enough to let her go? If she chose to divorce him—hell, she might have already signed the damned papers—would he let the divorce proceed?

And what if she stayed with him because of the baby? Could he live with her knowing he'd trapped her—twice—into marriage?

He checked her office. It was empty, neat.

Then his own office—empty.

Finally, he went to the kitchen.

And there she was.

Marnie.

Sitting on the sofa, staring out at the lifting sun, her face pale, her eyes a terrifying maelstrom of feelings and fears.

What could he say to her? What right did he have to explain?

He walked quietly and then crouched in front of her, directly in Marnie's line of sight.

'Have you slept?'

She blinked her eyes at him and then looked away, over

his shoulder, focussing on the colours smudged across the sky. 'I didn't leave.'

A muscle jerked at his temple. 'I'm glad.'

Her eyes flew to his again. Confusion. Hurt. 'Why?'

She reminded him of a wounded animal. He swore under his breath and dragged a hand through his hair. He needed to reassure her. To explain. She deserved at least that much. But his own questions were burning through him.

For a man like Nikos, not knowing what to say or how to negotiate on the terms of his marriage brought with it great frustration. He was used to commanding a room. He had not doubted his ability to bring people to his way of thinking for a very long time.

Business, though, was predictable—easy for a man like Nikos. He would discover what motivated a person and exploit that to gain his own success.

Marnie was motivated by love.

Loyalty.

Affection and faithfulness.

And he didn't want her to be with him for any of those reasons but one.

'You gave me divorce papers last night.' Her eyes had an unexpected strength in them. 'Why?'

He expelled a breath. 'Isn't that obvious?'

'You don't want to be married to me,' she whispered, the words a ghost of sentiment in the large room.

'I don't want you to feel *forced* to stay married to me,' he clarified.

She nodded, her gaze refusing to meet his. If only he *had* pushed her away! She'd ended up falling as much in love with him as ever, and now it was so much worse—for she'd tasted the mind-blowing bliss that came from sharing his bed and his life.

'You were happy to give me an ultimatum at one time. What's changed?'

Did he detect the note of challenge in her voice?

His smile was lacking any true happiness. 'We are married, but you are not my wife.' He stood, his back straight, his shoulders square. 'It turns out you can't really force someone into a marriage.'

'Isn't that what's happened here?'

He shook his head. 'I believed that having you as my wife would make you mine. It doesn't work like that, though.' His expression was bleak for a moment, before hard certainty crossed it. 'You will never be able to forget the way I propositioned you, and nor will I. I look at you and see the man I have become. A man I despise.'

'You have helped my father,' she said quietly. 'I could never hate you after what you've done for him.'

'You have to release us both from this. I can't live with how I've hurt you.'

She nodded, her throat raw from unshed tears. 'You *have* hurt me,' she whispered. 'Just as I hurt you. Does that make us even now?'

He stood up, moving angrily towards the glass doors and staring out. 'You were a teenager. A *grieving* teenager. You hurt my pride and my ego and I left. I should have stayed. It takes courage to stay and fight for what you want. But I didn't like how it felt to be rejected, so I went off like a sulking child.' He thrust his hands in his pockets. 'I didn't deserve you.'

She lifted her feet onto the sofa so she could rest her chin against her knees. 'Fighting would have been pointless. You would have only upset me more than I already was. I truly believed I had no choice but to end it.'

He nodded, thinking of the pregnancy test box he'd discovered. He turned slowly, but pain was a fresh wave crashing over him. She was a contradiction of fragility and strength. Broken but resolved. Determined and disappointed.

He strode to her, a guttural sound of angst tearing from his chest. '*I* have broken whatever we used to be—not you. If you are pregnant I will support you. I will make sure you have everything you and the baby need. But I will not let you use that as a reason to stay with me.'

Shock flashed over Marnie and her skin paled to paperwhite. 'The…baby?' She swallowed. 'How did you know?' What was the point in denying it?

'I found the box in our bathroom,' he responded, so close he could touch her, but not allowing himself to do so.

She hadn't bothered to hide it because she'd thought they would have a perfect dinner together, over which she would share with him the happy news. *Happy news!* Well, at least there was still some truth in that. Thoughts of the baby filled her shattered heart with a slight antiseptic against the pain.

'Is it true?' he asked, his words anguished.

Slowly she nodded, pulling her lower lip between her teeth. 'Yes…'

'Thee mou!' He groaned, standing and running a hand over his eyes. He seemed to stand there for ever, a heaving man, his whole body showing instant rejection of the idea of their child. Just as he'd said he would.

What had she expected? That he would welcome this news?

'I am so sorry.' He groaned again, dropping his hand and pinning her with the full force of his shocked gaze.

'Sorry?' she repeated, feeling numbed now, so fresh pain wasn't capable of sinking in.

'First I trapped you with blackmail and now you must feel trapped by our baby. But you can leave. You *must* leave. A baby is no reason to continue this farce.'

She sobbed and nodded. 'I know that.'

Neither spoke for a long time. Marnie was trying to imagine a life without Nikos and all she saw was the bleakness that had been her bedfellow for these past six years.

'If I could fix this, I would,' he said.

She nodded again, resting her cheek on her knees. She had chosen to stay and fight, but so far she had done a lot of listening and no actual fighting. She tried to find the strength in her heart, but it was in ruins.

'There is something else you should know.' He spoke with a grim finality to his words. 'I could not find the words to explain last night.'

'Explain what?' she whispered, wondering at the pain in her throat.

'I have bought Kenington Hall and put it in your name.'

She lifted her head sharply, almost giving herself whiplash in the process. Everything else disappeared from her mind. 'You've *what*?'

He expelled a sigh and crouched down on his haunches so that their eyes were level. 'You love the property, and I wanted you to know it to be safe. That no matter what happened to your father, or to our marriage, you would have the security of your family home.'

She let that statement sink in. 'When did you do this?'

'When I met with your father.'

She nodded, but nothing was making sense. 'Were you planning to divorce me even then? Was it to be my consolation prize?' Grief lanced her. 'What did I do wrong? I thought we were making this work…'

'You did nothing wrong, Marnie, except fall in love with an arrogant, selfish bastard like me.' He dropped his head into his hands. 'I didn't buy the house because I wanted to leave you. I bought it because I wanted you to understand that you have options. That you and your family are safe. Even before speaking with your mother I knew I had to give you back your freedom before I could even hope to make amends.'

'I have never considered myself to lack freedom,' she inserted seriously, her eyes sparkling, her mind moving quickly. 'So you *did* want to make this marriage a real one?'

A muscle jerked in his jaw. 'I cannot say if I ever thought of it in those terms.'

He dared to lift a hand and touch her soft hair. Fear at what he was on the brink of losing was all around him—a pit of despair he knew would swallow him if he didn't explain himself better than he was doing now.

'I knew only that I wanted you to look at me with the love you once felt. That I wanted to be able to smile at you with the love that is in *here*.' He tapped his hand against his chest.

Marnie made a sound of disbelief.

'You *should* leave me. You can go and it will not change how I feel about you. Your father is out of debt. Kenington Hall is safe in your hands. And I will be as involved as you allow me to be in our child's life. You must decide what will make you happy.'

Happy? That felt so far away.

She stood up, something snapping inside her. She could no longer sit still as though this were a normal discussion. Her temper flared. She spun round, her hands on her hips, her face showing the full extent of her rage. There was nothing remotely cold about her now. She was all feelings and flame.

'You're such an *idiot*!' she shouted at the top of her lungs. 'I have *always* loved you! Always! Even when I thought I was over you, how could I be? I married you! And—newsflash!—I didn't *have* to! Even to save my father's financial situation. I would only ever have married one man on earth. *You*. Only you.'

She wrapped her arms around herself.

'You were right before, when you said that you should have stayed and fought for what we were. I don't think it would have made a difference, but it's what you *do* when you're in love with someone. You don't bloody walk away. I'm not going to walk away now, because I love you—even when you're almost impossible to comprehend.'

He stared at her, but his expression was blank, as though her words were a problem he had to decode.

'I was furious with you when we got married. *Livid.* What a stupid thing you did, blackmailing me like this! But I still loved you. Every night of this marriage has been like slowly unwrapping a present, piece by piece, getting to find my way back to you—'

'I have pushed you away,' he interrupted, arguing the sense of her statement.

'Yes, you have—but you've also pulled me close. So close that I've been inside your soul. You've let me in. And you *dare* turn up with divorce papers, as though our marriage is a simple contract you can dissolve? You *dare* relegate our love to an agreement that you alone can end?'

Startled by her anger, he stood, wishing to placate her. He put an arm on her shoulder but she jerked away.

'No!' she snapped. 'I'm not finished yet.'

Her eyes held a warning and, fascinated, he was silent.

'You have been hitting me over the head with the fact that I flicked a switch and walked away from you six years ago. I didn't. I didn't flick a switch. I made the worst mistake of my life when I left you, and I'm not going to do it again.' She straightened her shoulders. 'If you want to divorce me—if you don't want me any more—then tell me that. You can make that decision. But don't tell me that leaving you is in my best interests—because I know what life is like without you and there is no life on earth that I want more than *this* life, here—right here with you.'

His breath was ragged, torn from his lungs. 'How can you feel that?' he murmured with a growing sense of wonderment. 'I have been—'

'You have been Nikos.' She cut across him, but softly, kindly, with the compassion that was always so close to her surface. 'Determined, arrogant and good.' She moved closer. 'Do you think either of us really understood what we were doing and why? You wanted to help my family. I believe that was at the heart of everything you did.'

He made a sound and shook his head, but she lifted a finger to his lips.

'Whatever motivated you to blackmail me into this marriage, I will never resent you for it. How can I? I've missed you and now I have you.' She paused, her eyes scanning his. 'I *do* have you, don't I?'

He wrapped his arms around her waist, crushing her to him. 'You have all of me, for all time.' The words were a promise against her cheek. '*All* of me. And you are the best of me.'

She shut her eyes and listened to the pounding of his heart. Her lips twitched in a smile that shone with true happiness.

Gradually Nikos pulled backwards, dropping a hand to her flat stomach. 'A baby was not on our agenda,' he said, as if just comprehending the reality of their situation.

'Apparently the baby had other ideas. I dare say it has a lot of your determination.'

He laughed. 'Let us hope that is balanced by your warmth and kindness.'

'Well, I guess we'll find out in about eight months.'

'And you are truly happy?'

'Nikos!' She laughed shakily. 'When I found out I was pregnant I wanted to shout it from the rooftops. I know it wasn't meant to be part of the plan, but it felt so *right*.'

He frowned, wondering how long she'd shouldered this secret. 'When did you first suspect?'

She smiled. 'Not until we were on the plane back to Greece.'

'And then I told you to leave me.' His face paled with remembered regrets. 'It was for *you*, Marnie. I didn't *want* you to go. You know this to be true?'

She nodded. 'I've never seen you like that.'

His smile was grim. 'I have only ever drunk to excess one other time in my life—the night your father paid me off and I took his money. Then, too, I felt like a shadow of the man I wanted to be.'

'Don't say that,' she murmured, resting her head against his chest. She stood there quietly for a moment. 'My father wouldn't have liked selling you the house...'

He breathed in her sweet fragrance and a sense of deep gratitude filled him. To think that he'd almost pushed her away for good! He would never make that mistake again. Not in his life.

'He...understood the necessity of it,' Nikos said after a moment. '*Agape mou*, I thought I would relish that moment. I had fantasised about seeing your father a broken man. I had dreamed of being in a position to throw my own success and wealth in his face and see him suffer. But at the first opportunity to do so I saw only you. I saw you and discovered that loving you meant loving *all* of you. Even your family. If you married me because you love me then you must understand that I have helped Arthur because I love you. It was not a payment for your marrying me.'

The words filled her with love and certainty—certainty that they were right where they should be. Together.

But she pulled a face of mock consideration. 'Well, it seems to me, then, that you haven't upheld your end of the deal.'

Sensing the amusement in her words, he answered in

kind. 'I suppose you're right. Is there something else I can offer instead?'

She pressed a finger to her chin and pretended to consider it. 'I can think of a few things…'

He surprised her by scooping her up and laying her down on the sofa. His mouth sought hers and he tasted her giddy delight there and answered it.

'Starting with right now?'

'I will expect the payment terms to be over a very long time,' she said, pushing at his shorts.

'Would the rest of our lives do?'

She sighed, her body firing with insatiable need for her husband. 'It just might.'

EPILOGUE

One year later

IT WAS THE ice sculpture that was the final straw.

She shook her head, torn between feeling cross and amused as she tore through the villa in search of her husband.

She found him by the pool, hands on hips, eyes staring out at the ocean. They'd been married for almost a year, and still the sight of him could stop her in her tracks. Her heart hammered roughly against her ribs, beating wildly as she approached him.

'A *swan*?' she said from just behind his shoulder, her expression one of utter disbelief. 'Seriously?'

His grin as he turned around skittled any discontent she had felt over his lavish decorations.

'It's summer,' she pointed out with a shake of her head, but her grumble was somewhat faint-hearted.

'Almost autumn.'

'Almost,' she responded archly. 'And it's as hot as Hades today. That thing's going to be iced water before anyone gets here.'

'So we will drink it!' He laughed. 'How many times does our daughter get christened?' he said, with such impeccable logic that all her objections were silenced.

'You're right.' Marnie smiled up at him, giving in to

temptation and wrapping her arms around his waist. 'And now I have another bone to pick with you.'

'Oh?' he murmured, his lips still pressed to hers.

She straightened, trying to be businesslike. 'The trust just called me to report that a rather sizeable donation has been made in Lulu's name.'

His smile lit the world on fire—starting with Marnie's heart. She was scorched with happiness.

'What else can I give you and our daughter on her christening? You will not let me buy you jewels or clothes… you insist she has all she needs. But this, I think, you *will* let me do.'

Marnie nodded, tears of happiness clogging her throat. 'But it's so much…'

'For a cause that means the world to you—and therefore to me. I still remember what you said to me, *agape mou*. That one day, through your efforts and the efforts of people like you, young girls like Libby might not get sick any more.'

He pressed a finger beneath Marnie's chin, lifting her eyes to meet his. She felt the love and commitment that underscored every decision he made.

'We have our own little girl now. How can you doubt my desire to work with you on this?'

Love coiled inside her. 'Thank you.' Her voice was husky. Emotions were too strong to contain. She lifted up on tiptoe and pressed a kiss to his lips. 'Why did we invite all these people over?'

He kissed her hungrily, his tongue exploring her mouth, his hands holding her tight against his body.

But for only a moment.

Then he lifted himself away, grinning as if he *hadn't* been shaken to the core by their molten hot connection.

'To see my ice sculpture,' he said, and laughed.

She rolled her eyes, but her mind was drifting. 'If only we had an extra hour…'

He grimaced, looking past her shoulder. 'If only we had an extra ten minutes…'

He saw their guests through the glass doors and kissed the top of her head.

'I will make you a promise,' he said in an undertone.

Marnie nodded. 'Oh, yes? I'm all ears, Mr Kyriazis.'

'Not from where I am standing.' He grinned at her, his handsome face a collection of lines and shapes that formed an inimitable image of masculinity.

Playfully, Marnie punched his upper arm. 'I believe you were making me a promise?'

'Soon we will be alone in our home again, and then I will show you just what that dress and you are making me want.'

Her pulse was lurching out of control. She lifted herself up on tiptoe again and kissed his lips, smiling as familiar sensations rocked her to her core.

'You'd better,' she said simply.

He wrapped an arm around her shoulder, pulling her to his side and knowing how right it was that they should be together. Everything in his world seemed to shine with the perfection that Marnie brought to his life.

'Your parents are here,' he murmured, looking down into the villa as Anne and Arthur Kenington made their way through the house.

Marnie took a moment to observe them, staying right where she was. Anne was her usual self—elegant and perfectly neat, despite the fact they'd come straight from the airport. Although a flight in Nikos's jet was hardly an arduous ordeal. Arthur Kenington showed the greatest change. He was dressed casually in a pale polo shirt and a pair of beige chinos. His hair was a little longer, and there were

more lines on his face now—lines Marnie chose to believe
were formed by happiness.

'Darling, there's a puddle forming in the foyer,' Anne
said with pursed lips as she swept onto the terrace.

A breeze lifted past them, drawing with it the tang of
the ocean and the sweetness of Libby's rose garden. Marnie inhaled, drawing strength from this reminder of her
sister before steeling herself to enjoy the next few hours.
Her parents were not perfect, but they were still her parents. And, fortunately for Marnie, despite their meddling
and strong opinions she and Nikos had found their way
together in the end.

'That would be the ice sculpture.' Marnie winked up
at her husband, then moved towards her mother, kissing
her cheek. She hugged her dad before returning to Nikos's
side. 'Thanks for coming.'

'Of course.' Anne nodded. 'Where is our granddaugh-
ter?'

'She's with her uncle.' Marnie grinned. 'Her honor-
ary uncle.'

Anderson emerged at that moment, their chubby dark-
haired little girl propped on one hip.

'Nothing honourable about *him*,' Nikos teased, with a
genuine smile reserved for their closest friend. 'Unlike
you, Lady Heiress.'

She shook her head, her hands extended for the baby
Elizabeth. But Lulu only had eyes for her father.

Marnie laughed. 'I see!' She shook her head. 'That's
the way it's going to be, huh?'

'It is because I am not often here when she is awake.'

'Sure it is,' Marnie said with another laugh. 'And also
because you spoil her silly. That's okay—I'm not offended.'

And she wasn't. How could she be? She had everything
she'd ever wanted in life.

It was a beautiful afternoon, filled with happiness and

joy. Finally, though, after the last of the guests had left and Lulu was fast asleep, Marnie went in search of her husband.

She found him on the terrace, his eyes focussed contemplatively on the shimmering moon. It was a cool night now, and Marnie wrapped her arms around herself for warmth.

Nikos noticed—as he did everything about his wife—and shrugged out of his jacket, placing it around her slender shoulders on instinct.

'Here, *agape mou*,' he said, pulling her closer to his warmth.

'Thank you,' she murmured, inhaling his intoxicatingly masculine scent. 'Have I ever told you there was a time when I hated you calling me that?' she asked softly.

'Did you?'

'It just reminded me of what I wanted from you. What I doubted you'd ever feel for me.'

Her eyes pierced his, and for a second those thoughts and feelings were right there before her. Such pain and heartbreak! How had that ever been their story when there was now such love between them? Such joy and trust?

She blinked to clear those dark vestiges of the past.

'Did you doubt, Mrs Kyriazis? Did you really doubt?'

His eyes held hers, and in them she saw the truth that perhaps she'd always held deep in her heart. The incontrovertibility of who they were to one another.

His soft sigh breathed warmth across her temple. 'I called you that, even when we were at odds, because I needed to believe we could be that to one another again. I wanted to feel that I had the right...'

Her smile shifted her features, taking his breath away completely.

'It sounds a little like *you* were the one who doubted we'd find our way here.'

He put an arm around her waist, his fingers feathering

over her hip. 'Not for a second.' His voice was gravelly. 'I could never accept a world without you in it.'

'Even if that meant blackmailing me?' she teased, finding it almost impossible to credit the start of their marriage with the state of it now.

'Even then.' He dropped a kiss against her hair. 'Will you ever forgive me for that?'

'Forgive you? Hmm…' She pretended to think, her eyes full of love and amusement. 'I can think of one way you could make it up to me.'

He smiled softly. 'Your wish is my command. Although in this case I think it is my wish also.'

The stars shone overhead and the rose garden was bathed with magical milky moonlight. Nikos Kyriazis kissed his wife, carrying her into their now quiet home.

And it *was* a home. Not simply a house, as it had been for so long.

Now it was a collection of walls that contained their family's life, that was filled with pictures and love and the kind of warmth he had only ever dreamed possible. It was a home he shared with Marnie and Lulu, just as he shared his heart and his being with them.

A man who had never known love was now overflowing with it, and always would be.

* * * * *

*Look out for more Clare Connelly titles
—coming soon!*

MILLS & BOON®

EXCLUSIVE EXTRACT

Natasha Pellegrini and Matteo Manaserro's reunion
catches them both in a potent mix of emotion, and they
surrender to their explosive passion. Natasha was a virgin
until Matteo's touch branded her as his and when Matteo
discovers Natasha is pregnant, he's intent on claiming his
baby. Except he hasn't bargained on their insatiable
chemistry binding them together so completely!

Read on for a sneak preview of Michelle Smart's book
CLAIMING HIS ONE-NIGHT BABY
The second part of her Bound to a Billionaire trilogy

'For better or worse we're going to be tied together by our
child for the rest of our lives and the only way we're going
to get through it is by always being honest with each other.
We will argue and disagree but you must always speak the
truth to me.'

Natasha fought to keep her feet grounded and her limbs
from turning into fondue but it was a fight she was losing,
Matteo's breath warm on her face, his thumb gently moving
on her skin but scorching it, the heat from his body almost
penetrating her clothes, heat crawling through her, pooling
in her most intimate place.

His scent was right there too, filling every part of her, and
she wanted to bury her nose into his neck and inhale him.

She'd kissed him without any thought, a desperate
compulsion to touch him and comfort him flooding her, and
then the fury had struck from nowhere, all her private thoughts
about the direction he'd taken his career in converging to
realise he'd thrown it all away in the pursuit of riches.

And now she wanted to kiss him again.

As if he could sense the need inside her, he brought his mouth close to hers but not quite touching, the promise of a kiss.

'And now I will ask you something and I want complete honesty,' he whispered, the movement of his words making his lips dance against hers like a breath.

The fluttering of panic sifted into the compulsive desire. She hated lies too. She never wanted to tell another, especially not to him. But she had to keep her wits about her because there were things she just could not tell because no matter what he said about lies always being worse, sometimes it was the truth that could destroy a life.

But, God, how could she think properly when her head was turning into candyfloss at his mere touch?

His other hand trailed down her back and clasped her bottom to pull her flush to him. Her abdomen clenched to feel his erection pressing hard against her lower stomach. His lips moved lightly over hers, still tantalising her with the promise of his kiss. 'Do you want me to let you go?'

Her hands that she'd clenched into fists at her sides to stop from touching him back unfurled themselves and inched to his hips.

The hand stroking her cheek moved round her head and speared her hair. 'Tell me.' His lips found her exposed neck and nipped gently at it. 'Do you want me to stop?'

'Matteo...' Finally, she found her voice.

'Yes, *bella*?'

'Don't stop.'